OCEAN OF STORMS

OCEAN OF STORMS

CHRISTOPHER MARI
JEREMY K. BROWN

This is a work of fiction. Names, characters, organizations, places, events, and incidents are either products of the author's imagination or are used fictitiously.

Published by 47North, Seattle

www.apub.com

ISBN-13: 9781503938779
ISBN-10: 1503938778

Cover design by Adam Hall

Printed in the United States of America

For my wife, Ana Maria, with love and gratitude.
What's real lasts.

—C. M.

For Alli, who never stopped believing and who loved me before I ever published a word. To the Moon and back, honey. Always.

—J. K. B.

PART 1: THE SIGNAL

Chapter 1

December 22
Institute for Geophysics and Planetary Physics
La Jolla, California
12:14 a.m.

Max Shepherd knew few people who loved working the graveyard shift. But for him, working nights at the institute was about as plum a job as he could have wished for. Just a year into his doctoral program, he had landed a position as research assistant to Dr. Elliot Seaborne, the noted seismologist currently heading up the Lunar Seismology Initiative. A NASA-sponsored project, the LSI was yet another component of the agency's increasing desire to mount a return to the Moon.

A new series of lunar missions had been talked about since Shepherd had been in grammar school. But since NASA had scrapped its shuttle program back in 2011, the Moon had become the agency's central focus. Yet despite all the talk about new missions, NASA still found itself in yearly battles with Congress over the costs of space exploration. Desperate for a way to convince Congress that manned spaceflight had not gone the way of the dinosaur, NASA was willing to listen to any theories that might generate some additional funding. That's when Seaborne had approached the agency with the plans for the LSI. The hope was that by demonstrating the Moon's geologic activity, they might be able to convince the politicians to set a firm date to mount another round of manned missions to Earth's nearest neighbor. Surprisingly, some initial funding had been approved. On July 7, 2010, an unmanned probe, Stellaluna, had been launched to the Moon. Once in orbit, it had sent several seismometers to the Moon's surface, devices considerably more sophisticated than the ones placed there by the Apollo astronauts more than forty years earlier. Now all that was left was for them to do their thing. Which is where Max Shepherd came in.

Pretty slow night up there, Shepherd thought as he glanced at Stellaluna's telemetry. He began surfing through the channels on the lab's thirty-six-inch flat-screen television. There wasn't much on any of the twenty-four-hour news channels, just some footage from the recent congressional hearings on human cloning. Some major biotech company was apparently on the verge of a breakthrough, and the age-old debate had flared up again. After ten minutes of flipping, Max muted the sound and turned his attention to the lab's radio antennas. He cranked the speakers, filling the room with the sounds of what was commonly called "cosmic debris," the collected noise of millions of radio, TV, and cell phone signals trapped in the Earth's atmosphere. The sound was eerie, like someone turning a wet finger around the rim of a crystal glass, but Max loved it.

Just as he was starting to relax, the seismic equipment monitoring Stellaluna's probes sprang to life. Needles and gauges flicked with such intensity that he was certain he was looking at a massive impact. The Moon was continually being bombarded by meteorites, but whatever had struck it tonight was a real whopper. Max scanned the readouts, searching for telltale signs. *If this is a meteor impact,* he thought, *it's a helluva big one.* He reached for the desk phone and punched in Dr. Seaborne's cell number.

"Unless the Moon just exploded, I don't care," came the sleepy voice on the other end.

"Sorry to bother you, Doctor," said Max, "but I thought you'd want to see this."

Seaborne sat up in bed, struggling to wake himself. "What've you got?"

"Something highly unusual. Massive seismic activity on an unheard-of scale." He tapped out a few keystrokes and e-mailed the data to Seaborne. "I'm sending you the numbers now."

There was a pause as Seaborne checked over what Max had just sent to his smartphone. "Impact," he deduced. "It's got to be."

"I thought so too," Max said. "But it's so damn big. It's like—wait. I've got an e-mail coming in from Big Sky."

Max often kept in touch with the astronomers at Big Sky Observatory in Montana. Whatever he heard, he reasoned, they might be able to back up visually.

"Um, Dr. Seaborne?" he said hesitantly. "They're saying that they're picking up debris on the Moon."

"Debris? There it is—it has to be an impact."

"I agree, but they're saying the ejecta pattern doesn't match an impact." Max paused, making sure he had read it right. "It's almost as if—"

Before he could finish, a high-pitched tone tore through the phone lines, nearly striking both of them stone-deaf. Max yanked the phone away from his ears and dropped it, expecting the intensity of the sound to diminish. He howled in shock and pain, but the sound was drowning out his own voice. It was everywhere—in the speakers, the TV, the stereo. It was even coming from equipment that normally didn't emit sound. The noise had a deep bass undercurrent that made Max think of a hive of angry bees. He could feel his bones vibrate from the sound. The experience was invasive, disorienting, and altogether awful. He crawled under a desk, praying that it would stop, or that he would die. The sound reached a fever pitch that seemed to resonate deep in Max's brain before spiraling madly down into silence. Almost instantly, the discord was followed by a second wave. This one cascaded through Max with locomotive force, bringing forth a powerful sense of vertigo. The coffeepot exploded, spraying hot liquid everywhere. Every lightbulb overhead popped and burst. Even his MacBook cracked open. All at once, the windows of the lab blew inward. Max blinked, stunned. He meekly picked up the phone, listening to see if Dr. Seaborne was still there.

Nothing.

Dead.

For a terrible moment, Max felt as if he were the only person left alive on the planet. He peered out the shattered window at the Moon, wondering just what secrets she had to tell tonight.

December 22
South China Sea
Off the Taiwanese Coast
4:14 p.m.

As a lieutenant colonel in the United States Marines, Franklin Wilson was not required to fly patrols. In fact, the act was frowned upon by other officers. But Wilson had volunteered. Every once in a while he just needed to get away, and he was never as free as when he was in the air. Stationed on the USS *Nimitz* off the coast of Taiwan, Wilson was overseeing the US initiative to protect American interests in the region. In recent months China had become increasingly adamant about its "one-China" policy and had expressed to the United States its view of Taiwan being a rogue province. Some feared that the situation, which had been escalating for some time, would ultimately lead to war.

If that's the case, let it come, Wilson thought. *It's better than all this damn waiting.*

Nearly forty years old, he had spent the first six years of the century as a pilot in his country's ceaseless campaign against terrorism and had fought in some of the most harrowing bombing operations of the conflict. Then he had applied for the astronaut corps and gotten in with no trouble, though he maintained his active-duty status. Today he was here more as a favor than in an official capacity. His experiences in Afghanistan, Iraq, and Saudi Arabia would prove useful should a combat situation arise, his superiors had thought.

That was fine with him. He had logged just one mission in space since 2011, when the United States had decommissioned its shuttle fleet. All attention was now focused on the new Phoenix project, which when Wilson last checked was still bogged down in cost overruns and research and development after his abortive test flight of the prototype Phoenix capsule. Wilson was slated to command another Phoenix mission sometime down the line, but at the rate the process was going, such a feat could take years. He figured a few weeks on an aircraft carrier would do him good. Plus, he had reasoned, they'd have to extend an officer a little courtesy and let him try out some new hardware. And that was just what he was doing right now.

"Mother Hen, this is Eagle One, over," he said, contacting the *Nimitz*'s control tower.

"Go ahead, Eagle One."

"Everything out here looks fine. No unfriendly skies, over."

"Roger that, Eagle One," the flight controller responded. "Why don't you come on back?"

"Will do, Mothe—"

Wilson's F-35 Lightning II was suddenly rocked by a powerful concussive force that struck him so solidly that for an instant he thought he had been hit by an object. His plane spun wildly out of control, caught in the mercy of the shock wave. He fought to right her, to no use.

"Mayday, Mother Hen, Mayday," Wilson said. "I've lost control and I'm going down."

No sooner had he said the words than every light on board blinked out and all the controls stopped responding. Wilson was handling a dead stick in a vertical dive.

He grasped the ejection-seat handle, praying that whatever had knocked his plane out hadn't screwed that up as well, and yanked it hard. With a whoosh, the canopy's explosive bolts fired and Wilson shot into the afternoon sky, his plane falling away beneath him.

"C'mon, baby, c'mon," he whispered. Almost in response, his chute snapped open, jerking him back forcefully, and he began floating gently toward the ocean. Deep in his stomach, he got a sinking feeling. He had been to enough classes on terrorist tactics to recognize the effects of an electromagnetic pulse. As he hit the water, he ignited the waterproof flares he carried in his flight suit, hoping the *Nimitz* would be able to pick him up. Treading water, he searched the horizon, wondering when both rescue and answers would arrive.

December 22
Taiyuan Launch Center
Taiyuan, Shanxi Province, China
4:14 p.m.

The rocket stood on the launchpad, ready for its journey to the stars. That journey, however, was still a few months away. This afternoon was simply a routine test of the capsule, which rested atop a new staged rocket the Chinese believed would jump-start their first series of manned Moon missions. On board were the two men selected to fly the craft: Commander Yuen Bai, a decorated officer of the People's Republic with a spotless service record, and Professor Bruce Yeoh. Although they were teammates, the two couldn't be more different. Yuen was a former fighter pilot in the People's Liberation Army, a cold-eyed black belt with an intense disposition, who had trained for this mission for almost five years. Yeoh, on the other hand, was Chinese born but American educated. A brilliant physicist, mathematician, and computer scientist, he had entered Caltech on a full scholarship, leaving Shanghai when he was just sixteen. His findings on gravitational motivation and Planck theory were considered some of the most groundbreaking scientific revelations in a generation. At twenty-five, he returned to his native country with his PhD and began applying his research to spaceflight. Four years later he was sitting here on the launch-pad, preparing to bring everything full circle. If the Chinese were going to be the first people to return to the Moon, industry pundits around the world speculated, Bruce Yeoh would be the man to help get them there.

"*Tai-Ping*, this is Mission Control," said the flight controller.

"Go ahead," answered Yuen.

"We are go for a preliminary test."

Yuen was about to respond when everything went haywire. Their headsets were filled with a horrible squealing sound; then everything went black. The lights and instruments on board the ship failed and, from what they could tell looking through the small viewport, all the lights on the pad had gone out as well. The two men sighed. It would likely be some time before they found out what had happened. They were strapped into their seats, and the hatches on these craft worked on an electrical locking mechanism. They were stuck.

Yuen, a disgusted expression on his face, looked at Yeoh. "Damned Russian technology."

December 22
The White House
Washington, DC
3:30 a.m.

"Is it nuclear?" asked General James Francis McKenna, chief of Space Command and NORAD, as he whisked down the hallway toward the Situation Room of the White House. He was almost afraid of the answer. He was sure only an electromagnetic pulse triggered by a nuclear detonation could knock out power like this, including emergency generators. Those on staff when the lights went out had resorted to using flashlights. Their beams cut wildly through the dark as McKenna walked with the President's advisers, including Aaron Stein, the secretary of defense.

"We just don't know for sure, General," Stein said. "We've only got sporadic radio contact with local NEST teams in and around DC. But there's no visual evidence of a detonation."

"Hell, I could have told them that," said McKenna irritably.

McKenna had been trained not to be surprised by anything. Sixty-five years old and tempered on the crucible of Vietnam, he had seen death as up close and personal as any man on this Earth. Over the next few hours, he would have to assess a possible threat that could ultimately lead to the annihilation of millions. McKenna didn't care how many years you'd spent in the game of war; that decision never came lightly.

These thoughts turned over in his mind as he strode into the Situation Room, which was lit by the halogen lamps of the emergency lighting system.

"Madam President," McKenna said.

"Morning, Jim," said the President. "What've you got for me?"

"Right now, we're in the dark, ma'am, literally and otherwise. Aaron's been briefing me on the way, and it looks like, at this point, we may be able to rule out a nuclear strike in the immediate vicinity."

"Can we be sure?"

McKenna and Stein exchanged worried glances. "Truthfully, ma'am, we can't," Stein flatly stated. "With the phone lines out, we've been unable to maintain continual contact with Nuclear Emergency Support Teams in the DC area, or those units in other cities. We're only able to raise them via radios operating on battery reserves, but the comm chatter has been a little chaotic. We're trying to clear it up now."

"Jesus Christ," the President muttered. "We'll have to dispatch people personally to every primary and secondary target in the area. Aaron—"

"Madam President," Stein said calmly. "None of our vehicles are working either. No electrical system is functioning at all. This has all the earmarks of an electromagnetic pulse."

"An EM pulse of this magnitude with no indication of a nuclear explosion?" the President asked incredulously. "Is such a thing possible?"

"That's what we're trying to ascertain now, ma'am."

The President turned back to McKenna. "Have there been any incidents of civil unrest?"

"Not as of yet. It's too soon to be sure, but it's something we may be facing should this crisis last the night."

"That's not good enough, gentlemen. We've got to deploy the National Guard, keep people calm."

"We've begun mobilizing them as best we can," said Stein. "We should be able to deploy them within the hour."

"We might want to consider calling in the army," voiced Amy Martin, secretary of Homeland Security.

"Posse comitatus forbids it," said the President.

"You could invoke the War Powers Act," she suggested. "A military presence could send a powerful message."

"The wrong message," McKenna broke in. "Madam President, you give the order and I'll roll a tank up to my blue-haired granny's house in Decatur. But, in my opinion, you'd be courting disaster. You'll put fear into every citizen, and fear will quickly give way to aggression. I've seen it a hundred times. Somalia, Liberia, Iraq. Trust me when I tell you it's the quickest way to make a bad situation worse."

"I agree," said the President. The two had known each other for decades. McKenna was the most sensible man the President knew. She trusted his views more than those of many of her closest advisers. She turned to Secretary Martin. "We're not there yet, Amy."

"If I may, ma'am," offered McKenna, "I think the best thing we can do right now is to get you, the vice president, and the Joint Chiefs to a secure location. We still don't know what we're facing and we need to maintain a working government."

The President shook her head. "I won't duck and run, Jim. It's not what this country needs."

"Ma'am," Stein protested. "I think you might be underestimating the severity of the situation."

"No, Aaron, I think I understand it perfectly. It's for that very reason I'm staying put."

McKenna smiled and shook his head. He'd known the President long enough to recognize when her mind was made up. "All right then," he said. "Let's pull up a chair and go over some—"

As McKenna was speaking, the lights suddenly snapped back on. Everyone froze for a moment, unsure if it was just a fluke. When the power appeared to be on for good, the room burst to life. Everyone ran back and forth. Phones began to ring, and laptops were popped open. Stein's secure satellite phone went off in his hand. The President nodded to him and Stein answered it. A few minutes later he switched off the phone, his face drained of blood.

"How bad?" the President asked.

"Madam President," Stein began slowly, "the preliminary reports indicate that the pulse wasn't contained to the DC area."

"What is it?" McKenna demanded. "Not the entire Eastern Seaboard?"

"No. Not just the seaboard."

The President leaned on the table. "Surely you're not telling me it hit the entire country?"

Stein shook his head. "We're getting initial reports from bases as far away as the Philippines. We believe this pulse or whatever it is knocked out power across the entire planet."

Over the next several hours, the President's staff began dissecting what had transpired. Preliminary reports were good. Most people across the country had remained calm, believing that the power outages had been isolated to their immediate area. Though details were sketchy at this point, there were almost no incidents of theft or looting. For the most part America had behaved exactly as she'd expected it would have. However, the report from Michelle Artus, head of the Federal Aviation Administration, was not as comforting.

"Ma'am, from what we've been able to piece together, we have several hundred downed planes. Casualties are thankfully pretty light across the country. Most pilots were able to make water landings or emergency touchdowns in fields and out-of-the way locations. Early estimates of fatalities are in the low thousands."

"The low *thousands*?" the President asked. "Can't we get a more specific number than that?"

"It could've been a lot worse," Secretary Martin suggested.

"Any number is too high," the President said quietly. "We haven't even begun to estimate things like car accidents, power outages at hospitals, and the like. How about international flights?"

Artus sighed. "We know of one plane so far that came down in a major city. We're still assessing the damage, but it looks like the death toll could be catastrophic."

The President sat down. "Where?"

"Hong Kong."

December 22
Lei Cheng Uk Han Tomb Museum
Kowloon, Hong Kong
4:14 p.m.

As she did every other month, Dr. Soong Yang Zi was leading a school field trip on a tour of the museum when it happened. Dr. Soong certainly didn't need to schedule the excursion. As one of the most respected forensic anthropologists in China, she couldn't really spare the time, but she loved the time spent with the children.

"Come along," Soong said as she led her charges to the entrance passage of the museum where the centerpiece exhibit, a tomb from the Han dynasty, was kept. Closed to the public for conservation reasons, its interior was only visible behind plate glass.

"This tomb was discovered in 1955, when a hill slope at Lei Cheng Uk village was being excavated," Soong explained. "According to inscriptions on the tomb and other findings, we think it is almost two thousand years old."

The ten children in Soong's group oohed and aahed at the number, and she smiled. After days on end of working in crime labs and university basements piecing together how a person lived and died, she found that leading these tours was the perfect way to recharge her batteries and reignite her passion for the work. As a student, Soong studied archeology at first but gradually became more interested in anthropology, wanting to know *who* the people she was digging up were. In time, she discovered that the greatest way to solve any puzzle was to break it down to its barest elements. On a whim, she took a course in osteology and never looked back. By studying the bones of a subject, she found that it was possible to determine where and how they lived, whether they were male or female, and even how they died. Her thesis on dental anatomy and its relation to primate and hominid evolution was received with nothing less than hosannas in academic circles, and she had her pick of just about any university placement she wanted upon graduation. However, when the bones of a murder victim were uncovered not far from her home, Soong offered her help in analyzing them. The team on the case discovered that the victim was a seventeen-year-old girl who had been missing for two years. Although the girl's family was devastated, Soong saw that they were relieved to at least know what had become of their daughter. Seeing the relief they got from having that closure was enough to propel Soong into the field full time. In the ensuing decade, she cracked some of the toughest cases the department had, as well as reopened a few cold cases with successful results. During her off-hours, Soong also found time to visit the university, where she often would work with some of her old professors, poring over bone fragments and trying to piece together some long-forgotten civilization. Still, as much as she loved it, it was very easy to get jaded in her line of work. Day after day spent with the dead could grow tiresome, to say the least. So to come here and see the innocent excitement with which these children viewed the pursuit of the past always gave her enough of a charge to keep going.

As she spoke, the room was filled with a terrible high-pitched sound. To Soong it sounded like the scream of an animal dying in extreme pain and fear. The glass surrounding the tomb cracked and then exploded, showering the entrance hall. Instinctively, she tried to draw the children to her, shielding them as best she could from the airborne fragments. Pots and vases forged thousands of years ago shattered in milliseconds against the onslaught of sound, which reached a wild fever pitch before lapsing into silence. After a moment, a terrible second wave hit them, filling Soong with a sense of vertigo not unlike what she felt when she was ten and climbed Mount Taishan with her father. The wave passed, and all power in the museum snapped out. Soong lay there a moment, huddled in the darkness with the children, then sat up.

"Is everyone all right?" she called out.

Miraculously, apart from a few nicks and scratches, they had all managed to avoid being cut to ribbons by the flying glass and shards of pottery. Soong gently stood up, brushing off debris. As she caught her breath, she heard another sound. This one was faint but seemed to be getting louder.

"What is that?" asked an elderly man, a security guard she knew as Li. He walked outside to have a look while Soong attempted to calm the children down. Almost immediately he ran back in, a look of sheer panic on his face.

"Get them to safety!" he cried, pointing at the students. "Now!"

Soong barely had time to react. She instantly herded them together and led them into the tomb's massive chambers. When the children were safely away from whatever danger was headed their way, she looked over to Li.

"What is it?" she asked. "What's wrong?"

Li frantically waved her away. Before Soong could open her mouth, the world around her exploded. A deafening roar like a derailing freight train filled her ears. Soong was blasted off her feet and into the chamber. The museum walls buckled and cracked, threatening to collapse and send several millennia's worth of history tumbling down.

The deafening cacophony overhead continued, the sound of shrieking and twisting metal stretched beyond its limits, blending with the symphony of shattering glass. Underneath it all, an unearthly sound of churning engines and turbines hummed. The combined sound was easily the most terrible thing she had ever heard or could even imagine hearing. To Dr. Soong, the gates of *diyu* had opened and the hungry ghosts of wicked souls were sweeping across the land.

Finally, with a last defiant cry, the tumult stopped. Without waiting, Soong crawled out of the tomb and led the children out onto the sidewalk. As soon as she got outside, she wished she'd stayed put. In the middle of the street, amid the wreckage of buildings it had destroyed in its death throes, sat a commercial airliner. Steam hissed from popped rivets and broken seams while its still-turning jet engines blew dust and debris everywhere. Soong looked at the ruin before her and back at the miracle of the still-standing museum behind her, at the people running to and fro, screaming and crying, at the buildings hollowed out by the devastation of the plane's landing. As she was surveying the carnage, a little girl from her tour group gently touched her hand.

"Is it over?" she asked.

Looking out at the terrible tragedy the afternoon had wrought, Dr. Soong could not help but feel that it was only just beginning.

December 24
The Pentagon
Arlington, Virginia
9:15 a.m.

We are all prisoners of our possessions, the President thought as she walked the Pentagon's long corridors, *and I'm the kid with the most broken toys.* Here she was the leader of the most powerful nation in the world, but she had been unable to do something as simple as address her own people on national television. It had taken two whole days for the American government to get their computer and communication systems up and running again. For those two days she had to rely on legwork and conflicting reports about the state of the nation. However, preliminary reports from the major cities were good. Few people had reacted violently, and most were trying to aid the thousands upon thousands who had been wounded when electrical systems all over the planet failed. People had been trapped in elevators, in cars, in planes and tunnels, on trains and bridges. The crash in Hong Kong had managed to kill several thousand people, and the damage to the downtown area was staggering. The President shook her head. The sheer magnitude of it all was almost overwhelming. But now, as things began to normalize, the general mind-set of the planet had drifted from outright panic to quiet terror. People were beginning to ask questions. People wanted to know what had caused this.

As the President entered the briefing room, everyone, including the Joint Chiefs, stood at once. The room was crowded, as the President had asked not only her entire cabinet to assemble but the various heads of space programs around the country as well. The sight of so many rumpled scientists standing around the table contrasted with the gleaming sharpness of military uniforms and the blue and gray business suits of professional politicians.

"As you were, ladies and gentlemen," the President said. She took her place at the head of the table but did not sit. "Sorry to keep you from your families on Christmas Eve, but as you no doubt realize, we're teetering on the edge of a worldwide panic, the likes of which no generation has ever seen. What you may not know is this: the world is a radically different place from the one we once knew." She paused, not for dramatic effect as she so often did (rather well, if you went by the editorial page of the *Washington Post*) during her other speeches. This pause came from a simpler notion. She honestly did not know what to say. After another beat, the President inhaled a deep breath and continued. "The cause of the anomaly on December twenty-second has been, to an extent, determined. As of right now, we have positive confirmation that we are not alone in the universe."

Knowing who was speaking, people tried their best to be respectful, but there was a collective rumble of gasps, groans, and *hmmms* in the room. A few of the more cynical attendees muttered a "Jesus Christ" or "Beam me up, Scotty."

The President silenced them with a look. "I know how it sounds," she said. "But we have at this point conclusive proof that the pulse emanated from something buried beneath the Moon's surface."

"From the Moon?" asked Aaron Stein, wiping his glasses with a monogrammed handkerchief.

The President answered Stein's query with only a slight nod. "For further analysis, I turn you over to Dr. Elliot Seaborne of the University of California at San Diego. He heads the LSI team that first encountered the anomaly."

Seaborne bustled up to the front of the room, a cluster of rolled-up maps and charts under his thin arms. A nervous balding man with a pinched face and a threadbare tweed jacket, he looked every bit the stereotypical lab rat. However, when he began speaking, he displayed a surprising confidence.

"Thank you, Madam President," he said, clearing his throat. "Okay, everyone. I should first give you some background on our work. As you are probably well aware, SETI has spent decades using giant radio telescopes across the country to search the heavens for any sign of extraterrestrial life. What you may not know is that in 1977 Jerry Ehman at the Ohio State SETI program received a strong narrowband radio signal that went on for seventy-two seconds. He was so excited by what he heard, he wrote the word *wow* in the corner of the page. Unfortunately, attempts to relocate the signal failed, and it was never heard from again. Still, it represented the closest thing we have to proof that intelligent life other than our own exists in the universe. Until now. We know very little about the anomaly at the moment. But we do know it came from a source of extreme power and originated from the Ocean of Storms."

"That's the landing site of Apollo 12," said Jack Sykes, director of the National Security Agency.

"Yes, sir," Seaborne said. "And as many questions as that raises, it also answers a few others. For starters, it all but exonerates Alan Bean from burning out the camera lens during the first extravehicular activity, or EVA, in November 1969."

"How is that?" asked Len Byrnes, a NASA scientist. "I thought he pointed the thing at the sun."

"He may well have, Dr. Byrnes," said Seaborne. "But in all probability, the camera had already been ionized by electrical activity at the site." He paused again. "Activity that most probably came from some sort of buried object."

The room erupted in murmurs. Some members of the NSA tried to keep poker faces, but beneath the veneer, a thin film of worry was showing.

Secretary Martin spoke up. "What other questions have been answered?"

Seaborne cleared his throat. "Well, for one thing, there's the water that was detected in the early seventies. At the time NASA thought it was just some kind of vapor released during a moonquake. We now believe that the water was most likely condensation of some sort from this buried object. Then there are the rocks brought back by the Apollo astronauts that contained bits of rusted iron. We theorize that the iron was driven into the rocks during the object's possible impact"—he paused—"approximately two million years ago."

McKenna set his coffee cup down. "How the devil can you know that?"

"Teams of geologists have been studying those rock samples since the 1970s, General," Seaborne explained. "The tests conclusively proved that the rusted iron ore found on the Moon was at least that old." Before letting this new development sink in, Seaborne plunged on. "The most fascinating discovery we have made during our studies of the site also stems from the days of the Moon landings. On November 20, 1969, when Apollo 12 blasted off from the Moon, astronauts Conrad and Bean sent the ascent stage of the LEM—that's short for the lunar excursion module—crashing back into its surface. Seismic equipment left behind recorded that the impact of the LEM caused the Moon to reverberate almost like a bell for over an hour. Dr. Frank Press of MIT explained the phenomenon by saying that the impact must have simply caused a series of avalanches and collapses on the Moon's surface. This explanation, however, does not account for the long, sustained seismic readings following the crash. Several experiments were subsequently conducted by NASA, which determined that the Moon—at least in that particular area—is hollow. The results of these tests have never been disclosed."

"That's NASA for you," one gruff military voice intoned. "Never A Straight Answer."

Seaborne cleared his throat again. "Spectrographic analysis of the Moon's surface around the Ocean of Storms reveals some clues that may point to an answer." At this point he nodded to an assistant at the far end of the room, who punched some keys on a laptop terminal. Instantly a crisp photo of the area appeared on a large television screen mounted into the wall behind Seaborne.

"These are pictures of the Moon's surface taken yesterday by orbiting telescopes. And that," Seaborne said, pointing at the photo, "is what we believe is the source of the EM pulse. Shortly before the pulse hit the Earth, this fissure opened up in the Ocean of Storms. As you can see, there is no discernible impact crater. The ejecta we see on the surface is new, previously unseen. Further, its dispersal pattern indicates that whatever caused this fissure to open came from the inside."

"Blasted out from the inside?" Stein wondered.

"Exactly. While shadows prevent us from peering too far into the fissure, by bouncing radar waves from our orbiting satellite, Stellaluna, at it, we can discern that this area of the Moon has an almost-hollow interior."

"And what exactly caused this area of the Moon to be so hollow?" Chairman of the Joint Chiefs of Staff Rick Gonzalez wondered.

"Well, General—and this is pure speculation—it appears that whoever put that object on the Moon had likely dug caves around it."

A palpable silence fell about the room. McKenna cleared his throat. "So what's the next step?"

"Well, that's where things get interesting," Seaborne said. "On a hunch, my team, in collaboration with some radio astronomers from

SETI, analyzed the EM pulse. We theorized that whoever sent the pulse may have been trying to make contact."

"But that's just a theory," General Gonzalez noted.

"Actually it's a little bit more than a theory," Seaborne replied. "We believe the incident occurred in three stages. First they used a source of immense power to open a fissure in the Moon's surface. Next they sent an electromagnetic pulse through that fissure to interrupt our way of life."

"Why would they do that?" Gonzalez asked.

"Well," Seaborne continued, "we believe they were trying to get our attention. The EM pulse worked on the same principle as the old emergency broadcast system. In the days of the Cold War, the government established the system to be able to break into every broadcast at once in order to get vital information out. These beings, whoever they are, decided to do basically the same thing. Here, let me show you."

Seaborne's assistant punched some more keys on his laptop, bringing up a graph on the screen.

"Moments after the power was restored around the globe, we began receiving a stream of binary numbers, on every frequency, in repeating patterns, for exactly twenty-four hours. Whoever sent this wanted everyone in the world—not radio astronomers at Arecibo, not government agencies—but *everyone* to pick up their heads and take notice. Once we broke down those numbers, we found this."

The wall display blinked over to an image that read, "3.04 S, 23.42 W."

"Latitude and longitude," Admiral Peter Reynolds offered from the far end of the table.

Seaborne smiled. "That's exactly what it is. The latitude and longitude of the Ocean of Storms."

"For what purpose?" Secretary Martin asked.

"Landing coordinates," Seaborne explained. "What we received was not a warning, not an attack. It was an *invitation*. As to our response to that invitation, I turn you over to John Dieckman, director of manned spaceflight at NASA. Deke?"

Dieckman stepped up and scanned the room, pushing his sandy-brown hair from his forehead. Youthful looking despite nearing his forty-fifth birthday, his well-trained former test pilot's body was only now beginning to develop a middle-aged paunch.

"Gentlemen, ladies, we at NASA believe that the quickest and best solution is to send a team to the Moon to investigate the signal, its source, and whatever else may be waiting there."

Aaron Stein glanced at him over the rims of his glasses. "And how do you propose to do that, Mr. Dieckman? From what I understand, the Phoenix program is still years away from a translunar flight."

"That's not quite true, Mr. Stein," Dieckman explained. "We have tested the command module in Earth orbit, and it has successfully docked with the ISS—"

"I've had enough of this," General Gonzalez grumbled, bristling at the idea. "I don't know about any of you, but I'm not prepared to sacrifice American lives so that NASA can get a budget increase."

"That's not the idea," Dieckman replied. "A hands-on analysis is the only way to ensure that we get an accurate picture of what's happening up there. We've done it before. Six times, actually. And we believe that, given the right timetable and the necessary funds, we can do it again quickly and efficiently with Phoenix."

Gonzalez remained unconvinced. "Who's paying the bills for this? The military? With respect, Madam President, I do not believe it would be wise to take money out of the defense budget for some kind of science fiction circus. Especially when we could be looking at some sort of . . . interstellar Armageddon!"

"And what exactly are we supposed to do, General?" McKenna demanded. "Wait for them to show up over our cities? Wait until they try something else, something far worse than an EM pulse?"

There were those in the room who had secretly harbored Gonzalez's fears. Now that he had displayed the courage to voice them, they quickly joined the fray. Those who disagreed spoke up even louder, and soon the room was afire with angry voices all trying to outshout one another. Dieckman looked around nervously as the meeting descended into chaos.

The President quieted the room by raising her hand. Her gaze swept over each of them before she spoke again.

"It's highly unlikely that after more than two million years there are any hostile forces on the Moon planning on taking over the Earth." She almost scoffed at the idea. "What's more likely is what SETI has suggested, that this was an automated signal intended to get our attention, nothing more." The President glanced around the room again. Each pair of eyes met hers, and they read the sincerity in them. "We stand on the threshold of a remarkable event in human history, the chance to leave our own world and make contact with those from another. To dismiss this extraordinary opportunity would be sheer stupidity. Future generations would remember us as fools, cowards who opted not to answer the call to incredible discovery"—she glanced at Gonzalez—"no matter what the risks."

She paused again, knowing full well that she had their attention. "'There is a tide in the affairs of men, which taken at the flood, leads on to great fortune,'" she said, quoting Shakespeare. "'Omitted, all the voyage of their life is bound in shallows and in miseries.' We are going to the Moon, ladies and gentlemen." She turned to Dieckman. "It's up to your people to get us there."

Chapter 2

December 25
Johnson Space Center
Houston, Texas
9:21 a.m.

Some present they've given me, John Dieckman thought as he stared at the miniature Christmas tree on the filing cabinet in his office.

Everyone had heard what the President said. They were going to the Moon. In six months. But there was only one catch: no one presently at NASA had ever been involved with a moon shot.

Dieckman laughed, shaking his head. Despite all the big talk he had spouted at the Pentagon meeting, he knew Phoenix was nowhere near where it needed to be for them to attempt another landing. In truth, NASA was a pale reflection of its former self. Back in the glory days of the late 1960s and early 1970s, the Apollo missions were pulling off miracles day in and day out. Six perfect lunar landings and one aborted mission, though thankfully the crew of Apollo 13 managed to return to Earth safely. Other than the probes sent to the outer planets and the Kuiper Belt, no one had been involved in any deep-space work since that time. This generation of NASA scientists and engineers seemed to consider the Moon to be a deep-space project, especially if it involved sending astronauts. And it was really no surprise that they did—no human being had left the confines of near-Earth orbit since Richard Nixon was president.

When a new series of manned lunar missions had initially been proposed back in 2004, the plan had been to slowly phase out the reusable but tragically unreliable shuttle fleet in favor of Apollo-style one-shot capsules, with the goal of reaching the Moon sometime in the next decade. The money was reallocated from existing NASA programs to the Phoenix project. The only problem was Phoenix was coming in painfully over budget and woefully behind schedule. At this point they had a working command capsule but no landing module or booster heavy enough to propel them to the Moon. In essence, they had built the seats to their little buggy to the stars but had no engine or any way to get out of the thing.

Before the shuttles had been decommissioned in July 2011, there had been lots of manned missions, plenty of them. Manned missions to launch or repair communications and spy satellites. Manned missions to adjust orbiting telescopes. Manned missions to the aging International Space Station, once considered a stepping-stone to deep-space exploration—a return to the Moon, a manned mission to Mars. Dreams of another generation, funded by a less pragmatic America.

But in the last two years there had been only three manned missions, each to test the fledgling Phoenix program in low Earth orbit. On two of the missions, the first and the third, the capsule had performed admirably. The second flight almost didn't count as a mission. Fifteen minutes after achieving orbit, one of the capsule's retro-rockets began misfiring and the mission had to be aborted. Only luck prevented the crew from being killed. A congressional investigation was held. It took NASA another six months to get the clearance—and money—to fly again.

The joke around NASA these days is that if not for military spy satellites, they would have less of a budget than the Park Service—any *one* Park Service in the country, that is. Everyone knew the arguments made by every skinflint legislator and administration who had diminished their budget: What's the benefit of going into space? What does it get us? Where's the bottom-line profit? And then there were the accidents over the years that helped cement those concerns. Apollo 1. *Challenger*. *Columbia*. All the lost probes. *NASA can't get anything right with the money they have,* the politicians barked—*why should we give them any more?* Never mind the fact that one can't build a better mousetrap without initial capital. From the political point of view, it was all no profit, no results, no funds.

Which left NASA officials with one fundamental problem: how to get to the Moon in a six-month time frame with the pittance they'd been allotted.

Oh the President promised more money, sure, Dieckman thought as he slumped in his chair, *but how much of that's actually going to get to us? The military's going to be clamoring for more funds now with the Chinese fleet conducting military exercises off of Taiwan.* Deke scratched out some rough figures for the mission on a legal pad and laughed. *There's no way they're going to give us this.*

But first things first. They needed to figure out how to get to the Moon in six months. Many of the younger engineers and designers with no living memory of Apollo were intimidated by the idea of sending astronauts across the translunar expanse. A number of wild ideas had already come across Deke's desk. The wildest of all was the one that involved building a giant orbiting magnet to yank the object out of the Moon. More practical ones involved unmanned landers with computer-guided robots on the ground that could dig out the object and analyze it there. But Deke knew that having people on the Moon was the best—and fastest—way of excavating the object. That was the only way to ensure getting to the Moon as quickly as the President wanted.

Deke clicked his pen absentmindedly as he looked out the windows behind his desk. *Yeah, it could work—using Apollo as a guide.*

With Phoenix 3, NASA had already shown that the capsules were capable of docking with another ship—in that case the International Space Station. The plan had been to continue to aid the Europeans and the Russians in supplying the station for the next couple of years while Phoenix's lander got off the drawing board. Now they would need to move it from the research-and-development phase to launch capability in just six months.

But even so, the capsule only needs to be reconfigured for the new mission using Apollo's design specs as an initial blueprint. We might even be able to do it on our budget—provided we freeze all projects currently in development. And we could practically guarantee the President that it would work. If only we had a few guys left from Apollo to help us with the modifications of the original design.

Deke stood up and stretched, jerking his tie down and his top collar button open in one motion. He glanced over at the models on his desk of the old Apollo command and lunar modules.

We'd need to send a bigger team, not just three men. That wouldn't be a problem with the capsule—modern computers take up a hell of a lot less space than what went into Apollo. We could put more guys into it easy. But we'd have to build a bigger lander . . . Actually the lander might have to be pretty huge, especially if the President wants us to bring the object or pieces of it back for analysis. A landing crew of at least three, maybe four. That would mean a much bigger booster. The weight's the issue . . . Those old Apollo vets were always worried about weight.

Wait a minute. Isn't old Cal Walker still alive? Deke remembered seeing him at the space center recently, at a party or something. *Christ, he's got to be pretty old by now—eighty if not eighty-five. But the old bastard was still sharp as a tack, rattling off all the reasons why the lunar module had to be so light, how they had to get rid of the seats in the original design, shrink the windows . . .*

I bet old Cal would love to sink his teeth into this, he thought with a grin, *provided he still has any.*

Deke picked up the phone and punched in his assistant's extension. "Mattie, can you come in here for a minute?"

A second later Dieckman's dedicated assistant, Mattie Kendricks, entered his office. Mattie, fresh out of Caltech, was the brightest assistant anyone could ask for—organized, intelligent, disciplined, in love with NASA and manned space exploration. Dieckman had no doubt that she would be sitting in his office chair one day.

"Yes, Mr. Dieckman?"

"Has the Astronaut Office come back with a list of teams for prime and backup crews for the mission?"

She handed an envelope labeled "Top Secret" across his desk. "It arrived just as you called."

"Good, good," he said, feeling the weight of the packet. "Seems they've given me enough options with the few astronauts we have."

"It sure feels heavy."

"Mattie, I want you to get Cal Walker on the phone. He was one of Wernher von Braun's assistants while they were working on Apollo. His number should still be in our files. I think he's in New York now doing some consulting for some big biotech firm."

"I've got his number right here," she said, handing him a small sheet of notepaper. "The company's Technical Genetics Incorporated."

"Old Cal's working for TGI? The biggest biotech company in the country? You're kidding."

"Nope. I thought you might want to give him a call."

He grinned at the number. "Always one step ahead of me, aren't you?"

She smiled and shrugged as she began to leave the office. "It's a gift."

"Oh and Mattie—"

"Yes?"

"Have the people down in the computer lab run a search for American archeologists. Have them cross-reference the names for experience and age. I don't want anyone younger than thirty or older than fifty. And then narrow down the candidates by marital status. I don't want any married candidates."

"You're not planning to send archeologists to the Moon, are you?"

"I'm not sure. It might be easier to train someone to be an astronaut than it is to train them to be an archeologist." He glanced at his Apollo models. "And what we'll need are experienced archeologists. God only knows what we'll find up there."

"I'll get right on it."

Deke winced. "Sorry to have to call you in here on Christmas Day and all."

"Not a problem," she said with an honest smile warming her face. "The Moon definitely outweighs mistletoe."

News about the pulse's source broke early and all over on Christmas Day. Though Dieckman was unaware of it at the time, the initial report had come out of California late Christmas Eve while he was flying back down to Texas. Amateur astronomers had reported seeing debris on the Moon's surface shortly before the effects of the EMP were felt worldwide. People quickly put two and two together after that. By Christmas morning, these reports had been confirmed by astronomers at professional observatories all over the world, many of whom were of the firm opinion that the EM pulse had originated from a recently opened fissure on the Moon's Ocean of Storms. At this point the major networks and twenty-four-hour cable news stations jumped all over the story, giving it almost equal time with reports about the death and devastation the EMP had caused. Expert after expert was carted into news studios across the globe, each ready to speculate on what might have caused such a fissure and such an explosive burst of electromagnetic energy to come spewing from the Moon.

It didn't take long for the public at large to begin to believe that an intelligence had been at work behind the EMP. It took even less time for them to suspect that this devastating burst of energy might be the precursor to an extraterrestrial invasion. Governments around the world initially remained silent on the issue. This in turn only fueled more speculation about the pulse's origin, especially after many governments sent out representatives to claim—on the condition of anonymity—that it had indeed emanated from a recently exposed fissure on the Moon.

The talking heads went wild with the news. Now some people not only believed that the signal was a precursor to an alien invasion but also that the aliens were using the Moon as a strategic staging point. Others argued that the EMP couldn't have originated from the Moon, that the Apollo astronauts had never reported any such electromagnetic activity. Contrary opinions argued that this meant that the source of the pulse had not been on the Moon in the late 1960s and early 1970s. A few believed that this conclusively proved that men had never walked on the Moon at all. Old grainy footage of the Moon landings was played on an almost continual loop. The effects of the pulse were broadcast over and over: the shots of windows being blown in before cameras worldwide blacked out; the image of a passenger jet lying in the middle of a busy Hong Kong street; the scenes of snarled traffic jams around Rome, London, Berlin, and other cities; the clips of people being pulled from car wrecks and subways and elevators in New York City.

By Christmas afternoon, the politicians had gotten into the act. All around the world reports were coming in that the major powers had placed their armed forces on full alert. An emergency session of the United Nations Security Council was called. Presidents and prime ministers, premiers and dictators addressed their nations, calling for—or ordering—calm. The prime minister of the United Kingdom asked for the public's patience as experts analyzed the data. The President of Russia read a statement from the Kremlin, noting that the country's forces were on the highest alert. The prime minister of Japan reported that national scientists were working around the clock to understand the source and meaning of the pulse. The President of France demanded that any response be channeled through the United Nations and noted that her government would not be involved in any preemptive attack, even if the signal proved to be coming from an alien source. Notably absent were the leaders of the United States and China, who dispatched representatives to address the howling press corps. Chinese warships continued their maneuvers near the coast of Taiwan; their American counterparts remained stationed off Japan and South Korea.

Across the world that Christmas Day, people either went to their houses of worship to pray or stayed close to home. In Atlanta a minister told his congregation that the pulse had been the first sign of the Apocalypse. In California people gathered around the Hollywood sign with banners welcoming the aliens. In London a man stood outside Westminster Abbey in the freezing rain holding a sign that read "Jesus Is an Alien." In Washington, DC, a protest was quickly organized on the Mall to denounce any military action against the aliens. In New York a fire broke out at an electrical station, knocking out power in northern Manhattan, and five hundred people were arrested for looting. In Vatican City a man was arrested for attempting to break into the pope's residence because he believed that the Catholic pontiff was an alien. Every news report seemed to indicate that a worldwide panic was imminent.

In Houston, Texas, Lieutenant Commander Thomas "Moose" Mosensen, United States Navy, nursed his first beer of the holiday and watched the television mounted on the wall of O'Driscoll's Pub with his friend and fellow astronaut, Lieutenant Commander Anthony "Benny" Benevisto. The bar was empty. The tinsel and the "Merry Christmas" signs decorating the dark-mahogany interior looked painfully depressing. Old man O'Driscoll was walking around the place in a Santa Claus hat and a dirty apron, shaking his head over the news. Benny was also shaking his head but was just a little more vocal about the situation.

"Fucking bullshit," Benny said. "It's all fucking bullshit."

Moose looked over his pint glass at his wiry little friend. "What makes you say that?"

"What makes me say that?" Benny laughed, lifting his pint of Guinness. "Oh my friend, are you kidding? I mean, wouldn't *we* know about it? I mean, we're astronauts after all. Don't you think that maybe NASA would let us in on this EMP business if we hadda go up there and look for little green men?"

"I'm an astronaut. You're just waiting by the phone."

"Whatever, Mr. I Went Up And Fixed A Busted Air Filter On The Space Station. I'm telling you we'd know. They'd haveta tell us."

"You've heard the reports, Benny. They haven't finished analyzing the data."

"And what're they gonna find when they analyze that data? Not that it's the precursor to some *War of the Worlds* invasion. It'll just be some bullshit. Trust me."

Moose scratched his blond buzz cut. "Seems to me you might be a little more hopeful about this pulse really being something. It might get you up there finally."

"Months of waiting for the go call is not gonna get me to pin my hopes on some crummy little EM pulse from space. Oh I'll go up all right. Fix a satellite or something. But to go looking for space invaders? Forget about it."

"You're a fatalist, Benny."

"I'm a realist, pal. It's not aliens."

Moose sipped his beer. "Maybe so."

"You're not telling me that you really buy into all this alien-invasion crap?"

Moose shrugged his thick shoulders. "I'm not ruling it out. If you were going to plan a global invasion, knocking out power all over the world would be the way to prepare for it."

Benny waved at him. "Aw, come on, that's your Cub Scout preparedness training talking."

"Eagle Scout. I was an Eagle Scout."

"Whatever. All that means is that you wore short pants and a sash until you were eighteen and still believe anything anybody in a uniform tells you."

"How'd you ever get by in the navy with that kind of attitude?"

"Simple, Moose. I followed your golly-gee-whiz lead and faked it."

Moose and Benny were known around the Astronaut Office as the Dynamic Duo, after the old Batman and Robin comic book characters, though Moose was hardly any vengeful Dark Knight Detective and Benny was no cheerful Boy Wonder. In fact, their roles were quite the opposite. Moose was very much the all-American boy, blond haired and blue eyed, six feet two and weighing in at an even two hundred pounds. He had grown up in a small town in Kansas on a farm owned by his family for four generations, the eldest child and only son out of five siblings. A high school honors student and football star, Moose missed his shot at playing for Notre Dame because of a debilitating knee injury suffered in his senior year. But Moose took the injury in stride, as he did any setback he experienced in life, and managed to regain the full use of his knee after a series of operations. At the same time the War on Terror had flared up again after the bombing of an American embassy in Cairo, so he joined the navy to serve his country. He became a pilot and flew bombing missions over a number of terrorist camps in the Middle East. While assigned to the USS *George H. W. Bush* he met Benny, who became the closest thing he ever had to a kid brother.

No one really understood why the good-natured Moose took to Anthony Benevisto, a dark-haired, scrawny little wiseass from Brooklyn who did nothing but brag about what a great pilot he was and break chops wherever he could find chops to break. Benny had joined the navy not out of any sense of patriotic duty but because no one in his family had left Brooklyn since they had arrived there from Italy in the early twentieth century. Like a lot of people from New York, Benny thought he knew everything about anything; he prided himself on his street smarts. He always felt someone somewhere was trying to pull a fast one on him and never took anything anyone ever said at face value. Every order was followed by a muttered wisecrack; every boast by a fellow pilot was met with cynicism. And then of course there was Benny's own bragging, which made him few friends among his fellow pilots.

Moose always felt that the source of Benny's arrogance stemmed from the fact that he had been a sickly child with an overprotective mother who never let him out of bed for fear that he would "catch his death." His mother also never let him play with the neighborhood kids—those kids were "up to no good." So Benny spent most of his childhood alone, taking apart old computers he found on the street and reassembling them into working order. Not only did he teach himself about computers, he also taught himself everything he could about airplanes. For as long as he could remember, he dreamed about being a pilot like the ones he had seen at all the air shows his father had taken him to as a kid. When he turned eighteen, he joined the navy and never looked back. Everyone in his family figured he wouldn't survive with his sickly constitution. He graduated at the top of his class in flight school just to prove them wrong.

When Moose applied for the astronaut program, Benny laughed, claiming that all he would be doing at NASA would be fixing a lot of busted satellites. He'd never get a mission to the space station. He'd be a space mechanic. He was throwing his career away. When Moose wrote him that he had been assigned to a repair mission for the ISS, Benny put in his application to NASA the next day. Now Benny strode around the Astronaut Office with his silver astronaut pin, pouncing on anyone in sight about getting a mission so he could earn his gold one.

On the TV behind the bar, the news was broadcasting a report about the scores of downed aircraft all over the world. Analysts remarked that the sheer number of damaged or destroyed planes might very well bankrupt several major carriers based in the United States, despite the White House's assurances that the airline industry would be bailed out by the federal government. This story was followed by an update from Taiwan, whose forces were on full alert as the Chinese armada was reported in firing distance of the island nation. Taiwanese officials were asking the American government for aid in the event of an attack.

Benny sipped his beer. "Dollars to donuts, Moose, that we'll be called back to active service to deal with that shit before I get a prime crew mission. Guaranteed."

"I hope it doesn't get down to shooting over there. I'm sure the President has people looking into the situation."

"Sure she does," Benny said. "And I'm sure ETs from the Moon really just sent that pulse to tell us to stop fighting and embrace the brotherhood of man." He polished off his beer and tossed another twenty on the bar. "Let's have another drink. It's Christmas."

Moose kept his eyes on the television. "Maybe we better."

December 25
The Empire State Building
New York City
2:15 p.m.

"So that's the long and the short of it, Cal. We could really use someone with your experience right about now."

Cal Walker sat back in his deep leather desk chair and glanced out at his panoramic view of midtown Manhattan. Though past his eightieth birthday, Walker was still very much the same steely-eyed missile man who had helped America reach the Moon decades earlier. His thin frame was still erect and strong, his ice-blue eyes still pierced fiercely whenever he caught someone's gaze, and his swept-back silver hair betrayed no sign of a receding hairline. Few men of his age could claim to feel and look so good. Since moving out of NASA and into the private sector in the mid-1970s, Walker had not only prospered financially but had also found a number of ways to keep himself feeling youthful.

"Thank you for contacting me, John," Walker remarked into his telephone. "I'm grateful I managed to catch your call. I'd be happy to help you in any way possible, though I doubt someone with my antiquated experience could help your young go-getters at NASA."

"You're being modest, Cal," Deke said. "No one here has your expertise with a moon shot. I don't know what we'd do if we couldn't get you on board."

"I just wish my return to space, as it were, were under better circumstances. I imagine that the President must be very upset with the most recent casualty reports."

"I can only imagine she is. That's why we're glad to get your help on the Phoenix redesign. The President's concerned that complete anarchy might be imminent now that the source of the pulse has broken on the news. She wants us up there investigating it ASAP."

"Understandable, of course. As I said, I am at your service. I'll see you in Houston after the new year."

"Thanks, Cal. I look forward to it."

Walker hung up the phone and turned his chair to face the man sitting on the opposite side of his desk. "Well, NASA's called me in."

The man gave an almost imperceptible shrug. "We were expecting this once the source of the EMP was analyzed."

"The President's put a rush on the mission. She wants a team to be on the Moon by the summer. Sometime in June, no later."

"That may work to our advantage."

"That's what I was thinking."

"Rushing to space can be a dangerous business."

"I know. But the President fears a worldwide panic if the source of the pulse goes unexplored."

"Then NASA has to attempt a mission."

Walker smiled thinly. "My thoughts exactly."

December 28
The White House
Washington, DC
5:43 p.m.

The President stood at the windows of the Oval Office with her hands clasped behind her back. She thought of her many predecessors, who had contemplated equally difficult problems. Harry Truman said he never lost a night's sleep over using the atomic bomb on Hiroshima and Nagasaki. Ronald Reagan navigated the end of the Cold War in this very room. Barack Obama made the decision to take out Osama bin Laden right here. She wondered what advice those men would give her regarding the current situations involving the Moon and Taiwan.

The casualty lists were almost more than she could bear. Thousands upon thousands of innocent people had been killed, most in transportation accidents as power cut off worldwide. In fact, power was still spotty across the country, and more people could die from contaminated water supplies or other such problems. The economic damage alone could plunge the world into a massive depression.

People had been trying to get their lives back to some semblance of normalcy over the last few days, but since the news about the pulse's source had broken, there had been an uneasiness in many American cities. The spike in crime alone indicated that. The populace was afraid of what all this news could mean, terrified that the warfare that had engulfed parts of the world since the turn of the century could be dwarfed by an imminent attack by alien invaders.

And even if she could convince Americans that there was no imminent threat from space, the report from the East was not good. The Chinese fleet was building in strength and numbers off the coast of Taiwan. Chinese rhetoric had been growing in recent weeks about the island nation, which they considered to be a breakaway province, rightly theirs. Generations of American presidents had supported the one-China, two-systems policy, and China in turn had left well enough alone.

Why are they doing this now? What's to gain from further provocation?

The President had ordered the Pacific Fleet to stand ready in the event of an invasion by mainland Chinese forces. Though the Cold War was long over, the policy regarding containment of Communist forces remained in place, if for no other reason than to protect viable new democracies like Taiwan from aggressive neighbors. But the world would not tolerate such a blatant act of aggression. *She* would not tolerate it.

So what do I do? Engage this country in yet another war while our forces are spread across the globe combating terrorism? When the threat of a full-scale biological or chemical attack is still possible?

A knock on the door stirred the President from her thoughts. In walked her private secretary, a step behind her General McKenna and John Dieckman. The President gestured for the two men to sit as her secretary shut the Oval Office door. She leaned against her desk but remained standing as they spoke. She liked to hear bad news standing.

"Madam President," the general began, looking somewhat embarrassed, "according to our latest intel, we believe that the Chinese maneuvers near Taiwan are a diversion."

"A diversion? A diversion from what?"

"Madam President," Deke said calmly, "the Chinese launched a rocket within the last hour. Everything indicates that it will head toward the Moon. The booster has almost twice the thrust of the old Saturn Vs that took Apollo to the Moon."

"My God. Is it manned?"

"We don't believe so," McKenna said, shaking his head. "We believe that it's an unmanned orbiter designed to study the source of the signal, similar to the one we currently have in orbit. But the booster's the real issue. If they've got a booster with that kind of thrust, then we have to assume it would be capable of sending a crew to the Moon."

The President rubbed her chin. "What's our probe telling us now, Deke?"

"The source of the pulse is definitely the Ocean of Storms. The fissure itself is pretty tremendous—a mile across, ten miles long. We haven't yet been able to ascertain its depth. We might not even be able to without readjusting our orbit."

"Do we have any clue what's inside it?"

"No, ma'am, not yet. But something's definitely down there. We're still picking up residual electromagnetic energy, but it's diminishing by the hour."

"General, what's the current status of the Chinese space program?"

"Fairly advanced, ma'am. Since putting up their first *taikonaut* back in '03, they've fine-tuned their Shenzhou capsules considerably. Most experts believe that their latest capsules are designed with the capacity to travel to the Moon. We believe that the Chinese have put a great deal of money into their program in the hopes of achieving a manned lunar mission by the end of next year. This probe gives every indication that they are attempting to accelerate that program in light of the recent developments in the Ocean of Storms."

The President sat down at her desk. "Are you telling me that they can get to the Moon *before* we do?"

"It's possible, ma'am," McKenna remarked. "They have a heavy booster and a working command module. Present intel indicates that they're having some troubles with a landing module, but we know they've been giving it a vigorous shakedown over the last two years."

The President turned to Dieckman. "And the status of our lander?"

Deke made a face. "Still in development, ma'am. We haven't yet had the funds to get it past the R&D phase."

"General, how do we know that the maneuvers are a diversion?"

"We have two subs shadowing the fleet, plus a Skystalker satellite over its position. It appears they're going in circles and making a big show of it but haven't made any further advances toward Taiwan in the last week."

"Okay, so we know they're not planning to attack Taiwan."

"Not *yet,* Madam President," the general added.

"Deke, what's our mission's status?"

"We're crunching numbers now, ma'am. But it looks as if our best bet to get to the Moon in the time period you've indicated is to modify our Phoenix capsules and copy Apollo ourselves."

"Can we beat the Chinese?"

Dieckman and McKenna looked at each other. Deke spoke up first. "I believe so, ma'am. I've just received a classified document from the air force regarding an experimental booster they tested in the early part of the century. Provided we conduct the operation as a crash program using modern modifications on Apollo's design specs."

"We can beat the Chinese, ma'am," the general said. "After all, we've done this before—they haven't."

The President nodded. "Fine. Just get us there before them. You'll get all the money you need."

"Madam President," McKenna said, clearing his throat, "I must strenuously disagree with a part of NASA's current plan."

"Oh what's that?"

"Ma'am." McKenna gave a sidelong glance to Dieckman. "They want to send *civilian* archeologists on the mission to dig up the damned thing."

The President leaned her elbows on her desk. "Archeologists, Deke?"

"Ma'am, with all due respect to General McKenna," Deke began with a reddened face, "we've trained scientists before. The geologists, for example, who undertook astronaut training in order to go on Apollo—"

"Geologists?" the President wondered. "Forgive me, but my NASA history is spotty. There were geologists on the Apollo missions?"

"There was one, ma'am. Harrison Schmitt went on Apollo 17, the last mission. We were planning to send more of them, but then the later missions were, er, cut, due to a lack of funding."

"Madam President," McKenna interrupted, "sending civilians, with the possibility that there may be a hostile force up there—"

The President held up her hand. "Jim, I understand your concerns, but we've been through this before. All the reports indicate that this object crashed into the Moon long ago. I'm sure the crew, if there was any, is long dead. Which to my mind suggests that we might make use of trained archeologists." She turned to Dieckman. "Do your boys have anyone in mind?"

"Well, ma'am," Deke said, pulling a folder from the pile on his lap, "this man came up as candidate number one. Dr. Alan H. Donovan. He's thirty-five years old, American, currently works for the Zell Institute in England. He's rated top of his field, though something of a maverick, but he's an experienced pilot, not trained by any of the armed forces—"

"Did you say the Zell Institute?" McKenna interjected. "You don't mean that this guy is running around with Elias Zell?"

Deke glanced over some papers in the file. "It says here he was Zell's protégé and now works with him at the institute."

"Zell's a goddamn cowboy, Deke," McKenna grumbled. "You've read all the newspaper reports about him. He's a glory hound, always dragging along reporters to his digs. We can't have someone associated with him go on this mission. Besides, it would mean involving the British—"

"I don't think we have to worry about the British, General." The President took the folder and glanced through it. "I'll take you at your word, Deke." She slid the folder back across the desk toward McKenna. "General, as head of Space Command, I want you to approach this man, feel him out. If you think he's a good match and he's willing to do it, I don't see why we shouldn't offer him the scientific find of a lifetime."

"But ma'am—"

"Thank you, gentlemen." The President stood up; Deke and McKenna followed her example. "Now if you'll excuse me, I have to look over the final draft of my address to the nation tonight."

"Madam President, if you don't mind my asking," Deke said. "Are you planning to tell the public that we're—"

"That we're going back to the Moon? No, I have to reassure the country about the pulse first. We can't show all our cards just yet."

Chapter 3

December 29
Qoriwayrachina Dig Site
Vilcabamba, Peru
7:15 p.m.

Dr. Elias Zell pushed back the mosquito-netting flap from his tent and stepped out into the evening air. The sun was slipping below the horizon, casting the entire dig site in a greenish-gold haze. Zell allowed himself a moment to take it all in. Since arriving in Qoriwayrachina, an Incan outpost that may have been a supply center for larger cities like Machu Picchu, they had been working nonstop and were just beginning to reap the rewards. Yesterday alone they had uncovered silver mines that went a long way toward explaining what the Incas may have been doing in such a remote location. Still, though, there was much work to be done.

The dig at Qoriwayrachina, located at the 12,746-foot summit of Cerro Victoria in the Vilcabamba Range, was just another day at the office for Zell and his team of diggers. As head of the Zell Institute for Archeological Research and Historical Study, he had spent his life in the pursuit of antiquities. The institute had been founded by his father, Thackeray Zell, a respected member of British society who had devoted a considerable portion of his family fortune to uncovering the past. Operating out of Greyhaven Mansion in Burford, in Oxfordshire, Thackeray had used the vast financial resources at his disposal to mount expeditions across the globe. Oh they had laughed at old Thackeray when he made his famous expeditions in search of Noah's ark and the Holy Grail; he almost destroyed his reputation when he attempted to uncover Atlantis. But the discoveries he did make, most notably the incredible underwater excavation of Cleopatra's tomb, distinguished him in the minds of mankind for all time.

Zell sighed, wishing he had some ice for his scotch. He sat down at his collapsible desk just outside his tent, wanting to write down the results of today's findings in his journal, but couldn't take his eyes away from Alan Donovan, his former student and now partner, scrabbling up the rocky slopes of Marcana, the mountain that abutted their camp.

Son of a bitch, he's still at it.

Zell shook his head and lit a cigar, half-hypnotized by the blue-gray smoke curling around his lantern. He knew Donovan should get some sleep and that they could do more at first light. But there was no point in saying anything. Once Donovan got his mind set on something, that was it. Zell knew that as soon as the question of where Qoriwayrachina got its water from was raised, Donovan would not rest until he found the answer. And so here he was, searching for the answers, even as the night closed in.

Zell wished he still had Alan Donovan's endurance. Though only twelve years older than his partner in archeology, every one of Zell's bones creaked, every muscle screamed out to remind him of his day's exertions. *I'm only forty-seven,* he thought. *Why do I feel like a hundred and forty-seven?* He looked at his scotch and cigar and smiled. *Ah, the causes and cures of so many ailments.* Zell knew he was being too hard on himself, that his drinking and cigars were only part of the problem.

He had lived the type of adventurous life few men in the twenty-first century still lived, had seen more places than most would ever see, had broken more bones, had come closer to death more times than he could count. If he wanted a cigar and a sip of scotch to blot out the aches, so what? He had lived enough for five men already and was glad of it.

He thought of Donovan again, out carefully sifting through earth for pieces of the past, the knees of his khaki pants no doubt thick with dirt. With a couple of drinks in him, Zell would tell anyone who was listening how Alan Donovan wouldn't even lift his head from the ground if the most beautiful girl in the world passed by—not that many gorgeous women sauntered by in their line of work. A bad joke, as he well knew, but that didn't stop him from repeating it.

"Elias!" came Donovan's voice from somewhere above him.

Zell sat upright. He'd been with Donovan long enough to read the tone of his voice. He'd found something. Zell stood up, hearing the electric pop of his joints as he did.

"This had better be good, Alan," he called. "I just was starting to review the day's work."

"Your scotch and cigars can wait," Donovan called back. "Now get up here!"

Zell began clawing his way up the embankment. As much as his bones ached, he knew better than to ignore when Alan Donovan had made a find. Alan was one of the brightest students Zell had ever seen. His mind absorbed history and ate up the technical aspects of the archeological field like nobody's business. But he was stubborn. Boy, was he ever stubborn. Once they had argued for days on the dating of certain skull fragments they had found in South Africa. Alan was convinced they had found a unique australopithecine specimen and did his damnedest to bring Zell over to his way of thinking. A fairly violent battle ensued between teacher and student, one that wouldn't have been tolerated if Alan had been any other apprentice. Yet, when they had unearthed the rest of the skeleton, Zell was forced to agree with his conclusions.

At last he reached Donovan's position. His old student was standing amid a set of hidden gullies, grinning almost madly as he watched the water roar past. The wind caused by the water's force whipped through his thick black hair. Donovan, his gray-blue eyes dancing, looked at his old friend.

"There's our water supply!" he said.

"Amazing," Zell marveled. "So what's your theory, Doctor?"

"There's got to be a second lake up there somewhere," Donovan said. "Maybe made up of meltwater from Marcana's snows. But that's not all—look."

Donovan led Zell to a section of the mountain where a line of stones seemed to form a channel that took the water more than five miles from the lake down to Qoriwayrachina. Zell looked at the channel a moment, the gears in his head now whirring.

"That's a lot of effort on the part of the Incas," he said. "Makes you wonder what was so important about this area that they'd go this far to sustain it."

Donovan clapped Zell on the shoulder. "Exactly!" he said. "All the more reason we need to get back to work at first light." He turned to walk down the mountain. "Come on, Luis and Cristian will want to hear about this."

As Donovan and Zell began to make the trek back to camp, Zell looked at his friend and spoke. "Your father would be proud, you know."

"My father?" asked Donovan. "He was a geologist, not an archeologist, remember?"

Donovan moved ahead of Zell, leaving him with his memories. Hunter Donovan had been one of the geologists selected for the Apollo missions, one of the many who never got the chance to go to the Moon, Zell recalled. But Hunter's case was different. It wasn't budget cuts that sidelined him but a minor heart fibrillation, so minor that many doctors questioned whether he even had one. Yet that didn't stop NASA's doctors from grounding him, though Zell long suspected there was more to their decision than that. Cal Walker, a top rocket engineer at NASA, hated geologists on principle, figuring that any astronaut could be taught to do what they did. And he had a particular hatred for Hunter, who was considered the best prospect for the geologist-astronaut program since he was also a trained pilot from his time in the navy.

That prick really screwed you good, old friend, Zell thought as he scanned the ghost of the Moon, now just coming into view.

Zell turned his attention back toward the past as he made his way down the slope. *Alan works himself too hard,* Zell mused. *He works himself because of what his father was and what his father became.* Hunter Donovan was the most disciplined man Zell ever knew, disciplined in such a way that if you pulled one piece from the way he was built, the whole man crumbled. Walker and NASA took that piece from Hunter and he was never the same.

He had been in awe of Hunter Donovan. Zell had met the man through his father, shortly after Hunter left NASA. Not only had Hunter been an ace navy pilot and chosen for the astronaut program, he had also received advanced degrees in geology and was one of the leading experts on the geological history of the Moon. He was a man not unlike Teddy Roosevelt, someone who could be a hundred things at once and never seem lacking in any category. Thackeray had selected him to accompany the institute on a dig in Antarctica. Hunter had helped them excavate and analyze thousands of meteorite samples on the East Antarctic ice sheet. But, in spite of his achievements, Hunter was well on the way to his ruination. As much as he had tried to block the disappointment of being grounded, and later the loss of his young wife to cancer, he couldn't stop dwelling in the past. His drinking finally caught up with him when he died of a heart attack. By that point, the only job he had been able to hold down was dusting crops somewhere near Modesto, California. Left without a father, Alan was taken in by

Thackeray and raised at the institute. Zell, then in his early twenties, became something of a big brother to the twelve-year-old orphan. Many times, when he was home on break from Oxford, Zell would tell Alan tales of the Han dynasty, the Ark of the Covenant, and the mysteries that lay scattered below the world's oceans. As he grew older, Donovan began joining Zell and Thackeray on digs all over the globe. When Zell took over the institute after his father's death, there was no question in Alan's mind where he belonged. Over the years, through scores of adventures, their friendship had evolved from mentor to student to a more equal plane, one built on mutual respect and admiration.

"Come on, Elias," Donovan called from the mountain's base. "What's the matter? Can't walk as fast without your cane?"

Zell dismissed him with a wave of his hand and walked over to the camp, where some of the other members of their team were working on the day's findings. One of them, a young man named Canessa, was reviewing his findings at a burial chamber.

"Look here," he said, calling Donovan and Zell over. "The bones we found, the woman. She's Inca, but nothing else about the cist is."

"And where's the skull?" wondered Donovan. "Usually that's the last to decay."

Cristian, another member of the Peruvian team, spoke up. "It's possible it's in another cist."

"Maybe," said Zell. "This woman was someone of importance," he noted, gesturing at some of the objects on the table. "Look at the silver pin. An average Inca woman fastened her shawls with copper."

As the team continued reviewing their work, a wind began to pick up, softly at first, then swirling with the force of a gale. Zell looked up into the sky, wondering why there weren't any threatening clouds overhead. Then he heard the almost silent whump-whump-whump of a muted engine and looked over the treetops to see the lights of an American black-ops helicopter coming toward their site. Donovan was running toward it, screaming and gesturing.

"The woman, the woman!" yelled Canessa, throwing a tarp over the bones.

All that work ruined, Zell thought. But before he could get as angry as Alan was, he began to wonder what a military helicopter was doing at their site. Not to evict them. Then what?

From the helicopter emerged a silver-haired army general about sixty years of age. He held his hat under his arm, and between his teeth was a large, unlit Havana cigar. The lights from the helicopter illuminated his green uniform, its sharpness contrasting with Donovan's disheveled attire. Zell crouched beneath the still-whirling blades and approached the newcomer. Donovan was already giving him an earful.

"Do you have any *fucking* idea how much work you've just ruined?" Donovan demanded.

The general kept his ramrod military bearing under the whirling blades, which was fine, as he couldn't have been more than five feet seven. "Am I speaking to Dr. Alan H. Donovan of the Zell Institute?"

"You're damn right you are. Who the hell are you?"

"General James Francis McKenna, at your service, sir."

"Well, General James Francis McKenna, what the hell gives you the right to—"

The general turned to Zell. "And you must be Dr. Elias Zell."

"I am, General. I assume you didn't just come here to destroy my dig and make small talk, so let's get down to it, shall we?"

"Sorry for any trouble we may have caused," he said, sliding a finger across his throat so the pilot would cut his engines.

Donovan looked as if he were ready to deck the diminutive general. "What's this all about, General McKenna?"

"It's a matter of national security, Dr. Donovan. I've been cleared to brief both you and Dr. Zell on it."

Donovan's eyes narrowed. "What matter of national security?"

"Well, Dr. Donovan, it's about the pulse."

"The pulse?" Donovan asked. "What's that got to do with us?"

"What's the pulse got to do with you?" McKenna asked, flabbergasted.

Zell stepped forward, a genial smile on his face. "Forgive my colleague, General. He gets somewhat absorbed in his work."

"That's exactly why we've sought you out." McKenna looked around at the team of diggers who had now gathered around the helicopter. "Is there someplace a little quieter, where we can talk?"

"My tent," Zell said, gesturing toward it. "That is, if your pilot hasn't blown it into the valley."

Donovan sat on Zell's cot, scratching at a week's growth of black stubble. He shook his head again and turned to Zell, who was sitting next to him trying to rekindle his extinguished cigar with his gold Zippo. The general sat in Zell's spare chair bolt upright with his hat in his lap. The air inside the tent was thick with the scent of expensive cigars.

"So let me get this straight," Donovan said. "NASA believes that this EM pulse came from the Moon, and they want me to tag along on some tossed-together mission and dig up whatever caused it?"

"That's the long and short of it, Dr. Donovan. The government ran a computer check of all qualified American archeologists, and your name popped up as candidate number one."

"And why is that?" Donovan wondered.

"Your experience in finding artifacts in hard-to-reach places," the general noted, "and of course your, shall we say, *unorthodox* methods that speed up recovery rates."

"This wouldn't have anything to do with NASA screwing my father out of a mission on Apollo, would it?"

The general seemed genuinely surprised. "I was not aware that your father was an astronaut, Dr. Donovan."

"He wasn't, thanks to NASA. They wanted geologists, and they got a ton, but when it came right down to it, it was a matter of who kissed the most brass."

"Alan," Zell said, shooting him a look. "General, now my field isn't electromagnetics, but isn't it possible that this pulse was caused by some kind of—I don't know—naturally occurring phenomenon?"

The general tapped some ash off his cigar in a nearby ashtray. "A lot of folks have said that. But they don't know what I'm about to tell you—a naturally occurring phenomenon doesn't send along landing coordinates."

"Landing coordinates?" A wave of shock overcame Zell's face. "Are you certain?"

"Positive. They're the landing coordinates to the Ocean of Storms. Some of the brightest minds at NASA have speculated that the fissure and the resulting EM pulse that emanated from it was just a way of getting our attention."

"It doesn't make any sense." Donovan ran a hand through his hair. "If what you're saying is true, that it's coming from the Ocean of Storms, then the crew of Apollo 12 should've picked up this EM energy. They had walked all over the damned—"

"Our best guess is that it was completely buried when Apollo 12 landed back in '69. It's possible that whoever buried this object there two million–odd years ago may have timed it to go off on a particular date." McKenna continued after letting that last thought sink in for a moment. "With this fissure having opened up over the suspected buried object, we believe it would be a relatively easy matter for an experienced archeology team to dig it up and—"

"A relatively easy matter?" Donovan laughed, looking at the lantern hanging in the center of Zell's tent. "Do you have any idea how difficult that work would be, even if it were partly exposed? We would be digging on the *Moon*, General, one-sixth the gravity of the Earth, in space suits not designed for the careful manipulations of an archeological dig—"

"NASA has promised to provide you with all the equipment and training you need."

"It's been my experience that NASA's promises aren't worth a hell of a lot."

"Alan," Zell said curtly. "General, wouldn't it be better for NASA to send an unmanned probe to the Moon to dig it out? The object on the Moon could be powered by some type of nuclear battery, which could be harmful—"

General McKenna waved his cigar. "NASA has a satellite in lunar orbit right now. All the spectral analysis indicates that no harmful radiation seems to be emanating from the object. Further, it would take several years to design and build an unmanned robot probe to dig it up. By that time the world could be thrown into a complete panic. Such a panic the President does not take lightly, especially in the current political climate." He sighed. "Besides, there's the Chinese to consider."

Donovan folded his arms. "What about the Chinese?"

The general gave a short, quick nod. "I've been cleared to give you this information. Spy satellites indicate that the Chinese sent an unmanned probe this week, with the possibility of sending a manned expedition sometime this summer."

"So that's it!" Donovan said, slapping the tent post. "You guys just want to beat somebody else to the Moon. This isn't about science at all; it's about sticking the Stars and Stripes in the ground and chalking up another victory for American ingenuity."

The general stood up and looked as if he was prepared to walk out. He turned and looked squarely at Donovan. "I can assure you, Dr. Donovan, that if this mission is successful, it *will* be due to American ingenuity. However, this mission is of vital importance to science, and we are treating it as such. It could very well mean that we're being contacted by beings who came to our solar system eons before humanity could rub two sticks together. However, the President believes that whatever information that object holds should be shared with all of humanity. The best way of sharing that information would be for the United States to mount a recovery mission. As you are well aware, the People's Republic of China does not share our beliefs regarding the dissemination of information."

"Wave that flag, General," Donovan chuckled. "But you're not convincing me. We'll go there, study whatever caused the pulse, and abandon the Moon as we did before, when you fellas in the military convinced the government that you needed a little more cash."

The general pursed his lips slightly. "So I take it you are not interested in serving on this mission?"

"Let me put it to you this way, General. Tell NASA to go to hell."

"Goddamn it, Alan!"

General McKenna ignored the outbursts. "I have been asked by your president to remind you that your country would be in your debt if you should choose to accept—"

"My country owes my father a debt, but he's not here to collect."

The general nodded stiffly. "Very well."

Zell cleared his throat. "I'll walk you out, General."

Donovan poured himself another scotch, holding the drink in his hand as he paced back and forth across the center of Zell's tent. *Some goddamn nerve,* he thought. *Let them get some other patsy to go to the Moon. What the hell did they come here and ask me for?*

Zell came in as the tent began billowing. He stood for a second by the flap, watching the helicopter lights disappear over the treetops. Then he turned and tossed his hat on the cot and refilled his glass.

"You're a stupid bastard," Zell said flatly as he stuffed the cork back in the bottle and sat down.

"Don't start, Elias."

He turned to look at his former student. Thirty-five years old and just as much of a hard case as when he was a child. "Do you happen to have any idea what you've just turned down?"

"I turned down a mission that will probably be scrapped the second NASA sends another probe and realizes they've got nothing more than—as you said—some naturally occurring phenomenon on their hands."

"And what if it's not? What if it is what they're saying it is—an ancient object placed there by a civilization that came to our solar system millions of years ago? What then, Alan?"

"Come on, Elias. That's science fiction. Do you really think it's all that?"

Zell slapped his thigh. "How could it *not* be, Alan? You heard the damn intelligence for yourself. But to turn down an opportunity like that without looking at any of their data, just because you've got a goddamn chip on your shoulder the size of the Rock of Gibraltar—"

Donovan waved his scotch glass at his mentor. "I do not have a chip on my shoulder."

"You do. You do and you damn well know it, Alan. You know what you just threw away? The dig of a lifetime. Goddamn stupid sack of shit is what you are."

"Well, there's no point in beating me up about it. It's gone, whatever it was. You think that brass hat is gonna come back here on his knees asking me to do this dig? Forget about it. I know these military types. When you say no, it's taken as such."

Zell smirked. "Are you so sure it was an absolute no?"

"What are you getting at?"

Zell stretched back in his chair with a sigh. "Let's just say I made sure you didn't slam the door."

"Come again?"

"I left the door open. I know what's best for you, even if you don't. I told the general you'd think about it. That I'd get you to change your mind."

Donovan shook his head. "You did what? Where do you get off?"

"Alan," he said after another sip of scotch, "you're a good archeologist. Perhaps as good as my own father was, God rest his soul. You're willing to take risks. To dare to imagine. That is, provided that your damn pride doesn't get in the way."

"So then you told him—"

"I told him that you'd look over NASA's data." Zell reached into his breast pocket and pulled out a one-terabyte flash drive. "This data. And that you'd get back to him first thing in the morning."

Donovan grinned over his scotch glass at the small black object in Zell's hand. "Oh you did, did you?"

Zell held it up to the lantern. "If you're not curious, I could just . . . toss this."

Donovan snatched it from Zell's fingers and sat on the bed. "Do you really think—"

"Alan, something no one can see from orbit is sitting about a mile below the surface. A fissure one mile wide and ten miles long opened up over this object just before the pulse hit the Earth. It sent landing coordinates to the Ocean of Storms. All it needs is a goddamn X to mark the spot. What the hell do you think it is?"

He smiled. "It's not ours. Definitely. Nothing we've ever built could hit the Moon at such a speed and bury itself that deep in the surface and still be able to emit a signal. It can't be ours."

Zell folded his arms. "And now you have the opportunity to go and dig it up. The first artifact from not only another age but from a civilization not even remotely human."

"Not even remotely human," Donovan repeated. "You know what this is?"

"I already told you. The dig of a lifetime."

"The Moon, Elias. It's been on the Moon all this time, since long before *Homo sapiens* walked the Earth. All those years of us shooting radio signals into the sky, and this has been sitting right in our backyard."

Zell picked up his laptop. "Do you want to look at the data?"

"Yeah. But this doesn't mean I'm going to join this little camping trip. After all, NASA hasn't given me everything I want yet."

"What the hell else could they give you? They're offering you all the equipment and training you need, a goddamn moon shot by the summer—"

Donovan rubbed his bristled chin and smirked. "There's one thing they haven't offered me yet. Choice over my team of archeologists. I mean, they can't expect me to dig this up all by myself."

Zell waved away that notion. "Ach, they'll give you whomever you want. They're nuts to beat the Chinese there. They'd give you anybody."

"Even you?"

"Me?"

"Well," Donovan said, slapping Zell on the knee, "if they want me, they're getting you. After all, we're a matching set."

Zell stood up, glass and cigar in hand, and went out to take in the night air. He chortled, shaking his head. "You *really* are a stupid bastard."

Donovan watched his friend go, then turned the flash drive over and over in his hand thoughtfully.

"And you really are going to the Moon."

Chapter 4

December 31
Houston, Texas
5:47 a.m.

The SH-60B Sea Hawk thundered across the dawn sky, en route to Houston. Two days had passed since Donovan and Zell first met McKenna, and they hadn't done much sleeping since. As they sailed over the landscape, Donovan peered out the helo's window, taking note of the occasional flickering dots of light that flecked the landscape.

"What are those lights?" Donovan asked the pilot.

"Fires, sir," he answered. "Cities all over are going up in smoke. A lot of folks think it's the end of the world. Over in Galveston, some cult calling themselves the Pillars of Revelation walked into a fast-food restaurant and killed everyone there with automatic weapons, then offed themselves on TV when the news crews arrived. A note left behind said that it was the first of many 'cleansings' that had to be done before God's hand wiped the Earth clean, or some happy crappy like that."

"Jesus," Donovan whispered.

"I'd be calling that name a lot more if I were you, sir," the pilot said. "Just last night a NASA scientist was killed in Houston because some nuts thought he had something to do with the pulse. Killers cut his throat with a butter knife, then tried to use it to saw his head off. Cops caught them in the act about three-quarters of the way through."

A material silence filled the helicopter's cabin. Zell gazed out at the smoldering world below him. He thought of his grandmother's stories about the war, of London burning during the Blitz as she and other children her age fled to the relative safety of the English countryside.

"Happy New Year."

Upon their arrival in Houston, Donovan and Zell were greeted by a security detail in an armored Humvee. The two men were then escorted to their accommodations, a motel right around the corner from the Johnson Space Center. Zell peered out the Hummer's window at the rather modest lodgings, then tapped the driver on the shoulder.

"My good man," he said, "is your GPS up to snuff?"

"Five by five, sir," the driver said.

"Then enter this address, if you please . . ."

In less than an hour, they were settling into the Zell Institute's regular luxury suite at Houston's famous Hotel Derek. The pair, who had spent the last month sleeping in a bug-infested tent in the middle of Peru, was eager to spoil themselves a bit. After a long workout in the hotel's weight room, followed by sixty laps in the pool, Donovan was sitting in the hotel room idly flipping through channels. From one end of the dial to the other, it was all the same. Chaos. The President's press conference had done little to extinguish the fuse on a powder keg that was already itching to go off. In a growing number of places in the country, people were rioting, looting, or just lamenting to anyone who would listen that the end had come at last. Others had decided to take advantage of the situation. Makeshift booths had sprung up in cities everywhere selling T-shirts ("The Man in the Moon Is Watching . . ." was the most popular one), bumper stickers ("E.T. Phoned *Me*"), and "authentic" moon rocks.

Some channels were still devoting attention to the TGI congressional hearings, which had become somewhat more heated in the wake of the President's speech. TGI executives were now making the argument that the human race may be poised on the brink of annihilation, and cloning may be the only way to stave off genocide. The argument was bogus, Donovan felt, but one that seemed to be turning the odds in the company's favor.

At that moment, the bathroom door swung open and a cloud of steam washed into the suite's common room. Zell stepped out of it in one of his monogrammed bathrobes, looking like a new man. He strolled over to the bar and poured himself a scotch with two ice cubes, then padded over to his suitcase, where, after a small amount of digging, he produced a box of Cohibas. Neatly clipping the end off, he lit the cigar, then sank into a chair across from Donovan and exhaled a haze of blue smoke. Donovan looked at his old friend and smiled. Zell could spend months sleeping in a ditch he dug himself with only a palm frond for a blanket, but put him in the lap of luxury, and he transformed instantly back into a proper blue-blooded English gentleman.

"What?" Zell said, noticing Donovan's look.

"Enjoying yourself?" Donovan asked, then gestured at the television. "While all this is going on?"

Zell dragged on his cigar. "It was your idea to bring me along on this little camping trip. They wanted you. I figured as long as I'm here, I may as well indulge myself a bit."

"It's NASA who's indulging themselves," Donovan said. "You know they're just going to pick our brains a bit, then send us packing while they take all the credit." Taking note of Zell's disinterested expression, he leaned in conspiratorially. "C'mon. You and I both know there's no way they're going to send two untrained men to the Moon. Two *civilians*. They barely did it in the heyday of the space program. Trust me, at the end of the day, they'll chew us up, spit us out, and send us off with a grant that will probably amount to what I made on my paper route."

"You never had a paper route," Zell countered.

Donovan stood up, exasperated. "You're missing the point."

"No, you're missing the point," his former mentor shot back, weary of Donovan's petulance. "At first we thought this was just going to be the dig of a lifetime. And it is, for certain, it is. But damn it, Alan, look around you. The whole damn world's coming apart at the seams, and we're being offered a chance to help put it back together. This has ceased to be just about you and your father. It's bigger than that now. Bigger than any of us. And unless you've got a glass navel, I'd suggest you get your head out of your ass so you can actually see what's going on here."

Donovan stared out the window for a moment, looking down on the street below. He thought a moment longer, then turned to Zell.

"Get dressed," he said, a smile cracking his face. "I'm buying."

Zell pointed at him with his cigar. "Now you're thinking, boyo."

Donovan went to get changed himself, then stopped and turned around. "Elias?"

"Yes, Alan?"

Donovan paused a second before speaking up. "A glass navel?"

Zell's baritone laugh filled the room. He shook the cubes in his glass. "A few more of these and it'll make sense, trust me."

As any good and responsible pair of scientists would do when faced with a world in upheaval, Donovan and Zell spent the evening getting good and soundly drunk. The men had a few good friends at the

Houston Archeological Society, as well as at the archeology department of Rice University. A few well-placed phone calls, and Donovan and Zell soon found themselves hosting a New Year's Eve steak dinner at the hotel's renowned Revolve Kitchen. Although the mood was somewhat more somber than New Year's Eves past, food was consumed, wine was poured, and tales were told, some taller than others. At midnight, the champagne corks were solemnly popped. For the two archeologists, it was a welcome return to the real world after a month in the field. And, in some ways, they knew it might be the last time they had an evening like this for a long while.

Around two that morning, they were seated in Derek's bar, nursing the last in a seemingly endless line of scotches. Donovan was well in his cups, but Zell, always the picture of control, looked as sober as a choirboy, despite having ingested enough liquor to make Winston Churchill blush. He was sitting quietly, dragging on one of his hand-rolled cigars.

Overhead the TV droned on, tuned to one of the twenty-four-hour news channels. Although news about the EM pulse and its effects had died down, there was still rampant speculation as to what was really going on up there. Right now a popular radio-talk-show host was rambling on about the conspiracies surrounding the events of the last ten days. As he talked, his Adam's apple vibrated wildly, causing his bow tie to bounce up and down in a curious rhythm. "I've been studying this topic for some time," he continued, spittle flying liberally from his lips as he did, "and I'm telling you that NASA has known about this alien presence on the Moon since the early days of the space program. And this presence has attempted to make contact long before then. In 1955, something blocked astronomers' view of the Taurus-Littrow area. In 1882, moving shadows were spotted in the Aristotle area of the Moon. And in 1587, astronomers reported seeing a star within the body of a crescent moon!"

Donovan watched this performance, then nudged Zell. "You see this?" he said. "This is what we're up against, here."

"What are you talking about?"

"This rampant paranoia, fear, distrust, all of it," Donovan answered. "This has gone beyond archeology. It's teetering on something bigger than the search for alien life. People are searching for something more."

"And that would be?" Zell asked, puffing away.

Donovan thought a moment. "Damned if I know."

January 2
Johnson Space Center
Houston, Texas
8:31 a.m.

Established in 1961, the Johnson Space Center was originally named the Manned Spacecraft Center. Only after former president and Texas native Lyndon Baines Johnson passed away in 1973 did it get its new name. If the launch towers and fiery rockets of Florida's Cape Canaveral represent the soul of NASA, then the JSC is most certainly its brain, and, some might argue, its heart. Every mission since Gemini IV has been handled from JSC's Mission Control. There men were first guided down to the Sea of Tranquility in 1969. Later the tense days of Apollo 13 played out in 1970, and much later staff watched helplessly as *Columbia* fell from the sky in 2003.

On top of Mission Control, the JSC was also home to the astronaut corps and the principal training site for all space missions.

While the JSC's primary focus was the stars, scores of scientists there also toiled daily to make life on Earth better. Everything from memory foam to scratchproof eyeglass lenses came from the JSC, using NASA technology developed for spaceflight. If travel to the stars represented the cutting edge of technological achievement, then the JSC was forever sharpening the blade.

After a much-needed day of rest and recovery, Donovan and Zell went back to work. They had been picked up at their hotel just after seven and briefed on the ride to the space center by one of the team members assigned to analyze the EM signal. After a cursory tour, they were ushered into a conference room, where John Dieckman was waiting for them.

"Dr. Zell, Dr. Donovan," he said, extending his hand. "It's a pleasure. I've read your dossiers, and I'm impressed."

"Thank you, Mr. Dieckman," Zell replied, grasping his hand firmly.

"Dr. Donovan," Dieckman said, "it's especially nice to meet you. I heard your father speak once. Here, actually. A lecture on geologic activity at Fra Mauro."

"My father?" Donovan said. "You must have been what—five years old?"

"Six, actually," Dieckman said. "I came here with my uncle. He was an engineer at Grumman and took me out here on a business trip." Dieckman paused. "It was that trip, and your father's speech, that first got me interested in working for NASA one day."

Donovan nodded, smiling inwardly at this slight validation of his father's work. "Thank you."

"Yes, well, now here I am, and here you are, and we've got work to do." Dieckman turned and reached into his briefcase, pulling out two large rocks. He placed them on a table with a thud. "Here are two rock samples from the Apollo 12 EVA in November 1969. It's not much to go on, but right now it's the only physical link we have to whatever's going on up there. Can you tell me anything?"

Donovan picked up one of the rocks and turned it over in his hands. "Well, I'm not a geologist, Mr. Dieckman," he said, "but the first thing that I notice is the abundance of refractory elements in the surface."

"Refractory?" asked Dieckman.

"Resistant to heat or decomposition," Donovan answered. "Could be something like titanium. What's unusual is that, on Earth, heavier elements are pushed to the core of the rock, while lighter materials are drawn to the surface. Here we've got the reverse."

"What do you think it means?" asked Dieckman.

"Again, I'm sure a geologist could tell you more, but it makes me think that these elements were somehow *brought* to the surface of the rock. How, well, I couldn't even begin to guess. To do that would . . ."

Zell studied the rocks a moment, then took out his key chain, which had, among various other knickknacks, a small magnet dangling from it. He held the keys over the rocks. The movement was slight but unmistakably there. The keys were slowly drawn to the rock. He looked at Dieckman. "You know these rocks are magnetized."

"That's right."

"But how? The Moon has no magnetic field."

"Residual from the Earth's magnetic field?" Donovan suggested.

"Impossible," replied Zell. "The Roche limit prevents the Earth from getting too close to the Moon."

"So your findings, gentlemen?" asked Dieckman.

"In my professional opinion," said Donovan, "there's definitely something weird up there."

Dieckman smiled. "I'm glad we flew you all the way from Peru for that assessment." He stood up. "Now, if you'll follow me, we'll get down to business."

"Business?" asked Donovan.

"You think there's something weird on the Moon?" said Dieckman. "Trust me, Dr. Donovan, you ain't seen nothing yet."

They left the conference room and made their way through the center's corridors. As they walked, Dieckman began filling them in on some of the stranger goings-on on the Moon.

"In a way, this whole incident shouldn't be entirely unexpected," he said. "If you look back at the history of lunar exploration, there's more that we *don't* understand about our nearest neighbor."

"Such as?" asked Zell.

"Well, for example, the upper eight miles of the Moon's crust are shockingly radioactive. Thermal readings taken by the Apollo 15 astronauts near the Apennine Mountains were nearly off the chart. Some experts thought this meant the core was hot. We now know that's not the case; it's quite cold, in fact. So the question remains, where's this radiation coming from?"

"And you think it might have something to do with our visitors?" asked Donovan.

"Your guess is as good as mine, Dr. Donovan, but it seems logical," Dieckman answered. "Here's one that'll get you thinking. Unmanned probes we've sent in recent years have shown that much of the Moon's surface is covered with a fine glaze, almost like glass."

"Couldn't that be caused by heat from meteor impacts?" asked Zell.

"Not to this extent, no," Dieckman said. "There's no doubt about it. Something, something big, scorched the Moon's surface so intensely that it paved most of the target area over with glass. Ah, here we are, Mission Control."

Located in building 30 of the Johnson Space Center, the Christopher C. Kraft Jr. Mission Control Center was the nerve center of NASA's operations. The three-story facility was primarily made up of two wings, one for mission operations and the second for operations support. After a rocket cleared the tower at Cape Canaveral, control of the flight was kicked over to Mission Control, where it remained until touchdown. From there, flight controllers handled every element of the mission, no matter how trivial. On the building's second floor, astronauts conducted simulated flights, running through every possible scenario to ensure that there would be no surprises in a mission. The second floor was also home to the Mission Operations Control Room, where every piece of information related to the flight, be it technical, operational, or even meteorological, was processed and displayed. Donovan and Zell were escorted to this room. Although neither of them had ever harbored more than average interest in space travel, they were awed by the sight. On the far walls of the room, a half dozen jumbo television screens provided an ongoing stream of data from the lunar orbiter Stellaluna while another set of screens seemed to be devoted to data coming from the ongoing mission at the International Space Station, where the current crew was also monitoring the situation on the Moon. On the ceiling, illuminated panels displayed the flags of various nations who had contributed to the ISS project. And all around them were workstations filled by technicians, physicists, and lunar experts, poring over lunar data and relaying their findings from department to department.

"Here's where it all happens, gentlemen," said Dieckman. "As you can see, we're monitoring the data sent to us by Stellaluna, the probe currently in lunar orbit. It's fragmentary, obviously. But it's enough to give us a sense of what we're dealing with. Plus, we've got every hi-tech satellite and earthbound telescope we could spare pointed in that direction."

"So what data have you got for us?" asked Donovan.

"Take a look at this monitor here," said Dieckman, leading them over to one of the massive LED screens. "Stellaluna detected massive concentrations of gravity, or mascons, located in and around the Ocean of Storms. These mascons were so great that, after rechecking Stellaluna's orbit, we found that the probe dipped slightly and accelerated when passing overhead. So what could cause a gravitational field like that?"

"A large concentration of dense matter beneath the surface," said Donovan, his eyes fixed on the screen.

"Right, and that's not all." Dieckman picked up a glass case from the desk and handed it to Donovan. Inside were small iron particles, almost like ball bearings.

"These particles, and others like them, were brought back from the Moon by the Apollo astronauts," explained Dieckman. "Incredibly, after nearly half a century on Earth, they show no signs of oxidization."

"Rustproof iron, eh?" said Zell. "Nothing of the kind exists in our world."

"Not true," said Donovan. "At the Quwwat-ul-Islam mosque in New Delhi, there's an iron pillar that hasn't rusted in almost two thousand years."

"That's right!" said Zell, snapping his fingers in remembrance. "To this day scientists can't identify the alloy."

"Either way," said Dieckman, "it's clear we're in uncharted waters."

"I'll say," said Donovan. "So what's the next step?"

"Well, we're launching a satellite tomorrow, the SIR-K," said Dieckman. "It's an imaging system that sends out its own radar signal and then 'listens' to the echo."

"Spaceborne imaging radar. Kind of like the Landsats you have in orbit that send digital data back to Earth," said Zell.

Dieckman grinned. "I've got to say I'm impressed, Dr. Zell. Yes, it's similar, only the Landsats use reflected sunlight to send an image. For more details, I should turn you over to the man behind the curtain, William Egan."

A shaggy-haired man wearing faded jeans, flip-flops, and a Rush T-shirt stepped up and put out his hand. He couldn't have been more than twenty-four years old.

"William Egan," Zell said. "The same William Egan who codesigned the AEV 22 Space Telescope at the Jet Propulsion Laboratory?"

"The very same, my friend," he said with a bit of a theatrical flourish.

"I remember reading about it in the *Science Times*," Zell said. "I thought you were recruited out of MIT."

"I was," said Egan, pushing his glasses up his nose. "Halfway through my sophomore year."

"Bill is one of the brightest minds we've got around here," said Dieckman. "He's also been helping design the ship that's taking you and the rest of the crew to the Moon."

"C'mon, let me show you how it works," said Egan with all the excitement of a kid at Christmas. He sat at his terminal, which was decorated with triathlon medals and cluttered with printouts and books that included a dog-eared edition of the Dungeons and Dragons *Fiend Folio*.

"Okay," he said, cracking his knuckles. "Basically, imaging radar is like a flash camera, right? A camera sends out a flash of light and records the light that's reflected back through the camera lens. Got it? So, instead of a lens and film, radar uses an antenna and digital computer tapes to record its images. In a radar image, one can see only the light that was reflected back toward the radar antenna. So, what we did was send one of our little birdies up there, ran a few imaging cycles, and *whap!*" He struck a few keys like a concert pianist finishing a sonata. Instantly an eerie image of the lunar landscape popped up. At its center was a dark-blue mass.

"There she is," said Egan. "Since the image is so dark, we can safely assume that it's a flat surface. Buildings or any kind of topography will bounce the signal off each other, what's called a 'double bounce.' They'll always show up white."

"She's big," Donovan said, letting out a whistle.

"And deep," Egan said. "About a mile down."

"So much for digging it up," Zell said. "We'll have to descend through the fissure itself, see what we can see from the inside."

"Couldn't dig it up anyway, even if we wanted," Donovan said. "Much of the surface in that area is made up of titanium, zirconium, and beryllium. I remember reading one of my father's old papers. He remarked that it was strange that these metals were there, as ordinarily they'd require extreme heat, somewhere around forty-five hundred degrees Fahrenheit, to fuse with rock."

Zell stared at the image a moment, lost in thought. Then he clapped Donovan and Egan on the shoulders.

"How's the coffee here, my boy?" he asked Egan.

"Detestable," came the affable reply.

"Excellent! Put on a fresh pot. We've got work to do. If we're going to uncover this Cracker Jack prize, we've got to know everything about where she is and, if possible, how in the hell she got there. Mr. Dieckman, I'll need every bit of information you've got on the Ocean of Storms, including the mission logs and transcripts from the 1969 landing."

"You got it, Dr. Zell," Dieckman said, enthused that progress was being made.

With that, they turned to leave. As they were heading out the door, McKenna stormed in.

"Gentlemen, I'm glad I caught you," he said. "I've got some disturbing news."

He tossed a file on the desk, spilling out some satellite photos.

"Two days ago, the Chinese launched a rocket, headed for the Moon," McKenna said. "We thought it was just another unmanned flyby. They had been sending them up even before the pulse occurred."

McKenna sifted through the photos, finally producing one seemingly taken from the Moon's dark side. "Skystalker satellites in geosynchronous orbit above the Moon picked this up last night." He pointed at the picture. "That's the Moon," he said. "And *that's* a manned command module."

There was silence in the room as everyone took this in.

McKenna turned to Zell and Donovan. "You just joined the second space race, boys," he said. "And the US is officially one lap behind."

Chapter 5

January 11
Johnson Space Center
Houston, Texas
6:12 p.m.

In many ways it's really not as bad as we figured. But in most of the ways that count it's a helluva lot worse.

John Dieckman sat at his desk in Houston and popped another pill. His acid-reflux disorder had been acting up again despite the corrective surgery he had undergone ten years earlier. His doctor said it was psychosomatic, that there was no evidence that the disorder had reoccurred. No matter the assurances, most days he still felt like he was drinking battery acid.

The Chinese mission had returned to Earth successfully. The craft splashed down in the South China Sea off the coast of Hong Kong in a manner not too dissimilar from the old Apollo landings. The splashdown gave further confirmation to American intelligence that the Chinese were indeed mimicking the Apollo program down to the letter, since earlier manned Chinese missions were modeled on the old Soviet Soyuz, which had come down on land.

The Chinese crew was alive and well and had returned to Beijing armed with film taken over the Ocean of Storms, as well as areas of the dark side of the Moon. The photos, which the Chinese government immediately disseminated to all major media outlets, conclusively proved that there was no apparent alien ship parked on the surface of the Moon, nor was there an alien armada lurking on the dark side, waiting to attack the Earth. This left most conspiracy theorists disappointed but alleviated the general panic in streets all over the world. The riots mostly subsided, people returned to their homes, and families went to cemeteries to bury those killed in the mass uprisings. The Chinese mission had done a service to humanity, much to the President's dismay.

The President's mood wasn't helped much by the Chinese ambassador's performance at the United Nations, where he displayed the photographs at a meeting of the General Assembly and touted the fact that the Chinese had undertaken this dangerous mission for the sake of "world peace" and to "add to the general and scientific knowledge of humanity." When asked by reporters if the Chinese were next planning to land on the Ocean of Storms to seek out the source of the pulse, the ambassador merely smiled.

At the White House, the President made it clear that she would tolerate no delays in the planned American Moon mission.

"The Chinese are using this stunt to boost their standing in the eyes of the world," the President declared. "We were this close to pushing through a NATO resolution condemning their threatening posture toward Taiwan. Now half the world, including the French, are suffering under the delusion that they're the saviors of humanity and that their only interest in the Taiwanese is to give them all a great big ol' hug. The bottom line is that if the Chinese get to the Ocean of Storms before we do, you can sure as hell bet that they won't be planning to share their discoveries in the same *generous* manner they've been displaying these pictures. We need to get to the Moon. Now."

Upon leaving the Oval Office, Deke felt as if he had just been scolded by a kindhearted but forceful principal who wanted him to make better grades in the future. But how? Deke couldn't see any way they could possibly design, test, and build a new lunar program that would not only get them back to the Moon but also get them there before the Chinese. All of McKenna's intel suggested that the Chinese had not yet built a viable lander, despite this successful circumnavigation of the Moon.

The plan was to have a manned flight in Earth orbit in two months' time to test the prototype command and lunar modules. The next flight would then be a manned mission that tested both modules in lunar orbit. That would be in early April. Then they would try a full-up mission to the Moon, including a landing, in late June. Six months to land on the Moon when no one's done it in over forty years. A rush job to end all rush jobs.

So all we need is to build the goddamn thing, Deke mused as he squinted out the window at the setting sun, *and hope we don't kill ourselves in the process.*

January 12
Johnson Space Center
Houston, Texas
10:50 a.m.

"You *understand* my concern," Cal Walker scoffed into his phone as he walked down a hallway at the JSC toward Dieckman's office. "Do you have any idea what a successful Chinese mission could mean?"

"I'm certain I do, Dr. Walker," a nervous male voice sounded on the other end of the line, "but believe me, we're doing all we can—"

"Obviously you aren't doing enough. I'm doing all I can here at NASA. Everyone knows I'll fulfill my task. And they also know that all of the heavy lifting that needs to be done must be accomplished on both of our ends."

"With respect, Dr. Walker," the voice urged, "I've spoken to the team leaders this morning. They've assured me that they have our full confidence and know that we're—"

"You've spoken—" Walker stopped in midstride. "Listen carefully, my friend. The next time you try to pull an end-run around me, I'll make sure you'll wish you were never born. Is that understood?"

The voice sputtered out something as Walker terminated the call. He looked around him apprehensively, wondering if any passersby had noticed his outburst. Not encountering any stares, he made his way over to a nearby water fountain and set his briefcase down beside it. The water was powerfully cold and made his teeth ache. The pain helped snap him back to reality. He hadn't realized how irritated he had become. He slipped a bottle of pills from his jacket pocket, shook one out, and swallowed it with another sip of water.

A moment of uncertainty hit him. It was more than just being back at NASA, he realized. On the drive over he had come to understand just how precarious his position had become. Did he still have it in him to see the project to fruition? All his life he had been willing to take risks, first at NASA and now in the private sector. In order to embrace the future, one had to be willing to dare to imagine, had to accept that morality was merely an excuse for a weakness of will. He had realized that early in life, while he was helping to adapt von Braun's deadly rockets into a means for humanity's journey to the heavens. Why should a man like Wernher von Braun have cared that the Nazis had used his rocket designs for the mass murder of thousands of Britons when he knew one day these same rockets would enable men to escape the confines of this planet? To wonder *if* they should use such devices was a dilemma Walker never considered. They *had* to be used in order for humanity to progress. If one were to invoke *morality*, nothing would ever be made. Every tool ever created had proven to have both positive and negative aspects. And what was the point of dithering about morality? If the earliest human beings had done that, none of us would have ever crawled out of the primordial ooze.

Odd, Walker thought as he straightened his tie, *odd how something I did so long ago could possibly wreck the future.*

Walker picked up his briefcase and continued down the hall. He wondered if his advanced age was clouding his judgment, not because of any degrading of his faculties, but because he knew most men his age didn't have the will to do the difficult tasks. For the first time in his life, he felt the sting of his own mortality. Despite the company doctors' assurances that he could well live another twenty years, he was envious of the young faces around him who would live to see the world he was helping to create.

Steady yourself, old man, he thought as he opened the door to Dieckman's secretary's office, *you still have enough will left in your body to get this job done.*

"I guess you've heard the news, Cal," Deke said as he gestured toward a seat in front of his desk. "Coffee?"

"No, thank you." Walker eased his slight frame into the overstuffed seat. "I heard about it. I'm sure the President is not pleased."

"Well, I got an earful," Deke said as he poured his third cup of coffee of the morning. "Needless to say, that rush job I was talking to you about has broken into a full-on space race."

"It really should come as no surprise, John," Walker replied, "considering the fact that we've just about given all of our Apollo technology away to every damned Chinese 'tourist' with a camera."

Deke held his tongue but went on. "They haven't got a viable lander."

Walker's face broke into a thin smile. "Well now, that's reassuring."

"Beyond working on the new rockets, we'd like to get your technical expertise on some of our designs." Deke reached across his desk and handed Walker an iPad. "These are the prototype designs of an air force redesign of the Saturn V, as well as a copy of our most recent design specs to the lander. The higher-ups have ordered work to begin on the lander immediately. The rocket's never been built or tested, but all the computer simulations suggest that it'll not only work but will have all the thrust we need to get to the Moon. Over nine million pounds of thrust in all, more than enough to carry a bigger payload. The only problem is that we've got to get it out of the R&D phase as soon as possible. That's where you come in. Once we're done here, I'll take you down to meet the engineers."

Walker pulled a pair of reading glasses from his pocket and surveyed the schematics. "The rocket looks promising, I'll admit. But the lander is far too heavy. One can see that at a glance."

"But as you can see, the air force specs indicate—"

Walker glanced at him over the rims of his glasses. "I don't mean to sound obtuse, John, but the lander *is* too heavy. Not to land on the Moon, but to achieve escape velocity from the lunar surface. The essential design is sound enough, but we'll likely have to—"

A knock at the door interrupted Walker's train of thought. Mattie Kendricks's blond bob appeared after a moment, an apologetic smile on her face. "Sorry to interrupt, Mr. Dieckman, but those gentlemen you asked—"

"Oh right, Mattie. Send them in."

A moment later Donovan and Zell entered Dieckman's office. Walker pulled off his glasses and turned slightly in his chair to look at them. Dieckman came from behind his desk to make the introductions.

"I thought you gents would like to meet Dr. Cal Walker. Dr. Walker worked here in the days of Apollo," Deke began. "Dr. Walker, this is Dr. Alan Donovan and Dr. Elias Zell, the archeologists who'll be going to the Moon."

Walker stood before his chair and held out his hand. "A pleasure. Your reputation precedes you, Dr. Zell."

"As does yours, Dr. Walker," Zell said, gripping his hand. "There are few names as closely linked to all aspects of the Apollo program as yours."

"You flatter me. I'm sure I can think of a few far more deserving of such praise." Walker turned to Donovan and shook his hand. "How do you do, Dr. Donovan?" he asked with a slight smile. "You know, I used to know a Hunter Donovan. You wouldn't happen to be a relation, would you?"

"I'm his son," Donovan said, forcing a smile to his face.

"I remember Hunter well," Walker said, looking at the ceiling. "One of the top geologists in the astronaut corps at that time. He never did make it on a Moon mission, did he?"

"I believe you would know, Dr. Walker," Donovan answered. "You were on the committee that recommended against his going on a mission."

"Yes, I suppose I was." Walker stroked his pointy chin. "Something about a heart condition? We were concerned about the g-forces, the stress on his system?"

"Something like that," Donovan muttered out of the corner of his mouth.

Deke rubbed his temples. How had he not noticed the connection to Walker in Donovan's file? "Dr. Walker will be assisting the engineers with building the Saturn VII, as well as helping us with the lander."

"Nice of you to come out of retirement to do so," Zell observed.

"Oh I'm not retired," Walker explained. "Just doing my part." He wandered over to the models of the Apollo spacecraft on Deke's desk, with that slight smile still gripping his face. "Strange, how it feels like I was here just yesterday. Hard to believe it was more than forty years ago. But still, the more things change, the more things stay the same. After all, here we all are, off to the Moon, NASA behind the gun, in a space race, and despite that *still* trying to train civilian scientists to be astronauts."

Deke spoke up before Donovan or Zell could answer. "By the way, guys. I just wanted to let you know that you've both passed your Class I physicals with flying colors. So you're a go for training. Tomorrow I'll introduce you around to the rest of your team."

"Well, that's good news," Walker said. "Congratulations, gentlemen."

Donovan forced another smile. "Thank you."

"Is there anything else, Deke?" Zell wondered.

"Nope," Deke said with a grin. "Though I'm sure with your connections you already know that the British prime minister has given her blessing to your going on this mission."

"I did, but I'm glad to hear it officially," Zell remarked. "I wouldn't want her to revoke my passport for making an unauthorized trip abroad."

"We should probably get going," Donovan suggested. "We were planning on getting in some weight training this morning."

"Certainly," Walker said. "Good day, gentlemen."

With a nod and a smile, Donovan and Zell left the room. Deke swallowed the rest of his coffee in a gulp and leaned on the edge of his desk, with his arms folded across his chest.

"You were part of the review board that grounded Donovan's father?"

Walker pulled his glasses from his pocket and began to study the schematics again.

"Oh that. I was on so many in those days. They simply wanted one of the rocket engineers to testify about the effects of the engines on someone in Hunter's condition, and I was selected."

"I'm sure his son isn't too happy about it."

Walker looked up from the blueprints. "I can't see why not. The stress certainly would have killed his father, and he wouldn't have ever been born."

Deke rubbed his cheek. "You said something before about civilian astronauts. I take it you don't approve of sending these men to the Moon."

"John, what does one old man's opinion matter?" Walker asked good-naturedly. "But for the record, I was never much for sending civilians to the Moon. Such a job involves years of training, and, even with that, only the best and brightest should go. But as I said, that's just my opinion."

"Cal," Deke began slowly, "we're all glad to have you aboard. *Believe* me. But my concern is the well-being of our astronauts. Those men are going to be a tremendous help to us once they get to the Moon. I'm not going to have them going thinking anyone here doubts they can do the job."

"I didn't mean to make any trouble, John. From now on I will concentrate on the task assigned to me," Walker said as he glanced at the tablet again, "which I will give my absolute attention."

January 13
Johnson Space Center
Houston, Texas
8:32 a.m.

The introductions lasted all of two minutes. Shortly after Donovan and Zell had arrived in Dieckman's office, he escorted them into an adjoining conference room. Sitting there were three men, each in blue NASA coveralls. The men immediately got up when Dieckman entered. The oldest of them, a black man of strong military bearing with a glistening, carefully shaved head, practically stood at attention. Standing to his left was a massive blond man whose face and piercing blue eyes betrayed a kindly, easygoing disposition, despite his best efforts to maintain military composure. The final man in the room was wiry and black haired and stood barely five feet seven but displayed all the easy swagger of an ace pilot.

"Dr. Elias Zell, Dr. Alan Donovan," Deke began, "this is Lieutenant Colonel Franklin Wilson. He'll be the commander of your mission."

"An honor, gentlemen." Wilson held out his hand to them. The handshake was firm and confident, the grip dry and cool.

"And this is Lieutenant Commander Thomas Mosensen, who'll be the lunar-module pilot."

"Call me Moose," Mosensen said with a big grin on his ruddy face as he extended his hand.

"And this is Lieutenant Commander Anthony Benevisto, the command-module pilot," Deke remarked, adding: "He'll be in orbit around the Moon, relaying intel to us while the rest of you guys are on the surface."

"Most everybody around here calls me Benny," Benevisto said as he shook hands with both of them.

"I don't envy your job," Zell noted as they shook hands. "Going all that way and not even stepping on the Moon."

"Hey, I'm getting ninety-nine-point-nine percent of the way there—a helluva lot farther than most people I know have gotten outta Brooklyn," Benny said.

Deke looked at each of them in turn, unable to suppress a smile. "Gentlemen, come this June, you will be the first men to return to the Moon."

Dieckman asked them to be seated as he stood at the head of the conference table, jingling the keys in his pocket as he glanced over some files. "Just to give Dr. Donovan and Dr. Zell a brief overview of the training: normally astronaut training takes up to two years, with candidates assigned to the Astronaut Office here at JCS. Owing to the fact that we're under considerable time constraints, that means you will be getting a crash course in how to be astronauts. All of your formal mission training will be compressed and overseen by Lieutenant Colonel Wilson, who is our most experienced astronaut. Assisting him in that capacity will be Lieutenant Commander Mosensen. Conversely, you gentlemen will be required to impart as much of your archeological training to other team members, since one of them will be on the lunar surface with you at all times. The days between now and the date of launch will be long and tight, but everybody here at NASA is confident that you will be ready when the time comes."

Zell leaned back in his chair and folded his arms against his barrel chest. "So what's the first thing on our agenda?"

"Glad you asked," Deke said, pulling a small remote from the table. He punched a button, and an engineering schematic of a rocket appeared on a small screen mounted to the wall behind him.

"This is the Saturn VII. Like the Saturn V that took the Apollo astronauts to the Moon, it has three stages. For the first two and a half minutes of flight, the first stage will push you out of the densest part of the atmosphere. When it is depleted of fuel, the first stage is jettisoned and the second stage kicks in. The second stage will burn for six and a half minutes until you gain orbital speed before it is also jettisoned. The third and final stage burns for another two and a half minutes, enough time to push you out of Earth's orbit and toward the Moon."

Donovan studied the screen. "What're the g-forces through all this?"

"About seven g's," Benny said with a good-natured laugh. "Enough to squeeze your eyeballs out through your ears."

Moose glanced at him. "Like you'd know."

Deke smirked. "At this point, I'll turn you over to Lieutenant Colonel Wilson."

Deke passed the remote to Wilson and took a seat. Wilson clicked a button, and another image appeared, this one of the Phoenix spacecraft itself. "Again like Apollo, Phoenix is composed of three parts: the command module, the service module, and the lunar module. The command module is the cone-shaped capsule you see at the top of the screen. This is where we will live and work for the majority of the mission. This middle section is the service module, which is connected to the command module and provides things such as oxygen, thrusters, fuel cells, and the propellants necessary to get in and out of lunar orbit. Once the third stage has put us into translunar injection, the command and service modules will turn around, dock with the lunar module, and pull it out of the third stage."

Donovan wrinkled his brow. "While we're going to the Moon?"

Wilson glanced at him. "It's a fairly standard procedure, docking with a spacecraft while both are in motion, Dr. Donovan. Just leave the driving to us."

"How do we get into the damn thing once we need to get down to the Moon?" Zell wondered aloud.

"We unlock the docking collar, which opens a tunnel between the command and lunar modules," Wilson explained. "Don't worry, we won't have to do an EVA just to get from one module of the ship to the next."

Zell leaned into Donovan. "Now *that's* comforting."

"So once we're in lunar orbit, then what?" Donovan asked.

Wilson turned to face him. "The four of us will suit up, and Mosensen and I will pilot the ship down to the Ocean of Storms."

"Basically it's like this," Deke explained from his chair. "The mission will last two weeks—three days for you to get to the Moon, three to come back, and eight days scheduled for exploration and excavation at the source of the pulse. You two will land on the Moon with Lieutenant Colonel Wilson and Lieutenant Commander Mosensen. You'll work in two shifts, with one experienced astronaut and one experienced archeologist working at the site. Right now there are no plans for all four of you to be on the surface simultaneously, but if the need arises, you will do so. Your task is to excavate the object—and if possible, return it or parts of it to Earth for analysis. Since we don't know how big the damn thing is or even if it will be possible to unearth, your space suits will be equipped with digital cameras and additional equipment so we can get a picture of what's going on there."

"Eight days is a pretty short time to do all that digging," Donovan noted, "especially since—if I understand correctly—the object is buried about a mile below the Moon's surface."

Zell grunted. "Hardly enough time to set up a wet bar, I should think."

"I'm afraid that's the maximum amount of time we can give you," Deke explained. "At eight days we'll have stretched the oxygen to just about its absolute limit."

Donovan leaned his elbows on the table. "What if we run into obstacles that prevent us from getting to the object—rock slides, things of that nature?"

Wilson clicked on another image. "These are prototype digging tools we'll be bringing with us on the mission. Apart from a major landslide, they should be able to handle any obstacles we run into."

"Those are rather large tools," Zell observed. "Even if we land right at the precipice of the fissure, how are we going to bring them down there?"

Wilson clicked the remote again. "The Mark II moon buggy. It will come equipped with a basket and a winch to bring tools down, and us back up."

Zell grinned. "Seems like you've covered all the bases, Colonel."

"If it's okay by you, I'd like to take a look at the gloves of our space suits," Donovan said. "I'm concerned that they might not be able to handle the careful manipulations of an archeological dig."

"Anything you can do to help us improve the equipment would be terrific," Deke remarked. "Any other questions?"

Donovan and Zell looked at each other. "No," Donovan added. "Except we're kind of champing at the bit to begin our training. We're getting a little bored with all the sit-ups and push-ups."

Wilson almost smiled. "We're going to take a little field trip to Ellington Field right after this meeting."

Zell sighed. "Do I dare ask what we'll be doing there?"

"Weightlessness training," Wilson said firmly, "aboard the Vomit Comet."

Zell squinted at the lieutenant colonel. "Did you say *Vomit Comet*?"

January 13
Ellington Field Joint Reserve Base
Houston, Texas
11:10 a.m.

"The honeymoon's over, sweetheart," Zell whispered to Donovan.

They were standing, along with Benny and Moose and a handful of other astronauts they hadn't met, inside a hangar at an airfield. Wilson had stepped away from them for a moment and was discussing something with a pair of pilots just outside the hangar.

Donovan looked over at the other astronauts, five men and one woman, and nudged Benevisto to ask who they were.

"Test-flight crews," Benny answered. "One group's gonna test all the hardware in Earth orbit, the other in lunar orbit, before we launch. I guess ol' Wilson wants them to get in some additional training, since they're all doubling as our backup crew."

"Pity," Zell muttered to them. "A fortnight's trip to the Moon could be made considerably more tolerable if a woman such as that were coming along for the ride."

"That woman's the best pilot in the astronaut corps, bar none," Benny declared. "Not that I'd admit out loud that anyone's better than me or anything. If she had more hours in space, she'd be the one taking us to the Moon, guaranteed."

The female astronaut they hadn't yet been introduced to was perhaps in her late twenties or early thirties and close to five feet ten, with black pin-straight hair upswept in a bun and greenish-gold eyes that didn't so much look at you as through you. Everything about her was smooth, straight lines, from the bridge of her nose to the slope of her shoulders to the taper of her wrists. Whenever Donovan found himself in her sights, he looked away, almost schoolboy embarrassed. Zell, on the other hand, seemed to be immune to her gaze and strolled right up to her. "Pardon me," Zell began, "I don't believe we've been properly introduced. I'm Dr. Elias Zell, and that fellow back there is Dr. Alan Donovan. We're the two draftees they've called on to dig up the Moon."

"Lieutenant Sydney Weaver, sir, call sign Blackfox," she replied. "Command-module pilot on the manned test flight. Nice to meet you both."

"A pleasure," Zell said. "And let me say, if you're half as good a pilot as you are beautiful, we're in excellent hands."

She popped her eyes wide and smiled brightly at him. "Gee," she said in an exaggerated swoon, "that's such a nice compliment—if it were 1960." She turned to Donovan. "Nice of you to bring along one of your fossils for show-and-tell."

As she walked off, Donovan looked at Zell, shaking his head reproachfully. "You never learn."

"Good morning," came a sharp voice that sliced the morning air. All heads turned to see Wilson in his immaculately pressed coveralls breeze back into the hangar. "For those of you who don't know me, I'm Lieutenant Colonel Franklin Wilson," he said. "I'll be leading you in today's training exercises. While many of you have already been through weightlessness training, I assure you this will be like nothing you've experienced before."

Wilson had the assembled crews' complete attention. Donovan was hanging on Wilson's every word, surprising considering Donovan's general disdain for authority. But he had been won over by some of the things he learned about Wilson from Moose and Benny on the way over to Ellington. Wilson was the closest thing NASA had to an old-school astronaut—cool under any and all pressure, and a tough-as-nails veteran of space, including three missions to the ISS and the second full-up manned test of the Phoenix capsule. Wilson was on the Phoenix mission that had to be aborted because of a misfiring retro-rocket. He received a drawerful of commendations for his quick thinking, which not only saved the lives of his crew but very likely the capsule as well. Donovan was not at all surprised that Wilson had been chosen to lead their mission.

Everyone strolled out onto the tarmac, where a giant plane sat reflecting the orange glint of the late-morning light.

"G-FORCE ONE," Wilson said, gesturing with his hand. "Welcome to weightlessness training, people. NASA hasn't officially used her for a few years, but we thought we'd dust her off and give the newbies a thrill. I hope you all ate light the last twelve hours."

Everyone nodded that indeed they had. Zell, thinking of the large breakfast he'd enjoyed that morning, remained poker-faced.

"Here's the way it works, for the uninitiated," Wilson continued. "The plane makes its ascent at an angle of about forty-five degrees. Once it hits apogee, you will be weightless for about thirty seconds. After that, it's straight down again."

"That sounds . . . disorienting," Zell muttered to Donovan.

"On the thirty-sixth parabola," Wilson went on, "we will experiment with an approximation of the one-sixth gravity of the Moon."

Zell turned to Moose. "Did he say the *thirty-sixth* parabola? How many loop-de-loops is that damn thing going to do?"

"Why do you think they call it the Vomit Comet?" Benny said, clapping Zell's shoulder. "C'mon, it'll be the ride of your life. Trust me."

"Have you ever done it?" Donovan asked.

"Couple times." Benny shrugged. "It's not so bad compared to some of the stuff I've done. I've pulled eight g's in an F-16, landed on a moving carrier at night. This'll be a walk in the park."

An hour later, the crews came off the plane, shaken but still mobile. Benny looked pale but had managed to keep his stomach under control. Zell, however, had not been as fortunate. His face was a sickly green color, and his clothes now had the appearance of having been slept in. As he descended the stairs, he weakly held the railing with one hand and clutched his now-empty stomach with the other. He noticed Donovan smiling at him and held up a stern finger.

"Not one word," he said. "Not even *hello*."

Donovan looked at his old friend and produced a Cohiba from his flight suit. He handed it to Zell, who took it gratefully. A moment after the cigar was lit, the color began returning to his face.

"Better not let Wilson catch you with that," Weaver said, suddenly appearing at their sides. "He wants to make up for lost time, so he's taking us all over to the gym for some work on the treadmills."

"Treadmills?" Zell blustered. "Is that man out of his mind? What about bloody lunch?"

"I guess you might be hungry," Donovan muttered. "Considering your breakfast is all over that plane's cabin."

"I hope your stomach's not too bad," Weaver remarked, unable to suppress a smile over Zell's misery. "Benny and Moose are thinking we should all go out for drinks at the end of the day."

"Drinks?" Zell's face practically lit up. "Lieutenant Weaver, you've just thrown a bone to a starving man."

January 13
O'Driscoll's Pub
Houston, Texas
11:35 p.m.

"Indiana Jones again?" Zell said with a groan. "Really? All of you think archeology is all about going on quests to find lost treasures. Archeology is about carefully reconstructing a past, learning how the objects you find were used in daily life a thousand years earlier. It's not about fortune and glory."

"That's what you say, Doc," Benny said as he drained his pint of beer. "Then why is it your picture's on the lead story of every major news website every other week?"

"Well, you exaggerate somewhat," Zell said, smiling at the lit end of his cigar, "but I do have some rather enthusiastic fans."

Zell had been holding court for hours, regaling all the assembled astronauts, from the two test crews to the flight crew, with stories Donovan either had participated in or heard a million times. Donovan knew his friend was in his element—an admiring audience, a scotch, and a cigar before him. But he also knew that Zell's tall tales had an edge of competition that went along with them. Both of them had been impressed with the stories Benny and Moose and Syd had told them of their missions in the service and in space. Zell knew he was in good company and wanted to let them know that when the time came, he could hold his own.

Donovan excused himself and took his empty pint glass to the bar for a refill. As he waited for the bartender to come down his way, he couldn't help but think how these astronauts had already made them both feel a part of the team. That was a distinctly different impression than he got from Cal Walker, who looked no more pleased that he and Zell were going to the Moon than he must have felt about his father and the rest of the geologists in the Apollo training program. Despite Walker's involvement, Donovan truly felt that everyone—from top brass like Dieckman and Wilson down to his fellow astronauts—wanted them on board. He was sorry Wilson had decided against joining them for a drink.

Donovan studied his face in the mirror behind the bar. He wasn't drunk. He was too tired to be drunk. He just looked tired. And a little haggard.

All these years of living in tents and on the move must be getting to me, he thought with a grin. *Wonder what it's like to settle down and live a normal nine-to-five life. Hell, is there even such a thing as a normal life anymore with the world going the way it is?*

As he waited for the bartender, Syd slid onto the stool next to his.

"Hi, sailor," he said with a grin. "Buy you a drink?"

"I think it's my round," she said, pulling a twenty. "What're you drinking?"

"Guinness."

She leaned her elbows on the bar, tilting slightly off the stool. "Hey Mike! Can we get a couple beers down here?"

Mike the bartender was over in a heartbeat. He seemed to know Syd well enough to know that she wasn't the kind of woman to wait around for anything. Syd ordered herself a Coors Light along with Donovan's Guinness.

Donovan smiled at her. "So that's how to get his attention."

"You can't wait around for a bartender. They'll never show up," Syd said. "What've you been living in, a cave?"

"Most of my adult life."

Syd snapped her fingers and pointed at him. "Right. A dumb thing to say to an archeologist, eh?"

"Not nearly as dumb as what Elias said to you this morning."

Syd laughed. "Don't worry, my opinion of him didn't rub off on you."

Mike stepped over with their beers. Donovan held up his pint to her glass. "So what should we drink to?"

"Success for the missions sounds too trite," she replied. "How about success in all things?"

Clink.

"So what're you doing over here?" Donovan asked as he set his pint on the bar. "Bored with Elias's stories already?"

She ran her finger around the rim of her glass. "I haven't heard anything yet that hasn't already been published. Besides, you look like you needed some company."

"Look that bad, do I?"

"Nah. Just lonely."

"You don't beat around the bush, do you?"

Syd shrugged her thin shoulders again. "What's the point? With this damn pulse and all those poor people dying, it just makes you realize how short life is." She shook her head. "I'm just glad I'm here, doing what I can to help. I'd hate to be one of those people out there, so afraid of everything that's going on that they just fall apart."

"I've always thought that myself," Donovan said, staring at his beer and thinking of his father. "It's lousy when people just waste their lives."

Syd leaned over, trying to look him in the eyes. "Got some stories to tell, Doctor?"

Donovan chuckled and turned to her. "Got a lifetime to hear them?"

"I dunno," Syd muttered as she tipped her glass to her lips. "For you I just might."

Chapter 6

March 1
John F. Kennedy Space Center
Cape Canaveral, Florida
7:05 a.m.

By the time the Saturn VII was ready for its first manned test flight into Earth orbit, the crew was beginning to function as a single unit. Donovan found himself particularly impressed with Wilson, Moose, and Benny. Despite having gone into training without the slightest understanding of archeology, they absorbed everything he and Zell taught them. He found Wilson to be a particularly good student, who would return to every lesson with pages upon pages of notes made in his off-hours. Further, he proved to be essential in getting the space-suit designers to produce gloves that would be adept at fine movements. Each prototype he brought in was better than the last, with the final ones being so light and flexible that they seemed as if they were wearing rubber gloves instead of gauntlets designed to protect them from the ravages of space.

Donovan was equally impressed with how well Zell had taken to his training, particularly the physical aspects. Each morning he and Zell would rise before dawn for a five-mile run around the space center, and each morning Zell had improved his time to the extent that he was now keeping pace with Donovan, who had been running all his life. Zell had even cut back on his cocktails and cigars, though he did sneak one of each now and then, much to the NASA physicians' dismay.

They all gathered in the Launch Control Center. Donovan was surprised to find that it hadn't changed that much at all since he was a child. Oh sure, there were advanced computers now and fewer slide rules and there were many more women and not nearly so many men waltzing around with horn-rimmed glasses and pocket protectors in short-sleeved white shirts, but it still had the same feel, the same eager anticipation. As dawn crept over the horizon, a second orange sunrise burst into life under the rocket's main boosters and lifted into the new morning. As Donovan watched the clock jump to life as the rocket climbed into the air, he knew that the rocket and the mission that went along with it were aptly named.

Phoenix.

Cheers burst around him as the rocket roared to life and lifted off into Earth orbit. Backs were slapped; hands were shaken; champagne was poured into Solo cups. Wilson gave Deke a firm slap on the back. Donovan felt a lightness in his chest. From his pocket he pulled his father's silver astronaut pin and watched the monitors.

I'm going to the Moon, Dad.

March 4
Neutral Buoyancy Lab
Sonny Carter Training Facility
Houston, Texas
6:15 a.m.

In gravity one-sixth that of Earth's, even the simplest tasks could become a challenge. Added to that the bulky environmental suits astronauts must wear, and those challenges could feel next to impossible. The only way to properly train to work in space was to find an environment that closely approximated zero gravity, which was where the Neutral Buoyancy Lab came in.

Built at the turn of the century while the International Space Station project was gearing up, the NBL was something of a big brother to the Johnson Space Center's Weightless Environment Training Facility. Although on the surface it appeared to be an ordinary swimming pool, the NBL was anything but. At over two hundred feet in length, one hundred feet in width, and forty feet in depth, it could easily accommodate full-scale mock-ups of the space shuttle, sections of the ISS, or any other craft NASA wished to test out. These mock-ups could be lowered into the water using two bridge cranes, each one capable of lifting over ten tons.

Wilson stood at the edge of the pool, his hands placed on his hips as the Phoenix crews filed in. "Good morning, people," he said. "Welcome to the Neutral Buoyancy Lab. Here is where you'll begin training to work in zero gravitation. Let's not waste any time. Suit up."

Donovan bristled at the notion of having to go underwater. Although he was a certified diver and had explored some of the most fascinating undersea sites in the world, he felt an icy sheet of panic wash over him nearly every time he dove. His fear stemmed from an incident when he went cave diving at sixteen with Zell in Bermuda. Somewhere along the way, the two had gotten separated and Donovan had found himself trapped in a small passageway with seemingly nowhere to go. Were it not for a lucky tap on the shoulder from Zell, Donovan was certain he would have run out of air and died there. In the years since, Donovan had not allowed his fears to control him. He continued diving, even in caves. But every time his head slipped beneath the surface, he felt that familiar trickle of dread.

As he was staring at the water, he felt a hand briefly touch his. Syd was standing beside him, a warm look in her gold-green eyes.

"Ready to take a dip?" she asked.

Donovan eyed the bulky EVA suit he was about to don. "Not my usual swimming attire," he said with a grin.

Weaver laughed. "Trust me," she replied. "This isn't going to be your usual swim."

Ten minutes later, the team was suited up and lowered into the water. For Donovan, it was one of the most alien experiences he'd ever had. All around him, the dive support team swam to and fro, floating ghostlike in the eerie still of the water. Donovan admitted he was glad for their presence. No ordinary sport divers, these were trained professionals adept at underwater rescue. Before joining the support team, divers had to prove their proficiency by lifting an astronaut in a flooded space suit to the surface in under a minute. Donovan tried to imagine carrying the combined weight of a human being and an EVA suit through forty feet of water in under sixty seconds and just hoped that today wouldn't be the day they'd have to do it for real.

"Okay, people," came Wilson's seemingly disembodied voice, crackling over the headset. "Today we'll be working with a mock-up of our command module, the *Carpathian*. Mosensen, Benevisto, you two, along with Furlong and Mongillo, are going to train for some basic EVA work. Donovan, Zell, you two are with me and Weaver. We're just going to run through some exercises to get you comfortable. As we get closer to launch, we'll start stepping it up."

"Stepping it up?" asked Donovan. "You mean we've got more of this to look forward to?"

"We run these tests over and over, Doctor," answered Wilson. "At the end of the day, you'll spend more time in the NBL rehearsing for this mission than you will carrying it out."

"Don't worry, Doc," came Moose's voice over the communicator, "we won't let you drown."

"At least not until *after* you've bought a round for the crew," said Benny, laughing.

"Cut the chatter," said Wilson. "We've got work to do." He turned to Donovan and Zell. "The term *neutral buoyancy* is applied to objects that have an equal tendency to float as they do to sink," he said. "Here we use the right amount of floats and weights to make objects 'hover' underwater, as they would in space. Thanks to the Vomit Comet, you know what it's like to be weightless. What we're going to do now is give you a feel for what it's like to work that way."

"As long as I can keep my lunch down, I'll be sound as a pound," said Zell.

They spent the next hour working with various instruments and tools, feeling their weight (or lack thereof) and learning how to compensate for the lack of gravity. The worst part for Donovan was working in the pressurized space suit, which gave him the feeling of walking in a balloon.

"Don't fight the suit," said Syd gently. "The suit's always going to win. You've got to learn to work *with* it."

"It's frustrating." Donovan grimaced. "It's like retraining my mind and body from scratch."

"That's *exactly* what it is," Syd replied. "You're learning already."

March 16
Cebada Cave
Chiquibul, Belize
2:07 p.m.

The Chiquibul system of caves was the longest in Central America, beginning in Belize and emerging twenty-five miles later in the Petén region of Guatemala. Consisting of four big caves and numerous sinkholes, the system was the underground bed of the river Chiquibul, which flowed west from the hills of Belize. Cebada was originally thought to be a separate cave, hence its name. However, intrepid divers found a connection when they underwent the first cave dive ever done at Chiquibul.

The inside of Cebada was a world unto itself. Explorers were as likely to stumble across the ten-thousand-year-old bones of a vampire bat as they were shards of pottery left twelve hundred years ago by the Mayans. Recent explorations had even revealed evidence of never-before-seen invertebrate species. For these reasons, among others, Donovan and Zell pressed NASA to allow for this trip. If their analysis of the Ocean of Storms was correct, the Phoenix team would find themselves in caves as elaborate, or even more so, than anything found at Chiquibul. Added to that one-sixth gravity and a quarter of a million miles from rescue, and it didn't take long for them to realize that a little preparation in a similar environment couldn't hurt.

"Come along, step lively!" called Zell as he slogged through the icy waist-deep water. Behind him trudged the rest of the team. Zell was particularly pleased by the fact that the astronauts had come to look forward to these field expeditions as a welcome break from the routine of training in Houston. His own crew, as well as the backup crew comprised of Syd Weaver, Mongillo, and Furlong, had arrived at Chiquibul courtesy of the Zell Institute's private helicopters and had spent the last three days exploring the environs.

"Here we are!" said Zell. "The Loltun room."

Everyone stopped to look at the incredible sight before them. If *loltun* was indeed the Mayan word for *stone flower*, then the room was aptly named. It looked as if a limestone garden was erupting from the floor, reaching up to the ceiling. The "flowers" looked like ordinary stalagmites but with leaflike protrusions sprouting out all around them. Wilson, who had never left New York before joining the marines, was in awe. Even the elaborate caves beneath the mountains of Afghanistan couldn't compare to the natural beauty here. After combat and spaceflight, he thought he had reached a point where the world held no more surprises for him.

"Stalagmites, right?" said Benny.

"Close," said Zell. "Splattermites. Notice the platy upright protrusions. They're usually formed in tropical caves. What happens is densely vegetated soils charge the drip waters with exceptionally high concentrations of carbon dioxide. This carbon dioxide is rapidly released as drip waters enter the cave atmosphere, 'splattering' onto the stalagmites. When that happens, you get calcite deposits and, in a few hundred years or so . . ."

"Stalagmites become splattermites," finished Furlong.

"Exactly!" said Zell. "So the lesson here is always look twice at whatever you see. Even if you *know* you know what it is, you'll be surprised." He clapped his hands. "Now, who's up for a little cave diving?"

Everyone in the group responded with enthusiasm, except Donovan. He smiled and shook his head. "Not this time, old friend."

Syd paused. "I think I'll stay behind too."

Zell waved a dismissive hand at the two of them while finishing getting on his gear. As the rest of the team joined him in the water, he snapped on his dive light and turned back to Donovan and Syd. "Be good," he said with a wry grin, and prepared to go under. Just before he did, he turned again. "As my father used to say, 'And if you can't be good . . .'"

"'Be careful,'" Donovan and Zell finished together. Zell simply laughed and dove out of sight. Donovan and Syd sat on a rock outcropping in the cave.

"He's something, isn't he?" said Syd. "I'm not really sure *what*, but he's something."

"Elias? Yeah. He's really the only family I've ever had."

"What about your father? I've heard Deke talk about him from time to time."

"My father? I never really knew him," Donovan said, dangling his feet in the water. "Well, not the man they talk about, anyway. He died when I was a kid."

"I'm sorry to hear that," Syd replied, looking around the cavern. "My own father thinks I threw away my military career when I joined NASA."

"Bet he thinks otherwise now."

"I don't know. He hasn't called yet," she said, then cleared her throat. "And so you threw your lot in with Elias Zell and have been paying for it ever since, huh?"

"You could say that," said Donovan, lost in memory. "He and I have been around the world and then some."

"The world. That's why I joined the service, you know? 'See the world.'" She sighed. "Not that I even want to see much of it these days, with everything that's going on."

"I know what you mean. I'm glad we don't have a lot of time to watch the news." He paused. "But I'm sure you have some stories to tell."

"I'm sure you do too." She looked at him and held his gaze. "Maybe we ought to make some time to tell them."

April 15
Johnson Space Center
Houston, Texas
5:25 p.m.

The crews finished yet another training day, their last before the manned test flight of Phoenix 5. Since Phoenix 4 had proven so successful in March, Weaver, Furlong, and Mongillo had been given final clearance to launch in two days. For Donovan and Zell and the rest of the Phoenix 6 crew, who still had two months before their launch, much of the classroom training had given way to extensive physical training, as well as hour upon hour in the simulator. As CM pilot, Benny's most important job would be to dock with the lunar module once the *Carpathian* had cleared Earth's gravity. This was a maneuver that required incredible precision. The final few feet of the docking procedure were covered at a rate of approximately a tenth of a foot per second. Any more or less and the chances of a catastrophic incident became more and more likely. Benny and Moose had run and rerun the simulation, each time filling up the comm channels with a blue streak. But in recent weeks they had fallen into a rhythm, each man working in tandem with the other, enhancing their strengths.

With the mission looming ever closer, the team was also working harder than ever to train their bodies for working in space. Six days a week they were required to undergo a ninety-minute workout, with another thirty minutes of vigorous cardiovascular training. Donovan, a fitness nut even before he signed on, took to the exercises like a duck to water. Zell, despite being in better condition than most men his age, was feeling the years of living the good life slowly creep up on him. At present, they were in one of the training rooms. Donovan was still running on the treadmill, fighting to keep his heart rate up to maximum. Zell was sitting in a hot tub, a wet towel draped over his eyes.

"My bones feel so frail, if I sneeze I might snap my neck," he groaned.

"Come on, Elias," Donovan said as he turned off the treadmill. "I've seen you fight in some of the toughest bars in the outback, arm wrestle Sherpas . . . Hell, you even got into the ring with that Samoan kickboxer that one time, remember?"

"You're talking about a different man, Alan," Zell said. "A younger man."

Donovan shook his head. "Bullshit. You talk like you're ninety."

"When I signed on for this, I thought it would be the adventure of a lifetime. Now, sitting here, I feel like the world's oldest child being told it's time to grow up."

Donovan wiped his face with a towel and walked over to his friend and mentor. "Listen, if Elias Zell has taught me anything about living, it's that when life knocks you for a loop, the only thing to do is hit back."

Zell grunted a laugh. "Remind me never again to give you advice. You just throw it in my face."

He looked at Zell, eyes glinting. "Don't worry, old friend. There's still a few more years in Neverland left for us Lost Boys."

At that moment the doors burst open and in came Benny, Moose, and Weaver clapping.

"What the blazes?" Zell protested.

"Congratulations, gents, you passed astronaut training, and you're still alive!" Benny said as he handed each of them a small piece of fabric. "You are now part of the club."

Donovan and Zell looked at what Benny had handed them: a pair of mission patches for the coming moon landing. They showed a Flash Gordon–styled riveted rocket blasting off from the Earth toward the Moon and an old-time radio tower poking up from the lunar north pole. Around this was emblazoned the mission's motto: *Ex luna, futura.*

"'From the Moon, the future,'" said Moose, translating. "We kind of borrowed it from Apollo 13. We figured Jim, Jack, and Freddo wouldn't mind."

"No," said Donovan, thinking for a moment of his father, "I don't think they would."

Benny smirked. "Let's just hope we have a little better luck with our mission than they did with theirs."

"Thank you very much," Zell said.

"Hold on," Moose said. "There's more for you, Dr. Zell."

"Oh really? What?"

"Well," Syd said with an impish grin, "we thought you needed a little something to see your way through this mission." With that, Benny stepped forward holding a stack of sick bags from the Vomit Comet.

"It's a long way to the Moon, Doc," he said, and the whole room, including Zell, broke up. After a moment, Benny waved his hands. "We still have one more gift. But this one's actually from you to us."

Donovan smiled at Zell. "I can't wait to hear this."

"First rule of astronaut training," Moose said. "Newbies buy the drinks."

"Finally," Zell said, pulling himself from the tub. "A NASA rule I don't mind following."

Now, if Elias Zell could have described his version of heaven, O'Driscoll's Pub in downtown Houston might have been it. Sawdust on the floor, dim lighting, and a host of surly patrons who looked as if they came here to get dead drunk and be left alone. Over the years, its ambience had made it a popular haunt for NASA crews.

They sat in a quiet corner of the bar. Benny, an avid music nut, had pumped the jukebox full of fives, ensuring that they would not be without tunes the rest of the night. An old Marshall Tucker song was playing as Zell regaled the group with yet another anecdote.

"So there I am, three hundred feet down in the mine shaft, when overhead I hear this horrible hissing sound. I look up to see that the walls and ceiling are *covered* with gray bats. Good-sized buggers with about a one-foot wingspan. Now, the one thing you never want to do with bats is rile them up. I've stepped onto their turf, and they're not happy about it. One little disturbance is all it's going to take to send them shrieking and flapping about. So I begin to quietly back my way out, when in bursts Alan yelling, 'Jesus Christ! The other chamber's full of bats!'"

Everyone laughed, clapping Donovan on the back good-naturedly.

"I was just a kid at the time," Donovan said.

"Yes," Zell mused, "a terrible thing to happen to a twenty-five-year-old kid."

"So you two have been just about all over the world, huh?" Moose asked.

"Everywhere on the map and a few places in between," Zell said with a flourish.

"Bet you never thought you'd be setting foot on the Moon, though," said Benny.

"No, that one was a bit . . . unexpected," answered Donovan, contemplating his beer.

"Well, don't worry," said Benny. "You're flying with the finest crew there is. Leave the driving to us."

"If we leave the driving to you, Benny, we'll be lucky if we get off the tarmac."

"Don't even start with me, Moose." Benny clapped his hands and rubbed them together. "So what's on deck for tonight?"

"Well, I don't know about the Eagle Scout there, but I'm a cheap date," said Zell, pouring a little more scotch. "Barkeep! Another round for these thirsty men!"

The bartender arrived with another pitcher of beer, from which Benny and Moose quickly poured.

"To the *Carpathian*," Benny said. "May she reach the stars."

"Or," said Zell as their glasses clinked, "may she rest in peace."

Outside the bar, Donovan and Syd were looking up at the Texas stars. It was surprisingly dark in the parking lot, so much so that the city's normal level of light pollution did little to dim the ribbon of the Milky

Way spiraling out before them. Each of its twinkling points was a reflection of the past, of stars likely long since dead.

"It always amazes me," said Syd.

"What's that?"

She looked up and twirled, her long neck arched all the way back. "How those stars might not even exist anymore but how we can still see them."

"It's because of the distance," Donovan explained. "The time it takes for the light of a very distant star to reach us—"

She looked at him, her head cocked to one side. "Duh. I know *why* it takes the light so long to reach us. I do work for NASA. I was just having a wow moment."

Donovan shook his head and laughed. "Okay, but I know what you mean. Sometimes, when I'm out on a dig, I'll stumble across something small. You know, a piece of pottery, plates, whatever. Something that in everyday life seems insignificant. I'll look at it and think, 'This belonged to somebody. This *meant* something to somebody.' Somebody who lived a whole lifetime before I was even a thought." He kicked at the dirt under his feet. "We think that we're living at the peak of history, Syd. In truth, we're just passing through."

She took his arm and drew him in closer. "Well then, we'd better make the most of it while we're here."

They looked for a time at the night sky. "So, next stop space, huh?" asked Donovan.

"Yep. Looks that way."

"Where to from there?"

"I don't know," she answered, turning her head toward him. "Where are you going?"

Donovan laughed. "You *know* where I'm going. I'll just be a couple months behind you."

"And after that?"

"After that?" He took her hand, thinking of the mission and of the woman next to him. "After that, the sky's the limit."

April 17
John F. Kennedy Space Center
Cape Canaveral, Florida
9:28 a.m.

Donovan, Zell, Moose, and Benny were standing at the NASA Causeway site with hundreds of other spectators, looking up at the Saturn booster that would take Weaver's crew into lunar orbit. There they would test all the systems the crew of Phoenix 4 had worked through in Earth orbit the month before, with the addition of the lander that would separate from the command module, descend toward the lunar surface, then fire its ascent engine and redock with the command module. A full-up dress rehearsal, like Apollo 10 had done, without actually landing on the Moon.

Donovan was amazed that NASA had been able to design and build the command module and lander so quickly. Much of this was due to the organization using Apollo's specs as a guide, but even more of the process relied on NASA's ability to use computer simulations to check for any defects or possible malfunctions. *Everything's running like clockwork,* he thought.

He couldn't believe that this was the same NASA he had come to only four months earlier. The designers, engineers, and technicians, the thousands of people working around the clock to get this mission off the ground, seemed to have been given new life with this task ahead of them. *Even the Chinese orbiter turned out to be a boon,* Donovan realized. *It got us to do what we needed to do in a hurry.*

He also realized history was repeating itself. Just as everything seemed to be flowing smoothly inside NASA as Apollo, and now Phoenix, was making its remarkable strides toward the stars, the world outside was falling into chaos. Even the President's announcement of a manned mission scheduled for June did little to comfort the restless masses outside these gates. The impact of the EM pulse was still being felt across the globe. Riots continued to flare up now and then. The conflict was not as bad as before the Chinese mission but still bad. Crime in every city was on the rise. Protests were a daily occurrence. Even the Chinese fleet had yet to return to port; they continued to circle Taiwan, waiting. The American ships stationed off South Korea, as well as the vast majority of the Pacific Fleet, remained on full alert.

Donovan tried to block out these negative thoughts and concentrate on the towering Saturn VII looming before him in the bright morning sun. Syd and her crew had been waiting on the launchpad, strapped tight into their seats, for well over an hour. No one wanted to give the go signal before every system was quadruple-checked.

"She sure is something," said Moose.

"Beautiful," agreed Zell. "I remember when they were half this size."

"So do I," said Donovan. Being here made him think of his father and how much he would have loved to be atop one of these boosters.

Suddenly, the group saw smoke begin to pour out from under the rocket as it prepared to launch.

"The clock is running!" Benny enthused.

Seconds later there was a deafening boom as the engines fired and the rocket broke loose from its moorings. Slowly it began to move, rising up from the launch tower with steady, determined speed. The thousands of onlookers gathered around the Cape cheered wildly.

"Go, baby, go!" yelled Benny.

"Liftoff! We have liftoff of Phoenix 5, a mission that will renew humanity's quest for knowledge in our—"

"Look at it go!"

The crowd at the Cape cheered madly, their euphoria seemingly boosting Phoenix from its moorings to the Earth. Around the world, their feelings were mirrored by the people watching in their homes, gathered in public places from Times Square to Red Square, standing together to watch this bold step into history. The tragedies of the past several months were temporarily forgotten and, in this brief moment, the world was united in the joy and promise of what lay ahead.

On the tarmac, the team watched with grim, serious expressions. Moose, watching Phoenix intently, was the first to notice the thin trail of smoke coming from the rocket's ascent engine.

"Oh my God," Moose said.

They saw the explosion before they heard it. A blast that sounded like a neutron bomb that came from above the launchpad. The rocket slammed back down into the launch tube with a sickening crunch. The burning fuel roared underground for a moment; then the entire Earth seemed to shift as it exploded. The fuel, now loose, began to ignite in the air, sending a torrent of flames up into the sky. With an aching groan, the toppling booster began snapping power cables and tearing through metal. Within seconds, the sheer heat from the rocket had melted the tower like wax. Whatever wasn't burned away was crushed by the weight of collapsing metal. After the rocket tumbled to the ground, shrieking and bellowing in its death throes, there was a pause. During that dreadful second, everyone hoped it was all over. Then came a powerful blast, knocking everyone to the ground.

"Syd!" Donovan yelled, getting up to run to the pad.

"No, Alan, no!" yelled Zell as he pulled him back. Donovan tried to fight him but eventually collapsed in a heap on the tarmac.

The launch area was consumed in a column of fire. Everywhere they looked, people were screaming, running for their lives. Another explosion rocked the pad as everything nearby was instantly immolated. A massive cloud of dust and debris consumed the area, covering all with a thick blanket of ash.

The crew stayed down for a second longer, then picked up their heads. Their world had just ended. After another second or two the smoke began to clear.

"My God in heaven," Zell said, looking out over the landscape.

The others followed his stare and were stunned. Where just ten minutes ago there had stood a pristine rocket ready for launch, there was now a burning crater belching out smoke and ash into the morning sky.

Chapter 7

April 21
The White House
Washington, DC
2:20 p.m.

"Now explain it to me again, gentlemen. But this time in plain English, if you don't mind."

The President sat in the antique rocking chair near the fireplace in the Oval Office. A chair once owned by JFK. Seated around her on plush cream-colored couches were General McKenna, John Dieckman, and Cal Walker. All of them, with the exception of the President, were shifting in their seats. Four days had passed since the accident that claimed the lives of Lieutenant Weaver and her crew. The three men had just spent the last twenty minutes explaining to the President, in very technical terms, what their preliminary investigation revealed.

The President thought they were purposely trying to obscure their findings by burying the causes of the accident in technical jargon. Either they weren't sure of what had caused the malfunction or they were trying to mask their own mistakes. The President assumed the latter.

The accident aboard Phoenix 5 did more than kill three Americans and injure scores of others who had gathered to watch the launch; it had reignited the panic that had followed the announcement of the signal. Wild stories were everywhere. Aliens had blown up the rocket in order to prevent their detection on the Moon. The invaders were masking their armada through some kind of *Star Trek* cloaking device, which rendered their ships invisible. Politicians across the world were engaged in a conspiracy that would allow them to remain in power while the aliens came down to serve as overlords to an enslaved human race. Such stories would be laughable if not for the fact that so many people—more than the President cared to admit—honestly *believed* them. It was as if the Chinese mission had never happened. And everyone had an excuse for the irrefutable Chinese evidence to the contrary that there were no aliens currently residing on the Moon. The pictures were doctored. The Chinese were in on the conspiracy. The news media caught every conspiracy theory and reported it as fact. On the Internet every half-baked idea burst into a full-blown exposé as if it were kindling. The President had gone on television the night of the accident to reassure the American public that the accident was just that, an accident. She asked for patience as the investigations went forward. She asked for calm.

Nothing she said did any good.

This morning she had declared martial law in New York, Atlanta, Chicago, Detroit, and Los Angeles. Two thousand five hundred people were arrested in a single night in a wave of looting and violence in Los Angeles. In New York, someone had exploded a pipe bomb in Saint Patrick's Cathedral, killing hundreds of parishioners, which led to a series of attacks on mosques across the city. She would very likely need to send the National Guard into several other major cities before nightfall. As much as she despised the idea of tanks in the streets of American cities, the gathering death toll was almost more than she could bear. She recalled history often and prayed she was making the right decisions. More often she thought of how history would look upon her own actions.

Dieckman, clearing his throat, was the first to speak. "Madam President, as far as we can tell, we believe the fire was caused by an exposed wire in the ignition circuit that ignited the fuel prematurely."

"And would you mind telling me how you know that?"

"We were lucky," Deke explained. "One of the first pieces recovered was the segment of the craft that housed the ignition circuit. The frayed wire was still there. It couldn't have been any clearer than if it had dropped right into our laps."

"Then explain to me one more thing," the President said, leaning forward slightly. "How in the hell did that get past the inspection teams?"

Walker shifted almost imperceptibly. "Impossible to say at this juncture."

"That's not good enough, Dr. Walker," the President declared in an almost too-quiet voice. "That's not half as good enough. We lost some good people on that launchpad. But moreover, we're losing more and more American lives each and every day as these riots go on. Riots, I might add, that are the direct result of Phoenix 5."

"I understand that, Madam President."

"I don't think you do, Deke," she said. "I don't think any of you do. Now again, what happened?"

Deke looked at the President sheepishly. "We screwed up, ma'am. Badly."

The President seemed momentarily satisfied by his admission of guilt. She maintained her fixed gaze on Deke, hoping to draw more out of the head of the Astronaut Office.

"Madam President," Walker suddenly interjected. "With all due respect, you are asking us to send a manned mission to the Moon by June with almost no lead time. This would have been impossible even in the days of Apollo. Why, we needed almost a decade to figure out how to—"

"But you figured it out, Dr. Walker. That part's done. We know *how* to get to the Moon. We did it six times, as all you fellas at NASA keep reminding me. We know what it takes. All I've asked of you gentlemen is to reassemble the pieces and make sure that we get there safely, before the Chinese do." The President turned to General McKenna. "General, what's the current status of the Chinese program?"

"Ma'am," McKenna began, "our latest intel indicates that the Chinese are still incapable of building a viable lander. We understand that they have conducted tests recently on military bases and have been unable to construct one that will be able to withstand impact with the lunar surface. They've had two accidents so far, both fatalities."

"So they have a rocket that can get to the Moon, and we have the know-how to land us there," the President mused. "Fine situation."

"Madam President," Cal Walker began, pressing the tips of his fingers together. "Perhaps we can still beat the Chinese there. After all, if they are still incapable of landing on the Moon, they surely won't send a mission they are certain will fail. If you would give us more time, perhaps postpone the mission indefinitely until after the review board—"

"Time, Doctor, is a luxury we don't have. We need to get to the Moon by June, if not sooner. If we wait any longer, then there might not be an America left for these astronauts to come home to."

"Ma'am," Deke said, "you don't mean—"

"Gentlemen, we are facing the possibility that we may have to put the entire country under martial law. There are reports of militia movements in the West planning an insurrection against the government in light of the recent declarations of martial law in major cities. If we don't do something soon to quell the panic in our streets, the entire situation may . . ."

She trailed off. Her eyes looked heavy and tired. All of them could see she was under tremendous strain. She cleared her throat. "We had word this morning that several European countries fear the overthrow of their governments. We're talking about anarchy, gentlemen. Possibly the end of civilization as we know it. This EM pulse has brought the world to the precipice of another dark age. And we're the Roman Empire."

McKenna, Dieckman, and Walker had all met with their share of presidents. They knew the levelheaded ones from the paranoid ones, the calculating ones from the honest ones. This president was, overall, both levelheaded and honest. For her to admit these things, they knew the world was in very serious trouble.

"So," the President said, straightening up in her chair, "I can't give you time. What can I give you in order to land a crew on the Ocean of Storms?"

The three men looked at one another. Again, Dieckman spoke first. "Engineers. Equipment. Round-the-clock access to factories."

"You've got it."

"We'll also need a considerable increase in funding, Madam President," Walker added. "And possibly the aid of the air force personnel who worked on the initial design of the—"

McKenna looked as if he had been slapped. "Ma'am, I'm as much in favor of this mission as anyone, but we've got to consider the costs, especially with the political situation being what it is. Besides the fact that we've spent the last decade-plus as the de facto policemen of the world, we have the Taiwan situation to consider. Additionally, we now have troops in major cities across the country, protecting the public. Any military pullback on our part would not only be seen as a sign of weakness, it would be political suicide."

For the first time in the meeting the President smiled. "So then you'll also need a change in the political situation. In other words, a miracle." She slapped her thighs and stood up. "I'll see what I can do about that."

"Mr. President, thank you very much for taking my call on such short notice."

The President of the People's Republic of China respectfully nodded at the President of the United States of America via teleconference. Sitting alone in the darkened Situation Room of the White House, she was grateful that her Chinese counterpart spoke English so fluently and that the connection linking them was so clear. What she had to say was something that only the leader of the free world could say to the man controlling the most populous country on the planet, and she needed to make sure that every word and every gesture was crystal clear. At this early juncture, even the translators were best left out of the talk, to keep the conference as confidential as possible.

"I appreciate the opportunity to express my condolences to you personally regarding the loss of your crew," he said quietly. "A most unfortunate accident."

"More unfortunate than you might imagine, Mr. President," she replied. "And moreover, the accident is specifically what I want to talk to you about."

"I'm not sure I understand your meaning, Madam President. Are you implying—"

"Sir, I am not implying anything. We both know that the loss of our rocket and space vehicle was an accident. We also know that we are both attempting to do something that will have massive political ramifications for the future peace of this planet."

"The People's Republic of China is committed to world peace, Madam President. That is why we are endeavoring to better understand the meaning of the signal coming from the Moon."

"Let's cut to the chase, Mr. President. We both want to get to the Moon. It would not only mean prestige for the nation who makes first contact with an alien species, it would also bring order to our troubled world."

"That it would. It would greatly aid your country in particular, which is facing such great civil unrest."

"We're still in the information age, sir. Despite all your best efforts, we know that similar unrest is brewing in your countryside, that your peasants are revolting and have been for some time. It may not be as widespread as the unrest in my own country, but it is there and it is a growing and gathering threat to the stability of your government."

"Be that as it may, Madam President, I still do not understand—"

"I would like to propose a joint mission between the People's Republic of China and the United States of America—one that would not only ensure that we would get to the Moon successfully but one that also would quell the panic growing every day around the world. What I am asking is that we set aside our differences and form an alliance, a true alliance, to promote world stability."

He smiled thinly. "Madam President, the current situation regarding Taiwan would prevent—"

"Taiwan is not on the table, Mr. President."

He sat back in his chair and lit a cigarette. "I see. So what do you propose?"

"We know your country is using Apollo-style technology to get to the Moon. You've successfully built a rocket and command module capable of circumnavigating the Moon. We have the know-how and the experience to build a lander that would set us down in the Ocean of Storms. We therefore combine our programs and missions, using a Chinese command module and an American-built lander to get to the Moon."

She watched her Chinese counterpart consider her offer.

"You are very practical, Madam President. But I feel I must offer a counterproposal. China must be represented on the *surface* of the Moon, for the sake of world unity and stability, if nothing else. So I suggest a full integration of materials and manpower, including an integrated team landing on the surface of the Moon."

"Fair enough, Mr. President."

"And as to Taiwan?"

"Taiwan will still be here when we get back from the Moon. The question is, will anything be left in a few months' time if we don't join forces to get there?"

He smiled again and stubbed out his cigarette. "I will be in contact with you shortly, Madam President."

April 22
Arlington National Cemetery
Arlington, Virginia
10:30 a.m.

The next morning Alan Donovan was standing in the whispering stillness of Arlington National Cemetery. Rain came down at an angle, wetting the side of his face, the wind whipping up the ends of his raincoat and soaking his pants. The earth around his feet bubbled into puddles. His socks were wet, and he shivered involuntarily against the cold. Beyond the hundreds of mourners before him was the President of the United States, paying tribute to three fallen American heroes, as she called them. Like the service members standing at attention around her, the President stood unflinching in the rain, braving it without the aid of a hat or an umbrella. Donovan couldn't look at the three flag-draped coffins lined up in a row. They reminded him of too many lost things.

His father.

Syd.

His father had been buried in the California sunshine in a little cemetery outside a clapboard church. Thackeray Zell had paid for his funeral. The sailors had handed Donovan, all of twelve years of age, his father's flag. The three of them made up all of the assembled mourners except for the sailors who had come to carry his father's coffin to the grave and play "Taps" on a hill nearby. His young mother had been buried in the same grave five years earlier. He spent most of the ceremony looking at his mother's name—Emily Donovan—on the headstone and wondering why his father's name wasn't there. As they left, he asked old Thackeray if they had forgotten to put the name on the stone. Thackeray brought him back a month later to prove the inscription had been added. Alan bent down and traced the deep grooves in the stone with his fingertips, first his father's name and then his mother's, over and over. He hadn't been back since.

A week ago Donovan awoke in his hotel room in Houston and was surprised to be reminded of his father's funeral—something about the way the light was coming through the drapes and casting long shadows into the room. Syd was one of those shadows. She was sitting by the windowsill and blowing on a cup of tea she had ordered up while he was still asleep. Her dark hair was hanging long and loose around her shoulders, freed from its normal military-style bun. Her profile in that light reminded him of the fact that she was a quarter Cherokee, something about the dark pin-straight hair, something in her long straight nose, her strong chin. She wore a silk robe half-slung on her body, open to her navel. She parted the drapes with two fingers and peeked out the window and into the morning light. Donovan watched her for a time before letting her know that he was awake. Looking at her then, no one would have ever guessed that she had been a rough-and-tumble navy brat who had traveled the world over with her father, who was only recently retired. Even fewer would have guessed that she had chosen a similar life for herself, ultimately becoming an astronaut. She looked every inch the picture of delicate feminine grace by those curtains, in that light.

For some reason, Donovan found it easy to tell Syd everything about his father. He didn't know exactly why, but he did. Maybe because both of their fathers had been in the navy. Maybe because of NASA.

But there was also something about Syd, the way her gold-green eyes pulled at him and made him say things he had never said to any other woman. Almost involuntarily he told her of the years after his mother's death when his father flew crop dusters out in Modesto. He told her of the long nights witnessing his father drinking until all hours, a bottle of Jack Daniel's and a framed picture of his mother on the kitchen table. He told her of how as a little boy he would put his father to bed and then help him get up in the morning. *You're a good kid, a real good kid,* he would slur as he leaned on his son. *You'd make your mother proud.* At first light Alan would brew a pot of strong coffee on their stove and wait until his father finished most of it, hoping it made him sober enough to get into his plane. Then he would ready himself for school. He wasn't bitter about these things. He wasn't angry. Alan was more embarrassed than anything else when his father drank too much. And he was only ever embarrassed if his father drank around other people. When the old man drank at home, he didn't mind. There Alan could take care of him; there he knew he was safe.

Alan always figured that he wasn't embarrassed by his drunk of a father because he knew what his father had been—an ace navy pilot, a geologist, a loving husband and father, an almost astronaut. In the years after his mother's death, his father often tried to sober up. Sometimes he would go weeks without drinking. Usually they were the weeks of school vacations, when they would hop into his father's old '74 Challenger and drive across country so Hunter could show off Mission Control to his son. Few people there at that time knew Hunter, so they never got any perks or were allowed into sensitive areas. Usually they would just join a guided tour and walk around the facilities. Hunter would bend down and point at the relics of Apollo and tell him stories. Alan loved those stories. He loved to hear the rising thrill in his father's whispered tales. His father had been one of the chosen few to qualify to go to the Moon. To Alan it was as if he had been chosen to become one of the apostles.

"You must've really loved him," Syd said one night as they were lying in bed. Her damp, recently shampooed hair was spread across his bare chest as he stared at the ceiling.

"He was my hero," Alan told her. "No comic-book superhero could hold a candle to him."

Alan often compared his father to superheroes. The ones he liked best were a lot like his father. Spider-Man had problems paying the bills in his secret identity of Peter Parker. As mutants the X-Men were outcasts living in secret in a school in upstate New York. Iron Man was the best of all. He was a genius who had invented this supersophisticated suit of armor, but he was also an alcoholic. Those superheroes always managed to overcome their problems, both ordinary and extraordinary. Alan always assumed his father would do the same.

Syd had the same hero worship of her own father. Because she traveled all over the world with him, she always imagined he was a part of America's first line of defense against any and all enemies. She loved the way he looked in his pressed and starched uniform. She loved touching the medals on his dress uniform when his jacket was draped over a chair. Most of all, she loved how, despite all the concerns he must have had protecting the United States, he still had time to come home and play with her and call her his Sugar Pop. She said it was like something out of an old black-and-white movie, the way he loved her.

The only problem Syd ever had with her father was that he thought she was throwing away her military career when she joined NASA. He never saw much good in the space program and believed she was wasting her talents as both a leader and a pilot by joining the astronaut corps at a time when NASA's next-generation space vehicle had yet to go into production. They had fought bitterly and then hadn't spoken much since despite all her mother's efforts to get them together. But no matter how much she loved her father, she couldn't resist going to space. In American bases all over the world, she spent her nights looking up at the stars. She wanted to be up there with them, even if it was only in low Earth orbit aboard the International Space Station.

"I love the navy," she told Donovan, "but sometimes it limits your perspective on things. Everything's an order to be carried out. Everything's procedure. Everything's just what you're told. But out there," she said, nodding up into the sky above the rocket that would take her life, "there are no limits, no perspective to limit you but your own."

No one was supposed to know about them. Syd made him swear to keep things a secret. Zell knew, of course—how could he not? But he was tight as a drum about the whole thing. Never said a word. Syd really got to like him because of that, even if she still ribbed him about being an alcoholic lecher. As far as Donovan knew, nobody still had any knowledge about the extent of their relationship.

Donovan looked at Syd's parents. Her father's face was a stoic mask, though the eyes reflected the depth of his loss. Syd's mother's face was cracked and broken by grief, probably beyond repair. Donovan paused a moment before retreating into the rain. It was better this way.

Loss isn't eased by another mourner.

April 25
John F. Kennedy Space Center
Cape Canaveral, Florida
12:30 p.m.

If Elias Zell could describe a vision of his own personal hell, it would be that he would spend eternity doing nothing at all. Zell was, if nothing else, a doer. He had to be occupied at all times both intellectually and physically. He and Donovan had spent the days since the accident drumming their fingers while everyone else at NASA was busy conducting their investigation. He tried to occupy himself by rereading

Herodotus and going to the gym to keep up his training, but such activities did him little good. Yet as badly as he had been faring, he knew Donovan was doing much worse.

They had returned to Florida two days ago. As most of the crew was reassembling Phoenix 5 inside a hangar, Donovan was grabbing whomever he could lay a hand on to pester them about getting involved with the investigation. He had been rebuffed at every turn. Zell was now watching his friend lean on Benny, who was trying his best to be sympathetic.

"Look, Donovan," he said, slurping his fifth cup of coffee that day, "what can I tell you? If it were up to me, you guys would be in there helping us with the investigation. But the suits don't want you in there. It's protocol to have only NASA investigators involved with this kinda stuff."

"Fucking bullshit, Benny," Donovan said, leaning into him. "Elias and I are archeologists. We're used to sifting through pieces."

"Again, what can I say? Those are orders."

"Fuck orders. You know we can be of more use than any goddamn pinheads in the military—"

"Present company excluded from such condemnation, of course, Commander," Zell muttered.

Benny looked to Zell and then Donovan. "Sure."

"Benny, look," Donovan said, running a hand through his hair. "All I'm asking is for you to talk to Wilson. I haven't been able to get a hold of him since—"

"I know, I know. But he's on the primary investigation team. Whaddya want me to do, kidnap him and bring him to your hotel?"

"I don't know. Just do something."

Benny glanced at his watch. "I've gotta go, Donovan. I'll see what I can do."

With that, the pilot walked toward the hangar.

Zell touched Donovan's arm. "Alan, you're pushing."

"I'm not pushing, Elias."

"Let them do their jobs. I know you're upset about Syd—"

Donovan jerked his arm from Zell's grasp. "I'm not upset. I just don't trust these guys. I don't want to get aboard that goddamn thing and have the same thing happen to us."

Just then Moose came strolling toward them. "Dr. Zell, Dr. Donovan. I'm glad I found you guys. Wilson wants to see the whole crew right away."

"What for?" Zell asked.

Moose shrugged. "Didn't say. But it sounded pretty important. I'm supposed to assemble you guys ASAP."

"Good," Donovan said. "I've got a thing or two to say to our mysterious leader."

Moose gave Donovan a quizzical look.

"Lieutenant Commander, I believe you'll find Benevisto in the hangar."

A few minutes later they were all assembled in one of the briefing rooms outside Launch Control. Through the windows, Donovan could clearly make out the top of the hangar that housed the remains of Phoenix 5. Around him, Zell, Moose, and Benny were buzzing with questions. Benny was sure the mission was canceled. Moose was as ever more optimistic, believing that Wilson was going to come in and tell them the mission had been pushed back until the investigation was concluded. Zell countered that by remarking on the latest news broadcast, which claimed that over four hundred people had been killed in riots across the country just this week. Donovan scratched the short hairs on the back of his neck and paced the floor.

Wilson entered the room a moment later with an attaché case and jerked his sunglasses off with a quick snap, tucking them into his breast pocket. He stood at the head of the sun-brightened oak table and looked around at his assembled crew.

"I'm here to inform you that the mission has been changed," Wilson said crisply.

"Terrific," Benny groaned. "So what're you saying, sir? It's been scrapped?"

"What the hell're you trying to pull, Wilson?" Donovan demanded. "Are you telling me NASA's just going to let those people die in vain?"

Wilson reached into his attaché case and tossed a book at Donovan. Then he slid a book across the table at everyone else.

"Chinese-English dictionary?" Zell mused.

Moose cleared his throat. "If you don't mind my asking, sir, what are these for?"

"Better brush up on it, Moose. This just became a joint mission."

"A joint mission?" Donovan peered up from the dictionary. "Explain."

"There's really not much *to* explain," Wilson said with a piercing look. "Politically, it makes sense to the government. Financially, it makes sense to NASA. Setting aside the lives lost aboard Phoenix 5, NASA has lost *billions*. If the rocket has—as we believe it may—a fatal flaw, there's no money to redesign and build a new one. If there's also a flaw in the command module, we have the same problem. Moreover, we've lost *time*. If we're to divert a panic on this planet, we need to get to the Moon on schedule—and the only way to do that is to combine forces with the Chinese. The Chinese have already proven they have a working CM and rocket—they've already flown it around the Moon. The President opened up a dialogue with her Chinese counterpart, so here we are riding to the Moon on the back of the dragon."

"But why?" Benny asked. "What's in it for the Chinese? I mean, NASA's all but ruined. Why don't they just take their ship and fly it right over our houses on the way to the Moon?"

"Good question, Benevisto," Wilson said. "The simple reason? They can get there, but they have no way of getting down to the surface."

He hit some keys on the desktop terminal, bringing up satellite photos that showed what looked like the lunar surface strewn with wreckage.

"Skystalker satellite imagery reveals that they attempted to land an unmanned LEM on the surface when they circled the Moon. It failed.

Our intel also indicates that their two earthbound tests have had similar problems, resulting in the deaths of both pilots. Over here, we're looking at the opposite problem. We've been touching down landers in San Bernardino light as a feather since Valentine's Day, but as for a rocket—"

The room fell silent as everyone recalled the horrific events in Florida. Zell's eyes flicked over to Donovan, whose searing gaze was fixed directly on the table.

"Anyway," Wilson continued, "our boys upstairs have struck a deal."

Zell folded his arms across his barrel chest. "Why do I not like the sound of that word?"

"What's the deal?" asked Donovan.

Wilson paused. "The Chinese have agreed to give us five slots on the mission. Providing we give them a working lander. And—"

"And what?" Benny asked.

"And one of their taikonauts is first out the door."

Again, silence struck the room as everyone processed this. They all knew they were being silly. In this day and age, it shouldn't matter who was first. Hadn't the country come so much further than where it was in 1969? Wasn't this mission about something bigger than petty politics? It shouldn't matter. *But it did.*

After a moment, Moose spoke. "Who pilots it down, sir? The lander, I mean. Who's on the stick?"

"The lander will be, for all intents and purposes, an American spacecraft," Wilson replied. "I will pilot her down, along with Donovan, Zell, and two Chinese crew members. Mosensen, your new assignment will be co-CM pilot along with Benevisto. Orbiting the Moon along with the two of you will be a Chinese crew member who, as I understand it, essentially designed their spacecraft."

"This is ridiculous," Benny said, tossing a pen on the table. "This whole mission's turned into a joke."

"But we still are going, aren't we?" Moose said, leaning his elbows on the table. "In the end, that's what it really boils down to. We're still going to the Moon."

"Maybe it's better this way," said Donovan soberly. "The message, or whatever it is, isn't just for Americans after all. And we're supposed to be going there for science. Not to plant some flag in the dust."

"You say that now," said Benny. "Just wait'll the media puts their spin on it."

Donovan turned to Benny. "And what spin is that?"

"That we're limping to the Moon with our tail between our legs, the Chinese holding our hands the whole way!" Benny stood up. "I don't know about any of you, but I'm pretty ashamed right now. And if Syd were still here, she would be too."

He turned to leave. Instantly Wilson was blocking his path. Benny glared at Wilson. "Listen, Wilson, it's none of your goddamn—"

Before he could even complete that thought, Wilson was up in his face, his dark eyes fixed on Benny's. "Stand *down*, Benevisto. You're talking to a superior officer."

Zell was behind Benny in a moment, a light hand in the crook of the pilot's left elbow. "Commander, Colonel Wilson is only the messenger. We can't kill him for being the bearer of grim tidings."

Benny paused a moment, then turned away. Still defiant, he refused to sit but deferred to Wilson by remaining in the room. Meanwhile, Wilson turned to face everyone else. "Listen up, people," he said. "We have a long road ahead of us. Once that Chinese crew gets here, we're on *their* turf. At least until we get into the LEM. If we start fighting now, if we can't stay unified, then this mission doesn't stand a snowball's chance in hell."

With that, Wilson spun on his heel and exited the room. The remaining crew members milled around, now less sure than ever about their place in this mission.

Benny spoke up. "So now what do we do?"

Their silence was answer enough.

Chapter 8

May 2
Johnson Space Center
Houston, Texas
9:09 a.m.

In the week before the Chinese crew arrived, the surviving members of the Phoenix program had been thrown into a crash course. On top of the regular daily training, there were nightly lessons in Chinese language and customs, as well as endless run-throughs in the simulator, which had been quickly redesigned to match the specifications of the Chinese craft. Compared to the relatively cramped *Carpathian*, this new craft, named *Tai-Ping* ("Great Peace"), was like a ballroom. Configured to hold eight people, it offered plenty of elbow room. Benny wished they could say the same about *Copernicus*. While an improvement over the lunar modules of the Apollo days, holding five people versus the older model's two, it still felt like piling into a phone booth. Benny was grateful that he would be sitting this one out, although he felt for Moose, who had lost his slot to the Chinese commander.

"Damn it, Benny! We slammed into the LEM again!"

Moose's angry rebuke shook Benny out of his thoughts. He sighed in frustration. They had been cooped up in the *Tai-Ping* simulator since six that morning, running and rerunning the docking procedure. The problem for Benny was that the Chinese Shenzhou ship was a different model than what he was used to. Whereas the *Carpathian* had its roots in Apollo, the Shenzhou ships came from the Russian Soyuz designs. The differences were subtle, but when flying a seventeen-thousand-pound craft in an airless vacuum with around four thousand pounds of thrust behind it, *subtle* takes on a whole new meaning.

Benny shook his head. "Sorry, Moose. This thing's kicking my ass."

"Yeah, I know. My dad always said that if you were going to do something, you might as well take your time and do it right. Come on, let's run it again."

As they waited for the techs to reset the simulation, Benny and Moose talked about everything they'd been through.

"This whole joint-mission thing still got you messed up?"

"Shit yeah, Moose. Don't tell me it's not bugging you."

"I'm not saying it's not. But when I think about it long enough, I realize that the only reason why it's bugging me is on account of ego. I wanted to fly that bird down to the surface."

"I'd be plenty pissed if I were you."

Moose laughed. "That I know. In a way I'm glad it's not you who got bumped."

"How come?"

"Because you're my friend and it always hurts more to see a friend hurt than to be hurt yourself. That and the fact that you'd be so pissed off you'd probably crash the whole thing right *through* the Moon."

It was Benny's turn to laugh. "Got me pegged, eh?"

"You might say that."

"I tell you, man, I wish I had your cool about this. I dunno how you do it."

Moose turned to him, a hand running through his scruff of blond hair. "Everything happens for a reason, man. Maybe this is God's way of showing us that we need to join together to solve this thing. Donovan's right: this object was placed there for all of humanity. It only makes sense that the Chinese come along."

Benny looked at his friend. "You're kidding, right?"

Moose grinned and turned his attention back to the instrument panel. "I was raised in the heartland, friend. We don't joke about the Big Guy."

Before Benny could respond, the comm channel buzzed in their ears.

"Sim's been reset, boys," the chief technician informed them. "Time to let 'er fly."

A knock on the sim's viewport startled them. They glanced up from their instrument panels to see Wilson's face staring back at them. He pointed toward the sim's hatch. Benny threw Moose a glance as they made their way over to the portal. They found Wilson standing at the top of the ladder.

"I wanted to speak to the two of you about the other day."

Benny folded his arms across his chest. "Sir, if this is another pep talk—"

Wilson shook his head. "That's your problem, Benevisto. You've always got a smart-ass remark ready before you know what someone's going to say."

Benny's face flushed visibly. "I'm sorry, sir. Go ahead."

"What I wanted to say is that I understand your concerns. I don't very much like that you got bumped from the lander, Mosensen. And I don't really like the idea of having one of the Chinese taikonauts looking over your shoulder, Benevisto. If it were up to me, this would be our show all the way. But I also understand the practical reasons for making this a joint mission, and I need the two of you to help convince Zell and Donovan of that. I'm fairly certain they don't trust us any more than we trust the Chinese."

Moose glanced at Benny, then back to Wilson. "I think we understand that, sir. But we're all willing to do what it takes to make this a successful mission. However, I do have to agree with Benny, in that I think there will be some negative media coverage once this story breaks."

"Then get ready," Wilson said with a sigh. "As I understand it, the President will be breaking the news this afternoon."

"You're thinking bad, sir?" Benny wondered.

Wilson smiled halfheartedly. "The worst."

May 3
Ellington Field Joint Reserve Base
Hangar 616
Houston, Texas
5:13 a.m.

Despite Wilson's fears, the President's speech went over better than anyone had anticipated. In measured, even tones, she explained to the American public—as well as the world at large—why the United States and China had to mount a joint mission. Point by critical point she had laid out her argument, stressing how the significance of the object buried on the Moon required the two most powerful spacefaring nations in the world to join forces. She even hinted at the possibility of reconciliation by suggesting that the mission would foster better diplomatic relations between America and China. Mutual cooperation would be likely as the two nations studied the object and disseminated their findings to humanity.

"If the object placed on the Moon so many millennia ago suggests anything," the President remarked in her address to the nation, "it is that mankind is not alone in the universe. The question before us now is whether or not humanity reaches out to that intelligence together—or if we choose the path of divisiveness, pettiness, and distrust. With this joint mission, we have chosen mutual cooperation. We have chosen unity. We have chosen to reach across the expanse in brotherhood and in friendship. We have chosen to greet the future not as a group of nations, but as a single people, resolved and united for the common good and the peace of our world."

The speech received high marks and helped ease the tensions that had erupted into street violence following the Phoenix 5 accident. Moreover, the President's words gave many people hope that the Taiwan situation would soon reach a peaceful solution. Yet some in the press looked at the President's speech and the forthcoming joint mission more cynically. Famed syndicated columnist Goldie Mae Horning wrote that America had "resigned not only its preeminence in space exploration but also its moral authority by capitulating once again to China's demands of sovereignty over Taiwan." None of these sentiments, however, prevented representatives of the world's press corps from descending on Houston the day the Chinese taikonauts were due to arrive.

In order to avoid a media circus, American and Chinese officials had agreed that the crews would meet at Ellington instead of at the Johnson Space Center. The Chinese crew had arrived overnight and been spirited away to an isolated corner of the base. Despite having gotten only an hour's sleep on the long flight, each of them had arrived at the hangar precisely on time. The same could not be said for the Phoenix team, who straggled in ten minutes later, bleary-eyed and complaining about the unseasonably cold morning air. When they spotted the Chinese crew patiently waiting, the American astronauts felt the urge to clean up their act. They eyed the new members of the team. One of them, a steely military man with a close crop of black hair, was standing almost ramrod straight in an impeccable dress uniform. The second, neatly clad in jeans and a black golf shirt, sported shaggy hair under a Yankees baseball cap. He peered at the world through a small set of round wire-framed glasses. The third was a smartly dressed woman with shoulder-length hair in a charcoal-gray business suit. Even though she had spent nearly the last entire day flying across the Pacific Ocean and half the American continent, she looked as sharp, refreshed, and alert as if she was about to address an academic committee. Donovan, Zell, and the others greeted them and were met with polite, but curt nods.

"Good morning, crew!" Wilson's voice sounded like a rifle shot. He strode into the hangar at a brisk clip. "I'm sure you've all had a chance to get acquainted, but let me formally introduce our guests." He motioned to the silent military man. "This is Commander Yuen Bai, PLA Air Force. He'll be leading the team on the surface. Additionally, he'll be the first out the door when we arrive at the landing site. Next to him is Dr. Bruce Yeoh, the noted computer specialist and physicist. As Dr. Yeoh helped design the *Tai-Ping*, his job will be to make sure everything runs smoothly on the mission, as well as relay intel from the surface back to Mission Control.

"Dr. Yeoh and Lieutenant Commander Benevisto will work together as tech support," Wilson continued. "And lastly, this is Dr. Soong Yang Zi, a forensic anthropologist."

"Anthropologist?" Benny wondered. "With all due respect, sir, why do we need one on the crew?"

Yuen cleared his throat and stepped forward, his hat tucked in the crook of his right arm. "It is the belief of the Chinese government that the dig site will likely contain the remains of whatever species left that object on the Moon. Since it did not occur to your government to provide an expert in anthropology, the People's Republic of China has secured the services of Dr. Soong."

"How generous of them," Benny muttered to Moose.

"Even in the unlikely event that we are unable to recover remains," Yuen continued, "Dr. Soong's expertise in forensics, as well as her professionalism, will prove invaluable on this mission."

Yuen stepped back and gave the direction of the meeting back over to Wilson. Wilson turned to the new crew and spoke in perfect

Mandarin. "It is our honor to have you here," he said, bowing respectfully. The crew bowed in return. After a moment, Wilson spoke up again. "Okay, people, we have a lot of ground to cover, so let's head over to the training center and get started."

With that, Wilson turned smartly on his heel and walked off. Zell walked over to Soong. "Dr. Soong," he said, extending his hand. "I read your thesis on DNA fingerprinting in the *International Journal of Osteoarchaeology*. Interesting stuff, though I think your research could benefit from the experience of working in the field."

Soong raised an eyebrow at his outstretched hand. "Do you?" she asked in slightly accented English. "Well, from what I know of the Zell Institute, I think you and I have a slightly different assessment of fieldwork."

"And what do you know of the Zell Institute, my dear?"

"Only that your approach to archeology could benefit from less media coverage and considerably more discipline."

She dismissed him with a nod and turned to leave the hangar. Zell stood there a moment, unsure of what had just happened.

Following the first day of meetings between the two crews, Wilson headed straight for the gym. He needed some time to himself before the press conference tomorrow morning. The gym was always the first place he went when he had things on his mind. He went through his workout almost on autopilot, blazing through calisthenics with no effort, punching the heavy bag with determined, graceful speed. He then hit the track, his feet pounding the clay in an unbroken rhythm. After forty minutes he slowed down, then came to a stop, finally out of breath. Wilson put his head between his knees a moment, then looked back at the track. Six miles a day, every day since he was a teenager. He figured he must have run halfway around the world by now. He smiled at that thought, remembering jogging with his dad and barely being able to keep up.

Wilson's childhood in Yonkers, New York, was still the happiest time in his life, he thought. Every day when he came home from school, there'd be a note from his father, a mechanic who'd flown a chopper in Vietnam. Usually the note would be just a few words long. "The Revolutionary War" or "Adolf Hitler." Wilson would read it, then dash into the dining room, where the *World Book* encyclopedias were kept. Wilson would take all the relevant books down to the basement and sit under the stairs, eating a peanut butter sandwich and reading by flashlight. Every night, he'd hear the door open and his stomach would jump. He'd sprint upstairs and run right into his father's waiting arms. To this day, Wilson associated the smell of grease and oil with unbridled joy. After dinner, and only after dinner, Wilson and his father would retreat to the living room, where his dad would smoke a Camel—the only vice he had—and discuss what Wilson had learned. These talks could last anywhere from fifteen minutes to two hours and often would travel lazy, winding routes. A talk about the Declaration of Independence might branch off to a story about Medgar Evers, or the history of the Delta blues, before circling back to where they started. One time, Wilson came home to find just one word written down:

Space.

Looking back, Wilson realized that the boy who had gone down into the basement that golden October afternoon was a very different one than the one who emerged three hours later. His whole life had changed as he pored over the stories of Gus Grissom, Neil Armstrong, Sally Ride, and, of course, Guy Bluford, the first African American in space. When he stepped back into the ebbing daylight, Franklin Wilson knew he was going to be an astronaut.

When Wilson was twenty-two, his father, after years of twelve-hour days and six-day weeks, died of a heart attack. After the small service at Mount Hope Cemetery, Wilson stood over his father's grave and swore that everything he did from that day forward would justify all the sacrifices his father had made for him. By everyone's standards, he had more than succeeded. During the war in Afghanistan he had flown several rescue missions and led the air raid during the liberation of Kabul. For his services, Wilson had earned a Congressional Medal of Honor and his choice of assignments. Without a second's hesitation, he had chosen the astronaut corps.

Wilson had always thought that he had joined the astronaut corps because he had grown tired of war, tired of fighting, tired of death and destruction. Though he had no regrets about serving his country all these years, he had wanted to do more, give something back to humanity. He had also wanted to challenge himself as a pilot and as a commanding officer, and to his mind there was no greater challenge than going into space. Yet now, reflecting on the complexities of this joint mission, he realized that he had also wanted to join the astronaut corps to get away from politics. As a commanding officer, he often had to field questions from the press about the justifications of military actions. Those games exhausted him, and he expected the politics surrounding this joint mission would deplete him further. He just wanted to do his job. But as coleader of this mission, he knew he would have to do much more than that.

It'll have to be all smiles and glad-handing at that press conference, he thought. *Yes, Mr. Reporter from the* Times, *we're happy to have the Chinese aboard. Certainly, Ms. CNN Correspondent, we feel the Chinese will be an asset to the mission. How do we get along, Mr. Tabloid? Why just peachy—like old friends.*

Wilson shook his head and laughed to himself. So here he was, a lifetime of accomplishments behind him, and the greatest one yet to come, provided he could get these two crews to work together. If he could do that, he could stomach all of the asinine questions the press threw at him, especially the ones about how it would feel to be the first black man on the Moon, a matter he had dismissed as too trivial in this context to even consider. For Wilson, going to the Moon meant one thing: his father hadn't spent more than half his life toiling in a grease pit for nothing. He looked up at the sky, seeing the sun begin to slip down over the horizon. He figured there was time for a few more laps. Standing up, Wilson stretched his legs, exhaled, then began pounding the track again. As he ran, he saw the Moon fading into the twilight sky.

Be seeing you soon.

May 20
Johnson Space Center
Houston, Texas
9:34 a.m.

Benny and Yeoh were sitting in the flight simulator, running through some last-minute checks. Though not speaking about it, they were both surprised that they had become such fast friends in so short a period of time. After reading Yeoh's file, Benny was surprised that someone like him—a physics genius—could be so easygoing and self-deprecating. He also appreciated Yeoh's love of American music, particularly Chicago blues, one of Benny's favorites. Yeoh was equally impressed with Benny, especially after learning that most of the lieutenant commander's computer knowledge was self-taught. The two sat in the semidarkness, their faces lit by the instrument panels.

"So," Benny said as they reset the simulator, "whaddya think is waiting for us up there?"

Yeoh looked up from the tattered notebook he was scribbling computations in. "It's interesting you should ask. I've spent so long trying to get this mission off the ground that I've hardly had time to consider what could be up there. The short answer is that I don't really know.

Whatever it is, it has the potential to change the world in ways we've never dreamed."

"As if it hasn't already."

"This is true, but just think for a moment. Whatever we find on the Moon, it means that some sort of spacecraft had to bring it there. For a craft to travel here from another star system . . . Just for them to have survived the trip means that they're far more advanced than we are."

"You're talking about faster-than-light travel," said Benny. "It's impossible."

"Not if they traveled through a black hole," Yeoh replied, tucking his pencil behind his ear.

Benny laughed. "Black holes? Come on! They're so dense that any matter even approaching one would be torn to bits."

"Not true," said Yeoh. "It's that very density that may hold the key." Yeoh smiled at him, having heard it all before. "Look, from what we've learned, the inside of a black hole collapses the fabric of the universe into a point of infinite curvature—what's called a space-time singularity."

Benny nodded. "In a singularity, the laws of physics don't apply, right?"

"Exactly! Imagine what that means: perhaps inside such singularities, access to whole other universes, other realities completely unlike our own. These singularities can have strong and weak elements, sections that aren't as destructive as others. A ship passing through the right section could conceivably enter a wormhole and pass through to the other side of the galaxy."

"Maybe," Benny said, "or maybe they'd be crushed into subatomic particles."

"Well, there's the problem," Yeoh said, laughing. "It's a theory, but no one can get close enough to a black hole to try it."

"Not to mention that the closest black hole is about three thousand light-years away. I dunno about you, but I don't exactly have that kinda time to spare to make the trip."

Yeoh nodded, flipping some overhead switches in preparation for the next simulation. "Well, I suspect you won't have to wait that long before we learn all the answers."

May 25
Forensic Anthropology and Computer Enhancement Services Laboratory
Louisiana State University
Baton Rouge, Louisiana
10:13 a.m.

Since opening in 1980, the FACES lab, as it was commonly known, had grown from a center for the analysis and curating of skeletal remains to one of the foremost crime labs in the world. Using computer-assisted age progression, facial reconstruction, and photo enhancement, the laboratory was able to piece together detailed analyses of crime scenes using only the bones of a victim. Under the leadership of Mary "The Bone Lady" Manhein, the lab had handled over six hundred cases for the FBI, local law enforcement, and the Center for Missing and Exploited Children.

Knowing there was a chance that the crew might come across the bodies of whoever planted the object there, Soong felt it would be a good idea to run through some of the basics in her line of work. She had put in a request with LSU to use its facility for a bit of training, and the university had graciously agreed. The crew, eager to get off the base, was thrilled at the chance to take a road trip. Soong, her face partially obscured by a surgical mask, pulled on a pair of latex gloves with a snap and looked down at the bones.

"The first thing to do when trying to analyze human bones is to remove any putrefactive tissue that could obscure vital clues."

"Putrefactive?" asked Moose.

"Rotten, Commander," answered Soong. Moose nodded, his pallor turning slightly green.

"After that, you want to assemble a profile. Look here," she said as she pointed to the skeleton's left leg. "See the fractures along the tibia and fibula? The bones were broken once at some point during her life."

"*Her* life?" asked Benny. "Call me crazy, but that seems like something you'd have a hard time telling just from a bunch of bones."

"On the contrary, Commander," Soong answered. "The signs are everywhere. For one thing, look at this bone, right below the eyebrows. It's called the supraorbital ridge and is much more prominent in males than females." She gently put her fingers on the skeleton's jaw. "The mandible," she said. "Usually squared off in men, but rounded in women. And, the most obvious clue, the pelvis. Much wider in women." Here Soong allowed herself an uncharacteristic smile. "Otherwise we'd all have had a tough time being born."

"Excuse me, Dr. Soong," Moose began, "but I frankly don't understand why Dr. Yeoh, Benny, and I are here. I mean, we're not going to be going down to the surface. We won't be handling any bodies, if you should find any."

Soong fixed an impassive gaze on him. "If you are unable to stomach this lesson, Commander Mosensen, I suggest you leave. I have no time for questions which have already been answered."

"But you requested that we be here," Benny answered. "You might as well explain."

"I did not request your presence," Soong noted. "It was at the insistence of your government that you have come here."

Wilson cleared his throat. "Perhaps I can explain—"

"Your government doesn't trust us," Yeoh said sheepishly. "They wanted you—"

"No offense, Bruce," Benny interjected, "but with all the crap your government's been trying to pull with Taiwan? If it was up to me—"

"Benevisto," Wilson said sharply, then turned to the Chinese crew. "It was not our intention to seem distrustful. It just seemed a good idea to have everyone aware of what we might encounter on the Moon."

"What we might encounter," Yuen said suddenly, "is a species quite unlike our own. But the basics of anthropology allow us to have a general understanding of every species on Earth. That knowledge, imparted by Dr. Soong, will allow us to complete this mission successfully. For the time being, I respectfully ask you, Lieutenant Colonel Wilson, to have your man allow us to proceed. We have little time to spare for unnecessary outbursts from persons who are frankly unnecessary to this phase of the mission."

"With all due respect, Commander Yuen," Wilson said with an edge in his voice, "Benevisto has done no—"

Zell appeared suddenly between them, a grin creeping out from his graying beard. "Gentlemen, I have a suggestion. Perhaps a moment of tension like this could be eased by a friendly drink among fellow travelers and comrades?"

May 26
Spinning Wheel Bar
Baton Rouge, Louisiana
12:17 a.m.

Donovan thought Zell's suggestion was a good one, even if it didn't quite go off as he had planned. The crew hardly sat at the same table most of the night, with Wilson, Yuen, and Soong standing at the bar; Donovan and Zell at a corner table under a neon Samuel Adams sign; and Moose, Benny, and Yeoh pumping bills into the jukebox. As Zell got up from his chair to talk to Yeoh, Donovan watched Wilson excuse himself from Yuen and Soong and make a quiet exit. He wondered how successful this mission would be if its two commanders could barely socialize with each other.

Donovan thought back to the last time they had all been out drinking like this. So much had changed in so short a time. His eyes darted off to the bar, not very different from the one where he and Syd had first begun to hit it off. The stools were appropriately empty. He looked at his scotch glass and took another swallow. The liquor burned his throat, but he enjoyed the sensation. Occasionally he liked to be reminded that he was still alive. The only problem was, Syd wasn't. And Donovan knew it.

He also knew full well that the mission could fail, just like Syd's had.

Donovan wandered over to Zell, who was standing behind Benny at his table. Benny was trying to crack a joke, but it was met with only faint smiles before the table lapsed back into silence. Donovan wondered if he should try to coax Yuen and Soong away from the bar, but they looked like they were getting ready to pack it in for the night.

Suddenly, they heard an antagonistic voice call out, "Hey! Who brought the Chink?"

Benny looked up to see that Yeoh, who had left to buy another round for the table, was being bullied by a six-foot oaf in a food-spattered T-shirt and dark jeans. "Please," Yeoh was saying, "I don't want trouble."

"Is that so? Well, trouble sure wants you," said the oaf, punctuating his threat with a shove. "You're part of that goddamn mission that killed all those Americans. You proud of the fact that good Americans *died* so you could go to the Moon on *my* tax dollars?"

"I don't feel proud of that," Yeoh said, trying to defuse the confrontation. "I *am* proud to serve with an American crew."

"I bet you are!" With another shove, Yeoh fell back into a table, spilling its contents all over himself. Undaunted, he leapt back to his feet. Benny was up in a flash and shoved the man back a good two feet, this despite the fact that the man was a good half foot taller than Benny was and probably outweighed him by a hundred pounds.

"If you've got a problem with my crewmate, you've got a problem with me, friend," he said.

"I ain't your friend, peewee, and I'd sit down before you fall down."

Benny said nothing but did not back down.

"Don't say I didn't warn you," the oaf said, drawing back his fist. Benny and Yeoh poised for a fight. Before he could strike, a shout cut through the room. Every head in the bar turned to Yuen, who was striding over to the site of the confrontation. He eyed the man evenly.

"I do not believe you are looking for a fight," Yuen said in measured tones. "Please, let me buy you a drink."

The man laughed derisively. "Get this guy!" he bellowed. "You're going to be sucking egg-drop soup through a straw unless you step away right now."

Yuen did not respond but simply met his gaze with perfect reticence. This seemed to anger the oaf even more, and his fist came sailing at Yuen's face. Before anyone even knew what happened, Yuen had grabbed the oaf's hand and turned it toward him, the palm facing away. With his thumb and index finger, he rolled the knuckles up, contracting all the muscles in the man's forearm. The man went down to his knees, screeching in pain.

All of this happened in under twenty seconds.

"Please," said Yuen, his voice never losing its calm tone, "I do not want to hurt you any further."

As he was holding the oaf in his grip, one of the man's buddies crept up from behind, brandishing a pool cue. He swung it at Yuen's head. Without turning around, Yuen ducked, still keeping his hold on Yeoh's would-be assailant. The pool cue missed its intended target and instead collided with the man's head. He hit the floor like a sack of cement, out cold. Yuen spun around to face his attacker, who vainly tried to swing the splintered end of the pool cue at him. The commander deftly dodged the blow and subdued his assailant with one swift kick to the head.

The entire bar fell silent, an electric tension in the air. The crew looked around, realizing that they were on the verge of being in real trouble. Not wishing to complicate their evening any further, they simply ducked out the door. Once in the parking lot, they began walking briskly back to the hotel.

Yeoh looked at his companions. "Is this a common night out in America these days?"

Moose laughed. "If what just happened is any indication of how the populace feels about this mission, I'd get used to it."

Benny, meanwhile, had jogged over to Yuen, who was walking somewhat faster than the others. "Hey! Wait up!"

Yuen stopped.

"I just wanted to thank you," Benny said. "You know, for getting my back in there."

Benny extended his hand. Yuen eyed it, then took it firmly.

"If you had been injured, you could not perform your duties," Yuen said placidly. "The mission would have been compromised. Good night."

Yuen turned from Benny and walked away.

Benny stood for a moment in the cool late-night air, wondering if tonight's incident had brought the crew together or just served to remind everyone how far apart they actually were.

June 3
Inn at Little Washington
Northern Virginia
10:17 p.m.

Cal Walker was entertaining some senators at his usual table, dazzling them with stories of NASA's bold return to the stars. Just as his story was reaching its apex, his smartphone chirped urgently in his coat pocket.

He pulled it out, reading the number on the touch screen. His eyes narrowed imperceptibly. "Gentlemen, you will have to excuse me," he said, pushing away from the table. He strolled over to a quiet corner of the restaurant and tapped the screen.

"Yes?" he said tersely.

"The Chinese-American mission launches in twenty days," said the voice on the other end.

"I'm well aware of the launch window."

"It was never supposed to get to this point."

"It seems our commander in chief is more idealistic than I gave her credit for," said Walker. "She believes the Chinese to be trustworthy. Pity."

"The accident in Florida was supposed to put an end to this mission once and for all. Now things have gotten far more complicated."

"A contingency plan is in place," Walker replied. "The mission will fail, and your work will continue unabated. And our country will have a few more heroes to put in the ground."

PART 2: OCEANUS PROCELLARUM

Chapter 9

June 23
John F. Kennedy Space Center
Cape Canaveral, Florida
7:15 a.m. (6:15 a.m., Houston Time)

Shortly after sunrise the sky above Cape Canaveral in Florida was a bright blue, high and seemingly endless, almost indistinguishable from the gleaming Atlantic Ocean below. The sea was calm and few white-caps dotted the horizon. The relentless Florida humidity shimmered the air. Peering out toward the launchpad, tens of thousands of people squinted through crinkled eyes or binoculars at the giant white space vehicle, more than a hundred feet taller than any of the old Saturn V rockets that had launched mankind on its first exploration of its closest neighbor. In many ways the crowd appeared like so many others who had gathered at the Cape for a launch: they brought blankets and lawn chairs, drank coffee, and pressed ears to radios. On the surface, the scene was very much like a park filled with people enjoying a summer's day. But in fact the mood was much more somber. Many were obviously praying. Many more seemed to be searching for the faith to do so.

What they might have been praying for was not as obvious. Of course some were praying for the success of the mission—memories of the Phoenix 5 accident were still so fresh in everyone's minds. But people's prayers were about more than Phoenix 5 or the hope that Phoenix 6 would not meet a similar tragic end. The pulse had rattled the already-nervous generation who had come into the twenty-first century with so many hopes and dreams.

The twentieth century had been the most murderous century in the history of human civilization. Those who lived through the millennium celebration had all been eager to leave the old century behind, perhaps just as eager as the Victorians had been to leave their century to history. But two world wars, dozens upon dozens of regional wars, a cold war, disease, and famine had quickly wiped out the hopes of the Victorian era that the twentieth century would be a century of peace and prosperity. It had taken all of fourteen years. In the twenty-first century, it had taken less than a year. Since September 11, 2001, there had been a never-ending worldwide battle against terrorism, regional flare-ups in places like the Middle East and on the Korean peninsula, an AIDS epidemic that had killed millions in Africa alone. And the panic that had spread across the planet over the past six months had killed an estimated two million people worldwide. And now there was the imminent threat of war between the United States and China, just as representatives of these two nations were joining forces to discover the source of the pulse.

The crowd gathered at Cape Canaveral that bright June day was praying not just for these astronauts or even their miserable century, but also for themselves and their world.

"How do you read us, Phoenix?"

"Loud and clear," Yuen Bai replied into his mike. "Everything's five by five, Mission Control. Over."

"Copy that, Phoenix. Sorry for the delay, people. We're reading a slight flux in cabin pressure. Can you confirm?"

"Roger that," Yuen answered. "Negative, Houston. Cabin pressure reads nominal here."

Yuen couldn't help but feel annoyed by all the delays. More than two hours had passed since they had been strapped into their couches and the hatch sealed. He was normally a very patient man and understood the necessity of rechecking all systems before a launch, but something about all this waiting and staring out the window into an inviting bright-blue sky was getting to him. All told, this was his fourth spaceflight. Two hours' wait on a launchpad was not altogether unexpected. Before his first spaceflight he had waited almost three and a half hours for what ultimately became a letter-perfect mission.

To distract himself Yuen thought of home. There were his sons chasing each other through the house with the models of the *Tai-Ping* he had given them. And there was his wife chiding the boys softly and telling them not to disturb their father. Yuen saw himself reaching out for his wife's hand, smiling at her flawlessly beautiful face and telling her to let them be.

I wish I were home.

Yuen shook himself from his reverie and checked the cabin pressure again.

No, I don't. I wish I were on an aircraft carrier, waiting for the go call. I am never tense before a go call. My country needs me in that capacity at this moment in history. Not here. Not now.

Four days ago the primary Taiwanese separatist leader had been assassinated. The killers had shot him as he was emerging from a motorcade, and had escaped. A massive manhunt had caught no one and revealed no motives. The Chinese navy had responded to the assassination by blockading the island in an effort to prevent the killers from fleeing. The United States had protested this move as a violation of international law. Yesterday the US Pacific Fleet began sailing toward Taiwan in order to prevent a possible invasion by the Chinese.

So it begins, Yuen mused. *By nightfall my government may be at war with the very people with whom I am flying to the Moon.*

"Hey, Frank, you copy that?"

"Barely, Mission Control. I've got static on this channel. Can you clear it up? Over."

Franklin Wilson couldn't understand why his palms were sweating. He could feel the dampness through his insulated gloves, a thin layer of perspiration between his pressurized suit and his skin.

Wilson knew he didn't have concerns about the crew. Everyone was at the top of their respective fields. Even the archeologists had come through their training with flying colors. And the Chinese—he had never seen such intelligent and disciplined people. Despite himself, he particularly admired Yuen. Seeing him in training, Wilson wasn't the least surprised that the Chinese had asked him to be the commander of the *Tai-Ping.*

So why the hell are my palms sweating? It's the weight; it has to be the weight. This whole mission's a rush job to end all rush jobs. We designed the lander to carry four people to the surface, not five. All the engineers say it'll hold five plus a couple hundred pounds of materials we take back from the object.

Wilson squinted through the capsule's window into the morning sky. Yesterday's Moon was just fading away. It was almost a target in the corner of his window. All he had to do was aim and shoot.

I'll get the Copernicus *down. I'll set her down right between the remains of Surveyor III and Apollo 12.*

Do your job, Wilson. Think about the mission. Everything's nominal. Everything's on the line.

Benny groaned into his mike. "Lieutenant Colonel, are they gonna fix their little problem or what?"

"Frank," the capcom said, trying to stifle a laugh, "tell Benny if he keeps that up, we're going to have him wait for the next bus."

"Hear that, Benevisto?" Wilson said with a smile. "They're going to pull your hall pass."

"Let 'em try it, Colonel," Benny said, smirking as he did. "Let 'em try."

Christ Almighty, am I sick of this waiting, Benny thought. *Let's go, let's go, Mission Control. Go on, say it, Benevisto. You're scared. You'd crap your pants right now if it wouldn't set off fifteen alarms at the surgeon's console. Thank God they're not taking you down to the Moon.*

God. He shook his head inside his pressurized helmet. *If you hadn't gone into that church, you wouldn't have gotten your head so screwed up with this God business.*

Still, there was something about that church. Nothing about it reminded Benny of the Catholic churches back in Brooklyn, full of imposing statues and bloody crucifixes and marble and stained glass. It was just a simple white clapboard church on a little hill on the outskirts of Houston. Trimmed bright-green front lawn. Quiet. So simple he had never imagined it to be a Catholic church. When he saw that it was, he felt compelled to go in and light a candle in front of a statue of Saint Jude the way his grandmother had always done whenever she thought she needed the intervention of the patron saint of hopeless cases. Then that priest came by and smiled at him and went into the confessional. And Benny followed him in.

What had that priest told him in there?

God gives us all divine gifts and abilities, and we must be humble before them. Your gifts have brought you to a unique moment, and your abilities will guide you through it. The only question is whether or not you are willing to be humble enough to better understand the path upon which God has set you.

"Phoenix, looks like we've nailed down that little snag in the cabin-pressure reading. We're reading nominal pressure as well now. Please reconfirm your cabin pressure. Over."

"Roger that, Houston," Yeoh replied.

Here Bruce Yeoh was a crew member of the most important spaceflight in history, thanks to, of all people, Bruce Lee. Growing up in Shanghai, Yeoh and his brother, Xi, would always watch classic movies on Saturday mornings at the little theater near their home, where their uncle was the projectionist. He would never forget first seeing Bruce Lee's *Fist of Fury*. The moment Lee leapt into the air, shattering a sign that read "No Dogs and Chinese Allowed" with one swift kick, twelve-year-old Yeoh Kong-sang's life was changed forever. He immersed himself wholly in the study of the martial arts. His friends kidded him, called him "Bruce." The name stuck. As he tried to master Lee's ideas of moving like water, he saw how matter and energy were interconnected, one feeding off the other. Before too long, Yeoh's fixation on martial arts was second only to his fascination with physics. A door had been unlocked in his mind.

Yeoh sighed, remembering those fond times with his brother, Xi. As he flipped a few switches, his mind drifted back to a summer evening long ago.

We had taken Grandfather's boat out on Hangzhou Bay. Before we knew it, we rowed past the breakers and out into the East China Sea. I was so scared, but Xi had stayed calm, pointing back at the shore.

"See the lights?" he had said. "That's Shanghai. That's home. Row toward the lights, and we'll get home."

Over and over I said those words in my head. And when my arms gave out, Xi took my place at the oars and began rowing. "Just look at the lights, little brother. Look at the lights and think of home."

Yeoh peered out the small window at the top of the capsule, seeing a sliver of the Moon peeking out from the brilliant blue of the morning sky. So very far away from where he was now.

Look at the lights and think of home.

"Roger, Phoenix. All systems read nominal. We are restarting the countdown."

"About time." Benny looked through the edge of his visor at Moose. "Nice to know they're keeping their promises."

"Never doubted they would, buddy."

Benny shook his head. "Still waiting for the day something messes with your midwestern Zen, Moose."

Moose chuckled. *Man, Benny will flip when he finds out. He'll think I'm off my nut, especially after getting bumped from the landing.*

Makes sense, though. Ma had never wanted me to be a pilot. Too dangerous. Told her there was more of a chance of getting killed in a car than up in the air. Dad understands. But Ma's fears run deeper. She's afraid the family's going its separate ways after she's tried for so long to keep us together. You grow up and move away; you want to see the world. That's life.

Things had been difficult for his mother in running the farm since his father's stroke. Money, always tight, was especially so now that she had to pay for all that extra hired help. The strain on her face was clear when she came to visit Moose just before the crew had gone into isolation. She looked tired, old. Taking care of both the farm and his father—

She never asked me to come home. She just did that thing with her shoulders that she had always done whenever she felt funny about saying something, like she was bracing against the cold.

Mother and son tried to distract themselves from the mission by talking about the farm as they walked around the Cape. After a while, almost without meaning to, Moose told her he was thinking about coming home to take care of the farm after the mission.

I thought she was going to jump out of her skin, she was so happy. She didn't look so tired or old after that, just took my arm as I showed her around.

Before she left Moose to isolation, she took out a little plastic bag of soil from the farm—a piece of home to keep with him. Moose patted the spot where the soil sat in his pocket under his pressurized suit.

Promises to keep.

"T-minus sixty—"

"Dr. Donovan?"

"Yes, Dr. Soong?"

"Remember that Mission Control is not the only one who has promises to keep."

I honestly cannot believe that the Americans could find no better archeologist to join this mission than Alan Donovan. He is too unpredictable. In every single excavation scenario we have run, he has tried to find some way to bend the rules, if not break them outright.

Soong took a deep breath and tried to ready herself for liftoff. To block Alan Donovan from her mind. To be calm in knowing that all of the prelaunch procedures had gone according to plan.

Procedure matters. One follows rules, connects dots, delivers results. Yes, there is some room for improvisation. For original and creative thinking. But not for the brash, flagrant disrespect for rules that Donovan and his keeper, Elias Zell, employ. Still . . . they had produced results. If only they could stay in line long enough to uncover whatever truths are buried there . . .

Is anyone else's heart hammering as mine is? But I am not just uneasy. It is something else: yes, an overwhelming sense of elation. Years spent in the pursuit of justice by surrounding myself with death. Any victory—always wrought from human tragedy and suffering. Now the quest is not justice but truth. And such a wonderful feeling in seeking the truth. To be a part of this great journey . . .

Whatever we find there, it is impossible to believe that it will not be a joyous affirmation of life.

"Thirty-five, thirty-four, thirty-three, thirty-two—"

"Promise, Dr. Soong?" Donovan laughed. "I never promised you anything. I only said I'd make an effort."

Donovan flexed his fingers, trying to relieve his tension. *She wanted me to promise not to try anything outside of Mission Control's orders if the object proved irretrievable. Is she kidding? I'm not leaving the Moon until we find out what that goddamn thing is.*

Donovan hadn't gotten much sleep in the last week. Night after night he found himself lying awake in bed, trying to imagine the object in his mind. Trying to visualize it and know its purpose. Trying not to think of Syd or his father or of anything else that could keep him from completing his mission.

We have to show the world that this first contact is just a part of humanity's future, nothing else. As we go out into space, we'll probably meet dozens of civilizations. We can't be cowed by our own fears and taboos and just hide in our little corner of the galaxy because we're afraid. We need to make contact. We can't fear the future.

"Twenty-five, twenty-four, twenty-three, twenty-two—"

"Elias."

"Yes, Alan."

"What if it turns out to be an old Soviet probe? Some experimental thing that we never knew about?"

"Soviet probe, my ass," Zell grumbled.

Zell thought of his father. Oh if only old Thackeray could see him now! He wondered for a second if his father would feel the same humbling terror he felt at this moment, strapped into one of the most powerful rockets ever made by man, or if he would be elated by the grand adventure in it. He smiled to himself, knowing the answer.

Be brave, my lad, he would always say. *There's no fear in the unknown, only in the lack of trying to make it known.*

His father had always said that the more people learn as a race, the less they seem to have understood. Thackeray Zell knew that statement not only applied to his generation but to all generations of humanity going back to antiquity, when the Greeks believed Apollo pulled the sun across the sky each day with his chariot. Yet a new piece of information had always come along to prove so many of the previous generations' theories wrong. Newton. Galileo. Einstein. Any of those precious few who leapt beyond conventional thinking and saw the universe with new eyes.

And what have we learned from the experience? Not to stand in awe of the remarkable fabric of the universe, but to pat ourselves on the back after each of our discoveries. If we were really intelligent, we'd accept the fact that we hardly know anything at all. Perhaps then we could make the really great leaps in scientific understanding, leap beyond the limits of our own life spans and experience.

In order to be truly wise, we have to learn how to question things above ourselves, above time.

"Five, four, three, two, one—we have liftoff! Liftoff of Phoenix 6, through whose fires humanity's exploration of the Moon is reborn—"

As the rocket broke free of its moorings and thrust itself toward the stars, Zell thought of her name: *Phoenix*. Though pressed back into his couch by the excessive g-forces, Zell forced himself to look through the viewport as the blue of the firmament slowly evaporated into the darkness of space.

In your fires, he thought, *we are reborn.*

Chapter 10

June 26
7:17 p.m., Houston Time
3 days, 13 hours, 2 minutes, Mission Elapsed Time

The *Tai-Ping* glided through the vacuum of space with eerie silence. In the days since the crew had left Earth's gravity, the trip had been remarkably free of incident. Benny and Moose had docked with the *Copernicus* with no trouble and had fired the rocket's third stage to enter the lunar corridor, which would carry them the rest of the way to the Moon. From this point forward they were on a free-return trajectory, which would slingshot them around the Moon and back to Earth.

Aboard the ship, things had been less than cheerful. Donovan, though physically unaffected by the weightlessness, found his mind wandering along with his eyes to the tiny window, watching the Earth recede. Zell, on the other hand, spent much of his time wondering if a good cigar would cure his incessant nausea. His condition had made him ornery, leading him to perpetually lock horns with Donovan and Soong over how best to investigate the object. To make matters worse, none of them could agree on anything, switching sides so often in an argument that it became difficult to determine how they even got started. There had also been some tension between Yuen and Wilson, each one jockeying for the role of commander, but for the most part the two kept things civil, silently working their way through the day's tasks. Yeoh remained similarly reticent, although not so much out of disdain as out of pure disinterest in the day-to-day machinations of the mission. He spent most of his time poring over data and telemetry scans, forever looking for clues to the puzzle that awaited them. That left Benny and Moose, who at times felt like audience members to the world's most expensive soap opera. Luckily, there were enough tasks to keep them occupied, and Benny tried to face the situation with his usual good humor.

Whap!

"Son of a *bitch*!"

"Louder, Benny," said Moose, not looking up from the lunar chart he was studying. "They didn't hear you on Pluto."

Benny floated down from where he had been trying to sleep, still rubbing his head where he had struck it on a bulkhead. "How the hell'd you ever learn to sleep in zero-g?"

"You find a way," Moose offered. "Last time I was on the space station, one of the guys used to sleep with the EVA suits. He found that he could snuggle up against the arms and they'd just hug him tight. Me, I used to just free-float. You get used to it."

"When?"

Moose looked at his friend with a half smile. "About a week after getting back home."

"*Tai-Ping*, this is Houston, over."

At the sound of John Dieckman's voice, the astronauts on board sprang to attention.

"Houston, *Tai-Ping*. Go ahead," answered Wilson.

"First off, I want to welcome you to the Moon. You're officially in the influence."

This marked a significant moment for the crew. They had officially crossed the boundary where the Moon and the Earth's gravity balanced. From this point forward, the Moon was exerting the greater pull on their ship. Deke's announcement was met with applause from the crew.

"Copy that, Houston," said Wilson. "We're happy to be here."

"Okay, we've got you coming in at about four thousand feet per second, just shy of thirty thousand nautical miles from the Moon's surface. We want you to start making your preparations for a slight midcourse correction. That'll put you right on track."

"Roger that, Houston," said Moose.

"After that, we'll let you coast for about fourteen hours or so before we light the service propulsion system for lunar orbit insertion."

"Sounds good," Wilson said, checking over some data. "With reference to the midcourse, we're reading pitch and yaw at eight degrees and three hundred twenty-three degrees, respectively. Do you concur?"

"Roger that," said Deke. "Since you're using the reaction control system thrusters and not the SPS, your pitch and yaw factors shouldn't change much."

"Hey, Deke," said Benny. "What's the news like at home?"

Deke's radioed sigh told them all they needed to know.

June 27
Camp David, Maryland
7:30 a.m.

The President of the United States stood outside Aspen Lodge, the presidential cabin at Camp David in the Catoctin Mountains of Maryland, enjoying the morning sun. She knew it would likely be the most peaceful moment she would have all day. During her time in office, she had come to love the presidential retreat—its security and isolation, its natural beauty, its cool mountain breezes. First used by President Franklin D. Roosevelt in 1942 as a way to escape the stifling summer heat in Washington, DC, the retreat was initially called Shangri-La after the mountain kingdom in James Hilton's book *Lost Horizon*. Here, Roosevelt hosted British prime minister Winston Churchill in 1943 as the two men planned the Allied invasion of Europe during the Second World War. In 1953 President Dwight D. Eisenhower renamed the retreat Camp David for his grandson.

Ostensibly, presidents have come to Camp David for generations to relax. Since that first visit by Winston Churchill, however, it has also served as a place where many historic events have occurred, most notably the peace agreement between Israel and Egypt brokered by President Jimmy Carter.

The current occupant of the Oval Office hadn't used the presidential retreat nearly as much as some of her predecessors. She much preferred the comforts of her own farm in North Carolina, but seeing as Camp David was about a half-hour helicopter ride from DC, it made sense to take her vacation here. By taking a respite now, she wanted to give the impression to her fellow Americans that the current crisis off the coast of Taiwan was of little concern. Little did they realize she had gotten only a few scant hours of sleep each night since the crisis began.

The sun lighted the peaks of the mountains in the east as she began hiking a trail with Aaron Stein. Hiking some feet behind them and several feet before them was the usual detail of Secret Service agents.

Stein hated Camp David. He hated the bugs and especially hated what the mountains did to his allergies. But when he received the latest intel from China, he gathered his medications and handkerchiefs and top-secret briefings and headed out into the morning gloom, where the President stood whacking the tall grass absentmindedly with a stick.

The President held that stick now under her arm and paused occasionally on her hike so Stein could blow his nose.

"So what's the latest on the diplomatic front? Something pretty good, I imagine, for you to be up at this hour."

Stein put on his reading glasses and glanced through a folder. "The secretary of state's last report was filed two hours ago. She's made little progress in the negotiations since the last report."

"The Chinese are stalling. They know they have to do something in the face of this separatist movement. They can't back down and neither can we. But they know what this would look like if we went to war while we both had people on the Moon."

"That's what the secretary supposed." Stein flipped through a file and held out a stack of photographs. The President took them and glanced through them. "These are satellite photos taken within the last hour. It seems the Chinese are becoming well versed in brinkmanship."

"Are these—"

"China's missile silos, Madam President. The Chinese have readied their nuclear weapons and have targeted them on the nerve centers of the continental United States."

June 27
9:17 a.m., Houston Time
4 days, 3 hours, 2 minutes, Mission Elapsed Time

As the time came for the lunar orbit insertion burn, Moose floated into the command module, where Yuen was running some checks on the *Tai-Ping*'s systems. The Chinese commander had said very little in the hours since learning that his country stood on the brink of war with the United States. Where other members of the crew had flared up at one another, Yuen had remained quiet and continued to go about his work professionally. Though Wilson had done his best to calm the emotions of the crew, Moose could see that the possibility of war was eating at both commanders and wondered if the mission was at risk.

"Ready for this burn?" Moose asked affably.

Yuen flicked his eyes in Moose's direction and gave a curt nod. "I am—as you say—ready when you are, Lieutenant Commander."

Moose floated into the seat next to Yuen and strapped himself down. "Look, Commander, I know things look bad—"

"I should not be here," said Yuen, still looking at the ship's readouts.

"Well, none of us *should* be here, but there wasn't a whole lot of choice in it for us."

"It is a fool's errand. To sit here while our two countries prepare to go to war."

"That may be," answered Moose. "The only thing I do know is, whatever's going on down there, it doesn't mean much to us."

Yuen looked up at him, his eyes flashing. "How can you possibly say that, knowing that we—"

Moose pressed on. "Down there, they'll make a big fuss. Maybe it'll even get down to shooting. But in the end, a bunch of bureaucrats'll sign some papers and go about carving up the globe a little finer amongst themselves. And us, you and me? The grunts who won them their little strips of land? We'll just get scooped up and deposited in the next hot zone they want for their collections."

Yuen sized him up, trying to figure out if he was sincere. "So to serve your country, there is no honor in that?"

"Sure there is. If we're fighting to protect ourselves or our loved ones. When I think about my folks or my sisters, well—"

"There are many in my country who would argue that we are protecting ourselves by protecting Taiwan."

Moose rubbed the back of his neck and sighed. "Okay, look at it this way, then. Here we are, two supposedly sworn enemies about to fire a rocket that'll take us to the most incredible discovery in history. Maybe they're getting themselves all worked up about a war down there, but up here, we've got a battle ahead of us too. The difference is, if we pull this off, maybe there won't be a losing side. Hell, maybe there won't even be a war."

There was a slight pause; then Yuen began to laugh. "Such shining American optimism. You've watched too many movies, I think."

"Yeah, well, my mother always warned me—"

"*Tai-Ping*, this is Houston. Over."

"Houston, *Tai-Ping*, go ahead, Deke," said Moose.

"You're coming up on the Moon. We need to go over some LOI numbers before we initiate the burn."

"Copy, Houston," said Yuen. "Go ahead."

Deke went over several numbers to ensure that the *Tai-Ping* would enter the Moon's orbit exactly where she needed to be. She would then remain in position until the crew fired a second SPS burn to break out of orbit and begin the journey home.

"All right," Deke continued, "we anticipate this burn's going to last about four minutes and should slow you down by about three thousand feet per second. You should be getting a nice view of the Moon around that point."

"Roger, Houston," said Moose. "Looking forward to it."

"If all goes well," Deke said. "Okay, all your systems are looking good as you approach the corner. We'll see you when you come round."

"Roger that," answered Moose. "See you on the other side."

He switched off the VOX, the voice-operated switch, and gazed out the viewport. As the *Tai-Ping* slipped around the curve of the Moon, passing into the side that never sees the sunlight, Moose suddenly saw stars far more brilliant than he had ever seen on Earth. Without the sun to dim them, they shone brighter than on even the clearest Kansas night. He felt as if he was seeing the universe, its very vastness, for the first time. Even Yuen seemed moved.

Moose whistled. "It's something, huh?"

"My older son will be very jealous," said Yuen. "He's always peering through his telescope, trying to see further and further into the heavens."

"Just think of what you'll have to tell him when you get back."

After another moment of stargazing, the two got down to business.

"Do you have the orientation?" asked Yuen.

"Roger. I've got the Zeta Persei right where she should be." Moose smiled inwardly. Despite all the advanced technology at their fingertips, steering by the stars was still the tried-and-true method.

"Gimbals set?"

"Set."

"Very good. Prepare to initiate burn on my mark," said Yuen. "Three . . . two . . . mark."

As part of their mission, the Phoenix team was to deploy a small Chinese-built satellite in lunar orbit to monitor the site after their departure. Under the terms of the joint-mission agreement, whatever data was retrieved would be shared between the two countries. For the trip to the Moon, the satellite, the *Wan-Hu*, had been secured to the walls of the *Tai-Ping*, where Wilson was currently running last-minute checks. In order to keep himself steady in zero-g, he had braced one leg halfway into the hatch leading to the CM. Just as he was finishing up, the *Tai-Ping* was rocked by what sounded and felt like an explosion. Wilson was thrown violently aside. His leg, wedged inside the hatch, stayed where it was, snapping audibly at the knee. The pain was intense, expanding his understanding of the word far beyond his wildest imaginings. He slumped against the far wall, numb with shock. His eyes blurred from the pain, he tried to focus on his crippled leg. One hazy, distracted thought—*broken bone*—flew through his mind; then he passed gratefully into unconsciousness.

Donovan, Soong, and Zell were in the lander, going over schematics and plotting out the dig, when the force of the explosion rocked them. Donovan's head caromed off one of the viewports, striking the Plexiglas with dizzying force.

Zell looked up. "That didn't sound good."

Suddenly Benny's head poked through the hatch. "What the hell was that?"

"We thought you might know," Soong shouted.

"I dunno a damn thing," Benny replied. "But you better get up here. Wilson looks like he's hurt."

The three scientists floated up from the lunar module to the service module and saw Wilson's inert form drifting out from the center of the cabin.

Soong gasped. "Is he—"

"No," said Benny. "Just in shock. Any of you know what to do?"

Zell drifted over to him. "Looks like a compound fracture of the right tibia. I'm no doctor, but I've set enough of these in the field to patch him up. He won't be dancing any jigs, but it should be enough to get him home."

At that moment, Moose and Yuen floated down from the CM, their faces grim.

"What the hell happened?" asked Benny.

"We fired the SPS for the burn, and the whole damn thing went off like a roman candle," said Moose. "I don't know why."

"So what's going on now?" asked Soong.

"I can tell you this," said Yeoh from his computer terminal. "We're off course. Not badly, but it could affect the landing."

"Yuen and I attempted some minor corrections after the initial blast. What about communications?"

"Negative," replied Yeoh. "We're still in communications blackout. But the explosion could have knocked out the array."

"How long until reacquisition of signal?"

"It's impossible to say."

"We've got to get that engine working again," said Moose. "Otherwise we won't be able to get back on course. Forget about escaping the Moon's gravity."

Yuen's face set in determination. He turned to Benny and Yeoh. "Get up to the command module and get the ship back on course. Fire the aft reaction control system until you get us righted again." He turned to Moose. "How do you feel about taking a spacewalk?"

"What are you planning on doing?" asked Moose.

"Whatever I can."

A few moments later, the outer hatch of the *Tai-Ping* popped open and Moose and Yuen stepped out into the void. The Moon hung below them like an eerie, gray Christmas bauble, suspended in the blackness. The *Tai-Ping* drifted lazily, her orbit somewhat erratic from the force of the explosion. She currently tilted on an angle, the damaged service module above them on a slight incline. Tethered to the ship, they began to walk. Yuen, ordinarily unfazed by heights, suddenly found himself overcome by vertigo. He shut his eyes, willing the sensation to pass.

Moose clapped a gloved hand on his shoulder. "Try not to look down," he said.

"It's space," Yuen answered. "There is no up or down."

As Yuen and Moose worked their way slowly up the service module, the damaged engine came more clearly into view. Slightly above it, the dish-shaped main antenna array drifted limply, nearly broken off by the force of the explosion.

"Whoa, that thing is smashed," said Moose over the comm. "What do you think happened? Something electrical?"

"Possibly. It could have been a ruptured fuel line. Stripped wires. We may never know."

"You think we can fix it?"

"I think we have no choice but to try," said Yuen.

When they arrived at the engine, the astronauts began assembling their tools, each one fitted with a tether system, as well as a locking mechanism. Once a tool was locked into place, it couldn't be removed without a key. Thus, all the tools and their corresponding keys were tethered to the astronauts.

After getting everything organized, Moose turned to Yuen. "You work on the engine while I get started on the array."

"Are you sure you know what to do?"

Moose smiled. "Just like fixing the weather vane on my dad's barn."

Yuen shook his head, smiling slightly as he began work. Moose inched a few steps higher and took a look at the array. Suddenly he heard Yuen's voice call out.

"Commander Mosensen! There's something else—"

Before he could finish, there was another explosion, sterile and silent, but powerful enough to knock Yuen off the ship's hull and send him spinning. The debris from the second explosion whipped through space. Traveling at nearly five miles per second, they hit Yuen with ten times the speed of a bullet and a mass one hundred times larger. The small jagged pieces of metal peppered his suit, tearing through it like paper and severing his tether with surgical efficiency. In an instant he went sailing off into space, turning end over end in a wild circular motion.

"Jesus!" Moose screamed, trying to reach for his comrade. He barely had time to react when something told him to look over his shoulder. He did just in time to see the antenna array, now broken free from its moorings, flying toward him and striking him full in the face.

Moose's helmet shattered instantly upon impact. He fell back onto the hull, his faceplate gone. There was nothing protecting him from the vacuum of space.

Omigod omigod omigod omigod omigod—

Contrary to what was often shown in the movies, human beings could survive more than thirty seconds of total exposure to space. But the experience was sure to be the most agonizing thirty seconds of their lives, as Moose was beginning to discover. The air rushed from his lungs with explosive force. Fighting the urge to hold his breath and permanently damage his lungs, Moose skittered his way back down the ship.

Move.

The gasses in his body began to expand rapidly, and he felt a distinct sense of abdominal distention. He wasn't sure if he was just imagining it, but he thought he felt his skin beginning to swell. His oxygen-deprived blood began coursing up to his brain, and he felt his consciousness start to swim.

Move!

He closed his eyes against the pain forming in his temples as he fumbled with the hatch. Small cramps seized his body, a sure sign that the nitrogen in his blood was building up. As he wrenched the hatch open, he felt a strange sensation in his mouth and realized with horror that his own saliva was beginning to boil.

MOVE!

Moose pulled the hatch open and dove through, hitting the deck of the airlock with a thump. Gripping a handrail as he lay on the floor, spasms coursed through his body. Benny, knowing something was terribly wrong, repressurized the airlock. Moose took a deep breath, relishing the taste of oxygen in his lungs. At that moment, the door slid open and Benny dragged him back into the ship.

"What happened?" he asked frantically, propping Moose up in his arms. "Tell me what happened."

"There was," he gasped, "a second explosion. It was almost as if—" A series of coughs broke his sentence off. He turned to his side and disgorged a thin stream of blood from his ruptured lungs. After a moment, he tried to speak again.

". . . as if it was rigged to go off if anyone tried to fix it."

"Rigged?" asked Donovan. "Are you serious?"

Moose shook his head weakly, still trying to catch his breath. "I don't know."

"Where's Yuen?" Soong asked.

"Gone." Moose shook his head. "He's gone."

Everyone fell silent. In one horrifying instant, everything had changed.

"What's the situation like here?" asked Moose.

"Well," said Benny, "we managed to get her back on course, but that second explosion rocked us pretty good."

"I think I've fixed it," said Yeoh, coming down from the CM. "I've reprogrammed the computer to make any course corrections necessary to keep us in orbit. She should fire the reaction control system if anything goes wrong again. It's not perfect, but it should be enough to see us through the mission."

"And what about getting home?"

"If you and Yuen weren't able to fix the SPS, then we won't have enough thrust to break out of orbit," said Benny. "Unless we repair that engine, we're stuck here."

"To make matters worse, the *Tai-Ping* is dying," Yeoh said.

"Say that again," said Moose.

"The explosions have damaged her power systems. We're going to lose life support, telemetry, guidance, everything within the next twenty minutes or so. I'm trying to transfer everything over to the *Copernicus*, but we may have already lost some data."

Moose groaned, from pain as much as frustration. "No choice," he said. "We've got to use the *Copernicus* as a lifeboat and complete the mission."

"You mean to land on the Moon," said Zell, "with no chance of getting back?"

"It looks like we've got little chance as it is, Doctor," said Moose. "At least some good can come out of this."

"There may be a way to save the command module," Yeoh said. "I designed her with a remote power-up system for situations like this. If we transfer everything over to the *Copernicus*, we should be able to bring her up online again in a few days. I can't get the engine working, but who knows, maybe we can think of something between now and then."

"It's a fighting chance," offered Soong.

Donovan looked at Zell, his voice flat and numb sounding. "What choice do we have?" He hardly had time to process the horror of what they had just witnessed: Wilson injured, Yuen dead . . .

Moose finally made it to his feet and drifted back over. "Everyone better suit up."

"Better take it easy," Zell suggested as he tried to hold Moose in an upright position. "You've taken quite a beating."

"I'm fine. We've got to get the lander down."

"Moose, buddy," said Benny, "you can't fly the *Copernicus* in your condition."

"I can and I will." Moose nodded his head. "And you'll help me. Just like we did in the sim."

Within ten minutes, they were all piled into the *Copernicus*. It was an uncomfortable fit all around. Wilson, still in shock, had a seat to himself. Zell had been able to set his leg with a makeshift splint. Soong looked around at the desperate faces illuminated by the computer consoles around her, crammed as they were in the overstuffed lander, wondering how this could possibly work.

Benny and Moose were in the pilot and copilot's positions. Moose could barely sit up. Nonetheless, he gripped the stick with fierce determination.

"Hatch secure?" he asked.

"Secure," answered Benny.

Moose coughed. A trickle of blood ran from his mouth. "Prepare to detach on my mark. Three. Two. One. Detach."

The crew felt a slight bump as the *Copernicus* was released from her docking collar. She floated gently away from the *Tai-Ping*, upside down in the lunar darkness.

"We're upside down," said Moose, his voice strained. "Got to flip 'er over. Fire aft thrusters on my mark."

Benny peered out the window at the surface of the Moon, now growing closer and closer. *One crew member dead,* he thought. *Wilson critically wounded. A crippled ship, no way to get home.* He looked at Moose.

"We're not going to make it."

Chapter 11

From the moment Moose fired the *Copernicus*'s descent engine fifty thousand feet above the surface of the Moon, Benny realized they were losing altitude too quickly. He didn't need any instrumentation to tell him that, nor did he require any atmospheric drag pounding against their hull. In fact, he was grateful for the absence of sound. The soundless vibration tingling his skin was enough for him to know that the descent engine was firing and wasn't doing a damn thing to slow them down.

The lander was hurtling toward the Moon facedown. From their viewports the crew could see the lunar surface approaching fast. They searched for clues, details, anything that could tell them if they were on target for their landing coordinates. After several moments, as the long braking maneuver continued, the computer began pinging. They were closing in on their first set of landmarks.

"What's happening?" Donovan demanded.

Below them the crescent of the pockmarked lunar surface began to fill their viewports. The black void of space above the surface slipped out of their field of vision as the Moon grew larger and larger. Craters that had been no more than a thumb's length from their windows in orbit were suddenly the only features in sight, some of them more than a couple of football fields in length.

Forty-six thousand feet above the surface of the Moon, Moose adjusted the course of the *Copernicus* so that the ship was on its back and the landing radar was pointed directly at the lunar landscape. The Earth now peeked through one of their windows, an inviting warm blue marble in a sea of deathless black.

"No worries," Moose muttered as he tried to slow the *Copernicus*'s descent. "We're in the pipe."

"In the pipe, my ass," Benny groaned as he glanced at the altimeter. "Forty-three thousand feet, forty—we're burning *way* too much fuel, Moose."

Donovan held his breath as the ship continued its descent. He kept his eyes focused on the view of the Earth outside their windows and tried to blot out any image his mind was trying to create of their spindly lander descending on such an unforgiving world.

At forty thousand feet the computer activated the landing radar. At this point they had also expected the computer to automatically adjust its descent trajectory by firing *Copernicus*'s maneuvering jets, but it was signaling an overload of information, likely a result of their rapid descent. Moose took manual control of the lander and slowed their acceleration as Benny rebooted the computer and took a fresh reading of the radar echoes bouncing back from the Moon's surface.

"Twenty thousand feet, fifteen thousand. Still coming in too fast. Six minutes' fuel remaining."

"That's a lousy piece of real estate," Moose muttered impassively.

Zell glanced out to see a field of boulders, some the size of cars, hastily growing in size.

"Seventy-five hundred feet, Moose."

Halfway through the *Copernicus*'s powered descent, Moose punched in the command to throttle back the descent engine to half power. The crew found themselves growing lighter as the ship pitched over and moved into position for the final descent. At seventy-five hundred feet, the flat horizon outside their viewports was replaced with a vista of the Ocean of Storms.

"Four thousand feet, Moose. Descending two hundred feet per second. We're still coming in a little hot."

"I'm on it." Moose tapped the controls and kicked up the descent engine a third, slowing their drop to one hundred feet per second.

At fifteen hundred feet, Moose called out, "I need a fix on the site, Benny."

Benny's eyes dashed between his instrument panel and the landscape outside, searching for the landmarks he had memorized in so many training sessions. Then, almost unexpectedly, he caught some sunlight glinting off a metallic object.

"I see it! It's gotta be Apollo 12. Ten miles downrange. Yaw right ten degrees."

"Roger, go on that yaw," Moose replied, his voice level. "Continuing descent."

Benny's eyes moved from his window back to his instruments. Moose had managed to slow their descent, but the landing sites before them were either strewn with boulders or covered by massive craters. If he were to land the ship on any kind of slope, the *Copernicus* would likely tip over. Even if by some miracle it didn't, there wouldn't be much chance for their ascent engine to be in a position to fire correctly and allow them to reach orbit again.

At four hundred feet, a level field opened up before their eyes. Moose banked the craft to starboard and coasted toward that clear plain.

"Three hundred and fifty feet, Moose; down at six and a half."

"Shit, there's a crater," Moose muttered. "Got to get around it. Fuel?"

"Two minutes remaining."

As Moose slid the *Copernicus* past the crater, an alarm sounded. Benny punched a button to shut it off. They didn't need an alarm to know that every bit of forward thrust would burn up precious fuel. Once they hit ninety seconds left of fuel, they would almost be out of time to land. They needed at least twenty seconds of fuel to abort and reach an escape velocity.

Benny felt his mouth go dry. "One hundred feet. You're coming in fine."

Moose continued to slow his descent but suddenly found his chest constricting. He could hardly take a deep breath.

Jesus no Jesus no not now not now—

About three hundred feet in front of the lander, Moose spotted a small hill. He used it as a reference point to guide his descent. He leveled the craft and eased back on the descent engine and watched as his field of vision blurred with what appeared to be a rising fog.

Just a few seconds more please God a few seconds more—

"Picking up some dust, Moose."

Outside the windows of the *Copernicus*, dust was now whipping across their viewports. Moose kept his eye on his instruments as he brought the craft level. The ship was drifting slightly to port, but he ignored it, fearing that any correction in their descent would burn up precious fuel.

"Twenty feet."

"Do it right," Moose muttered, his voice a whisper. "Do it right."

A blue light appeared on Benny's console, indicating that the probes at the end of the lander's legs had touched the surface of the Moon. "Contact light!"

Moose punched a button to cut the engine. "Shut down."

Benny hollered with joy as he flicked switches. "Descent engine command override, off. Engine arm, off. Jesus Christ, we made it! Moose, we made it!"

Benny turned and touched Moose's shoulder. Harnessed into his seat, Moose fell forward only slightly. But it was enough.

A moment passed; then a crackle filled their headsets. "—this is Mission Control, do you read? Over."

"Repeat, Houston, we have landed in the Ocean of Storms. We're ascertaining our situation now and will get back to you in a few minutes." Benny rubbed his unshaven face glumly and cut off the live feed from their mikes. He glanced at Wilson, still unconscious. "They want a sitrep."

The survivors crouched around their prostrate mission commander as if he were a campfire. Behind them, still slumped in the corner over the controls, was Moose. Benny looked over at his fallen friend, shaking his head. "What happened?" he asked seemingly to no one at all. "What killed him?"

"His heart gave out," said Zell. "I'm sorry, Benny."

"It doesn't make sense," said Donovan. "After we brought him back on board, he was hurt but he seemed okay."

Soong touched Benny's shoulder. "Yes, but the damage was already done. The exposure caused the water in his body to vaporize, which expanded his venous system and shut down his circulation. He probably had a pulmonary embolism on the way down."

Yeoh looked solemnly at Moose's body. "The real miracle is that he held on for as long as he did."

"He had a job to do," Benny said, his voice a hoarse whisper.

Donovan looked out of one of the lander's two tiny windows at the desolate landscape. All around their tiny craft he could see the remnants of their recent flight, the gray lunar dust fanning out all around them in a circle from the blast of their descent engine. Looking southwest out of the corner of the window, he could discern the artifacts of the Apollo 12 mission on the horizon. The sunlight glinted off the legs of the lander and the other metallic objects in the area, though weakly, since they too were covered in a fine dust, likely the result of the constant bombardment of over forty years of micrometeors. He once read that researchers had calculated it would take almost two million years for such bombardments to obliterate Neil Armstrong's first footstep on the lunar surface. He grimly wondered if it would take as long for their remains to be obliterated by those same bombardments, should they never get off the Moon.

Donovan tried to think optimistically. Just by looking out the window he could tell that Benny and Moose had not only gotten them down safely but not that far off target as well.

The question is, just how far from the fissure are we?

"Okay." Zell cleared his throat. "So what do we tell them?"

"I don't think it matters," Benny mumbled with his head down. "Anything we tell them will give them an excuse to scrap the mission."

"Do you think they would really do that?" Yeoh asked. "Surely not after all that's happened."

Benny glanced at his new friend. "That's *exactly* why they'll do it."

"I cannot believe they would do that," Yeoh said, shaking his head. "Surely—"

"Commander Yuen is dead. Commander Mosensen is dead. Colonel Wilson is badly injured. And for all we know the *Tai-Ping* may be nothing more than a hulk in space," Soong said as she calmly removed her gloves. "As soon as they learn of what's transpired, they'll abort the mission and have us get back up to the *Tai-Ping* as soon as we can to see if we can repair it. The mission is now a nonissue."

Donovan stirred from his thoughts and turned from the window. "Do we even know if we'll be able to take off again? Do we even have enough fuel?"

"Fuel's not the problem," Yeoh said. "Something's wrong with the ascent engine. It could be something as simple as a power coupling shaken loose on impact. Or it could be shot. Either way we can't leave until we look at it. Either way it won't be anytime soon."

"But we can't stay here forever, Bruce," Benny added. "We expected to have five people down on the surface, not seven."

"Six," Soong said gently, a hand on his arm.

Benny winced and shook his head. "Right. Either way we had planned to have five people down on the Moon for eight days. Now we've got more people, and that means less breathable air, less food, less water among us."

"So how long do you figure we have?" Zell asked.

"Four or five days. Maybe six. I wouldn't wanna push it either way."

Donovan's face brightened. "But that means that we still have time to reach the fissure."

Benny shot him a look. "Donovan, are you nuts? Forget about the fissure. We've gotta figure out how to fix the ascent engine. And even if we do, we don't know if the damn thing's strong enough to lift the lot of us into orbit. And then, as if we didn't have enough fun, we've got to see if our bird in orbit is gonna fly again." He looked over at Moose. "Besides, we've got to deal with Moose."

"Benny," Donovan said, crouching near him. "I understand all that. *Believe me.* But Zell and Soong and I are of no use to you fixing this ship. We've got to go."

"Wouldn't it be a waste of Bai and Moose's sacrifices for us not to try?" Zell asked. "We only got this far because of them."

"Mission Control's never going to buy it," Yeoh observed.

"Let me talk to them," Wilson said suddenly.

"Sir," Benny said as he glanced at his commanding officer, "we didn't realize you were awake."

"I've been up for a while, Benevisto. You better let me get on the horn."

"Sir, with all due respect, you're gonna be the main reason why they'll want us to abort the mission. You let them know about your condition, and we'll be blasting off as soon as the ascent engine's functional."

Wilson smiled weakly and propped himself up on his elbows. "Then all the more reason for me to plead the case to them." He glanced at each of their faces. He had seen such faces before, unsure faces, despondent faces, faces that had looked to him as their commanding officer for assurance. "We've got a lot of people down there depending on us to figure this mystery out. Lives around the world besides ours are on the line. We have to convince Mission Control that we owe it to them . . . and to Yuen and Mosensen."

Before Wilson opened up the mike again, Zell did his best to make a splint around the lieutenant colonel's shattered knee, something more secure than the rush job he had cobbled together on the *Tai-Ping*. He fastened the splint over Wilson's space suit, since they would need to depressurize the cabin to get out of the airlock. It stabilized the knee somewhat, though not as much as Zell would have liked. After popping a few tablets of prescription-strength ibuprofen, Wilson signaled Mission Control. John Dieckman was on the VOX, waiting for him. Wilson's voice was as commanding as always, but everyone inside the cabin could tell that he was struggling. Nevertheless, he reported the situation in detail, excluding nothing except the severity of his condition. Only Zell suspected how badly shattered his knee was. At the end of the sitrep, Wilson firmly stated that he believed the mission could continue in a truncated state once they buried Lieutenant Commander Mosensen.

"We'd like to say you're a go, *Copernicus*," Deke stated. "However, we're not certain at this juncture that proceeding with the mission would be in the best interests of the crew. Over."

"Roger, Houston," Wilson said, masking his disgust admirably. "However, we're certain that Dr. Yeoh, Benevisto, and I can make the necessary repairs without the assistance of the archeology team. Over."

"Copy that, *Copernicus*," Deke answered. "Again, we reiterate that as we do not know your position in the Ocean of Storms, we do not believe it would be wise to do an EVA without an accurate read on the fissure's whereabouts. Over."

Donovan gestured at Wilson to ask if he could get on the line. Wilson nodded, trying to mask how grateful he was to not have to speak for a while. Donovan clicked his mike button. "Houston, this is Donovan. Over."

"Roger, Doctor. We read you five by five. Over."

"Houston, Dr. Soong has suggested that we do a preliminary EVA to release the Pigeon to ascertain our locale. Lieutenant Colonel Wilson believes it would be a wise use of our resources. Over."

"Donovan, this is Cal Walker. You do *not* have permission to engage in an EVA. Is that understood? Over."

"Houston," Donovan said, biting his tongue as he thought of all the people who might be listening, "are we on a live broadcast or private channel?"

He could just about hear the smile in Dieckman's voice. "*Copernicus*, nobody here but us rabbits. Over."

"Walker, now you listen to me, you son of a bitch!" Donovan yelled into his mike.

Zell put a hand over his mike and turned to Benny. "I'm sure that'll help."

"We can release the Pigeon when we have to go EVA to bury Mosensen," Donovan continued. "We're not that far from the Apollo 12 landing site; we can see it out the frigging window, for God's sake. Now, are you going to let us just sit here or are you going to let us do the job we came here to do? Over."

"Donovan," Walker cut in, "are you trying to pull some kind of—"

"I'm not trying to pull anything, Walker. What're you trying to pull?"

"Okay, Donovan. You've made your point," Dieckman interjected. "As you can well understand, Dr. Walker is concerned with the safety of the crew, as are we all—"

"Dr. Walker is trying to cover his own ass."

There was a momentary silence; then Deke returned. "We just don't want to lose any more lives up there, Donovan. Over."

"Fine. But if we can't get the ascent engine to fire, it won't matter. And the world will have missed the only opportunity we have to find out the source of the EMP. You don't want that on your conscience, do you, Deke? I'm certain the President doesn't. Over."

"Roger that, *Copernicus*," Deke said quietly. "Give us a few minutes down here, and we'll get back to you."

With that, Dieckman cut off the live feed to the Moon and popped another antacid, half under the impression that his stomach was trying to burn its way out through his chest. Then he picked up the telephone at the capcom station. "Madam President, did you hear all that?"

"I did, Deke," the President replied. "It seems to me that Dr. Donovan is right. They're there, and they might not get back home. We might as well give them their shot."

"With all due respect, ma'am, the Chinese might not want us to endanger the lives of their surviving crew members."

"Let me handle the Chinese. I'm sure they'll see it our way. How are we doing on repairing the orbiter remotely?"

"We think we have a fair shot, ma'am."

"Give it to me straight."

"We've got a one in five chance of restarting the backup systems from here. It looks like they took a pretty bad hit up there."

The President looked out the Oval Office window. "You're not planning on telling them that, are you?"

"No, ma'am."

"Good. Keep me apprised."

"Thank you, Madam President." Deke hung up the phone and returned to the VOX. "*Copernicus*, you are a go for a preliminary EVA."

"Roger that, Houston, over and out," said Benny. He switched off the VOX and turned to his teammates.

The crew, who had spent the time since their landing preparing for this, was ready to go. They suited up, ran through a few more last-minute checks, then opened the hatch, venting out all the oxygen. Below them now lay the answer to perhaps every question humanity had ever asked.

Donovan looked at Yeoh. "You're the ranking Chinese astronaut," he said over his mike. "This is your moment."

Bruce's head shook inside his helmet. "Respectfully, I must refuse my country's offer. I have never had a desire for fame." He gave a quick smile. "Just greatness."

Donovan looked over at Benny, who put up his hands. "No, no. It just doesn't feel right, you know? For me to play the hero. I mean, when all this started, we all made so much about who got the credit, who took home the glory. Then Bai and Moose. Now it just seems like maybe this isn't anyone's moment. Maybe it's everyone's."

Donovan nodded soberly. "You're right, but someone's still got to be first out that door."

Zell clasped Donovan's shoulder, his broad bearded face grinning through his helmet's visor. "Your father started this journey before you were born. Why not take the last few steps for him?"

Donovan looked around at the crew. Their faces all showed their support. He gave them each a nod of thanks, then took a second to take it all in before heading down the ladder. He couldn't quite tell what he was feeling or what he *should* be feeling. With communications back online, the whole world was now watching as he stepped down the ladder to become the first man to set foot on another world since 1972. He reached the last rung, then hung there a moment, feeling for one giddy instant that he should turn back. He had a wild flashback to second grade, when he climbed to the top of the ten-foot diving board at the public pool, only to retreat back down, his head hung in shame. Rather than entertain that notion even a second longer, he simply took his foot off the rung and planted it firmly in the lunar dust. He was down.

"This is Donovan. I'm down." He paused, then added with a smile, "Phoenix has landed."

In his headset, the cheers of both Mission Control and his teammates almost deafened him. Looking about at the gray wasteland, Donovan was awestruck by its sterile beauty. Over his head, he saw the Earth rise above him, a brilliant-blue orb in the ebony dark of space. In the last several hours, they had experienced unprecedented death and tragedy. But in this brief moment of triumph, Donovan felt a strange sense of joy. He thought of Syd, Syd with her broad beautiful smile—she would have loved this moment more than any of them.

He knelt down and, using his finger, quickly scrawled something in the lunar dust. He stood up and looked at what he had written, knowing that it would remain there forever, and no winds or rain would wash it away.

One word: *Blackfox.*

June 27
4:27 p.m., Houston Time
4 days, 10 hours, 12 minutes, Mission Elapsed Time

After a brief discussion with Mission Control, Wilson decided it would be best to deploy the lunar rover to aid in burying Mosensen. The rover's mounted backhoe would allow them to dig a proper grave for their fallen comrade. Without it, he suspected burying Moose would be next to impossible. Wilson and Yeoh would remain in the *Copernicus* working out the repairs to the lander and the *Tai-Ping* with Mission Control while the others prepared the burial and the deployment of the Pigeon.

The backhoe had been intended to clear through any debris that they might encounter on the way to the fissure. None of the crew had ever dreamed that they would be using it to bury a crew member on the Moon. Though their suits were considerably more flexible than the ones the Apollo astronauts had used, they simply weren't designed for digging graves. The backhoe would not only make their work easier, but it would also speed up the burial and help them conserve oxygen. Once Moose was buried, they could all get back into the lander and follow the transmissions from the Pigeon in shirtsleeve comfort.

The Pigeon was a small drone aircraft whose concept dated back to the old Predator drones used in the Afghanistan War and the Iraq War. It had a transmission range of about 250 miles and was about the size of a large shoe box. Unlike the Predator, it had no wings or rotary blades; instead it had a small ascent engine and maneuvering thrusters similar to the ones mounted on the *Copernicus*'s underside. Soong volunteered to deploy it as the others buried Moose. As they needed to conserve the precious amounts of air in their backpacks, there would be no way for her to attend the burial save through her headset.

Soong tried not to watch as Zell, Donovan, and Benny pulled Moose's body from the *Copernicus*. In one-sixth gravity the men had to hunch most of the way forward in order to stand upright. Once they brought Moose down the lander's steps, they realized that there was no way for them to lift their friend and carry him to his final resting place without falling over themselves, so they dragged him through the lunar dust to a shallow grave Zell had carved out with the rover's backhoe.

To unpack the Pigeon, Soong had moved some hundred yards from the *Copernicus* and the nearby burial site. She used the landing site of Apollo 12 as a guide and walked toward it, occasionally having to lift her helmet's sun shield for better visuals. The ugly little Pigeon was an engineer's dream, simple and efficient, but it was as gangly and strange as their own lander, upon which its design was partially based. She glanced down at the little drone and wondered if this was how an alien might see their ship—tiny, fragile, insignificant.

"Houston, how do you read us?" Benny's voice was hoarse, and his breathing was labored from his efforts. "Over."

"We read you loud and clear, Benny. Ready when you are."

There had been some discussion as they were making their preparations about whether they should televise the burial. After conferring with Mission Control, the crew had ultimately decided to film the burial for possible broadcast later, if Moose's family approved. For now his mother and two of his sisters watched the ceremony on a private-circuit television at Mission Control. Moose's father, disabled by his stroke, had no way of seeing the burial.

Remotely, Mission Control pointed the *Copernicus*'s main camera at the three astronauts gathered around the grave. Behind them flew the American and Chinese flags, put up before the camera was in position. The long shadows of the assembled astronauts stretched across the grave. Through the camera's eye, the grave itself was a black pit, made all the more deeper and blacker by the unfiltered sunlight on the Moon.

"We lay to rest not one man, but two: Yuen Bai and Thomas Mosensen," Benny began, his voice flat and grave. This was his friend, his brother. He struggled to find the right words. "One will find his rest in space, forever comforted by the warmth of our sun. The other will be laid to rest here on our moon. We owe them not only our lives but the lives of all who will be comforted by the knowledge brought from our mission. And we lay them to rest with the knowledge that all of mankind needs only to look to the heavens to know their sacrifices and forever honor their names."

With that, Zell mounted the rover and covered the grave.

Benny stood at its edge and watched as his friend's body was covered with some of the most ancient soil in the universe. Suddenly, something occurred to him. "Wait!" he called out.

Zell powered down the rover, craning his neck to see what Benny was doing.

Benny reached down into the grave, opening one of the pockets of Moose's space suit and extracting the small packet of Kansas soil his friend had brought with him. Benny poured it into his gloved hand, letting it mingle with the lunar dust.

June 27
7:30 p.m., Houston Time
4 days, 13 hours, 15 minutes, Mission Elapsed Time

Returning from their EVA, the crew members were surprised by good news. Mission Control had informed Wilson and Yeoh that they believed the *Tai-Ping*'s hull was not compromised. Houston also believed that they could reboot the ship's backup systems remotely so that the *Tai-Ping* could be warm and waiting for them upon their return. What the engineers and designers couldn't guarantee, however, was how well she would fly, but they felt that by using a free-return trajectory and conserving as much fuel as possible, the ship could handle the stress. As to food, water, and air supplies, Houston had calculated that the crew had roughly four and a half days remaining, provided that they strictly adhered to scheduled sleep periods. As far as the ascent engine was concerned, Mission Control's engineers and backup computers agreed that it was functioning within normal parameters. Wilson, however, wasn't convinced. He knew something was wrong with the engine and managed to coerce another approved EVA from Mission Control so they could inspect it.

Wilson cut off the live feed to Houston. "Benny, Yeoh, I think you might have to drag me out there so I can take a look at it."

"Sir—"

"I know what you're going to say, Benny. That wasn't a serious request. I guess you can use a helmet camera so I can take a look at it from in here." Wilson's face clouded with frustration. "Yeoh, if anything looks like a problem, could you disassemble it and bring it in here?"

"Disassemble it, sir?"

"Not the whole damn engine, just the power couplings."

"Sure," Yeoh said with a grin. "Why not?"

"Okay. That's what we'll do then." Wilson smiled at them. "But let's keep this in the family, okay?"

"In the family? I don't understand."

Benny nudged Yeoh. "Don't tell Mission Control, genius."

All they were waiting on now were the preliminary recon reports from the Pigeon. The six crew members gathered around Soong's laptop-sized portable monitor and cheered as the little drone blasted off. Soong had little to do other than the occasional course correction; its onboard computerized maps would seek out recognizable features of the lunar landscape and use them as a guide toward the fissure. Donovan removed his gloves and wiped the sweat off his hands onto his dusty space suit. He wondered if this was how Robert Ballard had felt as his robot submarine searched the cold North Atlantic depths for the debris field that would ultimately lead him to the *Titanic*.

Though the video on the Pigeon's monitor was clearer than any of the old Apollo films, it was still grainy enough on that tiny screen for all of them to be hunched forward and squinting. They tried to keep quiet as the Pigeon's control board lit up and pinged whenever the drone identified known features and adjusted course accordingly. Billions of years of geologic history flashed before their eyes. Practically anyone else would have been gasping at the sights, but to them all those craters and mountains and valleys were nothing more than signposts on a highway.

The flashes and pings on the control panel slowly built in intensity. Zell bit his tongue on several occasions when he felt that Soong was not adjusting the Pigeon's course quickly enough. He tried to keep his eye off the ever-decreasing fuel gauge.

"Wait," Wilson spoke up suddenly. "What's that shadow?"

"Zoom back over it," Zell suggested.

Soong glared at him but quickly brought the drone back toward the shadow. The shape was long and black and narrow, resembling a lamppost trailing down a sidewalk at daybreak.

"Jesus, would you look at that," Donovan muttered. "Soong, could all of that ejecta have come from our fissure?"

Soong glanced at the coordinates and let the drone hover for a moment. Each of them in turn studied the shadow and its outward-spanning fan of ejecta, looking very much like sand spread out by a child digging a hole at the beach. "The Pigeon says this is where it should be."

"That ejecta looks fresh," Zell mused. "It isn't at all pulverized by meteoric bombardment like the older specimens. That *has* to be it."

Benny leaned in over the monitor. "It's a helluva lot of it, in any case. Man, that thing's gotta be pretty deep for all of that to have been kicked to the surface."

"But what kind of a power source could blast that much material out of the Moon?" Yeoh wondered, a trace of excitement in his voice. "It has to be something phenomenally powerful—"

"Punch up the Pigeon's map of the fissure," Wilson ordered.

Soong tapped out a few keystrokes. "Got it."

Wilson arched himself up farther. "Now overlay it onto the picture we're receiving."

Soong clicked on the orbital photographs taken by the Chinese mission and dragged them onto the live feed. Despite the indistinctness of the orbital picture, the combined images looked like—

"A perfect match." Wilson grinned. "That's our baby."

Donovan leaned over Soong's shoulder. "Bring the Pigeon in closer. Let's see if we can take a look-see inside."

Soong nodded and decreased the Pigeon's altitude. When it was fifty feet above the fissure, she set the controls to hover and turned up the drone's belly lights to full. Despite the intense glare, the lights pierced the fissure's darkness no farther.

"We should be seeing much more than this," Soong muttered. "It doesn't make any sense. It should—"

"It's as if the fissure is absorbing all ambient light," Yeoh theorized, "almost the way a black hole would—"

Before he could finish his thought, a warning light flashed on the Pigeon's control pad and the image on the video screen winked out of existence.

"What happened?" Wilson demanded. "Have we lost the signal?"

Soong looked over her instruments and turned to Wilson. "It's as if the Pigeon just turned off. I'm not getting any readings at all."

Zell stared at the screen. "Curiouser and curiouser . . ."

"What's the range?" Wilson asked.

"Five and a half miles from our intended landing site." Soong was unable to suppress a smile. "Ten and a quarter miles from our present position."

Donovan returned her smile with one of his own. "Practically within walking distance."

Zell laughed and clapped Donovan soundly on the back. "Alan, they're never going to believe this."

Chapter 12

June 28
2:30 p.m., Houston Time
5 days, 8 hours, 15 minutes, Mission Elapsed Time

"Pain bad?" Zell wondered.

Wilson shook his head. "Not so bad."

"Here," he said, reaching behind an overhead panel and producing an embossed silver flask. "Single malt. Take a nip."

Wilson's eyes darted between the flask and the smile quickly spreading across Zell's bearded face. He grasped the flask and took a mighty swig and clenched his teeth as the sharp liquor coursed down his throat.

Wilson screwed the cap back on the flask and handed it to Zell. "This is against regulations, you know."

"Take it out of my pension," Zell replied. He clapped Wilson's shoulder. "No hard feelings, eh?"

"Dr. Zell," Wilson said with a shake of his head, "you've done so much to piss me off since we first met that I've pretty much become desensitized to your antics."

"Good, now you know how Alan feels," Zell answered, then looked around at the others. "So how do we look? I don't know about any of you, but after that catnap, I'm fairly eager to stretch my legs."

After the crew had lost the signal from the Pigeon, Mission Control had mandated that they take a four-hour rest period while they analyzed the data back in Houston. None of them was very willing to sleep except for Wilson, who had spent most of his waking hours since the accident fighting off the agony in his knee with just the occasional dose of ibuprofen. Despite themselves and the cramped quarters, the others also felt very refreshed after their rest—even Yeoh, who was half-convinced that he had been dreaming about the fissure the entire time he slept.

"Has Houston finished analyzing the data from the Pigeon yet?" Yeoh asked Wilson, not bothering to mask the excitement in his voice.

Wilson shook his head. "Not as far as I know. Any theories about what might be down there?"

"Just one," Yeoh answered. "It's the one I keep coming back to. I think we're looking at some sort of highly advanced nuclear reactor, probably fusion based."

"Fusion based?" Soong wondered. "Is such a thing possible?"

"With respect, Dr. Soong, you forget where we are," Yeoh replied good-naturedly. "If this object was placed on the Moon millions of years ago, it was obviously put there by a species considerably more technologically advanced than we are. They wouldn't have nearly the problems that we've had building a viable fusion reactor."

"You're about six steps ahead of me, Bruce," Benny said, "as usual. How do you figure it's fusion based? Why not something like our own fission reactors? Or solar powered? Hell, for all we know, it could be run on spit and baling wire."

"Even without the data from the Pigeon, we can discount it being powered by fission. Fission, as you know, gives off enormous amounts of radioactive waste. Both our unmanned orbiter and yours have given no indication of that. As for solar power, it isn't likely. Seeing as the object was buried for more than two million years, there's little chance of that."

Donovan crossed his arms. "But that still doesn't explain why we lost all the telemetry from the Pigeon."

"True," Yeoh replied. "It could be the residual electromagnetic energy from the EMP that knocked out the power on the drone. But the EM energy we've been recording for the last six months doesn't explain the power readings that have been coming from inside. Whatever is *inside* the fissure must have extraordinary power reserves—enough to power a small city."

Wilson rubbed his bristled chin. "So there's no danger of radiation?"

Yeoh shook his head. "Only fission reactors, like the ones we currently have in operation, produce harmful by-products. A fusion reactor wouldn't produce such highly radioactive wastes. If Houston confirms my theory, then I don't see any reason why the team shouldn't go out to the fissure."

"Fusion. Impressive," Zell said, turning to Donovan and Soong. "It sounds to me like we ought to lace up our boots and get out there as soon as possible."

Wilson's face clouded. "Wait. Could this residual EM energy knock out the life supports in our space suits as it did the power on the Pigeon?"

"Unlikely," Yeoh replied. "The life-support hardware is designed to be well protected from all kinds of radiation. I believe the shielding in the suits will hold."

Donovan's face burst into a grin. "So what're we waiting for?"

Wilson held up a hand. "Just a sec, Donovan. I want to confirm all this with Houston—no offense, Dr. Yeoh."

Yeoh shrugged. "None taken."

"So what do we do in the meantime?" Soong wondered.

Benny cleared his throat. "Well, we're go for an EVA to check out the ascent engine."

Wilson raised an eyebrow at him. "When did you talk to Houston?"

"About an hour ago, sir. They were asking for you, but I figured you could use a little more rest. They told me to have you contact them to confirm the order."

Wilson smiled at Benny. "Thanks for the added shut-eye. Okay then. Benny, Yeoh, suit up. I'll contact Houston and tell them we're ready."

"Well, folks," Benny said over the VOX, "we've got a pretty good picture of where we're at."

Inside the *Copernicus*, Wilson clicked his mike button. "Tell me good news, Benny."

"Would if I had any, sir. Basically, I'd start checking for real estate, because we're gonna be stuck up here for a *long* time."

Those remaining in the lander—Wilson, Donovan, Zell, and Soong—glanced at one another with apprehension. By now they all knew of Benny's fatalistic flair for the dramatic, but they could also sense a seriousness in his proclamation. Yeoh, accompanying Benny outside the ship, was also silent. That couldn't be good.

"Say again, Benny," John Dieckman asked from Mission Control. "Is the ascent engine repairable?"

"The ascent engine's smashed, Houston," said Benny. "Repeat: *She will not fly.* We must've come down a helluva lot harder than it felt. Right now you couldn't use it to roast a marshmallow."

"Can you jerry-rig something?" Wilson asked. "Even just to get us back in orbit?"

"I'm not sure, Colonel," Yeoh replied. "We should take some photographs of the engine and send them to Mission Control. Perhaps they might see a way to repair it that we cannot."

Wilson was quiet a moment, his coal-black eyes seething in thought and frustration. All the engines he repaired with his father flashed across his memory in an instant. He knew even with extensive damage, an engine could be repaired. Of course, that was how things were on Earth, when parts were usually only a ten-minute drive away at the local garage. They didn't have that luxury now.

Wilson looked up at Donovan. "I should be out there. I can fix an engine blindfolded."

Donovan shook his head. "You know you can't go out there in your condition."

"I know," Wilson muttered. "It's just that—"

"They've got the situation well in hand," Zell said. "If they need you, you can relay information from in here. But you're no good to anyone hobbling about the Moon."

"Frank," Deke said over the VOX, "let's get a look at some pictures before you start doing anything drastic. We've got a lot of good folks down here who know that engine inside and out."

"Don't sweat it, Colonel," Benny added. "We'll rig up the helmet cameras when we come out next. That way we can send them real-time video and still photos. You can guide us every step of the way. Think of it like operating by remote control."

"Understood, Houston," Wilson replied. "In the meantime, we'd like to prep the archeology team to go EVA to the fissure, if you agree with Dr. Yeoh's assessment that there is no harmful radiation at the fissure. Over."

"Roger that," Deke replied. "We concur with Dr. Yeoh and recommend that you suit up and get ready to depressurize the cabin. This way you can kill two birds with one stone by sending the scientists out and bringing Benny and Yeoh back in for a rest period."

"We copy, Houston," Wilson said. "We'll reestablish contact once we're ready. *Copernicus* out."

Wilson paused a moment and silenced the live feed.

"I know you're not used to sitting on the sidelines," Zell said, "but we don't choose the moments that define us. Just how we face them."

"Remind me to have that sewn onto a pillow when we get back," Wilson muttered.

"My mother already did," Zell said with a grin. "It's sitting in my parlor."

"You've got twelve hours of oxygen in your suits," Wilson told the archeology team. "Beyond that, you're surviving on bad breath and good luck. To be on the safe side, I'd like you back here in ten hours. No heroics." Wilson was quiet a moment. "How much intel can you bring back in ten hours?"

Donovan thought it over. "Not as much as we anticipated, but maybe enough to tell us what we came to find out."

Wilson smiled. "Then you'd better get moving."

June 28
3:35 p.m., Houston Time
5 days, 9 hours, 20 minutes, Mission Elapsed Time

As strange an experience as walking on the Moon had been, nothing had prepared Donovan for riding across its rugged surface in the Mark II moon rover. The Mark II was a significant improvement over the rovers that had been used on the last three Apollo missions. While it had the same amenities as its predecessor—a navigational computer, communications system, and cargo space for tools, rock samples, and maps—the Mark II was larger, capable of carrying four astronauts easily, and had an average speed of twenty-five miles per hour—considerably faster than the original rover's average of five to seven miles per hour.

Riding across the Moon would be disorienting to anyone, but it didn't help matters that Zell had insisted on driving to, in his words, "give the buggy a proper shakedown." Like many men of his wealth and stature, Zell had amassed an impressive collection of classic automobiles; unlike his peers, he didn't merely take them out to show off at auto shows on fine spring days, ever paranoid about scratching a fender. Instead, Zell drove one of his classic cars each day he was home in England, taking each hairpin turn on every winding English road as if his life depended on it. But Zell was far from a dangerous driver. He simply wanted to see just how far he could push those engines. This jaunt across the Ocean of Storms proved no different, except that in one-sixth gravity Donovan was doing all he could to keep himself from flying out of the rover.

Donovan sat on the rover's back bench next to some of the team's equipment. Soong sat in the passenger seat next to Zell. Occasionally her voice would fill Donovan's headset as she read off course adjustments from the onboard navigational computer. The computer was uplinked to the unmanned Chinese orbiter, which was acting as the backup Global Positioning System while the computers on the *Tai-Ping* remained inoperable. Donovan had little to do except hold on to his seat and watch the grayish-tan features of the Ocean of Storms unfurl before him as they cruised across the Moon at slightly more than twenty-five miles per hour.

Donovan knew he was no poet. He didn't have the words to describe the unearthly sights he was witnessing. Yet he felt the need to try to put into words what he was seeing and feeling. Most of his initial thoughts were about sensations—the feel of the buggy as Zell drove it across the most level part of the area he could find, the sound of Soong's voice in his headset, the crispness of the pressurized air against his face inside his helmet. Turning slightly in his seat, he could make out the rover's thick treads cutting their way through the Moon's fine, powdery surface. Though he couldn't hear anything in the vacuum of space, he imagined stones almost as old as the universe itself crunching under the buggy's wheels. Alongside them to the right, a debris field filled with boulders more than waist-high would've piqued the interest of any geologist worth his salt, most especially Donovan's father. Each interesting specimen they passed reminded him of an opportunity Hunter Donovan had missed. Looking out to the vista before him, he could imagine his father beside one of those rocks in a bulky Apollo-era space suit, hammer in hand, happily chipping off a piece of history.

Before them in the distance, a line of pockmarked hills and mountains beckoned with outcroppings of the Moon's mantle exposed by the impact of meteorites a million years old. He knew his father could've reached any of those peaks, moon rover or not. Despite what those NASA doctors had said, despite what Cal Walker had said, he knew his father's heart would've never given out. His heart only gave out when he lost the will to live.

In the end the only thing that ever gives out in people is their will. If they lose that, they lose everything.

Moose's will hadn't given out. Neither had Yuen's. Even with the dire news about the damage to the ascent engine, Donovan could sense no loss of will in the others either.

So why the hell do I feel so full of dread?

For a moment Donovan wondered if he had finally lost his will. The deaths of the others, coupled with the crippled ascent engine, had made him cynical about the outcome of the mission. He wasn't afraid of death. That wasn't it. He simply wondered if his own will would give out before he had a chance to discover what they had come here to find. What concerned him most was the possibility that the challenges of excavation would prove so insurmountable that he would just give up. If he feared one thing in life, it was the inability to complete a task, to be—in the end—of no use.

"Well," Zell said as he slowed the rover to a halt. "I believe we have arrived at our destination."

Donovan and Soong looked out across the desolate sun-bright landscape. The only feature breaking up the chaotic terrain of rocks and impact craters and hills before them was a remarkably straight black trench stretching across almost their entire field of vision like the parted lips of a long-dead god.

June 28
4:47 p.m., Houston Time
5 days, 10 hours, 32 minutes, Mission Elapsed Time

As Donovan was contemplating the odd sensation of riding across the surface of the Moon, Benny was crawling around underneath the *Copernicus*, trying to photograph the ascent engine. He shook his head and snickered to himself, thinking how the video and pictures wouldn't do Mission Control much good in any event. The engine had come down on a small outcropping of rock and was thus severely damaged in many places.

"Jesus Christ, is this damn thing shot!"

Yeoh winced as Benny's outburst crackled in his headset. "Please," he pleaded. "I'm right next to you. No reason to shout."

"Sorry, Bruce," Benny said as he crawled out from underneath the LEM. "I just don't see how we're going to get off this rock. The nozzle on the ascent engine is twisted up like cheap aluminum. From where I'm sitting, we're stuck here."

"Perhaps it isn't as hopeless as it seems. Mission Control might be able—"

"Might be able to what, Bruce? FedEx us a new ascent engine?"

After completing their photographic survey of the engine, Yeoh and Benny climbed up the ladder of the *Copernicus* and repressurized the cabin. As they pulled themselves out of their space suits, they looked around the inside of the lander, now coated in a fairly thick layer of dust. Try as they might, they had no way of preventing the grime from their space suits from entering the cabin. As they packed their suits away inside a locker, Wilson signaled Mission Control and uplinked the still photographs they had taken.

"I'd give us a couple of hours to study the video and the photos, *Copernicus*," Dieckman signaled from Houston. "By that time the engineers should be able to send you a preliminary outline for the repairs."

"You sound pretty confident, Deke," Wilson said.

"It's like you've always said, Frank: there's no engine not worth fixing."

"Especially not this one," Benny added.

"We'd like you to begin reviewing the schematics, looking for alternate solutions," Deke explained. "You might see something we could overlook."

"Roger that," Wilson replied. "One more thing, Houston."

"What's that, *Copernicus*?"

Wilson glanced at Yeoh and Benny. "We're all wondering how things are going with Taiwan."

Deke sighed. "I've been told I'm no longer supposed to discuss any topics not related to the mission over an unsecured channel."

"C'mon, Deke!" prodded Benny.

"The most I can tell you right now is that both the US and Chinese fleets are at this moment converging off the coast of Eluanbi. All traffic in and out of the region has been blocked. They've openly stated that they are prepared to take Taiwan by force, if necessary."

Benny stared at the others, shaking his head. "Jeez, and here I thought you were just sunshine and roses, Deke."

"Don't kill the messenger, boys," Deke muttered. "You asked for it. Houston out."

There was a silence in the cabin; then Yeoh spoke.

"My fiancée is in Oluanpi. She was visiting her mother when all this started."

"Your fiancée?" said Benny. "I didn't know you were engaged. When's the wedding?"

"September," said Yeoh. "At least, it was supposed to be."

"Setting aside my bitching for a second, Bruce, I promise we're getting you off this rock and to the church on time, if it kills us."

Yeoh smiled thinly. "An interesting choice of words, Benny."

Standing at the edge of the abyss, the archeology team thought that the fissure looked remarkably smoother than it had appeared in orbital photos, which was surprising since seemingly smooth celestial features, like the rings of Saturn, were usually rougher upon closer inspection. Standing more or less at the dead center of the fissure and looking down its length in either direction, they could discern no imperfection in its shape. In truth, the only thing that blurred its sharp edges at all was the amount of ejecta that had piled up around the fissure shortly after the initial blast. Beyond that—and the slight curvature of the Moon itself—the fissure seemed to be a perfect rectangle.

Donovan stood on top of a mound of ejecta and peered over the side. Darkness, complete and total, like nothing he had ever seen. Somewhere down there were the smashed remains of the Pigeon—and likely not too far from that debris field were the answers to all their questions. Dimly, a line from Nietzsche flashed across his consciousness: "And if thou gaze long into an abyss, the abyss will also gaze into thee."

Zell joined Donovan at the edge of the fissure, carrying the last of their equipment. He smiled and glanced over, hands on his knees. "Kind of makes you want to spit, doesn't it?"

"Would you care to try, Dr. Zell?" Soong asked with a laugh.

"No thanks," Zell replied. "You know what they say about curiosity."

"So," Donovan wondered, "are we set?"

"I signaled the *Copernicus* as you were preparing the winch," Soong informed them. "They're going to maintain radio silence but will keep an open channel in case we want to contact them. So we're free to proceed."

"Free to proceed," Donovan repeated with a chuckle. "Like we've got much choice at this point."

"Not getting second thoughts, are you?" Soong wondered aloud.

Donovan glanced toward the fissure again. "No, but I think I better go first in case I do."

"Certainly," Zell said with a broad gesture toward the fissure. "Your chariot awaits."

Their chariot was a collapsible mesh basket, no bigger than an elevator car, resting at the edge of the chasm. It was attached to an extensor arm they had fastened to the back of the rover. They had already locked down the rover and had attached the cable to the ring at the top of the basket. Though the setup might have looked frail to some, the team knew the cable and the basket were capable of holding up to two thousand pounds. Donovan began putting the lights and other necessary equipment into the basket as Zell got behind the controls of the winch.

Donovan climbed in and clamped his suit to the basket. "Don't miss me."

"We won't," Soong said. "Just remember to send the basket back up when you're down."

With a thumbs-up signal from Donovan, Zell lifted the basket from the edge of the ravine. He pressed another switch and swung the basket out over the edge and then released the brake. The basket slowly drifted out of their field of vision, Donovan's helmet the last thing they saw.

For a time Donovan decided not to use his suit lights to look around him. He knew he needed to conserve them for as long as possible. He was surprised that ambient sunlight from the surface was drifting down into the fissure, since at the top it appeared that no light could penetrate the gloom. Five minutes into his slow descent he was immersed in an all-consuming darkness. The total absence of light was disturbing, reminding him of nights as a child when he was scared of the dark or worse: Edgar Allan Poe stories about being buried alive. He flicked on his helmet lights. Nothing. The darkness seemed to eat luminescence. He could see no farther out than the edge of the basket. He tapped another button on the control pad mounted to his chest plate to activate the lights on his wrists. Still nothing. What the walls of this ravine looked like would remain a mystery.

Donovan flicked off his wrist lights and dimmed the helmet lights to half power, comforted by the idea that if he could see himself he would know that he was still alive. The minutes passed by endlessly. Five more minutes. Ten. He tried to imagine what he must look like—a frail tiny insignificant being needing a complex suit to survive in this environment, needing lights to comfort him, needing the grip of a basket's rail to remind himself that he exists. And all around, blackness. Nothingness.

Four more minutes passed, and Donovan still hadn't reached the bottom. At that moment he realized that he hadn't heard from Zell or Soong and thought it odd.

"Zell, Soong, can you hear me?"

His only answer was static. But he wasn't sure if they couldn't hear him, so he continued to transmit, likely as much for his sanity as anything.

"I don't know if you can hear me, but I still have no sense of what the interior of the fissure looks like. Repeat: I can't see anything at all. There seems to be nothing at all down here—almost as if the entire fissure is a vast cavern, as NASA suggested. I guess we've proved this part of the Moon is hollow, at least—wait, wait. There's something over there."

Donovan turned his helmet and wrist lights to full.

"Elias, there's a wall here! It's about thirty yards in front of me. It's like, it's like nothing I've ever seen. Black, obsidian. It's open at the top. I can make out three—no, four—very large circular objects in that opening. My God, each of those circles must be an eighth of a mile in diameter, but the wall—it goes on forever. I can't see the ends of it with these lights."

Donovan shone his lights to his left and to his right. It was useless. No matter how bright the lights or how far he stretched over the ends of the basket, he still couldn't get a sense of the wall's width. He arced the lights above him and below him. As he drifted down past the top, he could make out his lights dancing on the edge. But when he flashed his lights below him, all he could see was an endless black wall.

"There are no grooves of any kind—nothing to indicate that it was bolted together. No plating, no panels. Nothing. I think it's metallic—but it's not like any metal I've ever seen. But it was definitely made by some kind of intelligence. Elias, Soong—I don't know if you can hear me; I don't know if I'm getting through—but this thing, this object . . . I think it's what opened the fissure."

Soong and Zell never received Donovan's transmissions. In fact, they had no idea about what he had discovered until they too climbed into the basket and lowered themselves into the fissure via remote control. The massive object came as much as a surprise to them as it had been for Donovan. The main difference in their experience was the comfort derived from the arc lights Donovan had set up, which grew brighter as their basket descended.

When the basket reached the floor of the ravine, Donovan was there to greet them. He had been signaling them the entire time, each call growing more desperate as he spied the tiny basket above his position. Now on the ground, they still didn't answer his hails. In fact, they hardly noticed his presence. Their eyes were fixed on the unearthly wall before them.

"In all my life," Zell finally muttered, "I've never seen anything like it!"

"It's almost beyond comprehension," Soong continued, "as if it couldn't possibly be real at all."

Donovan took a step forward and ran his gloved hand down the surface. "Except for the opening at the top, it's perfectly smooth. Flawless. I've looked and looked, but I can't find any markings—not even a groove to indicate how it was assembled."

Soong approached the wall and slowly placed her hand against it as well. "But it has to have some kind of seam, plating. This is obviously man-made."

"Careful with your terminology, Dr. Soong," Zell reproached her as he held his helmet lights on a specific area of the wall. "This object wasn't made by man. No human being has ever made anything like this."

Soong turned to face them. "But what is it? A weapon?"

"Can't be. Not buried this deep," Donovan mused. "It didn't do anything but blast a very large hole in the Moon and cause a lot of electronic damage on Earth. If someone had wanted to destroy the Earth with this object, they would've put it on the surface, where it would do the most damage."

"Perhaps they hid it on purpose, Alan," Zell suggested. "Some form of sneak attack."

"A sneak attack planned two and a half million years ago?" Donovan shook his head inside his helmet. "It doesn't make sense. I think it was meant to go off at a specific moment in time. But how would anyone know when we were capable of going to the Moon?"

"A valid point," Zell added. "So it wasn't meant to hurt us, but just to get our attention?"

Soong thought of that horrible day in Hong Kong. "Tell that to all those who died."

"I can't believe that was intentional," Donovan responded. "I can't explain why I believe that, but it just doesn't seem like they wanted to hurt others. This was put here to bring us to the Moon."

"But why?" Zell demanded. "To see it? To see its power? Their power?"

"And why dig this cavern?" Soong asked as she flashed her helmet lights around the massive cave. "Look at it—smooth walls. I think those are some kind of braces down there keeping the roof up."

"I don't know," Donovan muttered. "But I do know now that they didn't bring us all the way here just to see this thing or this cave."

Zell turned to him. "Then what?"

"Come with me."

Zell and Soong trailed Donovan as he made his way deeper into the cave. They followed in his wake, careful to step where he had stepped, their gaze darting between the path before them and the lights on his helmet leading the way. Donovan had already ventured this far into the cavern, setting up lights here and there that revealed footprints from his previous walk. After about a quarter mile, Donovan stopped. He hadn't yet set up lights in this area. Their only illumination came from their helmets.

Donovan turned his helmet lights to full and held up his activated wrist lights to a corner of the cave's back wall. "I think they brought us here to find this."

Soong and Zell came up beside him and brought their lights to bear on the same spot. What the lights revealed was a smooth curvature, perhaps one hundred yards wide, poking out from the cave wall. The curvature was composed of the same seamless obsidian material the wall-like object had been made of.

"My God in heaven," Zell gasped. "What is it?"

Donovan's eyes never left the curvature. "I think it's a ship."

Chapter 13

Elias Zell took some careful steps toward the smoothly curving surface before him and crouched down as best he could in his space suit. He had made some remarkable discoveries in his years in the field and been involved with countless others, including his father's historic expedition to find Cleopatra's tomb. Nothing had prepared him for this. His chest felt tight, as if he wasn't getting enough oxygen. He checked the digital pressure gauge on his wrist just to make sure.

"A ship," he repeated. "It makes sense. After all, whoever sent the signal had to come from somewhere. As far as we know, the Moon's never been capable of supporting indigenous life."

"Maybe not as it is now," said Soong as she flashed her right wrist light along the length of the curvature, "but there are some who believe the Moon was once part of Earth, broken off after an asteroid impact."

"That's a possibility," agreed Donovan. "We knew that whatever was down here was considerably old. And some schools of thought argue in favor of outside influences on human evolution. History is rife with such examples."

"Yes," said Zell thoughtfully, getting out of his crouch, "the wheel of Ezekiel, Elijah's fiery chariot, the Baghdad Battery."

"Baghdad Battery?" said Soong. "I'm afraid you've lost me."

"An earthenware jar found outside the Iraqi capital in 1938," said Donovan. "Thought to be around two thousand years old. It contained an iron rod surrounded by a copper cylinder. When filled with an electrolyte-rich liquid, it produced a charge of about two volts."

Soong squinted at him. "So Alessandro Volta just reinvented the battery?"

"Maybe so." Donovan nodded. "Of course, some people also believe that the Ark of the Covenant was some kind of ancient capacitor capable of generating a powerful electrical charge."

"Maybe finding the ark should be the Zell Institute's next assignment."

Donovan winced. "His father already tried. Twice."

"We're floating off on a thousand theoretical tangents," Zell suggested, his eyes still fixed on the object. "While this could be some form of advanced terrestrial civilization that we've so far not detected, it isn't likely. I'm certain someone would've found some hint of that civilization's existence on Earth by now. I think Alan's right, that this is some sort of ship from an extraterrestrial civilization, which landed—or crashed—here on the Moon ages ago." He turned to them suddenly. "Could we have intercepted some kind of distress signal? An advanced SOS?"

"Possibly," said Donovan. "But why now?"

"Maybe they'd been trying for years and only now have reached us?"

"With an electromagnetic pulse that crippled the planet?" countered Soong. "I don't believe it. No, whatever signal they sent, they meant to send it when they did. Why they sent it is another question."

"Wait!" said Donovan. "My light just caught something. Hold it . . ." He shone his left wrist light on the hull again. "There it is."

"What've you got?" asked Zell.

"Writing."

Donovan approached the curvature. He reached into his supply bag and pulled out a brush, which he gently applied to the craft's surface, sweeping away sediment with care and precision. After a few moments, the symbols were more legible.

He scanned the symbols on the hull again. Could he be the first human in history to be glimpsing the language of another world?

"What do you make of it, Alan?" Zell asked.

"I don't—" Donovan began, then shook his head. "Wait a minute." He brushed away some more sediment until the symbols could be read clearly. "I can read this, and so can you."

"What?"

Donovan laughed at their foolishness. "It's Farsi."

"It's not possible." Zell approached the curvature and read the writing for himself. "In all the annals of history, there's never been a record of two completely separate civilizations coming up with the exact same language. Alan, this isn't possible!" He read the writing again. *"Khôsh âmadid."*

"'Welcome,'" Donovan translated.

"But why Farsi? What's the significance?" Zell demanded. "Why not English? Or Chinese? Or Spanish? After all, Farsi isn't the most common language on Earth."

"You're forgetting, Dr. Zell, that this object was deposited here more than two million years ago," Soong noted as she flashed her wrist light at the word. "No language on Earth had been invented at that time."

"Which leaves us with even *more* questions," Zell mused.

"Hold on," said Donovan, brushing away more dust. "Look, here it is again. 'Willkommen.' In German."

Without further discussion they began applying their brushes to the surface in earnest. Upon closer inspection they dismissed the idea that the material they were uncovering was any known type of metal. While it had metallic properties, the very gracefulness and fluidity of its shape suggested it could also be a form of advanced molded plastic—or some other material not known to humanity. As they cleared away more of the lunar dust, they found that the entire exposed area was covered in writing, all messages of greeting, in every language of the world, including ones neither Donovan nor Zell recognized. Even odder was that none of the symbols or letters seemed to be burned or chiseled into the surface, but were instead embedded there as if they had been natural details of the object itself. The words were the only imperfections on the entire surface.

"'*Ya'at'eeh?*'" Donovan read. "Don't know that one."

"It's Navajo," said Soong from behind them. "Loosely translated it means, 'It is good,' but the Navajo use it as a standard greeting." Seeing their admiring looks through their transparent helmets, Soong responded, "I studied the World War Two code talkers as a child. Fascinating subject."

Zell smiled. "So what do you make of our little discovery here?"

"Obviously whoever deposited this boat here wanted to make sure we knew they were friendly. All over this area it seems to be the same thing," Soong observed. "Greetings, welcome. I even found a few translations of 'friend' here and there. Except . . ." She led them down a few yards and shone her wrist light on another embedded symbol.

"Mandarin," Donovan noted.

"It's the symbol for *turtle*," said Soong.

Zell suddenly thought of the old anecdote in which a woman informed a prominent physicist that the world was a flat plate poised on the back of a turtle. "What is the turtle standing on?" the scientist of the tale asked bemusedly. The woman didn't flinch and answered, "It's turtles all the way down."

"Why a turtle?" Donovan asked.

"Turtles are significant in many cultures for many different reasons," Zell began.

"In Chinese mythology," Soong said, "a turtle was said to have risen from the depths with the eight trigrams on its back." She paused and turned to them. "A message of divination to the human race."

"A messenger," Zell said thoughtfully as he crouched down. He went to scratch his beard, as he often did when puzzling over a conundrum, only to have his hand brush over his space helmet. "I'm almost afraid to ask what the message might be."

"It still doesn't make sense," Donovan mused as he approached Zell. "Could it be possible that our languages are far older than we realize? That this is some relic from an ancient human civilization we never knew existed?"

"It can't be, Alan," Zell replied. "You know as well as I do that we can trace the evolution of languages, that Latin, as an obvious example, initially formed the basis—"

Soong had moved several feet away from Donovan and Zell as she spotted a fragment of a word that was poking out from the lunar dust. As she cleared more of the area, her very audible gasp made them turn their attention to her.

"What've you found?" Donovan wondered aloud as he approached her, Zell a step behind him.

Soong paused. "An airlock."

"How can you be certain?" Zell asked.

Soong took a step back and gestured at the newly revealed area with her brush. "Because it says, 'Airlock.'"

Donovan and Zell flashed their lights on the area. A series of words in various languages formed a rectangular pattern approximately eight by ten feet.

"This is too easy," Soong suggested.

Donovan turned to her. "Unless whoever built this *wanted* us to go inside."

"First dig I've ever been on with instructions built into it." Zell shook his head in wonder. "But I'm not one for looking a gift horse in the mouth. If this is an airlock, that means we can get inside."

June 28
7:44 p.m., Houston Time
5 days, 13 hours, 29 minutes, Mission Elapsed Time

"Houston, this is *Copernicus.* How're you guys coming with our little fuel-line problem? Over."

Lieutenant Colonel Franklin Wilson rubbed his eyes and strained to stare out the *Copernicus*'s window at the airless black sky over the Moon. As tired as he might be looking at computer consoles, he was even more tired of waiting for responses from Earth. Rationally he knew radio signals traversed the space between the Earth and the Moon in only a couple of seconds, but each time he radioed Mission Control, the delay felt longer. This one felt interminable. Benny and Yeoh had found the ascent engine's malfunction hours ago and were now doing a thorough survey of the ship's hull. They had relayed streaming video and still photographs of the damage to Houston at least two hours ago, but Mission Control still hadn't sent back protocols for making repairs.

Maybe they think it can't be fixed, Wilson thought as he scratched a half week's length of stubble on his face. *Maybe they're looking for a way to break it to us gently.*

The lieutenant colonel sucked tepid water through a straw. He exhaled and kicked the console with his good leg.

Son of a bitch . . . If I could only just get out there.

"*Copernicus,* this is Houston. Sorry about the delay," John Dieckman's voice echoed in his headset. "We're working out a number of repair scenarios right now and should have something to you before the day's out."

"Deke, are we on a private comm?"

"We are, *Copernicus*. Go ahead."

"Good. I don't want Benevisto and Yeoh to overhear us."

"What's on your mind, Frank?"

"What's going on down there? Are you guys giving up on us?"

There was another delay. "Of course we're not, Frank. We're just running a lot of sims down here and assessing the damage to the *Copernicus* and the *Tai*—"

"I know how busy you are, Deke, so skip the bullshit. How're we really doing?"

Dieckman cleared his throat. "Frank, as I told you—"

"You know they wouldn't have you on the horn with me every minute if it wasn't serious. So give it to me straight."

"Okay." Deke paused. "Right now we think the fuel line can be repaired. Once we've got it in working order, we'll be able to activate the system and see the situation. Most educated guesses down here think that you've got enough fuel to get back into orbit—but you'll be cutting it pretty close."

"And what about the *Tai-Ping*?"

"Frank, maybe we should worry about one problem—"

"The *Tai-Ping*. What's her status?"

"We've run the sims on the reboot procedure Yeoh told us about. It seems solid, but it's hard to tell without knowing what went wrong in the first place. If we're even one or two amps over on the power, the whole ship could be fried."

Wilson sighed. "Meaning if you don't get it to work, then there might not be any way for us to get back home."

"Let's not jump the gun on that one yet. We're still working on it."

"Working on it?"

"We're looking into the situation right now. Don't worry, Frank. We've got our best people working on the problem, both in the sim and—"

"Deke." Wilson was surprised to find his mouth dry. "What're our chances?"

There was a long pause before Deke answered. "One in five of getting the *Tai-Ping*'s systems rebooted. We're not sure if some of the backup systems were compromised by the explosion."

"So one way or the other we've got to take the chance and see if we're going back to a dead ship."

"That's the long and short of it, Frank."

Wilson propped himself up and glanced out the window at Benny and Yeoh making their last survey of the exterior of the *Copernicus*. His knee was throbbing badly inside the splint, but he took almost no notice of it.

"Houston, not a word to my crew."

"Understood. How's the knee holding up?"

Wilson couldn't help but laugh. "We're still assessing that situation, Houston."

"So what do you suggest we do, Dr. Zell?" asked Soong, still staring at the area around the airlock.

"I'm not the team leader, my dear. It's your call, Alan."

"Suddenly I love being the boss," Donovan said, grinning. "Let's crack this walnut."

"Now you're talking!" Zell said, clapping his hands together.

"Dr. Donovan," Soong said, stepping forward, "I, as much as you, would like to explore this mystery, but I believe we should contact the ship before we—"

"We can't, remember?" Zell noted. "If Alan couldn't contact us while we were on the surface and he was in the fissure, we certainly can't contact Wilson from here. Something—probably the cave itself—is interfering with the transmission."

Despite her concerns about being out of radio contact with the *Copernicus*, Soong followed them toward the area on the curvature marked with the word *airlock* in various languages. She suggested that they attempt to find the manual release or, barring that, the grooves around the airlock's seal. Finding themselves in agreement, the three scientists slowly began to sift away the ancient lunar soil. The dust flew around in strange directions in the lighter gravity before drifting down to the ground at a rate six times slower than it would have settled on Earth. To Soong's eyes, the odd gravitational effects were not nearly as strange as the object she was helping to uncover. Not only did the surface have the unusual distinction of seeming like the hardest metal she had ever touched, but it was also perfectly preserved, still shining brightly, as if it had been encased in a protective sheath. What was even odder was that the metal had no imperfections. Surely, if the object had crashed here, as they suspected, it would have developed some damage on impact.

"I think I found it!" Zell exclaimed.

Soong and Donovan hurried to his side. With their small brushes they began to clear away the last remnants of the lunar dust. Before them was a round indentation, about a square foot, with what looked like a handle in its center.

"Looks like a crank handle," Donovan muttered. "See if you can turn it."

Zell grasped the handle. "Opposable thumbs," he said, noting the handle's design.

"Not necessarily," Soong suggested. "Maybe they just built it so that we could let ourselves in."

Zell nodded and carefully exerted pressure on the handle. He feared it might snap off in his hand. Yet no matter how much force he exerted, the handle wouldn't budge.

"The damn thing's stuck," Zell muttered, his gasps of air audible in their headsets.

"I'll check for a seam," Soong said, picking up her brush. "Perhaps we can pry it open."

Donovan took his turn on the release. *Righty-tighty, lefty-loosey,* he thought, recalling the rhyme Mr. Arroway had sarcastically taught them in shop. *I'm turning it the right way. Why the hell won't it budge?* Then he laughed. *The right way for Earth, at least.*

"I'm unable to find a seam," Soong informed them. "Unbelievable—look at how much surface area I've cleared. Is it possible that the airlock is—"

Donovan shined his flashlight on the release again and noticed a button in the middle of the handle, not unlike a bathroom-door lock. He pressed it, and the crank popped up. He grasped the handle again, and it turned with ease.

"My God," Zell whispered. "Alan, look at the airlock!"

Donovan turned to see a seam appear seemingly out of nowhere, its perimeter deep inside the area Soong had cleared. As the seam solidified, the airlock sprang to life, and the three scientists watched as dust flew upward through the beams of their flashlights and into the vacuum of space.

"It's venting gas," Zell muttered. "This thing's still pressurized."

"Yeah, but with what?" Donovan wondered. "Oxygen or methane? Who knows what they breathe?"

"I don't know," Zell said, flashing his helmet's light into the airlock. "But whatever it is, it means that whoever was the last to step inside here never stepped back out. At least not this way."

Soong gathered her equipment. "We can check the air quality once we repressurize the lock."

Zell looked at her. "Are you mad? You mean we should seal ourselves inside this bloody thing?"

"It is the only way to tell," Soong observed. "Otherwise we might vent all the remaining atmosphere into space."

Zell groaned. "I'm not sealing this blasted thing behind all of us."

Zell's grumbling aside, Soong concurred with the assessment. Not all of them should go in at once. They decided that Zell would accompany Donovan inside the airlock, while Soong waited outside in case anything went wrong.

Zell snatched up his kit, grasped the edge of the airlock, and lowered himself inside. "The things you talk me into."

Donovan followed Zell inside. Donovan judged that the ship—if this was a ship—was pitched at a ten-degree angle and had settled slightly to what he guessed was starboard. The interior was even darker than the cave had been. At least the outer cave initially had the benefit of sunlight filtering down through the fissure. But this interior was darker than any place any of the explorers had ever been. They could see no more than a few feet forward. Walking the airlock's length and width, they judged it to be about twelve feet wide and thirty feet long. The walls were composed of the same odd curved metal found outside, unadorned except for two pairs of releases on either end of the enclosure, plus a pair of what they took to be pressure gauges. Above each release was a flat pad not unlike a small computer screen—the powered release, Donovan assumed. He pressed the button on the manual release and turned the crank. The exterior airlock door shut, and its seal disappeared.

"Better crank the other one."

Zell did as Donovan asked. Another rush of gas blew into the airlock as the interior door's seal revealed itself and the portal began to slide open.

Donovan monitored the air tester. "Amazing. I'm reading an oxygen-nitrogen atmosphere. We could conceivably take off our helmets."

"If it's all the same to you, Alan," Zell muttered as he flashed a wrist light through the open interior door, "I think we'd be well advised to keep them on. I can't speak for you, but when the temperature gets below two hundred degrees, I tend to catch cold."

June 28
The White House
Washington, DC
10:13 p.m.

The President peered out the Oval Office window. It was a remarkably clear night. None of the usual low-hanging summertime clouds blanketed the sky. As she stepped off the ladder of Marine One upon arrival at the White House that afternoon, the air had been hot and crisp and dry. So it remained as the night came on. The weather reminded her of a day long ago when she drove cross-country with a couple of college friends on spring break. They were in Arizona, and the only thing clearer than the air had been their heads. A long time ago. She glanced at the Moon one last time and stepped away from the window.

There was a knock at her door, and General McKenna entered. Despite the starched, pressed sharpness of his uniform, the President could clearly discern weariness on the general's ruddy face.

"You sent for me, Madam President?"

"Yes, Jim." The President gestured at a nearby couch as she took a seat in her favorite rocking chair. "Anything new from Phoenix?"

"None, ma'am. As you know, the archeology team's been deployed. NASA's coordinating repair efforts with Wilson's team."

"Good." The President nodded and scratched the back of her head, the skin on her face slack. "I just got off the phone with the Chinese president. He's none too happy that I gave the go-ahead for the mission without consulting him. Commander Yuen, it seems, was a very esteemed member of their military, and they felt we were . . . *cavalier* about his death."

McKenna tried to suppress his annoyance. "How cavalier, ma'am?"

"Let me play you the tape." The President cleared her throat and said to the room in a clear voice: "Activate recorder. Play telephone conversation of this date, sixteen hundred hours. Start six minutes in."

On the President's desk a small speaker stirred to life. "—certainly hope you will not be so cavalier when it comes to our sovereignty over Taiwan."

"I don't think it would be prudent to discuss Taiwan at this juncture, Mr. President," her recorded voice responded, "and certainly not while we both have people on the Moon and in danger."

"I disagree, Madam President. The Taiwanese situation highlights the need for cooperation between strategic partners. Without consultation, we would be guilty of—I believe the term is *cowboy diplomacy*. Surely you see the wisdom in consultation."

"You don't need to lecture me, sir. I know my obligations to both China and Taiwan."

"I do not mean to lecture you. Nevertheless, I must impress upon you the necessity of asserting our sovereignty over Taiwan if your government continues to make decisions regarding both of our nations without our consultation."

"I hope you're not threatening me, Mr. President."

"The People's Republic of China does not make threats, Madam President. We only claim what is rightly ours and will make our own decisions regarding it in the future."

"End tape." The President stood up and paced the floor with her hands in her pockets. "What do you think, Jim?"

"The Chinese have made threats like this in the past, ma'am, with no consequences."

"Still, the Taiwanese situation is pretty fragile since the assassination of their separatist leader. They might think they should declare their independence in reaction to it—especially if there's the slightest hint that Chinese agents were involved with it."

"You don't think the Chinese would be so bold as to assassinate—"

"No," the President replied with a shake of her head. "But we've still got to convince the Taiwanese of that. They're pretty hot on that idea right now." The President went back to the window but didn't draw the curtains. "It won't matter one way or the other that we have a joint mission to the Moon. If the Taiwanese declare their independence, the Chinese fleet will move in regardless of whether or not our fleet's in the vicinity."

"Should I alert the fleet, ma'am?"

"Yes. Meanwhile, I'll talk to Taiwan and make sure they don't make a move without us. We'll coordinate any defense of the island with them."

McKenna stood up. "I'll make the preparations, Madam President."

The President turned from the window. "Put whatever Skystalkers we have over the Chinese fleet. I want to know if they so much as twitch a hair on their asses."

Corridors. Seemingly miles of them. They arced this way and that, stretching down the length of the ship, slipping into darkness well past flashlights' beams. The walls looked like obsidian glass curving in a gentle arc over their heads. Unlike the exterior, however, the walls were completely devoid of markings—no writing or signs, no instrument panels, no comm system. If this was a ship, it was unlike any ship Donovan, Zell, and Soong had ever seen. Its walls betrayed no hint of its technological capabilities or purpose. Its interior revealed no remnants of its inhabitants. This was more than a strictly practical, form-follows-function design. The interior looked as if it had no discernible function except protection from the elements—which couldn't possibly be its sole purpose. *Could it be unfinished?* Donovan wondered. Yet even the most unfinished structure built on Earth betrayed some of its designers' intent during construction. This ship was like a stage set, devoid of furniture or paint . . . anything that might indicate what it would be.

Donovan looked down. He noticed some kind of phosphorescent lighting running in strips down the corridors, practically the same kind you would see in an airplane's aisle. Yet the lighting was also like some sort of bioluminescent organism, not unlike the ones he'd seen while cave diving as a younger man.

Were they there as markers? Could they be some remnant of the crew?

"Alan," Zell called over the comm, "better take a look at this."

Zell was standing at the end of the most recent corridor they had explored with Soong, who had joined them inside the ship. So far they had found three such corridors, each on top of the other, seemingly running what appeared to be the entire length of the ship. Each had been lined with a series of sealed sliding doors, each shut almost as tight as the airlock had been, except that these portals displayed obvious seals where the doors met the frames. They had managed to reach this level through a series of ladders running parallel to what they took to be the ship's main elevator.

As Donovan approached them, Zell's flashlight reflected off another door. "Unlike the others, this one was slightly ajar," Zell noted.

"Should we go inside?" Soong asked.

"Are you kidding?"

The door was open only about six inches and easier to force than the airlock had been. Together Zell and Donovan pushed the door into its housing with ease.

"I feel like I'm on the *Enterprise*," Zell said as he flashed his wrist light into the interior.

"Does that make you Captain Kirk?" said Soong.

"I always preferred Dr. McCoy."

"Hardly a surprise."

What they found inside was nothing like what could've been offered on an old television series. Before them was a deep and wide laboratory with dozens upon dozens of beds and a complex series of what appeared to be blank computer screens lining both the walls and parts of the curved ceiling. Yet, for a medical laboratory, there were no signs of any equipment. Not even anything that might have passed for a futuristic Bunsen burner. Not even buttons or controls for the vast array of screens. As they walked the lab's length, they noticed what appeared to be cabinet doors lining the walls under the screens. They tried to force open two or three of the doors, but none would budge.

"It would appear they made sure to keep all the medicine away from the children," Zell said after giving up on his door.

"It's so strange," Soong said more to herself than her companions as she walked around some medical beds. "How large was the crew to need so many beds?"

"Maybe it was a triage center," Zell suggested as he ran a hand over what appeared to be some kind of foam padding. "Maybe they had been anticipating a war."

"Maybe they had one," Donovan added. "And ran away from it."

"If that is so," Soong mused, "then where are the bodies? Come to think of it, if this . . . ship is as large as it appears to be, why have we been unable to find a single corpse?"

A ship. Donovan was convinced of it now. This was as much a ship as anything ever built on Earth that flew through the air or sailed the seas. It had decks and sections and cabins. And now a medical lab. Even the doors seemed to be of a fairly standard size—eighty inches by thirty-six inches, by the look of them. Whoever built the vessel had to have been humanoid; that was apparent. But who were they?

"I don't know if we'll find any, Soong," Donovan suggested as he flashed his light on some nearby screens. "Whoever came here probably did so millions of years ago—they had enough time to die and probably be buried by the survivors."

"So where are the survivors?" Zell wondered. "If this was their only means of transport, then the last surviving members of this crew must be here somewhere."

Donovan stepped toward him. "Elias, where would you go if you were the last man on the Moon?"

Zell thought about it for a moment and smiled. "The bridge."

"And why would you think that, Dr. Zell?" Soong asked.

"Elementary, my dear Dr. Soong. If the crew planned to blow a hole in the Moon, as we assume, at a certain time—say, early in the twenty-first century—then the way to do that would be from the nerve center of their technological universe—i.e., the bridge."

Donovan laughed. "You're a smart-ass, Zell."

"And where do you propose we might find this bridge?" Soong asked.

"I don't know," Donovan answered. "We'll probably have to search the whole ship."

"That could take days," Soong said, then looked at him. "Why, this ship is enormous."

Donovan looked around for a sign. "Any idea what deck we're on now?"

"Why, I thought it was the lido deck," said Zell. He looked around a moment. "Well, whatever planet you're from, up is up and north is north. If there is a bridge, that's the direction we're likely to find it."

It would have been difficult enough to climb the ladders to the remaining twenty decks minus their space suits, but with the protective gear the exertion was almost more than they could stand. The passageways had obviously been constructed for people not wearing backpacks—or at least with ones of a considerably smaller size. As it was, the trio had to squeeze themselves through each portal, often with the aid of someone else. Those were the moments Donovan feared the most. One wrong step, and they could tumble down to the lower deck. Luckily the ladders were staggered with landings, but one slip could still drop them a good twelve feet and shatter an ankle or worse. After three more decks, Donovan called for a break. Zell sounded as if he would collapse if he took another step. The air inside their helmets was thick and humid from perspiration. A second skin of sweat encased their bodies.

"All right," Zell said after a few moments, "let's get this show on the road."

They continued to climb, upward and upward. At last they reached what appeared to be the top of the structure. The ceiling rose above them, cathedral-like, its ebony surface mirroring the inky black of space. In front of the scientists was a door. Like the others they had come across, it was blank. The door was also completely sealed, with no apparent way to open it.

"Looks like the end of the line," said Zell.

"Think we should knock?" Donovan muttered.

Soong reached out and brushed her glove over the area's surface, searching for a manual release. There was a glassy texture to the door, a pliability. As her hand touched the door itself, she felt a very slight but noticeable tremor. She jerked her hands back as the door began to glow with a peculiar blue-tinted light. Instantly the door slid open with ease.

"Looks like we passed the test," Zell said.

Even with the dim illumination generated by their suit lights, they could tell they had entered a large, if not cavernous, room. The vaulted ceiling mirrored those they had seen throughout the ship, though much higher, stretching at least thirty feet overhead. Their flashlights bounced around, finding only the same blank obsidian walls. The sparse furnishings were comprised of comfortable-looking seats arranged in sections across the entire expanse. Most of them were facing what appeared to be large consoles or workstations. Each workstation, however, was just as blank and lifeless as every surface of the ship they had seen thus far. Donovan threw his flashlight's beam across one of the stations and stared down, finding nothing but his own reflection. No matter what they did, their efforts were frustrated by the fact that this ship—or whatever it was—apparently had no controls, nothing that would enable them to unlock dormant secrets.

"I'm guessing this is the bridge," Donovan muttered.

Zell approached him. "If it is, it certainly doesn't have much in the way of equipment, just these oblong tables and chairs. It could be the damn mess hall, for all we know."

"No buttons, no switches, no computer terminals," Soong muttered as she walked around, flashing her light on the array of stations before them. "This doesn't make any sense."

Zell sat in a chair before one of the oblong tables in the center of the room. In spite of his bulky backpack, he found the chair to be remarkably comfortable. He glanced at the blank surface before him curving upward into a half wall and slowly let his helmet's light drift across it. *A blank computer screen,* Zell mused. *The whole surface looks like an oddly shaped, blank computer screen.* He sent his wrist lights out across the room and watched as they revealed more weirdly shaped tables and consoles, all blank. *This whole ship is a blank—no controls, no buttons, nothing mechanical except for the airlock's release. How were they able to control this ship?*

Zell stood up and walked to about the dead center of the room, shaking his head. "I'd like to get some goddamn lights on in here."

And suddenly the lights came on, blindingly so. Each of them winced as brightness hit their dark-adjusted pupils.

"Elias!" Donovan called from where he was standing. "What the hell did you do?"

"It's not possible," Soong said quietly.

"Nothing," Zell answered. "All I did was—" He clapped his hands together and roared with laughter. "Voice activation. It's in sleep mode. The whole damn ship's been in a power-save mode for millions of years!"

Donovan looked around the bridge. For the first time since entering the vessel, he could make out colors. Far from the imposing black color they originally gave off, when illuminated the walls and other surfaces were a mottled bluish green, looking almost like the deep waters off the Caribbean. To Donovan, they seemed to ripple and move slightly, as if caught in a trade wind. They seemed powered, alive. Yet they still displayed nothing.

The room was far larger than they had previously imagined—at least a hundred feet wide and seemingly perfectly round. The ceiling was completely vaulted, a giant half sphere that reminded Donovan of the Hayden Planetarium in New York, which he had once visited with his father and Thackeray Zell.

"I don't get it," Donovan muttered as he scanned the vicinity for a control switch. "What's been powering her all this time?"

"It must have been a generator of some kind," Soong said into her mike from across the room. "Something kept this ship functioning. Something triggered the signal—"

"Dr. Soong," Zell said from the far end of the bridge, "I think I found your survivor."

The body was sitting in a chair facing the wall. Donovan and Soong approached it with little apprehension. They had both seen their fair share of corpses in all states of decay. And yet this body's condition bore little resemblance to any they had previously encountered. It appeared to be a man of above-average height dressed in a dark-purple coverall. The best way Donovan could describe its condition was mummified—with the exception that, unlike the dried mummies he had seen in Egypt, this one had retained a fair share of moisture.

"He was probably frozen solid," Soong surmised, "once the heat inside this ship dissipated after his death."

"He looks human," Donovan said.

"You sound surprised, Alan," Zell replied as he flashed his wrist light closer to the corpse's face. "Dark-red hair, from what I gather. An aquiline nose, strong jaw. I'm not sure if this was his actual coloring, but he seems to have had an olive complexion."

"Probably died at a fairly young age too. No more than twenty or twenty-five," Soong noticed as she bent closer to the body. "Large cranium, suggesting considerable evolutionary development. Remarkable. Human beings from another world. Virtual duplicates of us right down to the bone structure."

"What are the chances, eh?" Zell asked with a grunt. "A billion to one? A trillion?"

Donovan looked up from the body. "You sound as if you don't believe it, Elias."

"Believe what?" Zell scoffed. "That this man and his crew came from another world? You're both discounting what we've seen so far."

Donovan laughed. "Come on, Elias, you can't mean—"

"What we've seen so far is a technology far beyond our own," Soong said. "This ship couldn't have possibly come from Earth."

"All right, I'll keep my theory to myself, then. But whatever the case is," Zell said, "it's clear they were expecting us. You mentioned an oxygen-nitrogen atmosphere. Are you getting the same reading now? Is the air breathable here?"

Donovan turned to Zell. "Why don't you just ask the ship? It seems to like the sound of your voice."

Zell smirked at him. "I believe I might at that." He glanced around the room and finally up at the ceiling. "Is there—er—a breathable atmosphere in here?"

"THE SHIP'S ARTIFICIAL ATMOSPHERE IS FUNCTIONING WITHIN NORMAL PARAMETERS."

The ship's voice made Donovan and Soong jump, not because it was overpowering, but because it seemed to come from nowhere and everywhere.

And the voice was clearly human sounding, though its accent was unlike anything they had heard before.

Soong looked at Zell with surprise. "How did you know it would speak?"

"I didn't," Zell said. "I assumed it would give us a readout on one of these stations."

"Did it speak in an English accent?" Soong wondered.

"My dear, I have an English accent," Zell said proudly. "That's an American accent if I ever heard one."

"No way," Donovan said. "I've been all over the country, and I've never heard anyone ever speak like that. It's like it almost has no accent, like a trained newscaster."

"No, not that either," Soong said. "Dr. Zell, could it possibly be creating an accent by attempting a pronunciation after hearing us speak?"

Zell strode across the deck, looking around at the array of screens. "I doubt that. It's likely that a machine—even as sophisticated as this one—would need to hear more words than the few we've spoken here."

"But it knows English," Donovan said. "At least the designers of this ship did."

Zell cleared his throat. "Could you tell us how you learned to speak in English?"

"I AM PROGRAMMED TO SPEAK ENGLISH IN RESPONSE TO ALL QUERIES MADE IN ENGLISH."

Donovan looked up at the ceiling, half wondering if this was what Moses had felt like on Mount Sinai. "Does that mean you're able to speak other languages?"

"I AM PROGRAMMED TO REPLY TO QUERIES IN ALL KNOWN LANGUAGES SPOKEN ON EARTH."

"All the known languages," Soong said, looking at Donovan.

Donovan turned to Zell. "This isn't getting us anywhere."

"You're right. But let's be comfortable first. Can you raise the ship's temperature above the freezing mark?"

"YES. IT WILL TAKE ELEVEN MINUTES AND FORTY-THREE SECONDS TO RAISE THE TEMPERATURE TO ABOVE ZERO DEGREES CELSIUS. DO YOU WISH TO PROCEED?"

"Yes, ah, computer. Please do so, taking care not to boil us alive."

Donovan stepped toward Zell and Soong. "Minutes, seconds. Zero degrees Celsius. This ship seems to know an awful lot about human civilization. Computer, how do you know the human terms *minutes, seconds*, and *degrees Celsius*?"

"I WAS PROGRAMMED WITH AN UNDERSTANDING OF THESE TERMS."

"Donovan, it appears to be a tool, not an intelligence," Soong surmised. "If it is unable to answer complex inquiries, asking it questions could take us all day."

"What do you suggest we do, then?" Donovan asked.

"Ask it for the ship's logs," Soong said.

"A brilliant idea, Doctor," Zell said with a grin. "This way we can conserve the ship's power while at the same time figuring out where the hell it came from."

"Computer," Donovan again said to the ceiling. "Please play back the ship's logs. Start with the last entry."

"ACCESSING . . ."

Each of them expected to hear another voice coming from wherever the computer's voice was emanating. None of them expected the consoles and walls to shift from their murky sea-green color to instrument panels and controls, or for the empty seats to fill with people. Not ghosts, not images, but solid-looking people studying displays and running their hands over controls that appeared to be embedded in console surfaces. Soong stifled a scream as a purple-suited crew member passed right by her and walked over to the body sitting in its chair. With a mingling of horror and excitement, they watched as the crew member spoke soundlessly to the corpse. Then a ghostly figure with red hair and olive skin rose from the body and solidified as he stood near them in the middle of the bridge. He was a good five inches taller than Donovan, who stood six feet even in his bare feet.

Soong gripped Donovan's arm as best she could through her gloves. He turned to her.

"A hologram of some kind," he said, and reached out his hand, expecting it to pass through the red-haired man's shoulder. Donovan's hand instead smacked against the man's shoulder, but the man took no notice.

He was odd looking, very large and powerful and handsome, but not in a traditional sort of way. Each of them tried to peg his ethnicity, but his features seemed to be a combination of all the best features from all the races on Earth. He looked human; that was for certain. But he wasn't human in any way that they understood the term.

The man paced the floor around them. Zell, Donovan, and Soong in turn backed out of his way.

"What's he doing?" Soong asked.

"I think," said Donovan, "he wants to tell us something."

Chapter 14

Suddenly, violently, Donovan felt the room swim around him. Reality bent itself inward, twisting and curving into a Möbius strip of dementia. Donovan felt his thoughts turn to water as his mind rebelled against him.

There is a world outside. This is a room, not a world. We're on the Moon; we're in a ship; we're not here with what we're seeing.

Something was probing his mind, taking control. It was not a pleasant conjoining of thoughts. It was invasive, clinical. Donovan felt the floor drop beneath him and thought wildly of the time he rode the Rotor with Cynthia Evans at Playland, the centrifugal force pinning them to the walls as they spun round and round. Slowly, like a curtain being drawn back, he saw the fabric of infinite space unfold at his very feet.

There are worlds inside of this room. A whole solar system full of worlds. It's our solar system, isn't it? There's Jupiter and its innumerable moons. There's Saturn and its rings. But that's not our Saturn, not our Jupiter. They're all changed somehow; they're reshaped; the Moons have been transformed somehow into habitable worlds. People are walking around on Mars in shirtsleeves as water flows on its surface. And there are people—a hundred billion people populating those worlds, living under domes or in underground facilities or suspended in floating cities drifting with the currents on Europa's now-iceless ocean. But they're not people, not like us, men and women with flaws and imperfections and diseases and the fear of death clinging to their skins like cheap perfume. They're people, yes. But not like us.

These thoughts that were his and yet someone else's whirled violently inside his animal brain. Donovan thought the sensation would drive him mad. He saw the future, events that had not yet happened unraveling gaily, rocketing through his consciousness at limitless speed. Whatever it was that was invading his mind was taking over, letting him see through its—*his*—eyes. As he clawed at the ragged ends of his sanity, Donovan suddenly had one clear thought—*I am Joshua*—before the horrible mental roller coaster ratcheted up again.

No, I am not Joshua; I am Alan Donovan. I'm both and I'm neither. I've never—I don't know. This world will die. Civilization will die, and I don't understand how it came to be the way it is—no, damn it, the way it will *be—*

Was it a minute ago or seven hundred years ago or more than two million years from now that Zell asked the computer to play the last mission log?

The end began now. Here. In this time. In the twenty-first century. All we will become—all we have become—has already begun. And I must stop it. We must stop it.

Too many images, too many sensations, too many feelings. I've got to think; I've got to remember the chain of events, not this loop of lives lived, of lives interrupted so long ago, of lives not yet lived. Think of Elias—remember Elias—

Donovan screamed and covered his eyes, trying to block out the thoughts and experiences of generations not yet born. When he opened them again, he feared what he might see. But he was back on the bridge of the ship.

As the man finished speaking, his image, along with those of the crew members who had appeared with him, disappeared instantly, almost as if an unseen hand had snapped off a television set. Instead of merely facing a blank screen, however, Donovan, Zell, and Soong watched as the entire bridge reverted to its previous seemingly inert sea-green color. Where instrument panels and controls had just been operated by the apparitions of men and women, only blank consoles and walls remained before empty chairs. Each of them stared at the vacant spot where the red-haired man had just stood. The words of the crewman, whose body now sat before them, had chilled them so deeply that they were unable to speak. The room reverberated in a profound silence.

"Elias?" Donovan asked. There was a quiver in his voice. Whatever had just happened to him was still fresh in his mind. Looking at his comrades' pale faces, he knew they must have experienced something similar.

"Yes, Alan," Zell answered. "I felt it too. Something . . . trying to probe our thoughts."

"We're not alone in here," Soong whispered, looking around.

"Hello," a voice boomed. All three of them jumped in spite of themselves. They turned and saw the same man from the mission log, looking considerably less harried. Although they knew he couldn't see them—could he?—he appeared to be looking straight at them. The effect was unsettling. After a brief pause, he spoke.

"You've no doubt traveled a long way to get here, and not just in terms of distance. If our calculations are correct, accounting for your technological restrictions, it's sometime in the early twenty-first century. Don't be alarmed. We planned it this way." The red-haired man paused for a moment, walking toward them. The trio marveled at the click his footsteps made on the floor. "There's time for that. Let's start at the beginning. My name, the name I was born with, would sound strange to your ears. Our language is not quite like any of the ones of your time. Those of us chosen for this mission have learned many of them, but they are not regularly spoken, at least not in the way you do. We, and our vessel, were also given names so that you might better understand us. You can call me Joshua. You may want to get more comfortable."

Donovan, Zell, and Soong sat down as Joshua requested, never giving a moment's thought to the fact that they were taking orders from a man who had been dead for millions of their years.

"Your world, the world you know today, is in grave danger, although you do not know it yet. Even as you sit here, events are being put into motion that will unravel everything your race has sought to build for eons. Let me put it to you plainly. We, the crew of the *Astraeus*, left for your time more than seven hundred years from now. By that point, nearly all sentient life will be extinct."

"What does he mean?" Soong whispered.

"Please understand, it is almost as difficult for me to explain this paradox as it is for you to hear it. Perhaps you will better understand what I am telling you if you better understand what I am," said Joshua. "By your definition, I am not a human being. More specifically, I am a clone. A genetically engineered specimen flawless in design. But the seeds of what I am, what your world will become, were sown in your time."

Joshua took a step toward the center of the bridge, looking very much like a professor about to lecture his class. His eyes, however, never left their direction. He appeared to be looking right at them, which Donovan knew had to be impossible. A prerecorded message couldn't possibly know where its viewers would eventually be standing. As an experiment, Donovan stood up and crossed the room. Joshua's gaze suddenly shifted back and forth between his position and that of Zell and Soong's, just the way a speaker would shift his gaze back and forth before an assembly. He walked back toward his seat, and Joshua's eyes followed him. The hologram—if that's what he was—almost seemed to be waiting for him to stop fidgeting.

"At this point, I will ask our ship to adjust the life-support system to raise the temperature. Once this is done, you should be able to remove your helmets."

Okay, so the damn thing's not sentient, Donovan thought as he cautiously removed his helmet, remembering that they had already asked the ship's computer to raise the temperature. Soong and Zell followed suit, carefully sniffing the air. The temperature was still on the cool side, but it was well above freezing. If they needed to, they knew they could remove their space suits and walk around in their coveralls.

Joshua returned his gaze to them. "Now that you're ready, we can begin. Rather than having to explain what is to come, it was decided that you should be *shown* your future. In order to achieve this, your cerebral cortex was probed and the proper images implanted. This is something that is quite common in our time, but for your brains, the experience will no doubt be . . . disorienting."

And with that, reality washed away from them.

They see their world. Not an image of their world hanging in the blackness of space. Not as snapshots or sounds. But their entire world, all at once, every corner of it, as it exists here and at this moment. Their senses flood with an unyielding array of sights and sounds and smells and tastes. They're in crowded city streets and on dusty village roads, atop mountains and in valleys, sailing on the ocean and roaring at supersonic speed across the skies. And they aren't just in places; they're also surrounded by images and events indicative of their times. There's a double helix, and now here's a partial map of the human genome. Suddenly they're on a farm with Dolly the sheep, the first mammal cloned from an adult cell, created at the end of the twentieth century. Other images and sensations quickly replace the ones they're witnessing—stem cells and in vitro fertilization, sonograms of children in the womb, researchers working in laboratories, filling vials, peering through microscopes, holding test tubes to the light.

Their minds are being bombarded as well, almost as if they're living each of these moments in an instant.

"This is your world today." Joshua's voice resonates in their minds. "A world on the brink of discovery. But it is also our world as well. Our genesis, if you will. Your race is about to embark on a series of what you will consider to be miraculous discoveries—from things as simple as parents choosing the sex of their children to the development of stem-cell research that will unlock the cures for a whole host of diseases. Our history records show that in your early twenty-first century, there was considerable debate about the ethical uses of this new technology. Some feared that researchers were 'playing God' by manipulating human genes. Others claimed that religious and ethical taboos were preventing your political leaders from grasping the true benefits of genetic engineering." Joshua looks at the floor wistfully. "These debates will soon wash away."

More experiences now. Their time again as historical playback. Smoke rises up into an image of a bright-blue sky, now covering what had been the entire breadth of the ceiling. The effect is disconcerting; the sky and surrounding village seem to go on for miles. To their senses they are standing in the center of a village in what they assume to be the Middle East. Their noses find in the air the sickening smell of burning rubber, the stench of human decay. Their ears are filled with the sounds of mourning as survivors of this attack scurry around them to find loved ones. And now all around them are corpses—women clutching their dead children to their breasts, men collapsed in doorways and on dusty streets. All of the bodies look strangled, ruined. *The Iraqi poison gas attacks on the Kurds,* Donovan realizes.

They're in a crowded Japanese street. Hundreds of Japanese men and women are fleeing a subway station, their mouths covered with handkerchiefs and shirts. The scientists flinch as this terrified mob runs toward them and then through them, disappearing as quickly as they had appeared. The three move from scene to scene with wrenching speed. Suddenly they're standing in deserts with mushroom clouds exploding overhead; they're running with hazmat teams in full gear as they enter office buildings; they're postal employees sorting mail in respirator masks and latex gloves; they're soldiers in gas masks—and always the smell of death, of so many, many bodies, hangs in their nostrils.

"Terrorism," Joshua mutters as he materializes in the center of this swirling mass of death and carnage. "The great scourge of your age. And more than simple terrorism"—here the images shift to familiar scenes of car bombs in Israel and Iraq and Northern Ireland, of the Twin Towers of the World Trade Center crumbling into dust—"but chemical and biological terrorism of a kind you have only begun to witness. Soon attacks will come in such unimagined ways and cause so much death and destruction that the populace at large will forget its qualms about the manipulation of human genetics. The public will soon demand protection from chemical, biological, and nuclear attacks. Funded by government grants, researchers around the world will join forces in a global effort to cure or lessen the effects of smallpox, ricin, mustard gas, anthrax, nuclear radiation, and the like. And more remarkably, the gene-therapy cures will come with stunning frequency. The world will rejoice in the knowledge that many of the most insidious forms of terrorists attacks will be a thing of the past."

Happy voices now. An electric thrill fills the air. And around them a cacophony of overlapping images of scientists and politicians, doctors and nurses, scholars and ordinary people from all walks of life praising the work of researchers and geneticists. Donovan and the others marvel at the sight of so many familiar faces, eminent people of their era, talking about things that haven't happened yet. These events might well be in the future, but it's their world they're seeing, their time.

Joshua's voice rises over the din of conflicting sounds. "Terrorism would not end soon. There would still be deaths—too many deaths—from more conventional means of attack. But terrorism would be dealt a crippling blow, as its perpetrators realized that it could not evolve into more hideous forms. And the human race would come to understand the remarkable benefits of genetic engineering—as your corporations would soon realize."

Donovan's mind explodes with thoughts, images, feelings—all not his own. He's drifting down a river of rationality, each obstacle in his path being overcome by sheer force of nature. Or perhaps force of *will.* With this new technology, humanity has been given a new choice. And making the choice is as inevitable as taking a step, as likely as all the previous choices had been. In the twentieth century, more and more people gained the freedom to choose what type of education they would receive, what types of jobs they wanted to apply for, what neighborhoods they wanted their children to grow up in. Even now, in his own century, Donovan could see how new technologies would allow them to improve their overall health and well-being in unimagined ways. He understands the choice being made implicitly, though not as Alan Donovan. He views the world of his time as Joshua would and is ashamed.

No, he thinks as he fights to retain his identity, *I'm Alan Donovan. I'm a man, and I'm alive here and now. I'm thirty-five years old. I've been sick. I've known pain. I had my appendix removed when I was twelve. I have scar tissue on my lungs from pneumonia. I'm imperfect. I'm human.*

More images now, coming faster and faster. Scenes of congressional committees and laboratories, of people discussing issues, working, *acting.* Scenes of mass immunizations, of people lining up in hospitals and clinics to receive vaccines. Now scenes of people in wheelchairs walking, of men and women and children smiling and leaving hospitals.

Elapsed-time images of cancer cells shrinking, of severed nerve cells growing, of lives again and again given a second chance.

This is what genetic engineering gave to your race. Donovan hears Joshua's voice ringing in a far corner of his mind. How much like his own it sounds now. *The ability to prolong and improve your lives from the very moment of conception. Once geneticists were able to unravel the coding of human DNA, they could target specific defective genes and either eliminate or repair them. Does your family have a gene for heart disease? In your near future, that gene can be repaired as easily as replacing a defective part in a clock. And why stop at curing diseases and preventing chemical and biological attacks through mass inoculations? Why not remake humanity itself better, smarter, stronger, more beautiful? It was, as one chairman of an American genetics conglomerate put it, "a market waiting to be exploited."*

They are moving into the middle of the century now, 2040 or so. They're in an endless room filled with bodies. But the smells surrounding them are not of death and decay but the antiseptic aroma of a medical facility. Surrounding them are lengthy rows of headless bodies attached to life-support machines, each monitored by technicians with electronic notepads. Kept alive by artificial means, these bodies exist solely for the purposes of organ harvesting, medical testing, and the collection of raw material for further genetic testing. Though such clones do not exist in Donovan's era, he finds these clones to be strangely primitive. And somehow he also knows that these early clones open up entirely new fields of medicine.

In an instant, they are whisked into an operating room—white, clean, bright. Doctors are attaching cloned legs and hearts to patients. They're in a medical laboratory. The clones are being shot up with drugs, their DNA sequences manipulated in an effort to accelerate the development of vaccines.

It only makes sense, Donovan realizes. *It's inevitable that we will cure cancer, AIDS, all the great scourges of our age. And it's just as inevitable that, for people who could afford to, gene therapy and cloning will be used to improve appearance and overall health.*

It's October 2042. They're in the streets of New York around Times Square, the LED lights illuminating angry faces. Protesters swirl around them, marching with signs declaring "Clone Rights." In another moment they're in the midst of another demonstration, this time with people carrying signs for "Human Rights" on the Mall in Washington, DC. And now the smell of incense fills their nostrils as they stand in a church, listening to a priest condemn the sin of vanity and beg his congregation to think of the importance of the next life. And now there's the taste of disinfectants in their mouths again as they walk through a hospital, looking at withered, haggard people dying in their beds. And now they're in a living room with a family watching a news broadcaster talking about the widening health-care gap between rich and poor in the United Kingdom.

It's the middle of the century now. A new world order is emerging. Those able and willing to have their own clones grown and maintained throughout their lives do so. Those with ethical reservations or without the means to grow their own clones do not. And between them, those fighting for the civil rights of clones, people lobbying for better, more ethical treatment of clones. They argue that it's a violation of basic human rights to grow headless clones solely for medical purposes, and propose adding higher consciousness to the basic matrix.

Donovan's thoughts fly like leaves in a hurricane.

But no one's listening. And why should they? There's too much money being made in making headless clones for the privileged to have genetic corporations legislated out of existence. Separate societies are emerging, with the ethical, religious, and poor on one end and the rich and powerful on the other. By the early 2060s, the disparity between the two groups has grown so great that many countries are on the brink of civil war.

They see images of riots in the streets, of buildings burning and police descending on mobs with sophisticated laser-like stun guns, of assassinations and explosions and chaos. A man holding a placard is trampled to death. A doctor entering a cloning center is knifed by a waiting mob. Building after building explodes, debris descending like a man-made snowstorm.

They're in government offices now. Politicians are bickering with one another around tables. All of the rooms smell of sweaty panic and fear. Their rule teetering on the brink of overthrow, the lawmakers begin to act. Political realities force countries to fall into line like dominoes. Universal health care is granted to all citizens, thereby pacifying a large portion of the population by allowing the poor access to cloning privileges around the world.

August 31, 2072. A special session of Congress has been called to pass the first clone-rights bill in the United States. The bill bans the creation of headless clones in favor of clones with full intelligence. Whoever wishes to create a clone, either of themselves or a deceased loved one, is allowed to do so. Within a decade, the clones are working and living so closely with ordinary humans that most people cannot tell the difference.

More laboratories. Medical techniques are being perfected; organs are being cloned without needing to create headless bodies. Yet, at the same time, the need for cloning human body parts or organs is diminishing as the human beings with the means to do so are reaching unparalleled levels of physical and mental perfection in utero. These new genetically perfect humans have come to be known as the Purebreds. Both they and the clones are generally doing jobs better and more efficiently than most ordinary humans, an ever-shrinking portion of the population growing more and more marginalized in the new societal hierarchy by clinging to an outmoded definition of humanity.

It's 2092. They are surrounded by people, almost impossibly beautiful people, doing even more impossible things. A man is running a mile in under two minutes. A female scientist is demonstrating a new type of fusion energy. A doctor is administering a new childhood vaccine to an infant. A baseball player is heading for home plate, having broken the single-season home run record of one hundred and sixty-five. Astronauts are inside their spaceship, zooming out to Pluto at one-half light speed. And among them, not a single human being untouched by genetic manipulation.

Why shouldn't we be at the top of every field? Why shouldn't we be the greatest scientists, doctors, professors, financiers? Weren't we bred for this? Weren't our bodies designed to exceed what you thought was the peak of human perfection? Isn't it only logical that only Purebreds and clones win all of the Nobel Prizes, break sports records, reinvigorate your stale scientific pursuits? Weren't we designed to dominate?

Weren't we designed to rule?

January 2101. They are in a crowd, shivering against a cold gust as they stand on the steps of the Capitol in Washington, DC. The first clone is being sworn in as president of the United States. His vice president is a Purebred.

Clones and Purebreds now make up almost two-thirds of the population, thinks Donovan, now completely seeing the world through Joshua's eyes. *The Purebreds are used to harvesting DNA and genetic material for further experimentation. We are what humanity has always striven to become. We're greater than the sum of our frailties and weaknesses. We're no longer bound by them. We're Purebreds. We're clones. I am a clone. I have lived for fifty-five years and have not yet lived even a quarter of my life span. I have strength and endurance and intelligence. I am embarrassed by what our race once was. It's good that we have moved beyond what we were. It's good that we wiped them out so long ago. It's good that we've destroyed every last vestige—*

Destroyed? the part of him that is still Alan Donovan questions. His voice rises inside his mind, shouting at Joshua. *What has become of the human race?*

By 2150, a distinct underclass of nongenetically engineered, non-cloned humans emerges. Unable to compete with the upper classes, they are forced into menial labor jobs across the solar system, willing to do anything to survive. The Purebreds and clones, however, do nothing to help the original humans' status, seeing them more and more as a distinct—and inferior—race.

The last war between the Purebreds and clones and the original humans occurs in 2230. The conflict begins with an attempt by the human population to rise up against its masters.

The battle is swift. Those humans not killed are banished from our society, relocated beyond the borders of our cities to areas without light, shelter, or adequate food or water. We call these places the Shadow Territories.

The stench of these lands fills Donovan with equal parts revulsion and pity. He walks among sick and dying humans, feeling the crunch of dirt, gravel, and bones beneath his feet. Men and women and children huddle together beside garbage heaps, burning whatever they can for warmth, their skin thin and slack on their prominent bones. Some of the men hunt whatever wild game is available with crude bows and arrows or spears. Others agree to work in labor camps on the Moon, mining minerals, or on Jupiter's moon Europa, where water is a central export. Years pass, but human hardship never does—more squalor, more disease, more war, more death. He is standing in a blasted-out house. Rotting timbers lay strewn about. Pictures are scattered and broken. He bends down to pick up what seems to be a doll's head and realizes that it is a child's skull.

Within two or three generations, by the dawn of the twenty-fourth century, the last original humans are extinct, Joshua's thoughts inform him, *killed off by disease, malnutrition, and fighting among their tribes for dominance. We Purebreds and clones hardly notice, as we are more interested in perfecting our utopia without disease, crime, or other ailments. We continue to spread across the solar system. And we are already looking toward the stars.*

Donovan and the others watch as technologies almost beyond their comprehension transform the solar system. Centuries pass in an instant. Mars is terraformed into an Earthlike environment; the seas under Europa's ice begin to be exploited. Over the next two hundred years, the Purebreds and the clones alter the environments of all of the solar system's planets and moons, creating entire worlds for them to populate. Then they turn their attention back to Earth.

Having been abused by the original humans for so long, Earth, a slag heap of humanity's imperfections, must also undergo a transformation. We Purebreds and clones terraform it, bringing it back to a more natural state. All remnants of original human civilization are eliminated, leaving only a few ultramodern cities of our own design and wonderful natural preserves. Before long, nothing remains of the original humans. Their cities, their monuments, their history, even their bones . . . all gone.

Earth is now a Garden of Eden.

Our garden.

Donovan is standing on a hillside. Beneath him is a green-blue sea crashing against the rocks. Far into the distance, he can see more hills rising through dense forests. They burn pure gold in the light of early morning. White spires jut up from them, a city reflecting that same light in a brilliant array. The sight is so beautiful it fills him with anguish. *We died so this world might live,* he thinks.

Suddenly, in the distance he sees a flash of blinding-white fire, then a muffled sound like a thunderclap. He knows this from somewhere. Another time and place. A moment later, something streaks into the sky, a plume of white smoke trailing behind. *A rocket,* he marvels, his mind childlike in the wake of all that he has seen. *A rocket to the stars.*

The first faster-than-light ship on its way to Alpha Centauri, he realizes. He remembers, though the launch has not yet happened. *Those who made the trip return home to a hero's welcome. They tell of new worlds to exploit and prepare to spread out to the stars. What no one knows at the time, however, is that most will never live to make the journey.*

"A plague," says Joshua, his voice tingling at the edge of Donovan's mind, growing fainter. "It's the only word for it. A mutant strain of disease from beyond the stars and for which we had no cure. We had no frame of reference for what it was. We did not even know why we were getting sick. There had been no record of disease on Earth for the better part of five hundred years. People continued to work, sleep, eat, and travel—around the world, around the solar system. Within six months every outpost was seeing plague outbreaks in record numbers. By the time we knew what it was we were fighting, it was too late. You see, in accelerating the human-cloning process, we had altered certain sequences in the DNA strand. Most notably, those involving the immune system. Before long, people were dying off so quickly we had neither the space nor the time to bury all of them. Bodies were unceremoniously cremated in an attempt to stop the spread of the disease."

Joshua appears before him, his face worn with horrors that had yet to come into being. The connection between their minds is broken, and Donovan's consciousness is his own again. They stand on the hillside, looking over the tranquil green sea.

"DNA can repair itself, copy itself. But for reasons we cannot ascertain, our DNA could not repair the damage done by this plague. We returned to the original map of the human genome made in the late twentieth century and attempted to repair the damage to our own DNA by using your people's genome as a template. But having the map didn't lead to a solution. We then tried to genetically engineer viruses and bacteria to fight the plague. Again we were thwarted. The plague continued to mutate as more and more of our people died. We were faced with extinction. And so we came up with a desperate plan. We needed to harvest samples of original human DNA. Hair follicles, blood and tissue samples, anything that we could find. It was our belief that, with these unmolested samples, we might have been able to synthesize a vaccine. Here our folly was revealed. The terraforming of Earth had removed all traces of original human DNA from the planet. All was lost, so it seemed. Until one scientist came forward with a radical idea. For decades he had studied wormholes and their movements. He and his team had devised a way to create wormholes . . . and send matter through them. Time travel. Imperfect, but the process worked, at least according to a few preliminary tests. We now saw that, if we could send representatives back from our era, we could stop this future from taking place. Work together to create a society where our kind and yours could live in harmony. A potentially flawless plan. But as you can see, we failed. Either the wormhole proved unstable or our calculations were incorrect—in any event, we were deposited here on the Moon about two and a half million years before our target date: Earth in the early twenty-first century. Now unable to contact your race and warn them, we developed an alternate plan. We would use the Moon's vast supplies of helium-3 to maintain our ship, with the idea of blowing open a portion of the Moon in order to attract your attention sometime in the early twenty-first century.

"Here, in this preliminary overview, I have given you a general understanding of how our society evolved from yours over the last seven hundred years." Joshua takes a step toward them and gestures at the central consoles on the bridge. "In the memory banks of the *Astraeus*, you will find a more complete history of our mission to travel to your time. In addition, we have included information on how to cure many of the ailments that are still rife on your world. A gift, and perhaps a conciliatory offering. We will never know if we were successful. But know we died with the knowledge that our deaths would help to bring about a future more prosperous than the one we left behind. I can think of no greater honor. That is all I have to tell you. My mission is now yours. You must return to Earth and tell your governments what you have seen and learned here. Take back the mission logs from the ship and show them to your scientists. If you do not, then our mission will be in vain. Mark my words: the future of the world is in jeopardy. We have precious little time left. Good luck and farewell."

Donovan felt himself being lifted up, up, up into the sky, watching the ground recede beneath him before being unceremoniously dropped back into his body. He scanned the *Astraeus*'s bridge, then collapsed onto his knees. He looked up and saw Soong and Zell both prone on the deck, breathing heavily. Joshua's tour of the future had wreaked havoc on their minds as well.

They lay there in silence. After a moment, Zell spoke. "I think I would have preferred little green men."

"I saw it all," Soong said, turning over to stare at the ceiling. "I saw it all through his eyes. I saw our world end; I felt it die."

"So did I," Donovan said.

"We all did," Zell replied soberly. He was uncharacteristically quiet for a time. "It's fitting, isn't it? Nature, the very thing we've spent generations trying to buckle to our will, will ultimately prove to be our undoing."

"Well," said Soong struggling to her feet, "let's not waste time discussing it. Let's get to work and figure out what we can do *now*."

"Soong's right," said Donovan. "There'll be other chances to debate the philosophical implications here." He stood up as well. The promise of action wiped away the remnants of Joshua's mind connection. "We need to figure out how to contact the *Copernicus*, get Benny and Yeoh down here. We'll need them to download as best they can everything this ship has got."

"Do you think they'll be able to?" asked Zell. "Remember, this ship is seven hundred years ahead of us."

"True," replied Donovan, "but their mission was supposed to succeed. They had *planned* to give us this information on Earth. There must be data ports somewhere on board that can adapt to our technology."

"While the two of you are working on that problem," said Soong, "I'd like to perform an autopsy on Joshua. I'm certain his physiology will reveal as much as his message." Soong cast a long look around the ship. "I'm afraid I'm not up on my Greek mythology. Who was Astraeus?"

"One of the Titans," said Zell, thinking of the terrible future Joshua had shown them. "The god of dusk and the coming of night."

Chapter 15

The Chinese and American fleets were first seen converging off the coast of Taiwan on June 29. A local Taiwanese television station was the first to broadcast images of the seemingly endless array of ships, but American stations quickly picked up the story and shifted their focus from the Moon mission to the South China Sea. Each channel then related the events of the past few weeks in an endless loop, from the assassination of the Taiwanese separatist leader to the announcement of Taiwan's declaration of independence. This was followed by a declaration from the President of the People's Republic of China, announcing that the Chinese government would be sending its fleet to ensure that "no armed rebellion would occur in the Chinese province of Taiwan." His statement was followed by one from the President of the United States, who said she would be sending the Pacific Fleet to "reaffirm Taiwan's position in the 'one-China, two-systems' arrangement."

News commentators and pundits filled the airwaves on every twenty-four-hour news station. Many compared the situation with that of the Cuban missile crisis of October 1962. While few believed that a nuclear war was imminent, most ominously predicted that a conventional war between the United States and China could be under way in a matter of hours.

"Whatever they tell you now, sir, is frankly bullshit," Benny groused as he sat in his dusty space suit inside the *Copernicus*. "There's no way that ascent engine's gonna get fixed. It's crumpled up like a tin can."

Wilson glanced again at the computer screen image before him of the ascent engine's mangled nozzle and nodded stiffly. He had come to the same conclusion hours ago. He popped another Advil for his knee, still forgoing anything stronger in the interest of keeping his mind sharp. The way he saw it, they would likely have to rebuild the entire engine from scratch. And even if they had the spare parts for the work, they wouldn't be able to complete the job before their air scrubbers were finally overloaded by carbon dioxide. Something about the tone of Mission Control's progress reports over the last eighteen hours had been the clincher, each more assuring as the hours progressed. They were working on repair scenarios for the ascent engine—just be patient, they said. But Wilson knew in his gut that they were just biding time. Maybe they wanted to hold out hope until the last minute. Or maybe they were just trying to find the courage to tell them that the *Copernicus* would never leave the Moon.

"So," Wilson said, looking up from his computer screen, "is that also your assessment, Dr. Yeoh?"

"Truthfully, Colonel," Yeoh said with a sigh, "I had pretty much thought that the first time I got a good look at the engine. The rest of the ship is running A-OK, considering. I've been running diagnostics on the remote power-up procedure for the *Tai-Ping*. But . . . from where I'm sitting, the *Copernicus* cannot fly."

"So what do we do now?"

"We build the thing from scratch if we have to, Benevisto. And we get Houston to help us out on a repair scenario the two of you devise."

"But sir, the oxygen—"

"I'm not giving up, Benevisto. You shouldn't either."

"Colonel Wilson," Yeoh began, "have you heard any more news about the Taiwan situation?"

"Nothing. They haven't moved."

Benny patted Yeoh on the back. "Don't worry, Bruce. These guys are all a lotta hot air. They're just making a big show like we did with the Russians back in '62. Nothing's gonna happen."

Yeoh nodded, eyes on the floor. "You're probably right."

"Sir," Benny said, trying to divert attention, "what about the archeology team? Any word?"

"Not since they descended into the fissure."

"Probably interference from the cave," Yeoh mumbled. "They can't get a signal out."

"Regardless of our archeology team's status, it doesn't change our job," Wilson said. "We've got to fix that engine even if we have to cannibalize the rest of the ship. We're getting off this rock if I have to get out and push."

Donovan rubbed his eyes and let out a sigh. In the time that had passed since they had received Joshua's download—as they were now calling it—they had been sifting through the memory banks of the *Astraeus*. What they had found was no more heartening than the future they had witnessed. A civilization thriving, bursting with pride at the magnitude of its own technological accomplishments. Then undone by its own conceit.

How very much like our own, he thought, grimly realizing the bitter truth of that sentiment.

Soong had found a stretcher to take Joshua's body down to the medlab to conduct an autopsy. Zell, meanwhile, had been busying himself trying to further probe the ship's technology. While they had found that the *Astraeus* was powered by some sort of engine located deep within its core, they had been unable to determine how the vessel itself was controlled. Finally, Zell discovered, much to his shock, that by simply using a voice command, the ship could generate consoles and controls using the same holographic technology it had used to play Joshua's message. The readouts were fully interactive and real to the touch. As Zell ran his hands over one of the panels, he could imagine the rivets holding the console together and the circuit boards humming underneath. When he took his hand away, the screen suddenly resolidified and reassumed its inert purple hue.

"That's impossible," he breathed, awestruck. "These screens are some kind of matter-energy conversion ports. But it can't be. The amount of energy needed for such a device would be—"

"Likely created by a civilization capable of moving a ship of this size through time," Donovan said.

"That is . . . quite impressive," Zell said. "Somehow seeing these screens go through their permutations makes me believe in time travel all the more."

"Wait. Are you saying that you actually doubted what you experienced in Joshua's download?"

"No," Zell answered. "Not really. But this," he said, tapping the screen lightly with the tips of his fingers, "is more in keeping with our life experiences—having controls, looking at screens to procure information. It somehow seems more *real* as a technology than having an overview of future history downloaded directly into our heads."

"Strange as it is to say, but I believe all of this, Elias. The time travel, the clones, all of it. These people really came from the future to change the past."

Zell smiled in agreement as he studied the screen. "But to the specific matter at hand. Let's think about this. If there are no apparent controls for the ship—"

"Then the crew just simply generated whatever controls or tools they needed. It's like a souped-up 3-D printer, capable of creating anything in an instant." Donovan clapped his hands. "Let's try something. Computer, could you activate the, um, bridge's navigation controls at this station?"

"Why the hell do you want navigation controls?" Zell wondered.

"I'm curious."

A second later the purple screen before them winked out of existence and was replaced by a series of buttons, not dissimilar to the buttons displayed on a tablet's touch screen. The top half of the screen seemed to be devoted to a real-time image coming from an exterior monitor or camera, but at present displayed nothing more than moon rocks.

Zell rubbed his chin. "Miraculous."

The crackle of their communicators broke up Donovan and Zell's reverie. They picked up their headsets as Soong's voice rang in their ears.

"Gentlemen," she said, "I think you might want to come down to the medlab."

"What have you found?" asked Donovan.

"I'm not entirely sure."

After a long hike belowdecks, the two men arrived outside the medlab. The space was set up in a makeshift manner, with Soong using whatever tools she was able to carry with her into the crater. With power up and running, the area was now flooded in light. Joshua's body lay on the slab in the center of the room. He had been opened up with a traditional

Y-incision, running from the shoulders to midchest, then down to the pubic region. His entire chest cavity was on display. Although both Donovan and Zell had uncovered numerous bodies in their careers, there was something so real, so immediate about what they were seeing that both men raised a cautionary fist to their mouths.

"There's very little blood," Zell observed.

Soong walked about the table, snapping off her latex gloves. "A corpse has no blood pressure, Doctor. The only blood we ever see is that which is produced by gravity. And in an environment like this, in gravity one-sixth that of Earth's, that's apt to be very little."

She walked over to her instrument tray, pulling out a set of pincers. She drew on another pair of gloves and walked back over to the body. "Let me show you what I've found." She sat down and leaned in close to the open cavity, poking around. After a moment, she turned her head over her shoulder. Donovan and Zell were still rooted to their spot.

"Would you please come here?" she said. "I am certain he won't bite."

The men cautiously padded over.

Soong shook her head. "Donovan and Zell. The fearless adventurers." She resumed her explanation. "Now here we have Joshua's chest cavity. Notice anything strange?"

Donovan and Zell peered in, looking in earnest, then picked their heads up and shook them almost in unison.

"Nothing?" Soong said. "Nothing at all?"

She was met with the same blank stares. Soong stood up, eyeing them both with a mix of surprise and the kind of exasperation a teacher might have for a slow student. She fixed them with a chiding glare. "Put your hands over your hearts."

Instinctively, each man placed a hand over his heart in the traditional Pledge of Allegiance maneuver.

"Good," she said. "You know *something* about anatomy. Now look here." She pointed to where Joshua's heart was. "Notice the two chambers?

One atrium and one ventricle. Humans have a four-chambered heart. Two atria and two ventricles."

"What you're describing is impossible," Zell said.

"Not really," Soong said. "Two-chambered hearts can be found even on Earth today."

"They can?"

"Absolutely," Soong said. "In fish."

The men fell silent a moment. Then Donovan spoke. "So he could breathe underwater?"

Soong laughed. "He's got a two-chambered heart, not gills. Although I'll admit that I did check for them. You see, fish have what's called a 'single circulation' system. Blood comes in through the heart, is oxygenated, then pumped through the gills and into the body. Humans have a 'double circulation' system. Blood enters the heart, leaves the heart, travels to the lungs, then back to the heart and out into the body."

"So if he doesn't have gills, where's the blood going to be oxygenated?" Donovan asked.

"Good question, and I wish I had the answer. My setup here is much too primitive to get the kind of information we're looking for."

"Okay," said Zell. "Here's what I want to know. We know they're engineered. So this discovery is less shocking than it could be. However, some things still don't add up. Number one, if the purpose was not to have him breathe underwater, then why give him a single circulatory system?"

"Again, that's something that a more complex autopsy might reveal. However, it might shed some light onto the kind of world Joshua was living in." Soong paced in an effort to jog her thoughts. "All right, mammals have a four-chambered heart because they have a greater demand for oxygen. Just maintaining our body temperature requires more energy than fish or frogs. We also absorb more oxygen through the lungs than we do through the skin, again unlike fish. In order to meet these high demands, we need two extra chambers to create more pressure to force the blood through the body."

"So maybe their demands weren't as high," Donovan said. "Maybe they'd found some sort of way to conserve body energy longer."

"Or maybe there were changes in the atmosphere on Earth in their time," Zell said. "Or on one of those terraformed planets or moons. Maybe they need less air or have found some sort of way to conserve the air they have. The other question I have is, how were they able to do this?"

"I don't know," Soong said. "I've heard of Nazi experiments that attempted to crossbreed humans and animals with horrifying results. Somehow, and for some unknown reason, these people seemed to have figured it out. I want to get a look at the files Joshua has in the memory banks of this ship. For all we know, fish aren't the only animals they've experimented with. They could be using different pulmonary types for different tasks, different environments—especially if the worlds they terraformed weren't exactly Earth normal. The list is endless."

Zell ran his hands through his hair. "Whatever the case is, there's more to the puzzle than we ever knew. Now, if only there was a way to communicate with the *Copernicus*. They could probably talk us through downloading all of Joshua's information and getting it back to Earth."

"Maybe there is," Donovan declared.

Soong turned to them. "You think the computer can contact the *Copernicus*?"

"I wouldn't put anything past a technology that can download seven hundred years of history into someone's mind or conjure up consoles out of thin air."

"Be careful," Soong warned. "We're really working without an instruction manual now."

Zell spoke up. "Computer, can you find the ship located on the surface, in the Ocean of Storms?"

"YES."

"Do you have the capability to make radio contact with it?"

"YES."

"Open a channel," Donovan commanded, then smiled at his comrades. "I always wanted to say that."

"CHANNEL OPEN. YOU MAY NOW PROCEED WITH YOUR TRANSMISSION."

"*Copernicus*, this is Donovan. Do you read me? Over."

A second later Wilson's voice filled the medlab. "Donovan, this is *Copernicus*. How the hell are you sending this transmission? Are you back on the surface?"

"Not exactly, Colonel." Donovan couldn't help but smile. "We're talking to you from the starship *Astraeus*."

June 29
Johnson Space Center
Houston, Texas
3:31 p.m.

John Dieckman poured himself another cup of coffee. He knew it would probably fill his stomach with acid, but he needed the caffeine badly. He hadn't slept much in the past thirty-six hours, refusing to leave his post despite the gentle warnings he had received from his superiors. He needed to be in Mission Control. There seemed to be no one else who still believed they had a ghost of a chance of repairing the *Copernicus*. Nobody had said as much as of yet, but he could tell by the eyes of his engineers that they had given up hope long ago. So much for the can-do spirit of NASA. He peered at the *Copernicus*'s blueprints again through his reading glasses, hoping to find some way of cannibalizing the ship's systems to repair the engine and get the crew back into orbit.

A hand gripped his shoulder, and he flinched at the touch. He turned to find Cal Walker standing behind him, a beatific look on his face.

"Any progress, John?"

Deke pulled off his glasses and rubbed his bleary eyes. "None. How're things on your end with the sim?"

"We're not having much luck either. When we designed these systems, we never planned for a complete rebuilding of the ascent engine on the Moon's surface."

Deke smiled weakly. "I thought you Apollo boys planned for every contingency."

Walker lifted the blueprints from the desk. "Not for a catastrophic failure of the ascent engine. It breaks your heart to know that nothing can be done."

Dieckman stood up. "I'm not ready to call it a day just yet. We've managed to get the *Tai-Ping* up and running. We'll fix this problem too."

"Of course, John," Walker said, patting him on the shoulder. "I meant to imply nothing else. Perhaps I'm just too old and not of much use with this refit. Or perhaps I just keep thinking in the back of my mind of the scrubbers. Even if we find a way to fix the engine, the scrubbers may give out long before the crew can effect any repair."

"I'm not at that step yet, Cal," Deke said, taking the blueprints back. "I've got to fix the damn engine first."

Walker glanced at his watch. "Perhaps we both need some rest. We'll see things better after a little shut-eye."

"You rest, Cal. I want to look this over a little more."

"Of course. I'll see you in a couple of hours."

Walker stepped out of the room and walked down the hall. Around him he could hear the tired voices of engineers and mission controllers debating repair procedures. He pulled his phone from his pocket and dialed.

"This is Walker. I just wanted to give you an update. It looks like NASA will be unable to make repairs in time. Our work won't be threatened."

June 29
4:23 p.m., Houston Time
6 days, 10 hours, 8 minutes, Mission Elapsed Time

"So to sum up, Donovan, you're on a ship, from the future, that came back into the past to stop genetic engineering from causing the extinction of the entire human race?" Wilson said in an even tone. "And you got this from the interactive hologram of a guy who's been dead for about two and a half million years?"

Donovan sighed. It had taken him about a half hour to bring Wilson up to speed about their situation. It took additional time to convince Wilson, Benny, and Yeoh that no one had been drinking any of Zell's smuggled scotch down in the fissure. Once Donovan had finally convinced his crewmates that the tale of the *Astraeus* was at least plausible, Benny and Yeoh began peppering him with questions about the ship's technology and power supplies while at the same time explaining the difficulties they were facing in repairing the ascent engine.

"Helium-3," Yeoh said, shaking his head in amazement. "Incredible. Powering that ship for millions of years."

"If we could tap into it," Benny added, still in a state of wonder over the scientists' discoveries, "then we could repair *Copernicus* in a flash."

"What if we didn't have to?" Yeoh wondered, a smile in his voice.

Zell lifted his head from his screen. "What do you mean?"

"Well," Yeoh began, "the ship is able to generate stable wormholes that move through both time and space. If we could figure out how to use one, then it could be possible that the ship could transport all of us back to Earth."

"It didn't work too damn well when *they* tried it," Zell grumbled. "These 'stable wormholes,' as you call them, deposited this ship on the Moon more than two million years in the past."

"Assuming this is all true, people," Wilson said, clearing his throat, "Dr. Zell's right. It's too risky."

Yeoh chimed in. "But maybe we could do a test run to see if it works."

Wilson looked unconvinced. "What've you got in mind, Doctor?"

"If we can figure out how to generate a stable wormhole, maybe we could send something small from the *Astraeus* to here and back again. If it works, then we can recalibrate the parameters to move us from the Moon to the Earth."

"Better be careful with your coordinates," Zell added. "We don't want to wind up in the middle of the Antarctic or the bottom of the ocean."

"That's what the test would be for," Yeoh replied, his clipped tone showing uncharacteristic annoyance.

"Not on a person or anything," Benny stressed. "At least, not initially."

"But we need to figure out how to make it work first," Soong added. "And that's been the problem we've had down here: giving the computer the right commands."

Donovan pulled a small rock hammer from his pocket. "I'm for it. How's about we try it on this?"

"Let's not get ahead of ourselves," Wilson said soberly. "I certainly haven't approved this."

"Well, I certainly don't approve of it, Colonel," Zell said. "But have you a better idea of getting us home?"

June 29
The White House
Washington, DC
5:30 p.m.

"That'll be all for now, ladies and gentlemen. Thank you."

The President's national-security team gathered up their papers and rose in unison. As they began to file out of the Oval Office, the President walked back toward her desk and took off her suit jacket.

"General McKenna, could you stay for a moment?"

McKenna looked up from collecting his briefing papers. "Certainly, ma'am."

The President waited until the last of her staff left the office. Once the door clicked shut, she gestured for the general to take a chair and offered him a drink. The President made up two neat, short glasses of scotch and handed one off to McKenna.

"Jim," the President began as she swirled her drink around in its glass, "what if I told you that there might be a way out of this Taiwan mess?"

"Ma'am?"

The President took a swallow. "Despite the official line about us having cut off diplomatic relations with China, our two countries have maintained contacts through informal channels. I've just received a proposal from the Chinese government that could very well save our necks."

"Ma'am, I don't understand."

"I'm sorry." The President rubbed her temples. "I don't mean to be mysterious. I'm just tired. The long and short of it is that the Chinese are willing to back off and leave Taiwan alone provided we share all technologies we discover on the Moon with them and them alone."

The general nodded. "But surely they know we've already promised to share our findings with the world."

"Of course. But they're assuming—probably rightly—that no other country will be able to get to the Moon to verify what we've discovered for at least the next decade or two. Russia has no plans to get to the lunar surface in the near future. The Europeans don't have the money and haven't shown any real interest in human spaceflight. India could do it, but if they divert money to their fledgling space program, they'd stand a chance of hurting their economy."

McKenna sipped his drink. "Even if we agree to such a proposal, Madam President, there's no guarantee we'll be able to deliver. The latest reports from NASA indicate that there's a strong chance the crew won't make it back from the Moon."

"And with them all knowledge of whatever they might have uncovered. I know. But the Chinese seem willing to venture to the Moon with us again if need be. And if there's any chance to avoid bloodshed—"

"If you're asking my opinion, ma'am, I'd agree to the deal—provided that the Chinese sign a nonaggression pact with regard to Taiwan."

"I doubt I could get any public promise. More likely an under-the-table gentlemen's agreement."

"The Chinese are good to their word, ma'am. But they also need to find a way to save face."

The President set her drink down on the desk and sat on the edge nearest McKenna. "I want an honest assessment from you, General. If this thing goes to the mattresses, what're our chances?"

"In a conventional war? Not good, ma'am. Our forces are more technologically advanced, but as far as actual manpower is concerned—"

"I know. I guess I just wanted someone trustworthy to tell me. The rest of the Joint Chiefs have been assuring me that we've got the manpower ready, but I can read numbers. Our forces are dispersed all over the world. China's are concentrated in the mainland. They wouldn't even have to call in additional forces from Tibet to take us on." The

President shook her head. "So we just have to hope for a miracle from the Moon."

June 29
10:31 p.m., Houston Time
6 days, 16 hours, 16 minutes, Mission Elapsed Time

Donovan had been surprised that Wilson was so willing to keep the discovery of the *Astraeus* out of his transmissions to NASA. He had assumed the lieutenant colonel would want to issue a full report ASAP, but he seemed more than willing to hold off until they had completed their wormhole experiments.

"They wouldn't believe it anyway," Wilson had assured him, still not entirely convinced he believed it all himself.

Things must be more desperate with the ascent engine than Wilson let on, Donovan realized.

It took more than three hours for Benny and Yeoh to figure out the right commands to give to the computer that would allow them to download the *Astraeus*'s wormhole protocols. During that time, Benny and Yeoh had been relaying instructions to Donovan and the others with relative ease. Their initial issue was with regard to the vessel's energy reserves. The *Astraeus*, according to their best estimates, likely had enough power left to send them home but far less than would be needed to move the entire ship through time and space. So the *Astraeus* would remain on the Moon, but Benny and Yeoh were confident that it would be able to get the six of them home.

Donovan knew little about physics, but Zell and Soong knew enough about the subject to explain stable wormholes to him in layman's terms. The *Astraeus* had been designed with both standard ion-propulsion engines and a wormhole drive. The conventional engines were intended to bring the ship to a point in space far from any celestial objects it might run into as it made the jump in time. Once in the right position, the crew set coordinates and a date into the main computer. Then the ship would accelerate while at the same time generating a stable wormhole. Once it reached the event horizon, the ship would instantly arrive at the point in time and space the crew had plotted.

However, since the ship itself wouldn't be going anywhere, there would be no need to engage the conventional engines. Yeoh had extrapolated that any vessel with the ability to form matter from energy would also likely be able to generate smaller versions of wormholes to move objects back and forth within its confines. What he planned on doing—generating one of those wormholes to send the lot of them back to Earth—would be an extension of that program but not a great one. All they would be asking the computer to do would be to invert the wormhole—put it inside the ship instead of outside it—and send them to Earth approximately one minute after they would leave the Moon. They just needed to plot very specific time and space coordinates, which, as Zell liked to point out, was easier said than done.

Yeoh lifted his glasses to his forehead to rub his tired eyes as they finished their calculations. All looked right; the numbers added up. But creating wormholes, moving matter through space and time—he found it hard to believe he was about to test out a theory that was completely beyond their capacity only a day earlier.

Yeoh cleared his throat and asked Donovan to place the rock hammer at the central coordinates of the bridge. The computer aided him in this endeavor by shining a single light on the exact coordinates.

"You got that hammer in the right spot?" Benny asked, his Brooklyn accent bellowing through the bridge.

"It's in the center of the beam."

"Refresh my memory, gentlemen," Wilson interrupted. "How exactly is that computer going to know where to place that hammer on the *Copernicus*? I don't want it popping through a bulkhead or a window and depressurizing the cabin."

"It's pretty straightforward," Yeoh explained. "I'll send the computer the exact coordinates to the center of the *Copernicus*." A pause was followed by, "Soong, do you see them on one of the screens?"

"All of them, in fact," Soong replied.

"Roger that," Yeoh replied. "Okay . . . so now all you have to do is ask the computer to send the hammer to the coordinates displayed on the bridge's screens."

"That's all?" Zell asked incredulously.

"What were you expecting, Doc?" Benny asked. "To pull a big lever or something? The whole ship is rigged for voice commands."

"Ostensibly, yes," Zell replied. "But remember that this technology failed the builders of this ship, so how do you expect us—"

Donovan touched his shoulder, a warm grin on his face. "Have faith, Elias. Nothing has ever been accomplished by believing it couldn't be done."

"Where'd you hear that rubbish?"

"Your father used to tell us that all the time."

"Which only proves that you shouldn't listen to old maniacs."

"Whenever you folks are ready," Wilson said with some irritation.

"Computer," Donovan spoke up, trying to keep his voice steady. "Do you read the coordinates displayed on the bridge's screens?"

"YES."

"Please send the rock hammer located in the center of the bridge to those coordinates exactly ten seconds into the future on my mark." Donovan glanced at his watch and waited for the second hand to reach twelve. "Mark!"

"ACCESSING WORMHOLE PROTOCOLS. INITIALIZING TEMPORAL AND SPATIAL COORDINATES. WORMHOLE FIELD INTEGRITY AT ONE HUNDRED PERCENT. ACTIVATING WORMHOLE."

Donovan, Soong, and Zell watched from a safe distance as the hammer became immersed in the wormhole. The effect was odd. At first the hammer seemed to be encased in an ever-thickening vortex, not unlike a whirlpool. As the tool became hazier inside the vortex, they could hear its metal edges clanging against the deck plating. A slight breeze then brushed past their exposed cheeks as the air sucked in to fill the vacuum that had emerged inside the vortex. A second later the hammer had blinked out of existence.

Ten miles away, the remaining crew aboard the *Copernicus* watched as their mission clock counted down ten seconds from Donovan's mark. A bubble began to form in the center of their cabin, a few inches above the flooring. The bubble seemed to morph Wilson's perception of Yeoh's face, which had suddenly taken on the properties of a fun house mirror—wide in the jaw at one moment, then narrowing at the forehead, then eyes bulging. Yeoh's face became obscured as the bubble darkened. A moment later it was gone and the hammer appeared in midair, dropping to the floor in a rush of air and a definitive clank.

The three men stared at the hammer for several long seconds. Then Benny picked it up, half-disbelieving the slight weight he felt in his hand.

Wilson pressed his mike button. "Donovan, your . . . package has been delivered."

"Are you okay?"

"We're fine, Donovan," Benny said as a smile broadened on his face. "The hammer's fine. And we're going home."

"Wait a minute, Benevisto," Wilson said suddenly. "We can't go anywhere until we run some more tests. Besides, you two have to get on the ball and help Dr. Donovan download those files from the *Astraeus*'s memory core."

"I'm sorry, sir. It's just that—"

Wilson patted his shoulder and hit his mike button again. "Donovan, we'd like to run another test. Are you ready to bring the hammer back?"

"Sure. All we need from you guys are the protocols."

Yeoh pressed his mike button. "Doctor, all you have to do is tell the computer to reverse the wormhole and bring the hammer back to the same coordinates."

"Is it back in the same location?"

Benny placed the hammer back where it fell on the deck. "Affirmative, Donovan. We're all set."

"Roger, Benny. We're all set down here."

Donovan did exactly as he was told. Wilson, Yeoh, and Benny watched and waited for the bubble to reappear, but nothing happened as the clock ticked off ten seconds. As the men glanced at one another wondering what went wrong, they were suddenly seized by an incredible sense of vertigo. The hammer began to clatter on the floor as the floor itself fell beneath them. Wilson tried to look away, but he could barely turn his head to see the moonscape around him clouding with dust.

The vortex was opening up around the ship.

They were falling. They tried to hold on to the cabin interior, but the ship itself was falling as well. Wilson wondered if an underground cavern had opened up beneath them. The sensation was not unlike the time his plane was hit by a SAM missile in Iraq, but then he could still move, still blow his hatch and parachute to safety. Now he was frozen inside his own body, inside this vertigo, inside the vortex.

Ten seconds later a much larger vortex materialized in the center of the *Astraeus*'s bridge. Zell and Soong stood transfixed as the bubble in the air began to solidify. Donovan grabbed them by their collars and shoved them over a console just as a rush of air knocked them flat.

Zell stood up first and saw the *Copernicus* sitting serenely in the center of the bridge. "My God in heaven. Alan, Soong . . ."

Soong and Donovan helped each other to their feet and peered over the console as the *Copernicus*'s hatch began to open. A moment later Yeoh appeared on the porch in his grimy space suit and shot a stream of vomit onto the deck below. Donovan rushed up the ladder to steady him. He glanced inside. Wilson and Benny were alive but groggy.

Benny smiled weakly from his prone position. "Well now, that didn't work out quite right."

Donovan, Zell, and Soong soon helped their comrades down the *Copernicus*'s ladder and onto the deck of the *Astraeus*. Yeoh pressed his face against the cool plating and groaned. Wilson asked for some water and watched in amazement as Zell ordered some from one of the ship's omnipresent screens. He reached into the screen's belly and handed a cold glass off to each of them with a grin. Wilson eyed his water suspiciously but drank it anyway.

"You look pretty good for three men who were just sucked down the drainpipe of the cosmos," Zell said, unable to contain his amusement.

"Never in my life," Yeoh muttered as he sat up. "It was incredible—there's no describing it."

Wilson wiped his mouth and glanced at Benny and Yeoh. "You two want to tell me what the hell just happened?"

The two men looked at each other sheepishly. "I don't know," Yeoh said finally. "We placed the hammer exactly where it materialized. It was in the right coordinates—"

Benny shook his head. "No, it wasn't, Bruce. It materialized a few inches above the deck. Setting it down on the deck must've screwed up the computer's targeting mechanisms."

"So it took the *entire ship* with the hammer?" Soong asked.

"The computer must have located the hammer in the general vicinity," Yeoh explained, "but was forced to widen the field in order to receive all of the targeted object."

"Receive all of it?" Wilson asked. "You're telling me there's a chance that the wormhole could've split the hammer—and therefore us—in half?"

"There was that possibility," Yeoh said, his face reddening. "We figured it wasn't likely to happen though."

"Well, now at least we understand how this ship wound up on the Moon," Donovan added as he looked around the bridge. "They must've been off with their coordinates somehow."

"And wound up crashing into the Moon instead of landing on Earth," Zell added.

"But that doesn't explain how they wound up two and a half million years in the past," Soong noted. "Remember, Joshua said that they planned on going to the early twenty-first century."

"If they couldn't get *where* they were going right, what makes you think they were any better at *when* they were going?" Benny said with a groan. "That's all beside the point now. What the hell are we gonna do now stuck inside this ship?"

Yeoh smiled at him and sat up farther. "You're far too cynical, Benny. We're *much* better off than we were."

Wilson sipped a little more water. "Care to explain that, Yeoh?"

"Well, Colonel, from what Dr. Donovan has said, this entire ship is a fully interactive matter-energy converter, a massive 3-D printer as it were. We've just seen it generate water out of thin air. It's likely the ship is also able to generate mechanisms in the same manner. Why else would it have no controls? No spare parts lying about? We could program the ascent engine's specs into the computer and, in theory, receive a perfectly functioning duplicate."

"Yeah," Benny said, "sure that'll work. But how the hell are we gonna get back to the surface?"

Yeoh shook his head. "Benny, we know the wormholes work provided we give the computer very specific coordinates. All we have to do is repair the engine, send the ship back through the wormhole, and blast off from the surface, as we had been planning to do."

"Go back through the wormhole?" Zell repeated. "Are you out of your mind? The damn thing almost killed the three of you!"

"You said it yourself, Elias: they look pretty good," Donovan said. "Aside from a keen sense of vertigo, the trip doesn't seem to harm human beings. To me, it seems like our only shot of getting out of here."

"Wait a minute," Benny jumped in. "Why not fire up a wormhole to take us straight back to Earth?"

Yeoh shook his head. "We know the wormholes are stable across short distances. But a quarter-million miles? That didn't exactly work out well for the people who built this ship. I'd rather reverse what we just did, since we know it works."

"Suits me," Donovan said. "Let's go."

"Donovan," Soong said impatiently, "I know you don't mind risking your life, but I for one—"

Wilson held up a hand. "I agree with Donovan, Dr. Soong. It's our only shot." Wilson turned to the others. "Yeoh, you're in charge of plotting our next wormhole jump. I don't need to tell you to make sure you get the coordinates right. Benny, you're in charge of getting this computer to repair our ascent engines. As soon as that's done, I'll help you effect repairs. Then we'll all concentrate our efforts on downloading the *Astraeus*'s files." Wilson grabbed the edge of a chair and forced himself up from the floor into a sitting position. "We're going home, people, and we're not going home empty-handed."

Donovan stepped forward. "Wilson, what about Mission Control?"

Wilson smiled. "If you'd be so kind as to help me get them on the horn, I think they might like to have another sitrep."

June 30
Johnson Space Center
Houston, Texas
8:08 a.m.

Deke walked back to his office and collapsed in his desk chair. He had listened to every single word of Wilson's transmission. He half wondered if Wilson was hallucinating because of his injury. But after letting it sink in, he chose to believe the report. How could he not? The important thing was that the crew was alive and would be able to blast off the Moon and ultimately come home. But everything else—the story of the *Astraeus*—was completely beyond him. Not in his wildest dreams could he believe that humanity would ultimately be capable of such a thing. Although skeptical by nature, he had never been a cynic. And what would the news ultimately mean for humanity? Would the world finally be able to stop all this madness, all this death and war, and be able to live with one another in peace? Would humanity finally become wise enough in their decisions with regard to genetic engineering? *Maybe this generation,* he mused, *but we're creatures of short-term memory*. He doubted the lessons learned from our future would guarantee a safer one. And could the future even be changed by having foreknowledge of it? He put his head in his hands and rubbed his tired eyes.

He had equally been disturbed by the lockdown in Mission Control following his conversation with the President. She hadn't informed him that the military would be involved and forcing anyone affiliated with the mission to sign nondisclosure statements under penalty of treason. In fact, the President had been warm and friendly on the phone, apparently pleased with the news. She even informed him that she thought the mission's success would help to ease tensions with China over Taiwan. Why then the media blackout? Why all the secrecy? What the hell were they planning on doing?

Deke sat at his desk, staring out the window, thinking of the crew, of that ship from the future, of all the unbelievable things that had blown into his door and upended his life. When he finally thought to glance at his watch, more than an hour had passed. He had sat with this new world long enough.

There was only one thing to do. He knew it was right, even if it meant betraying his country.

He pulled his cell phone from his pocket and dialed.

"Hi, Mom?"

"Johnny? Johnny, what time is it? Is anything wrong? Did something happen with the mission?"

"No, everything's fine. Looks like we're going to get the crew home."

"Oh thank God, those poor people."

"Mom, uh, is Dad there? I want to tell him the good news."

"Yes, certainly. He's right here. Hold on."

A shuffle was followed by his father's rich baritone voice. He imagined the old man sitting up in bed and smoothing his silver hair down before reaching for the phone. His father always hated to look messy, even if he was only on the phone.

"Son, is everything all right?"

"Yes, Dad. Everything's fine. The crew's going to make it back home."

"That's wonderful news. Incredible. You guys must've pulled a rabbit out of your hats."

"You're not far off. Dad, are you still sitting on the committee to approve funding for genetic-engineering companies?"

"Yes. Why?"

"I need to see you soon, Dad. I might have some information for you."

"Final check of the outer hull is complete," Donovan heard Yeoh say through his headset. "We're coming back in."

Donovan circled the *Copernicus* once more, not so much looking for any flaws in its structural integrity but just looking at the craft in amazement. It was sitting in the exact spot where the crew had landed, its legs in the exact same impressions they had first made on the Moon. The *Astraeus*'s targeting systems had proved flawless. The trip itself through the wormhole had been another matter.

Regardless of how many times he thought about it, Donovan still couldn't believe the ease with which they were able to repair the ascent engine inside the *Astraeus*. The ship's computer had been able to scan and replicate an entirely new engine indistinguishable from the old one. Wilson had double-checked its systems and declared the engine functioning within normal parameters.

"Okay, I'm heading up the ladder now," Yeoh said. "You coming, Benny?"

Benny looked off in the distance and sighed audibly. "Yeah, I'm coming."

Donovan walked toward Moose's shallow grave underneath the American and Chinese flags. So much of the mission had gone so terribly wrong. The explosion in orbit. The damage to the ascent engine. Yuen and Moose. Yet, somehow, they had been able not only to fix the engine but also download the *Astraeus*'s files and return to the surface with relative ease.

He wished he had had more time to examine the ship, do a proper survey. But that was a mission for another team somewhere down the line. His job was over now.

"Dr. Donovan," Wilson's voice echoed in his headset, "we're just about ready up here."

"I'm sorry. I'm coming."

Donovan pulled open the Velcro flap of his left pocket and carefully pulled out his father's silver astronaut pin. He placed it at the foot of Moose's grave and made his way back toward the *Copernicus*. He smiled.

"You made it, Dad," he said, feeling the years of anger and regret wash away. Donovan looked at the Earth, a giant blue bauble in the lunar sky. He sighed. It was time to go home.

They had work to do.

Chapter 16

July 1
The Tai-Ping
Lunar Orbit
8:55 a.m., Houston Time
8 days, 2 hours, 40 minutes, Mission Elapsed Time

For everything that the team had endured by going to the Moon, and for all that had transpired while on its surface, the journey back to the *Tai-Ping* in lunar orbit had been positively uneventful. Benny, with Wilson's aid, had piloted the *Copernicus* with relative ease back to a gentle docking. The two astronauts marveled at how, considering everything she had been through, the *Copernicus* actually flew *better* than she had before.

The *Tai-Ping* herself was almost as much of a marvel. Using the restart procedures Mission Control had given them, Wilson, Benny, and Yeoh powered up the cold and seemingly dead module with relative ease. Despite the freezing temperatures inside the craft, they took their time, confirming each step in the restart program with NASA's engineers back in Houston before execution. Systems soon began humming to life all around them. Heat and fresh air began to flow through the ventilation system. Once they knew everything was functioning, they conducted a detailed inspection and made any necessary repairs. After several hours of intense work, the *Tai-Ping* almost looked as if it had never been switched off.

Wilson drifted through the tunnel connecting the *Tai-Ping* to the *Copernicus*. While the others were still getting reacquainted with weightlessness, he found himself more comfortable than he had been in days. His broken knee hardly bothered him, though he had to make doubly sure not to smack it against any equipment. As the others stowed gear in the *Tai-Ping* for the trip home, he made one final inspection of the *Copernicus*. He knew they had already transferred everything they needed from her, but he wanted to take one final look to be sure—and to say good-bye to the ship that had been their lifeboat during their perilous journey to the Ocean of Storms.

Wilson whirled around in the center of the *Copernicus* and used his momentum to shoot himself through the tunnel to the *Tai-Ping*. Benny was waiting for him on the other side, a knowing look in his eye.

"Ready, Skipper?"

Wilson nodded. "Seal the tunnel and get ready to jettison the LEM."

The lieutenant colonel continued his way up through the *Tai-Ping* to the command module, where he would activate the controls to send the *Copernicus* into the depths of space. He didn't know whether the ship would ultimately be captured by the sun's gravity or continue to hurtle through the cosmos for all time. He thought about Yuen Bai and wondered where he was now. He shook off such thoughts and slid himself into the pilot's seat.

"Are we all set, Benevisto?" he asked over the mike.

"All set," came Benny's voice through his headset. "Should I tell everyone to strap in, in case we have a little bump?"

"Better do that. We'll be going for trans-Earth injection soon enough."

In a few minutes, Benny and Yeoh were strapped in next to Wilson in the command module. Just behind them sat the three scientists. All kept their eyes on the viewport before them, now filled with their last sight of the *Copernicus.*

"Ready?" asked Wilson. "In three . . . two . . . detach."

With a muffled thump, the *Copernicus* broke free of her moorings and began her lazy orbit into the void. Watching her tumble end over end as she drifted from sight, the crew was surprised at the sadness they felt looking at what was now ostensibly another piece of space junk littering the solar system.

As the *Copernicus* sailed on toward destiny, framed by the stars, Wilson whispered a line from James Flecker: "'I have seen old ships sail like swans asleep.'"

A half hour later, Wilson fired the *Tai-Ping*'s engines to break free of the Moon's gravity. Excepting the possibility of a midcourse correction to adjust their trajectory, the crew had little to do but kill time for the next three days before they made their final approach to Earth. Wilson decided that he would break the crew up into two rotations. Benny, Donovan, and Zell volunteered to take the first shift. Wilson gratefully strapped himself into his bunk and went to sleep. Yeoh and Soong soon joined him, too exhausted from their experiences to be all that bothered by again sleeping in a weightless environment.

Zell heated water in the ship's oven to make instant coffee. After passing lidded mugs out to the others, he climbed into one of the seats of the command module and watched the bright-blue Earth grow larger through their viewport. For hours the men talked of what they had uncovered on the Moon and what it might mean to humanity once the truth was known. Both Donovan and Zell expressed some concern about whether the Chinese and American governments would give the whole truth to the public, but Benny was surprisingly optimistic about the situation.

"The way I see it is like this," Benny muttered as he sucked hot coffee through his straw. "They need to keep things kinda quiet for now. Otherwise they'd have a helluva bigger panic than the one they had on their hands after the pulse."

"So you think they'll just let us talk, once they find a way to break it to the public?" Donovan asked.

"Sure. But what're you worrying about, Donovan? You'll get a sweet book deal out of this, guaranteed."

"I hope you're right," Zell muttered as he glanced out the viewport at Earth.

"But that's not what's bothering me," Benny explained, leaning in almost conspiratorially. "What's bugging me is the mission itself. Has anyone else noticed that this moon shot has had more than your average run of bad luck? First there was Syd's accident; then the *Tai-Ping* nearly explodes in lunar orbit; then we barely got the *Copernicus* on the Moon before she broke down."

Donovan leaned forward. "So how are we talking here? Hypothetically?"

Benny answered with a shrug of his lean shoulders. "I dunno, Donovan. How're we talking?"

"What are you suggesting?" Zell asked. "That this mission was sabotaged?"

"Like I said, I dunno." Benny grimaced. "But it doesn't seem like it was a mission that was supposed to succeed, now does it?"

"You've got the mind of a conspiracy theorist, Commander."

"It doesn't make sense," Donovan said. "Why would NASA spend billions of dollars and waste so much time, energy, and manpower on a mission they *wanted* to fail?"

"All right, call me a crackpot," Benny replied. "But did you ever think about the fact that there's a lotta people who might not want information about that ship to get out? People like Cal Walker, who made a buttload of cash in genetic engineering and pharmaceutical companies?"

"Walker worked for a pharmaceutical company?" Donovan asked.

"A bunch of them since he left NASA in the seventies," Benny answered. "The most recent one is an outfit called TGI. He was on its board of directors before John Dieckman called him in as a consultant on Phoenix. At least that's the watercooler gossip."

Zell's grin retreated from his face as he glanced at Donovan. "I think he's got us there, Alan."

"Wait a sec. This makes no sense." Donovan shook his head. "There's no way he—or anyone else for that matter—could've known what we would find up there."

Benny smirked. "Unless he already knew it was there."

"But how?" Zell demanded. "The damn thing's been up there two million years or so. Walker's not quite *that* old. There's no way for him to have known."

"That's what Bruce and I are trying to figure out," said Benny. "I laid my theory on him earlier, and he's curious. We're planning on going over the *Astraeus* files, as well as snooping around in Walker's files as soon as we get back to Earth. If there's a connection, we might find one there."

"I'm not sure, Benny," Donovan mused. "This is an awfully big stretch. As much as I'd like to pin Walker's hide to my wall for a whole host of reasons, it just doesn't seem likely that he would know about a ship that's obviously been abandoned for eons."

"One more question. If Walker was trying to *keep* us from getting there," Zell asked, "why not just scrub the mission altogether? That plan seems far easier than plotting out a series of sabotage efforts."

Benny slurped coffee and smiled. "You want my whole conspiracy theory? Okay. Here it is. He didn't have the authority. The mandate for

Phoenix came down from the President. Walker's hands were tied. The best he could do was try and keep us from getting down to the surface. If the mission failed, they could simply chalk it up to human and mechanical error. Then, excusing presidential decree, Walker could use his connections to tie up plans for another mission for years."

Zell leaned in. "You're making an awfully serious accusation, Commander. And one that's based on purely circumstantial evidence. Just because Walker's doing consulting for NASA and *happened* to be on the board of a genetic-engineering company and we *happened* to find a ship from the future, which *happened* to warn of genetic engineering—"

"I know, I know," Benny said. "But considering all the lives that've been lost, don't you think we ought to check it out?"

One look at Zell told Donovan that his former mentor was convinced. "Okay, but let's keep it quiet. Let us know what you find."

"Will do, boss," chimed Benny as he headed out of the cabin for a refill.

Donovan looked at Zell. "The dig of a lifetime, huh? Just what the hell have you gotten me into?"

July 3
Johnson Space Center
Houston, Texas
8:12 p.m.

Cal Walker stood at the window of the office NASA had furnished for him. The sun was setting over the Texas landscape. He always enjoyed this time of day. His mother had called it the gloaming. Truthfully, he had never known what that meant. He had always thought it was an unnameable time of day, a nebulous time when the Earth hung in the balance between light and shadow. A time when secrets could be illuminated, or just as easily hidden.

Walker eased himself into his black-leather office chair and glanced at the Phoenix blueprints scattered across his desk. Despite all the considerable efforts they had made, Phoenix was back on its way to Earth.

If ever there was an aptly named mission, Walker mused, *Phoenix is it.*

The phone rang as he was ruminating. He hastily picked it up, irritated at being interrupted. "Yes?"

"We have a situation," said the voice on the other end.

"I'm aware of it," Walker replied.

"They weren't supposed to see it. You said if I did everything you asked, they—"

Walker glanced at his nails and noted that he hadn't had time for a manicure. "Then obviously you didn't do everything I asked. The team was more resourceful than you had anticipated."

"How much do they know?" asked the voice.

"Only pieces of the whole," said Walker. "But enough to cause some . . . consternation."

"Can they trace any of it back to us?"

"I doubt it," said Walker. "But we have a crew of very stubborn people up there. They might dig until they find something."

"We have to do something. Too much is at stake."

"Too dangerous," countered Walker. "Taking any of these people out could draw undue attention. Better to let me handle this through more *diplomatic* channels. You wouldn't want to jeopardize everything we're working toward by acting too hastily."

"You don't have to tell me that, Walker." The line was silent for a moment. "Okay, we'll do it your way. But I won't let anything threaten the project."

"I know you won't," Walker replied, twirling the phone cord around. "You are in something of a bind now, aren't you? The project is his only hope."

The line went dead. Walker shook his head in disgust. Emotion clouded the minds of too many men. He turned his eyes back to the window, but the sun had set, and the world was covered in darkness.

General McKenna knew better than to let the likes of someone like Cal Walker push his buttons. In his more than forty years of military service, he had seen too many smooth operators like Walker manipulate the emotions of soldiers like himself, twist them to make the kind of gambles they would have never taken under any other circumstances. But this was a far different situation.

McKenna pulled himself out of his desk chair and wandered over to his liquor cabinet, a half-smoked cigar still gripped in his right hand. He uncorked a bottle of scotch and poured himself a stiff three fingers' worth in a square crystal glass. The amber liquid went down smoothly. He paced across the room, cigar in one hand, glass in the other. He glanced at the far wall, now in shadow since the sun had set. The photos lining that wall told his life's story. There he was as a young chopper pilot in Vietnam. And there he was in his dress uniform in his wedding photo, his young wife radiant, her eyes eager with anticipation for a wonderful new life together. And there he was a few years later in a studio portrait, himself, Ingrid, and their three sons: Jim Junior, Frank, and Danny. Just boys then, barely out of diapers. But strong already. He could see that in their eyes. Even then they were strong and smart and brave and full of potential.

McKenna brushed past the rest of the pictures, of himself receiving various promotions, of himself with congressmen and generals, presidents and kings. He went to the last photo in the line, one of Danny in his Notre Dame football uniform. The photo was taken on a crisp fall day, the sky high and bright blue above his son's head, the wind ruffling his thick, wavy brown hair. He took the photo off the wall and sat back in his chair.

McKenna puffed on his cigar and took another swallow of scotch. He looked at Danny's photo and recalled how he had met the current president of the United States right around the time his youngest son had been born. Thirty-five years. The President had a daughter right around Danny's age. McKenna remembered how they used to joke of setting them up when they got older. It was hard for McKenna to think of either the President or Danny without realizing that his friendship with the President had grown as his son had grown. They were connected in his mind, an interlocking set of events in the same chapter of his life.

McKenna sighed and chugged down the rest of his scotch. He took a key from his pocket and unlocked his bottom right-hand desk drawer. Inside was his father's service sidearm from the Second World War, an army-issue .45-caliber M1911. McKenna slid the clip into the pistol, chambered a cartridge, and laid it on his desk. He smoked his cigar and looked at the gun on his burgundy blotter. Simple enough. No one was home. Ingrid was out visiting Frank and his family in Baltimore. She would be home late in the afternoon on Sunday.

It was strange to think that his life had come down to making a simple choice. He could continue to betray the woman who had given him both friendship and his elevated status in Washington, *or* he could condemn his son to a continued life of torment, *or* he could finish it all here and now. If he chose the final option, he would leave no note, no hint of scandal. Just a family wondering why.

McKenna picked up the gun. The light from his desk lamp shone dimly on its barrel. It was heavier than his own Beretta. But it was his father's gun. It only made sense to use the gun of the man who had given him life in the first place. A complicated situation became a perfect circle.

He stubbed his cigar out in his ashtray.

McKenna gently placed the gun under his chin. As he did, he spotted the most recent family portrait on his desk, one taken in his backyard at a Fourth of July barbecue, his wife at his side. Around them were Jim Junior and his family, Frank and his family, and Danny in his wheelchair. He could never look at his son in that chair without recalling the night he got that call from a friend of Danny's—a girlfriend maybe? His son had been in a car accident. A drunk driver. He remembered that girl's voice, her every word, as if he were hearing it now for the first time. He had never heard that voice again. He had never heard any of the voices of any of Danny's so-called friends again, not a single one of them in the last fifteen years. A star quarterback had a whole host of friends. A star quarterback got the most beautiful girls. He had NFL potential. He could have a wife and children and a full life. A cripple had his memories and nights of unfulfilled dreams.

McKenna eased the gun from his chin and unloaded it. He ran a hand up to his nose, wondering if he had a nosebleed. The fingers returned to his sight wet, not bloodied. Almost as if in a dream, he realized he had been crying.

He picked up Danny's football photo. He would get his boy's life back even if he had to betray the President of the United States to do it.

July 5
The Tai-Ping
Approaching Earth Orbit
1:20 a.m., Pacific Time

Aboard the *Tai-Ping*, preparations were being made for reentry, which was coming up in less than an hour. In keeping with the unusual element that had pervaded the entire mission, the splashdown was going to happen in the dead of night on the West Coast, a first for any manned lunar mission. "We're gonna give them one hell of a show!" Wilson had said when he heard the news. And indeed he was right. All over the world, people were already gathering in crowds to watch the *Tai-Ping* make her fiery return to Earth.

"For the love of Christ, Bruce," Benny groaned for what felt to him like the twentieth time, "will you *please* turn that down?"

Bruce was working through the reentry procedure NASA had sent them. Given the stress the ship had endured, the return to Earth had to be meticulously plotted out. Already there was uncertainty about whether the heat shield would hold and how well the drogue chutes would deploy after spending so long in the cold of space. Bruce always worked better when he had some music playing. Today's choice was a personal favorite, Jethro Tull's *Heavy Horses*.

"This is a classic!" protested Yeoh, enjoying getting Benny's goat yet again.

"The '70 Rebel Machine," Benny said. "*That's* a classic. This—this is something else."

"It helps me concentrate."

"Well, that you'd better do," Benny replied. "I don't want to end up deep-fried."

"The shield will hold," Yeoh insisted.

"Even if it does," Benny continued, "there's no guaranteeing that those drogues won't be three Icees when they open."

"Good old American optimism," Yeoh chided. "It's a miracle you made it out of the twentieth century."

"All right, you two, that's enough," Wilson said, gliding into the cockpit. "We've got work to do. How's that reentry procedure coming?"

"I think we've got it pretty well mapped out, Colonel," said Yeoh.

"Good job. We're coming up on Earth, and I want to have everything laser tight. Benny?"

"Yes, sir?"

"Take your seat."

Benny noticed Wilson was gesturing to the command chair. He looked at him and shook his head. "Sir, I may have brought the *Copernicus* down, but this is your show."

"She's yours to fly," Wilson said, but Benny heard what was behind his words.

Benny smiled. "Shut up and take us home, boss."

Wilson grinned like a kid, a look that almost surprised Benny, then slid into the pilot's chair as gently as he could with his splint. He got on the VOX. "Attention, archeology team, we're about to make our final preparations for reentry, so you'd better pack up and strap in."

"Jeez," said Zell, hastily gathering up his materials. "You'd think we'd get more notice." He looked over at Soong and saw that she was already seated in her chair.

"He did tell us to start preparations fifteen minutes ago."

"Just make sure you've got your copy of the *Astraeus* files," Donovan said as he floated into his seat.

Soong's face went white with concern as she patted down her space suit for the flash drive. After several seconds of watching Donovan's face flush with frustration, she pulled the drive from a compartment in the arm of her chair and laughed. "I'm sure Commander Benevisto has his copy."

Donovan shook his head and smirked. "Whoever said you had no sense of humor was dead wrong, Soong. A bad one, yes. But no humor? Definitely not."

On Earth all eyes had turned skyward. Even the news that the crisis in Taiwan had been averted and the American fleet was steaming home seemed almost trivial compared with the event that was about to transpire in the heavens. Traffic had ground to a halt in all the major cities, and the streets were flooded with people. Even though the landing was at night, schools had closed for the day and businesses had ended work early. People had spent most of the last twenty-four hours watching the news coverage of the Taiwan situation, alternating with bulletins about the reentry. The landing was scheduled to happen at 2:15 a.m., Pacific time, so America would be getting the best show. Elsewhere in the world it was dusk or still daylight, but it promised to be no less enthralling. NASA had targeted the Pacific as the landing zone, which meant that California was particularly frenzied. Many people had left both Los Angeles and San Francisco, heading north to escape the light pollution. Fittingly one of the largest gatherings was in Modesto, the hometown and final resting place of Hunter Donovan.

In a small field on the outskirts of Modesto, almost two thousand people had gathered to hold a small service to pray for the Phoenix team. Nearly every major religion was represented. Priests, rabbis, and imams each gave readings from their respective books and encouraged others to do the same. Even those who had no formal beliefs were moved to get up and offer words of encouragement. The whole of America was gathered there in that field, men and women, Jews and Gentiles, blacks and whites, gay and straight, young and old, immigrants and the native born, rich and poor. Their gathering was a microcosm of the breadth of American society, which in itself was a microcosm of the remarkable diversity of the human race.

As all eyes turned upward, someone called out, "There it is! I see it!" Every head shot upward and was awed at the sight that greeted them. A ball of fire, streaking downward toward the Earth like a shooting star. Almost instinctively, many people joined hands, clasping on to the closest person to them in the dark. One little boy perched on his father's shoulders shook the sleep from his eyes and cried, "Daddy! Make a wish!"

On board the *Tai-Ping*, the crew heard the heat roaring around them as their ship forced itself through Earth's atmosphere. Although it was hot enough to melt titanium outside, they only felt a mild increase in temperature, barely enough to break a sweat. *The heat shield's pushing the inferno away from the craft,* Donovan thought with some relief. *It's holding.* Still, nothing could protect them from how bumpy the ride was. To Wilson, a veteran of so many missions, the sensation was comfortingly familiar. To everyone else, the ship seemed ready to fly apart at any second.

Soong looked out the portal; all she could see was a cascading wall of flame. She thought of the fairy tale she heard as a child in which a girl became a dragon, incinerating Anchin, the boy who refused to return her love. She knew how Anchin must have felt.

Benny, thrust back in his seat by the incredible g-forces, barely heard Wilson give the order to deploy the chutes over the roar. Straining his hand against the force, he reached forward and pulled the lever.

There was a powerful jolt, and suddenly all the tumult stopped. The landing capsule of the *Tai-Ping* was floating gently down toward the ocean. The chutes, far from being blocks of ice, were working perfectly. Donovan peered out the portal and could make out the green phosphorous churned out by the carrier that had been sent to pick them up. As much as he couldn't believe it, they had come home.

"Houston, this is Phoenix," Wilson said. "We're on approach, and everything looks five by five."

The cheers that broke out at Mission Control came over the VOX with deafening clarity. All around the world a similar sound was heard as people welcomed back the astronauts with unbridled joy. On board the ship, Benny and Yeoh looked out the front viewport at the lights of the West Coast, now coming into view.

"California, here I come," Benny sang, and everyone on board cheered in agreement.

A moment later, the capsule splashed down into the ocean, its heated and charred outer shell sizzling on contact with the water. At once, Wilson, Benny, and Yeoh got to work, securing the ship and powering her down.

"Houston, this is Phoenix," said Wilson. "We are at stable one; the ship is secure."

"Roger that," replied Dieckman. "Welcome home, team. We're glad to see you. Sit tight awhile. The carrier *Ronald Reagan* is on its way to pick you up. She'll be looking for your tracer flares."

"Copy, Houston. This is Phoenix signing off."

The crew spent the next few minutes collecting what they would need to take with them. As they packed up, Donovan stole a look at Benny, who nodded in understanding as he tucked the backup flash drive into his space suit. When they were done, Benny climbed up to the hatch and burst the seal. Fresh ocean air rushed into the cabin, the sweetest thing they had ever smelled or felt. The spray of the ocean washed in, dotting their faces with salt.

Wilson looked out at the approaching carrier, her lights sparkling on the horizon. He turned to Zell. "Here's to coming home."

"Amen to that, my friend."

Chapter 17

August 10
Johnson Space Center
Houston, Texas
9:35 a.m.

Donovan sat in the office of Ted Bremer, special liaison from the NSA, and one of the seemingly endless string of people in charge of debriefing the Phoenix team. In the five weeks since the crew had returned to Earth, many of his days had played out in rooms much like this one. Not only had they not been allowed to talk to the press, who had been clamoring for interviews, but they had also been unable to leave the confines of the space center since they arrived home. Each night they gathered around the television and flipped from station to station as a parade of familiar faces from NASA gave the various talking heads standard lines about how the Phoenix crew was eager to tell their story and vague promises about granting interviews in the near future. He suspected these lines were designed solely to mollify the press long enough until they lost interest. Right now he didn't care if he talked to the press, NASA, or a brick wall; he just wanted to get out of Ted Bremer's office.

Bremer had the pinched, worried face of a lifelong bureaucrat. What made matters worse was the fact that he had one of those pendulums with metal balls that clicked and clacked against one another endlessly. After sitting in his office for nearly forty minutes, Donovan began to suspect that Bremer had timed all of his movements to the metronomic precision of the knickknack. With every click, he would loudly lick his thumb and turn pages of the report he had been given. He would then exhale and read for exactly two cycles of clicks and clacks, only to repeat the entire process again. At first Donovan had found this an amusing diversion from the tedium. Now the pendulum was beginning to slowly but surely drive him certifiably nuts. Finally, and perfectly timed, Bremer exhaled again and looked up at Donovan, staring at him a moment over the silver rims of his bifocals.

Click.

"So, Dr. Donovan, you stand by everything that's in this report?"

"Absolutely. As far-fetched as it may seem, everything we've told you is true."

"Mmm-hmm," Bremer said. "You realize that this kind of a story might be extremely hard for the public to swallow?"

Donovan squinted at him and shook his head. "Harder to swallow than prehistoric aliens sending a signal so powerful it causes a worldwide blackout?"

Bremer paused again. Donovan could tell that he was not used to people questioning his opinions or suggestions.

Clack.

"What I'm saying, Dr. Donovan, is that the world was prepared to accept the idea that we are not alone in the universe. What they are *not* ready to accept is the notion that we are headed into a civil war with some sort of superintelligent clones who will ultimately drive us to extinction."

"But Joshua came here to *prevent*—"

"That's immaterial at this juncture, Doctor," Bremer said. "Right now, the world is entering into a period of reconstruction. The news that it may all be in vain could cause a global panic and plunge us right back to where we were."

"Look," said Donovan, "I'm not saying that we should climb every bell tower and shout that the sky is falling. But we have a responsibility to learn from what Joshua told us. To tread carefully from here on out."

"And we will, rest assured. As you are aware, there are a number of biotechnology corporations the government has already asked to study the materials you brought back from the Moon."

"With respect, Mr. Bremer, that knowledge is not a comfort to either myself or my fellow crew members. We have reason to believe that Joshua picked this particular time to contact us because he felt that one, if not all, of those very same biotechnology companies may begin the chain of events that will lead to mankind's destruction."

Bremer wiped his glasses with a monogrammed handkerchief as he leaned back in his chair. "Surely, Dr. Donovan, you don't expect us to believe that these companies are secretly—what?—planning the downfall of humanity? The very notion is, forgive me, absurd."

Donovan leaned forward. "But I've already told you it was an accident. At least these people from the future thought it was. The division of humanity into various factions was simply a by-product of their experiments to prevent us from suffering from the effects of chemical, biological, and nuclear terrorism. They didn't know . . ."

Click.

Bremer held up a hand. "We've already gone through that," he said, shuffling his papers. "Your report is satisfactory, but please keep yourself available should the NSA or any other US government agency need to question you further, Dr. Donovan."

Clack.

Donovan laughed. "That's kind of funny. Keep myself available. You guys have us locked up."

Bremer stared at Donovan blankly across his wide mahogany desk.

Donovan got up and began walking toward the office door but thought better of leaving so abruptly. "You have to get a team back up on the Moon. There's more research that needs to be done."

Click.

"We have people looking into it as we speak," he said.

"You're going to blow it," Donovan said. "You people have the opportunity of a lifetime here, and you're going to throw it away and cover it up under some government-issue party-line *bullshit.*"

Clack.

"Might I remind you, Doctor, that you have been a paid consultant to the United States government for the better part of a year and lived quite comfortably at the expense of the American taxpayer."

"That's beside the point."

Click.

"Might I *also* remind you that the government is prepared to fund whatever projects you and Dr. Zell choose to embark on."

"We don't need your payoff," Donovan said. "The Zell Institute is more than self-sufficient."

Clack.

Bremer leaned his thin elbows on his desk. "Then let me be candid, sir. This project is a government-funded operation. Like it or not, you are a government employee for the duration of your involvement. Further, as part of your astronaut training, you were required to sign nondisclosure agreements pertaining to your lunar mission if you encountered anything there which might prove a threat to national security. The government has read your report, as well as the reports of your fellow crewmen, and has come to the conclusion that your findings indicate a threat to the security of the American people, if not the entire human race. We cannot afford to make any public disclosures until such security threats have been analyzed and neutralized."

Click.

"Is that a threat?" Donovan asked.

Clack.

"We're the United States government, Dr. Donovan. We don't make threats."

Almost four weeks later and what seemed like several thousand pages of nondisclosure forms later, the Phoenix team was released from their "quarantine." Despite government hopes to the contrary, news agencies had been unrelenting in their efforts to find out what the crew had seen and experienced on the Moon. Following a carefully guided script, the crew had been brought together for their first news conference, also marking the first time that any of the American team had seen Soong or Yeoh since members of the Chinese government had hauled them off.

At the news conference, the crew members each took turns describing their mission. They recalled in full detail the deaths of Commander Yuen and Lieutenant Commander Mosensen. Wilson gave a very technical description of their attempts to reboot the *Tai-Ping* remotely and their efforts to repair the ascent engine. And that was where the omissions began. No mention was made of the fact that the *Copernicus* was sucked onto the bridge of the *Astraeus* through a wormhole. No mention was made of their generating spare parts for the ascent engine through the future ship's extraordinary matter-energy converters. And no mention at all was made of Joshua and the message he brought from the twenty-eighth century.

Neither Donovan nor Zell liked lying to the press. But they did as they were told, careful not to mention anything about what the *Astraeus* was. They regaled the press corps with a detailed analysis of the enormous engine that was used to blast a hole in the Ocean of Storms to emit an electromagnetic pulse. They showed a photographic record of the inside of the ship. And they admitted to not knowing who or what had built it or what its purpose was—but kept stressing that it was immensely old and contained no evidence of an imminent attack on the Earth.

The press corps had more questions at the end of the conference but left more or less satisfied. The nightly news reports and editorial pages seemed content with what had been revealed. Donovan and the others had helped pull off one of the most elaborate deceptions in the history of civilization and were released from their captivity with no injuries except those inflicted on their consciences.

They had decided to play along for the sake of humanity. But none of them expected to stay quiet for long.

Donovan's suitcase hit the bed with a decisive thump. He was glad to be leaving the confines of the government facility that he had reluctantly called home since returning from the Moon. He was aching to get back to the Zell Institute, to see familiar things again. But he had hoped that Benny or Yeoh would have uncovered something in those backup files by this point. He knew that there was more on those records than they had already seen.

Just then there was a knock on the door. Figuring it was the Reuben he had ordered from room service, Donovan strolled over. When he opened the door, he was surprised to see Benny.

"Merry Christmas, Doc!"

"It's September, Benny. What are you doing here?"

"That may be," said Benny, "but I've got a gift that keeps on giving."

"Okay, okay, come in," said Donovan. "Thrill me."

Benny walked into the room, looking around suspiciously. He pulled out his phone and tapped out a number. Suddenly Donovan's own phone rang. He picked it up and then showed the display to Benny.

"Why are you calling me?"

"Just answer," Benny said.

Donovan complied, and Benny put his phone on speaker, holding it up and waving it around the room, near the lamps, television set, refrigerator, and windows.

"Care to explain?" Donovan asked.

"Uncle Sam could be listening," Benny said. "Cameras and microphones give off an electromagnetic field. If we hear a click, it means the phone is interfering with the field."

Benny searched the room a bit longer, then hung up the phone, satisfied. "You got a laptop here?" he asked.

Donovan reached over to his bag and pulled his computer out, popping it open and starting it up. "What've you got?"

Benny hopped over to the laptop and inserted a flash drive into the USB port. His fingers danced over the keys, going through a number of decryptions before opening the needed files. "Something you're never going to believe. Remember how Joshua said there were other survivors from his era?"

"What're you saying?"

"Wait for it." Benny tapped a few more keys and turned the computer toward Donovan. He peered at the screen and was surprised to see schematics for another vessel.

"There's a second ship?" he asked.

Benny grinned broadly. "There's a second ship. The *Eos*. They came through the portal not long after Joshua's team did, in hopes of completing the mission."

Donovan's eyes went wide as he studied the schematics on the computer screen. "Why didn't Joshua tell us about this?"

"Remember, you only got the overview of what Joshua wanted to tell us in that download. He knew we would eventually look at the complete logs." Benny tapped on a few more keys and punched up a series of transmission logs. "But he was in contact with the captain of the *Eos*. It seems that it was pulled through the same unstable wormhole that the *Astraeus* had gone through. Except that instead of crashing into the Moon, it crash-landed on Earth."

"Jesus, are you sure?"

"The logs confirm that much," said Benny. "And as to where, I reran some diagnostics on the energy pulse that came from the Moon, and there it was. A major electrical surge concentrated on one fixed point on the globe."

"How come no one else found it?" asked Donovan.

"No one else was looking for it. Once the word got out about the Ocean of Storms, anomalies on Earth seemed positively Victorian."

"I'm confused," admitted Donovan. "Are you saying the EM pulse powered up this second ship?"

"I think it was accidental. Both ships were made from the same technology. My guess is that when the pulse arrived it simply recharged whatever circuits and gizmos this one had on her."

"So where is it?"

Benny hit a few more keys, then sat back, cracking his knuckles. "Tanzania," he said. "In East Africa."

At that moment, the bathroom door opened and Zell stepped out, freshly showered. He was clad in a terry cloth robe and clutching a tumbler of scotch.

"Pack your bags, Elias. We're taking a trip," said Donovan.

"Oh Jesus, Alan. The ice hasn't even melted in my drink yet. Where are we off to now?"

"Africa," said Benny. "There's a second ship."

Zell almost dropped his glass. "A second ship? Does anyone else know?"

Donovan looked to Benny for the answer.

"They might, but as far as I know, NASA's still spending a lot of time looking over what went wrong on our mission. But the surge wouldn't be that hard to discover once you start looking. And once you find that, it's pretty easy to find the logs."

"Then the race is on!" he said with a flourish. "I'll call Andre and have him fuel up the jet. Oh and the lovely Dr. Soong must be a part of this as well. We leave tonight!"

He was about to enter his bedroom to change when he grabbed a cigar and lit it in celebration. He looked over at Donovan and Benny, his eyes aglow.

"Step lively, lads," he said, grinning. "Now the game is truly afoot!"

PART 3: THE CALDERA

Chapter 18

September 9
Kariakoo Market
Dar es Salaam, Tanzania
5:15 p.m.

In its 150 years of existence, Dar es Salaam had grown from a small settlement and prospective summer home of Sultan Seyyid Majid to one of the largest cities in Africa, with a population of more than four million. People from all over Europe and Asia poured into its streets daily, jockeying for space with local tribesmen. Dar es Salaam was a disorienting experience for the first-time visitor. Hawkers and peddlers sold their wares in the crowded streets. Muslim women scurried by, shrouded in *buibuis*. Indian traders enticed prospective buyers with a myriad of spices and silks from the world's most exotic corners.

Most disorienting was the Kariakoo Market, filled with the sound of chiming marimbas and ceaselessly clucking chickens along with the combined aromas of sizzling meats, fresh fish, and burning incense. Casual shoppers glancing around the market could find anything they needed, including herbs, potions, and concoctions for almost every ailment, usually in small bottles collected from local hospitals.

Benny, strolling through the marketplace, found the scene almost overwhelming. Despite having been to some of the most unique places on Earth throughout his naval career, he had never gotten quite used to the way different cities assaulted his senses—so many new sights and smells and sensations. In the midst of such vibrancy, life, and heat, he struggled to believe that not so long ago he had been stranded in one of the most hostile and unforgiving environments known to man. Though Dar wasn't his home or even remotely like it, he was glad to be immersed in so much humanity again. He never wanted to be so alone again.

"So where're we supposed to meet your guy and Zell and Soong?" he asked Donovan, who was walking alongside him. The group had opted—wisely, to Donovan's way of thinking—to split up so as not to attract undue attention. Zell and Soong had arrived earlier that day at a private airfield funded by the Zell Institute and were planning on meeting up with Donovan's contact in about an hour. To Donovan's surprise, getting out of the States had been easier than he expected. He assumed that most officials had figured he agreed to play ball and weren't about to question his actions. Still, he knew he and his colleagues should play it safe. After taking Zell's private jet from DC, they had split up in England. He and Benny arrived at Dar es Salaam in a chartered plane from Amsterdam, while Zell had quietly taken a cargo plane on the institute's payroll and Soong arrived on a jet Zell had procured for her.

Donovan laughed to himself about their almost-paranoid secrecy. Soong had been back home in China for just a few days before Zell had her quietly spirited out of the country. Zell had promised to make a generous donation to fund the repairs to the Lei Cheng Uk Han Tomb Museum, on the condition that she accompany them to Tanzania with no questions asked. This desire to not attract attention was part of the reason Donovan had chosen Dar as their meeting place. He had been to Tanzania several times before and knew it was a good place to stay anonymous.

"How'd you know this guy, Badru?" Benny asked.

Donovan smiled. "How long do you have? Badru came to the institute when he was fourteen. He met Thackeray on a dig in Tanzania, and the old man was impressed with his eagerness to learn and his sharp instincts. He lived at the manor and studied at the institute for almost ten years." Donovan paused as they pushed their way through yet another crowd of merchants trying to sell them more objects of dubious origin. "After my father died," he continued, "I came to live at the institute as well. Badru and I became fast friends. I guess both of us felt a little out of place. When I was ready to start my fieldwork, Badru and I teamed up. He and I have found ourselves in some of the stickiest situations I can imagine, and more often than not, he was the one who saved my neck."

"So you trust this guy?"

"With my life," Donovan answered.

"Well," Benny said, peering around the marketplace, "let's hope it doesn't come to that."

September 9
Kilimanjaro Airport
Tanzania
6:05 p.m.

Two men stepped off a British Airways 767 with 314 other travelers who had come from London's Heathrow Airport. The waning sunlight drew their long shadows out before them as they stepped onto the tarmac. To anyone else on the plane, they appeared to be two men in their early thirties on a trip to Africa—perhaps backpackers in search of adventure or journalists on assignment. Their dress was casual enough: faded jeans and matching black golf shirts. A closer inspection would reveal the US Navy SEALs trident emblazoned on their forearms, but no one would get that close. For as unassuming as the two men looked, there was a hint of menace about them. The taller one's eyes were hidden behind mirrored sunglasses, and the African sun glinted off his shaved head. The most casual inspection revealed that he spent several hours a day on the weight pile, his body a knotted mass of ropelike muscle. His partner was smaller, his lithe frame moving like an uncoiling sidewinder. He brushed his dark, shaggy hair out of his gray eyes and peered about the airport. Years of training had conditioned both of them to anticipate threats, even in the most benign situations. Everyone was a threat, and no one was above suspicion. After so many years immersed in wet work, they had come to think of themselves as the only "real" people on the planet. The bags of meat that passed them by were as faceless as their own shadows, worthy of neither recognition nor compassion. Only when a price was named did those shadows step out into the light and become something altogether different. To their minds, if you weren't a shadow, then you were a target.

These men had names once, changed many times for many similar jobs. Their true identities represented other people, different lives. For although they still proudly wore the emblem of the SEALs, they had not been members of that elite unit for nearly a decade. In truth, their former shipmates would most likely frown on their current profession, seeing it as a dishonorable use of their training. They could live with such judgments, though. Money had a funny way of keeping one's conscience quiet.

For this mission they were traveling as Miller and Sherwood, names that could be corroborated by passports, driver's licenses—even birth certificates and Social Security cards. It was amazing what could be bought for the right price.

Amazing, indeed.

Miller picked up his ringing cell phone.

"Yes," he said. "Uncle John! How are you?"

"Very good," came a gruff voice on the other end. "Have you arrived safely?"

"I sure did," he said in a voice affected with a slight midwestern twang, the accent he often used when doing business at an airport. No one ever looked twice at another American tourist talking loudly on a smartphone.

"Do you know who you're meeting?"

"Well, gee, Uncle John, I think we covered all of that back at the ranch," Miller said, running a hand through his thick hair.

"It seems there are other members of the party that we didn't know were attending, a Chinese sales rep and an English one," the voice replied. "People who might be able to get there before you can bring the hors d'oeuvres."

"That would be a shame," Miller replied. "Me and ol' Sherwood are getting a car now and heading out to meet them."

"Very good," said the voice. "Just make sure you stay until the party's finished."

"You know me, Uncle John," said Miller. "Do I ever leave a party guest feeling neglected?"

He ended the call and jerked his head at Sherwood, signaling that they should leave the airport. Ten minutes later they were in a rental car that had been arranged for them, heading to their appointed destination.

"What's our directive?" asked Sherwood as he drove, his eyes hidden behind ebony glasses.

Miller didn't look up from the Glock he was cleaning. "The same as ever," he said, with a certain hint of glee creeping into his voice. "Interception with terminal force."

"A clean hit," said Sherwood.

"Exactly. But it looks like we've gone international, buddy. It seems that Soong and Zell are here too."

"Any special arrangements for them?" Sherwood asked.

"Same as the others," Miller answered. "Just make sure nobody ever finds them."

September 9
The White House
Washington, DC
10:40 a.m.

General McKenna had been in a national-security meeting for the last hour and hadn't heard a word anyone had said. He knew the meeting had been called to address the latest series of car bombings in and around Baghdad, but beyond being told to train some Skystalker satellites over the Iraqi capital, he had little idea about what was being said. His thoughts were quite literally half a world away.

When the meeting ended, McKenna gathered up his reports and briefing papers and headed out to his car. As he glanced out the window, his thoughts drifted, as they often did, to his son Danny. He had spoken to him that morning, as he did almost every morning. They talked sports. They talked about Jim Junior's upcoming birthday. And they talked about Danny's physical therapy. As always, Danny tried to sound upbeat and McKenna tried to sound encouraging. But in his heart McKenna knew such conversations were as futile and as hollow as Danny's therapy. Such thoughts stiffened his resolve as McKenna thought of the men he had sent to Africa in pursuit of Alan Donovan.

McKenna's smartphone chirped, and he dug into his pocket to retrieve it. He wasn't surprised by whose voice was on the other end of the call.

"General McKenna," Cal Walker said calmly. "You've left the White House?"

"Yes, I'm on my way home now. What can I do for you?"

"I'm at the Lincoln Memorial. Meet me there in fifteen minutes. Come alone."

The line went dead. McKenna stared at the phone for a moment, then told his driver, Corporal Hayes, to head for the Lincoln Memorial. McKenna knew Hayes would take the change in plans in stride. Hayes often had to drive him to unusual locations at a moment's notice. However, when they arrived at the memorial and McKenna asked him to remain in the car, McKenna noticed the faintest twinge of surprise on his face. McKenna rarely went anywhere in public without an armed escort.

The Lincoln Memorial was still crowded with tourists. On such an especially beautiful September day, thousands of people tended to visit the memorial. As he climbed the steps, McKenna knew he looked somewhat out of place in his dress uniform among so many tourists, many of whom were still wearing shorts. Reaching the top of the steps, the general realized why Walker had chosen such a public meeting place. As a government official high up on the food chain, McKenna could be easily exposed for what he was doing.

McKenna found Walker standing directly under Abraham Lincoln's gaze in the midst of a crowd of tourists. To one side of him stood a group of Cub Scouts reading an inscription on the monument. On the other were groups of families, each posing before Lincoln for a series of snapshots. Among them Walker looked like a college professor or someone's grandfather. Above all, he looked completely anonymous.

Walker smiled broadly as he gripped the general's hand firmly in his. "So good to see you." Walker jerked his head to the side and added quietly, "Walk with me, General."

As they walked toward the columns at the front of the memorial, Walker continued speaking in a loud and conversational tone.

"Remarkable man, Lincoln. There are many that say he overstepped his authority as president many times during the Civil War. The suspension of habeas corpus is the example most often cited. But if Lincoln hadn't done those things, we wouldn't have the republic we do today, now would we? Nor would many of our citizens enjoy the freedoms we hold so dear. Great men must often go *beyond* what is deemed morally right in their times to achieve the greater good."

McKenna grabbed Walker by his forearm and was surprised by its firmness. "What did you bring me here for, Walker?"

"General," Walker said with a slight grin, "I think you know exactly why you're here."

McKenna glanced around and turned his back to the crowds. "I wasn't going to risk my son's future once I learned that Donovan and the others were heading to Africa."

"So you decided—on your own—to take care of it?" Walker asked with some disgust. "Really, General, did you think I wouldn't find out? Did you think I would allow Donovan or any of the others to reach the dig?"

"I didn't know what to think," McKenna said. "All your goddamn talk of diplomatic solutions didn't keep them from finding out about the ship."

Walker took a step forward. "Understand this, General. My company's spinal-cord drug trials begin in a month's time. You go behind my back and carry out another of these independent operations, and you'll find your son's name *very* far down that list."

"You son of a bitch," McKenna said. "You do that, and I'll—"

"You'll what?" Walker laughed. "Expose me? Expose yourself? What will you do, General? You'll not only doom your son to a life in that chair, you'll be revealed as a traitor to your country and your president."

McKenna felt the blood pulsing behind his eyes. "The men are already in the field. There's no way—"

Walker shrugged. "Then we won't recall them. But let's hope they are as good as you think they are, General."

Walker strode away from McKenna and headed toward the steps. At the top step he turned around and grinned again. "You know what I like most about the Lincoln Memorial? How open it is. Great men should be seen in the light of day." He tipped his hat. "Good day, General."

Donovan and Benny were seated at an out-of-the-way table in one of the many restaurants that lined the streets of Dar. Often doubling as tobacconists, the corner shops were just the place for people not wanting to be noticed. As Donovan and Benny sat, a waiter brought them a plate of the Asian dish that gave the shops their name.

Benny stared a moment at the triangular leaves in front of him. "What is this?" he asked.

"Paan," said Donovan, pushing the plate toward him. "It's a mixture of spices, nuts, syrup, and white lime, wrapped in leaves."

"I suppose a cheeseburger might be too much to hope for?"

"Too much, and then some," Donovan replied. He looked out the door at the crowds streaming past. "Benny, I haven't really thanked you for this. Putting your whole career on the line just to chase down a wild goose—"

"Look, Donovan, I was there with you on the Moon. I saw that ship. If we let them cover it up, if we let what Joshua warned you about happen, then our friends—all of them—have died for nothing."

"It's too bad Bruce couldn't have joined us," Donovan said.

"Yeah," replied Benny. "Christ knows what we'll find if we make it to the ship. We sure could use his brain down there. But, after everything we went through on the Moon, the Chinese government requested his presence in Beijing. I think they're very interested in what he saw up there."

"Aren't we all?" said Donovan.

"Enjoying the city?" said a gruff English voice behind them.

"It sure took you long enough," said Donovan, looking up at Elias Zell and Dr. Soong.

"You travel here in the belly of a C-130, and we'll see how punctual you are," Zell retorted.

"So," said Soong, taking a seat, "I can only imagine the precautions you've taken mean that you've found something."

Donovan leaned forward. "There's a second ship."

"What?" asked Soong. "Another one like the *Astraeus*? When did it arrive here?"

"That's what we're trying to figure out," said Benny. "We think it may have come here sometime after the *Astraeus*'s mission failed. Possibly as a rescue mission or backup plan."

"Whatever brought the ship here," said Donovan, "the crew no doubt has the same files that the *Astraeus* had. Maybe even more. The information they're carrying could prove everything the government's trying to sweep under the carpet."

Soong sat back a moment, deep in thought. She sprang forward suddenly.

"The Laetoli footprints!" she said with all the excitement of a ten-year-old exclaiming her favorite flavor of ice cream.

"I'm surprised you believe that story," Donovan said.

Benny leaned in. "Care to explain?"

"In 1978, archeologists found a trail of fossilized footprints seemingly made by upright-walking hominids. The prints were dated at around three-point-six million years old," said Soong. "It's proof undeniable that there were humans walking upright millions of years before anyone thought they did."

Zell laughed. "So what're you saying? That those footprints were made by our friends from the future?"

"It doesn't follow," Donovan interjected. "This second ship arrived here, we speculate, around two and a half million years ago. A million years *after* the footprints were supposedly made."

"I know it's a leap," said Soong. "But after everything we've seen, I'm willing to make it. And who's to say if our dating methods are completely accurate?"

"Why, Dr. Soong, you're beginning to sound more and more like my father."

She gave him a sidelong glance. "And that's a good thing?"

He raised his glass and gave her a wink. "To me, my dear Dr. Soong, the best of things." He put his drink down. "Now, where is our friend?"

Donovan nodded toward the front of the shop. "He's been here for ten minutes."

"What's he waiting for?" asked Benny.

"He's sizing us up," said Zell. "He wants to make sure we are who we say we are."

"But he knows you and Alan," said Soong.

"Yes," Zell answered, "but not you two. And, what with everything we've been through, it does no one any good to take chances."

After a moment, the towering man up front strode to their table, exuding confidence, almost like a prince striding forward to claim his crown. His fierce obsidian eyes seemed to size them up with only a glance. He stopped at the table, peering down at the four of them.

"Hujambo?" he asked Donovan in a bass voice that resonated from deep within his khaki shirt. *Are you well?*

"Sijambo," Donovan replied, nodding his head cordially. *I am fine.*

Suddenly, the man leapt across the table, grabbing Donovan by his shirt with an oak-like arm and yanking him to his feet. Soong jumped out of the way, while Benny stood up, ready to mix it up with this newcomer. At once, the man's smile broadened, revealing one missing tooth, and he let out a belly laugh that almost shook the glasses on the table. He pulled Donovan close, and the two embraced.

"Your friends are jumpy," he said, still laughing.

"You would be too, in our shoes," Donovan said.

The man then turned to Zell. "You still hanging around with this loser?" he asked.

"Depends on which one of us you're talking to."

The man laughed even louder, gripping Zell in a massive bear hug. Once Zell was released, he turned to the table.

"Badru," he said, making the introductions, "this is Anthony Benevisto and Dr. Soong Yang Zi."

Badru shook hands with the two of them.

"Badru studied at the institute under my father," Zell explained. "He and Donovan spent years together in some of our African expeditions."

"We had our share of adventures," Donovan said. He punched Badru in the shoulder. "Then he decided to get respectable."

"Well, for me it came down to a simple choice," Badru said. "More money or more broken bones." He laughed again and turned to the table. "Donovan has told me about you," Badru said to Benny and Soong.

"Not everything, I hope," joked Benny, still a little taken aback by what had just happened.

"What he didn't tell me, I was able to fill in for myself," Badru replied, tossing a newspaper onto the table. The group peered at the headline, which was in Swahili.

"What does it say?" asked Benny.

"More of the same from the White House," said Zell. He read aloud. "'The President reports that the alien ship represents the greatest discovery in human history, and she thanks the Phoenix team for their incredible service.'" Zell tossed the paper aside. "She goes on to say that, conveniently, further missions will be postponed until a proper analysis of the data recovered from the ship can be made." He sighed in disgust. "A lovely piece of fiction."

"So what are you saying?" asked Badru. "That your president knows something she's not telling the people? Something you also know?"

"That's exactly it," Donovan answered.

Badru laughed again. "That's why I like you, Alan. When you see a tiger trap, you always find the best way to walk right into it. So what are you telling me, my friend?"

"I'm telling you there is no alien ship."

Badru took a moment to absorb that, then pulled up a chair. "Why do I get the feeling that your presence here might be frowned upon by members of your government?"

"You've had those sinking feelings before," Donovan said, smiling.

"Yes, and they usually led to an extended stay in the hospital," his friend remarked, grimacing. "So what are you all involved in?"

Badru listened as the group explained everything that had happened in the Ocean of Storms. The ship, Joshua, the devastating future that awaited the world. When they got to the part about the second ship, his eyes flickered with recognition.

"What you're saying, however incredible it is, is sounding less and less like fiction," he mused.

"What are you getting at?" asked Donovan.

"Two years ago," said Badru, "men began coming through here. Men with trucks, helicopters, making a lot of noise. They set up camp out on the crater."

"Crater?" asked Benny.

"The Ngorongoro Crater," said Donovan. "Based on the input you've given us, I'm pretty sure it's where the second ship lies."

"These men," Badru continued, "they moved my people off our land, telling them there was a plague that would soon kill off the wildlife and plants in the area."

"That's a raw deal," muttered Benny.

"Not as bad as you may think," Badru said. "My people are Maasai. One of the oldest and, at one time, most powerful tribes in Africa. We are seminomadic, moving with the changing seasons. Besides, we are used to being shuttled from one place to another by someone's government. We are the last tribe to resist such requests to adopt a more sedentary lifestyle. As a result, we're not all too popular with most people. Except tourists, of course."

"And this plague they told you about?" Zell asked.

"Most people can't get near the crater, but my university credentials have gotten me close enough."

"Close enough for what?"

"Close enough to snap these shots." He put a handful of pictures on the table and leaned in. "Close enough to see that there's no plague, no pestilence, no wildlife left dead or dying."

Donovan looked at the images. Although blurry, he could make out machinery, tents, people running back and forth.

Badru spoke again: "If there's a plague, where are the hazmat suits? Where are the clean rooms? There's not even a surgical tent." Badru leaned in. "Alan, I've been an archeologist for more years than I can remember, so I know what I'm looking at." He paused. "Those men are digging for something."

September 9
National Naval Medical Center
Bethesda, Maryland
7:08 p.m.

Franklin Wilson shifted uncomfortably in his bed. The healing of his shattered leg was going slower than he would have liked. While the makeshift splint he had employed on the Moon had probably ensured that he would walk again, it had also allowed some of the bones to fuse in a less-than-perfect fashion. As a result, doctors had been forced to rebreak the leg and start from scratch. At best, he was looking at a return to active duty within a year. The good news was, thanks to his part in the Phoenix mission, he could write his own ticket. While many believed he would return to the marines, those who knew him best saw a different kind of flicker in his eyes.

At present, he was propped up in bed, his laptop open. The door clicked open, and Wilson looked up to see Aaron Stein stroll in, his face looking more nervous and pinched than usual. Reflexively, Wilson closed his laptop.

"Colonel Wilson," Stein said, extending his hand.

"Nice to see you again, Mr. Stein," Wilson answered, gripping it firmly.

"How's the leg?"

"It only hurts ninety-five percent of the time now," said Wilson. "So I'm feeling pretty good."

"Good to hear it," Stein replied, shuffling through some papers. He pulled a chair up next to Wilson's bed. "Now, Colonel, I need to talk with you about your shipmates on the Phoenix mission. As you may or may not have heard, all of them, with the exception of Dr. Yeoh, have gone missing. We've checked with Interpol and the Chinese government—nothing. Might you have any idea as to their whereabouts?"

"Not a clue, sir," Wilson said, his eyes fixed.

Stein settled back in his seat, taking off his glasses and chewing on them thoughtfully. "We know Zell called you three days ago, just before his plane took off from Dulles. He must have said something."

"He merely said he was returning to the institute."

Stein eyed Wilson a moment, then leaned forward, his tone more serious. "I know your record, Colonel. I know you're an honorable man, the kind of man who wouldn't betray his friends. I also know you're a man who knows the rules." He leaned in even more. "The kind of man who knows the penalty for obstructing a federal investigation."

"I wasn't aware there was an investigation, Mr. Stein," Wilson answered, his voice remaining even.

"In the NSA, Lieutenant Colonel," he said, chuckling, "there is always an investigation." He paused, shifting his voice to a "Let's be pals" delivery. "You've got a bright future ahead of you, Frank. You're on the fast track to the top. Maybe all the way. Are you really willing to see that derailed by a couple of loose cannons?"

"Those 'loose cannons' risked their lives for this country," Wilson said.

"That may be," Stein replied, "but they've decided to take this matter into their own hands, and in doing so have risked causing an international incident."

"An international incident?" Wilson raised an eyebrow. "Really?"

Stein's lips thinned as he stood up. "If you hear anything, you know where to find me."

"Of course."

"Good evening, Colonel," Stein said, turning on his heel and leaving the room.

Wilson watched him leave, then looked out the window.

Whatever you're looking for, guys, you better find it quick.

September 10
The White House
Washington, DC
10:45 a.m.

"What do you mean, you can't find them?"

The President did not raise her voice often. For years she had used to her political advantage the fact that she had a remarkable ability to hide her emotions. This wasn't to say that she wasn't a passionate woman—far from it. Still, few legislators could ever gauge her feelings on any particularly controversial bill. On Capitol Hill they even had a nickname for her: the Poker-Faced President. However, upon hearing that the survivors of the Moon mission had just up and disappeared, her usual restraint had evaporated.

John Dieckman and General McKenna eyed each other cautiously as they sat before the President's desk in the Oval Office. They had been the ones in charge of keeping the crew on a tight leash, at least the American ones.

"All we know for a fact is that Lieutenant Commander Benevisto is AWOL," McKenna explained. "And that he was last seen visiting the Watergate Hotel, where Donovan and Zell were staying. They checked out and Benevisto hasn't been seen since."

The President leaned back in her chair and folded her arms. "What about the Chinese crew members?"

"Dr. Yeoh took a flight out to Taiwan about the same time," Dieckman noted. "It seems he's got a fiancée there and wanted to see how she was holding up after the recent activities."

"And Dr. Soong?"

McKenna grimaced. "Missing too. And she was last seen with Zell."

"Well, that's just terrific," the President said, slapping her desk. "All they need to do is shoot their mouths off once, and the whole arrangement with the Chinese is out the window."

"I don't know about that, ma'am," Deke added. "The NSA people were pretty clear about the fact that their discoveries were top secret."

The President glanced at Dieckman, her voice level. "You sound like you don't approve, Deke."

"Truthfully, Madam President, I don't. These people are heroes. I know it's not politically correct to throw that word around these days, but they are. And we've essentially—"

Dieckman's thought was interrupted by a knock at the door, followed by the entrance of the secretary of defense, Aaron Stein.

"I'm sorry to interrupt, Madam President, but—"

"Have some good news for me, Aaron."

Stein glanced around him at the other people in the room. Seeing that it was okay to speak, he did so. "We've found them, ma'am. They boarded Zell's private jet at Dulles International shortly after they checked out of the Watergate. All of them—Zell, Donovan, Soong, and Benevisto."

"Where the hell did they go?" McKenna demanded. "Back to Zell's institute in England?"

"That's what we thought at first," Stein said as he skimmed some papers in his hand through his half-moon reading glasses. "But according to the FAA, the plane refueled at Heathrow and immediately took off again. This time only Donovan and Benevisto were on board. It seems that the larger group split up in London but all arrived at the same destination."

"And that destination was?" the President asked irritably.

"Dar es Salaam."

"Tanzania?" Deke said, looking at Stein. "Why would they be going there?"

"A good question," the President mused. "Do we have an answer?"

"If they're all together, my guess is that it's something to do with the Moon mission," McKenna added. "Deke, did you find anything in the *Astraeus*'s records to suggest—"

Stein shot the President a look, then turned back to Dieckman and McKenna, eyebrows raised.

"Well?" the President wondered. "Do you know, Aaron?"

"I can take a guess, Madam President," Stein began slowly, "but I'm not sure you're going to like it."

"It doesn't matter if I like it, Aaron."

"Well, ma'am," he said, pulling his glasses from his face, "what do you know of the Ngorongoro Crater?"

Chapter 19

September 10
The Hotel Harrington
Dar es Salaam, Tanzania
6:45 p.m.

After dinner Badru and Donovan left the hotel in search of transportation to the Ngorongoro Crater. Both Soong and Benny were bothered by Donovan being mysterious in not permitting them to tag along. Knowing Donovan as he did, Zell did his best to ease tensions by offering them both a drink in his room while they waited. The day had been too hot to be dragging themselves across the city anyway, he decided. With the end of the dry season, the air was heavy and thick, made worse by the smell of garbage and automobile exhaust. To Zell's mind, such weather served as the perfect excuse for relaxation before their long journey.

Zell poured some scotch for Soong and Benny and lit a cigar. Soong immediately went over to the hotel-room window and opened it wide, hoping to draw some cleaner air into her lungs. Unable to find any outside, she sat back in the window seat, watching the ceiling fan twirl and begrudgingly accepting her fate. Zell smiled and continued to puff away as he eased himself into a nearby rocking chair.

Benny was in the corner, idly flipping through a Tanzania travel guide. "Wait a minute," he said, sitting up. "This Ngoron . . . goro . . . whatever you call it . . ."

"Ngorongoro Crater," Zell said.

"Yeah," Benny said, "it's actually a collapsed *volcano*?"

"That it is," Zell said with a grin. "The world's largest unflooded and unbroken caldera, as a matter of fact."

"English, please."

"Essentially a crater with a diameter considerably wider than the volcanic vent which created it," Zell answered through a haze of blue-gray smoke. "The volcano's center usually collapses in an enormous explosion of some kind. In this case, two and a half million years ago, the lava inside formed a lid over the crater. But when the magma subsided, this lid collapsed the entire volcano, leaving behind an extremely large and unbroken rock wall."

"At least that's the theory," Soong said.

"You sound as if you don't believe it, Dr. Soong," Zell answered with a grin.

"It's just that in our line of work, we theorize so much about a subject that such theories often become biblical truths," Soong said. "I for one have many times seen evidence which disputes even the most highly held theories."

"I agree—no one knows for certain how it collapsed," Zell replied. "But volcanologists believe that the volcano once rivaled Kilimanjaro in size."

"I'm not disputing the fact that it was a volcano, Dr. Zell," Soong noted. "It's just that I've been mulling over a theory." Soong sat forward in her seat, pressing her thin elbows into the knees of her khaki pants. "We estimate that the *Astraeus* crashed on the Moon roughly two million years ago and that her sister ship crashed in Africa around the same time. Now, if we buy into Dr. Yeoh's notion that time travel acts as a river, bringing objects to the same point in time—"

"Then the second ship could've caused the collapse of the volcano." Zell took another drag and smiled through the smoke. "That's a leap of faith worthy of Alan Donovan. Or my father. I didn't think you had it in you, Yang Zi."

Soong smiled. "Let's say my ability to jump to far-fetched conclusions has increased somewhat recently."

"But still, entirely plausible." Zell got up from his chair and rustled through the backpack on his bed and pulled out a map. He set it on the table near Benny. "See here," Zell said, pointing at the map. "That's the Ngorongoro Crater, six hundred meters deep, with a diameter of about nineteen kilometers."

Benny rubbed his chin. "Well now, that's a big goddamn hole in the ground."

"And an important one, if those coordinates you downloaded from the *Astraeus* prove accurate. The whole area is a treasure trove of fossils, but I can't imagine anyone has ever found a fossil like the one we're going in search of."

"But how do we get to it?" Soong approached the map and leaned over it, tucking a black strand of hair behind her ear as she did. "If the village is here, outside the crater, but the main roads are blocked to visitors because of this supposed outbreak, how do we get to it?"

Zell traced a finger across the map. "If the walls of Jericho cannot be breached, they must be scaled."

"You mean climb up over that rock wall you were talking about?" Benny said.

Zell smiled. "Exactly, Commander. We ascend over the rock wall in a discreet location, then descend into the crater. From there our global-positioning equipment should lead us right to the spot."

Benny rubbed his chin. "I hate to ask how high the damn wall is."

"More than twenty-one hundred meters above sea level," Zell replied. "It gets fairly brisk up there at night, so I hope you brought your winter coat."

Benny sank back in his chair. "Terrific. And here I only brought my suntan lotion."

Just then Badru and Donovan entered the room. Zell offered them a drink, which they eagerly accepted before he returned to his rocking chair.

"So I'll assume that you gentlemen have procured means of transportation by now?" Zell asked.

Badru and Donovan gave each other a look. "Well, Elias," Donovan began, "*procure* might be too strong a word."

Benny took a sip of his scotch. "Don't tell me you just dragged us halfway across the world and haven't even chartered a private flight out there?"

"A private charter flight would be too risky," Badru explained. "Too many eyes would be watching the airport."

"So what've you got in mind?" Soong asked. "Overland, by Jeep?"

"Still too risky, Soong," Donovan said. "If anyone's looking for an archeology team heading for the crater, they'll be expecting us to either come by plane or by caravan."

Soong shook her head. "Then how can you possibly expect us to get all of our equipment to the site?"

"Badru's arranged to have our equipment shipped incognito to his village." Donovan smiled sheepishly. "We'll be arriving separately."

"Oh Jesus." Zell's face flushed with dawning realization. "Not the damn bus!"

"The bus, Elias," Donovan said flatly.

Benny looked to Donovan and Zell, and then back to Donovan again. "What's wrong with the bus?"

"Well," Zell said, contemplating his cigar, "give it some time. You may find yourself wishing you were still stranded on the Moon."

September 10
Ngorongoro Crater, Tanzania
8:05 p.m.

There was no single technological advancement that Dr. Joseph Cuevas detested more than videoconferencing. If no one had ever thought of it, he might have been able to mask his nervousness in an ordinary telephone call. Instead, he had to face the wrath of Cal Walker full-on, protected only by the thousands of miles that separated them. And, at the moment, even that distance didn't feel like much protection.

For a thin old man, Walker had the amazing ability to fill an entire computer screen. He always drew himself in close, the top third of the screen filled by his silver-gray hair, the bottom two-thirds by his ruddy yet still youthful face and shoulders. Cuevas wondered if he sat that way because he was nearsighted, but then thought better of it. If Walker was good at anything, it was intimidation. And he knew the best way to do that was through a face-to-face confrontation.

Cuevas watched the old man's visage grow larger on the screen. The ice-blue eyes never seemed to blink. "I was made to understand that the project would be completely shut down this morning."

"With respect, Dr. Walker," Cuevas began, absentmindedly running a hand through his thinning black hair, "what the company expects is impossible. They're asking us to completely abandon a project many people have worked on for nearly two years, knowing how much progress we've made in the last six months alone."

"No one *asked* anything, Dr. Cuevas." Walker leaned back slightly, exposing his shoulders to the screen. "What was expected was for your team to shut down operations and seal the dig site by seven this morning. I cannot continue to give excuses to the board."

"Sir, if you only give us a little more time. We should be able to—"

"You have another hour, Doctor. Beyond that I am afraid that matters will be out of my hands."

Cuevas watched as Walker sat back and his thick-veined hand reached toward the keyboard, tapped a key, and ended the transmission. The researcher sat for several long seconds before the blank screen, then turned to the members of his team who had gathered around the periphery of the terminal.

"You heard the man, ladies and gentlemen. We've got another hour."

The team dispersed with worried glances and muttered comments. He knew as they did that their entire careers were now on the line. Walker and the other members of the board had the power to destroy them. Cuevas pulled a handkerchief from his pocket and patted down his glistening brow as he scanned around him. They couldn't disassemble all the equipment they had brought with them, but he knew they had to take as much as possible before they sealed up the dig. He didn't fully understand the urgency about shutting down operations so quickly, but having experienced all the secrecy surrounding the project—including the incredible outbreak story—he could guess why. Someone had discovered what they were doing, someone who was likely heading toward their position at this moment. Whoever was coming was obviously beyond the control of Walker and the others.

Cuevas almost wanted to meet such a person. He knew the company had more than its fair share of competitors, but there were few people they outright feared.

Cuevas was a geneticist. Not that he bragged about it, but he knew he was at the top of his field. That's why TGI recruited him so many years ago. That's why they invited him to lead this project six months ago. But he didn't have the stomach for this kind of cloak-and-dagger business. He knew that the moment he had signed all of the confidentiality papers before heading off to Africa. But the money—and the prestige—that came with such an offer were far too tempting.

Cuevas pulled himself from his seat and strolled down the central aisle of workstations and computer banks under the rigged fluorescent lights bolted into the roof of the cavern. At the end of the aisle sat the ship, still half-buried in earth and volcanic muck. Though the archeology team had excavated several hundred feet of the vessel over the last two years, much of it still remained underground. Its sheer enormity overwhelmed him. They could still only estimate its actual size and shape by walking around inside the craft. And much of that was barred from them. The ship had long been exposed to the elements and was heavily damaged in many sections, making them inaccessible. The best-educated guesses suggested that the ship was at least nearly two miles long and more than half a mile wide.

Still, it was remarkable that so much of the ship had been preserved after roughly two and a half million years. But the vessel was composed of a metal unlike anything any member of his team had ever seen. If it really had been piloted through time and space as they now suspected, its builders must have known the ship could survive burial in a volcanic antechamber.

Though his team had disassembled many of its components, the *Eos* still very much looked as it did the first day he beheld it—like a massive prehistoric beast trapped in a tidal wave of nature. And like any prehistoric fossil, this ship looked out of place in his own time—except that its time was not a past age but a future one. He had discovered that much in the last six months. Before him rested a piece of humanity's collective future.

Cuevas pulled his pipe from his coat pocket and stuffed it with tobacco. He knew he was breaking his own rule by smoking in the cavern, but it wouldn't matter all that much now. In an hour this place and its secrets might well be sealed for the rest of his lifetime. He struck a match and touched it to the pipe's bowl as he strolled before what they had decided was the bow of the ship. The pipe calmed him. He ran a hand against the ship's hull, which still had an almost-living warmth.

He knew the rumors surrounding the ship's discovery. Supposedly, a little over two years ago, a Maasai warrior who lived in a nearby village had led a British archeological team to the ship. The Maasai had described falling into a cavern while walking through the Ngorongoro Crater one day. Wielding a torch composed of shreds of his robe and a tree branch, he explored deeper into the chamber. Before him was a metallic wall. Scrambling up out of the cavern, he returned to his village to inform some of the tribal leaders about the discovery, who in turn informed a dear friend who was also a British archeologist. The leaders told their warrior to tell no one else of what he had discovered. And true to his word, the warrior kept the secret and was allowed to lead the team back to the cavern.

Beyond that, Cuevas knew little of the British team's story, aside from the fact that they were found, along with their Maasai guide, shot to death inside their vehicles on the road leading out of the crater. Local government officials had claimed that the team had been murdered by thieves intent on robbing them of their supplies and vehicles. Apologies were issued to the British government, and compensation was made to the members of their families. The Maasai remained silent on the subject. But no trace of where the exploratory team had been or what they had been doing on that road had ever surfaced. And neither had the killers.

Two weeks later, an American team of archeologists was called in. They surveyed the cavern and unearthed a fair portion of the ship over a year and a half. Six months ago the dig was subcontracted out to TGI. Cuevas didn't know how his government had managed to take the dig away from the British, but once a genetic team was clearly needed at the site, TGI was given the project. He knew his employer was well connected inside the American government—the amount of political campaigns the company had contributed to over the years was testament to that—but he didn't know how high up those connections went. For all he knew, the President herself might be aware of the *Eos*, though that didn't seem likely. If anything ever smacked of a case for plausible deniability, this was it.

Someone cleared his throat behind him. Cuevas pulled his pipe from his mouth and turned to face his assistant director, Dr. Arnold Anderson.

"What's up?"

"Joe, we've got the specimens all packed away. But we're not sure about what to do with the research. Should we load it all onto one truck, or should we split it up?"

"Better split it up, Arnold. Make sure each truck has copies of our records. This way if anything gets damaged we'll still have a complete record somewhere."

"What about the components from the ship?"

"Same drill. Split them up. I know we're not completely sure how they work, but the computer people seem to think each station is a complete microcomputer in itself."

"Okay."

"What's wrong, Arnold?"

Anderson wiped sweat from the back of his neck. "We're still leaving a lot behind. Too much."

"I know. But we have to take what we can and hope it's enough."

"There's still a lot of questions."

"I know," Cuevas said, looking back toward the *Eos*. "And in less than an hour no one may ever learn the answers."

Donovan had to admit he was impressed. Benny had gone all of two and a half hours before he began complaining about the more-than-thirteen-hour bus ride from Dar es Salaam to the Ngorongoro Crater.

Still, he was amazed that Benny could be complaining at all, especially when one considered all the discomforts they had to endure during their trip to the Moon. But, as Benny said frequently throughout the bus ride, he had been trained for that. No training he had ever gone through had prepared him for the inadequacies of the developing world's public transportation.

The bus was old and without air-conditioning. And despite all the wide-open windows, the air inside the vehicle was thick and gamy. The smells reminded Donovan of many of the farms he had visited as a child when his father went crop dusting. Here the open windows did little more than blow dust inside from the roads to coat the worn, cracked seats with grime. About four and a half hours into the trip, the driver pulled to the side of the road and announced that they had a one-minute bathroom break before pulling out again. As soon as Badru translated what the driver had said, Benny burst from the bus in pursuit of the other passengers who had scrambled into the brush for a moment of privacy. In one minute exactly, the driver blew the whistle he wore around his neck, and everyone raced back into the bus, Benny trailing behind as he pulled up his pants.

They all knew better than to laugh at him. All of them, that is, with the exception of Badru, who burst out in hysterics.

"Keep it up, pal," Benny said as he buttoned up his pants, "and I'll knock your teeth out."

Badru wiped tears from his eyes. "I'm sorry, my friend," he said, "but I've got a head start." He smiled widely, revealing his missing lower front tooth.

"What?" Benny joked. "You piss someone else off worse than me?"

"Not quite," Badru said as he regained his composure. "It is a rite of passage for all Maasai males. When we come of age, one of the elders knocks it right out, pop!" He slapped his hands together for emphasis.

"Neat trick," Benny said.

Badru nodded. "Not only does it mark us as having completed the journey to manhood, but should one of us succumb to the heat while in the wild"—he clenched his teeth and broadened his smile—"it makes for a convenient place into which to pour water."

"Huh," Benny said thoughtfully. "Sounds like your tribe is really something."

"Once, we were the most feared tribe in East Africa," Badru said, his voice becoming reflective. He then chuckled. "Some say we are one of the ten lost tribes of Israel."

"And others believe you're the living ancestors to the ancient Egyptians," Donovan added.

Badru nodded thoughtfully. "Based primarily on the braided hair of our warriors. I think that theory is rather dubious."

"As are most theories," Zell said, glancing at Soong, "until backed up with solid facts."

"Perhaps it is better to believe in myths then, Elias," Badru noted. "Myths are never as disappointing as facts often are."

Donovan took a breath. "Or as dangerous."

September 11
Arlington, Virginia
2:12 a.m.

"Jim, did I wake you?"

"Not at all, ma'am. I was sitting up waiting for you."

The President laughed. "That's bullshit and you know it."

McKenna sat up in bed and stuck a cigar in his mouth, unlit. He glanced over at his wife, who stirred slightly in their warm white sheets, and took the cordless phone down the hall into his study, where he struck a match. Easing back into his desk chair, he watched as the smoke curled off the cigar and into the well-worn volumes in his bookcases.

The phone call at two o'clock in the morning came as no surprise to McKenna. For as long as he had known the President, he knew she couldn't sleep when she had something on her mind. And after that meeting with Stein yesterday, he was surprised that the President had waited until two to place the call.

"I guess I don't have to ask what's on your mind."

"I can't believe this mess we've gotten ourselves into, Jim. I understand all this plausible-deniability crap, but something like this—"

"I know, ma'am. But that's the goddamn NSA for you. Who the hell knows what they're doing?"

"Well, I mean to change that," the President said firmly. "You'd think we'd have learned our lessons after 9/11, not to keep all our cards so close to the vest that nobody knows what the hell anyone else has their fingers in."

McKenna glanced at his desk calendar. He couldn't believe he had forgotten the anniversary. Obviously the President hadn't. What sitting president could in this day and age? Though the ceremonies to mark the attack had become less and less ornate over the years, McKenna knew that he was going to participate in just such a ceremony at the Pentagon that very morning. For a few moments, he found himself unable to respond to the President. Since his involvement with Walker, he had become quite good at compartmentalizing the various aspects of his life. He felt ashamed to have shoved the anniversary to some barely used broom closet of his brain.

"With all due respect, ma'am, this is a card that had to be played close," McKenna answered. "And this is coming from the head of Space Command. If anyone besides you should know about it, I should."

"I know. But I've been doing some thinking. We can't have Donovan and that bunch on the loose. But we can't do it through ordinary channels."

McKenna sat up in his chair. "Ma'am, are you asking me—"

"Jim, prep a team. We need reliable people, trustworthy people. I don't care where you get them from or how you get them, so long as we keep this thing quiet."

"What about the British prime minister? She might not like this, since it also concerns a British citizen."

"I'll handle her. I'm sure she'll understand our wanting to take extraordinary measures to be discreet."

"Understood, Madam President. Thank you, ma'am."

McKenna switched off the phone and tossed it on a pile of papers on his desk. He stood up and paced around his study absentmindedly, reading the spines of his books, cigar in the corner of his mouth, hands behind his back. His gaze fell as it so often did to the photo of his son in his wheelchair. So many had sacrificed so much for so long to keep this country safe. They had sacrificed their families and their lives for the good of the whole. He thought of men he had known in combat, of those passengers aboard Flight 93 who brought that plane down in a field in Pennsylvania to keep it from hitting the White House. For most of his career McKenna took comfort in the idea that he was one of those few who had sacrificed for the many. And now, and now—

He made his decision. He picked up the photo and ran his hand across the glass. "Forgive me, son."

He reached for the phone and dialed a number he didn't often use but knew by heart.

"Colonel Casey? Jim McKenna. Sorry to call you so late, Mitch, but I've got a job for your boys."

Badru's village was poorer than Donovan remembered. All around him red-robed Maasai warriors drifted by, eyeing them with caution, their spears ever at the ready but with eyes and arms too tired or weak from malnutrition to use them. Once Badru was spotted among their group, the warriors let down their guard somewhat, but the exhaustion in their eyes remained. The continuing battles between the Maasai and the Tanzanian government had left the tribe on the edge of extinction.

Ever since settlement of the Ngorongoro Crater had been banned by the government back in 1974, the Maasai had experienced numerous difficulties in trying to maintain their traditional lifestyle. The first came in the early 1990s when cattle grazing was banned from the crater and the tribe was unable to find pastures for their livestock in the dry season. Without hunting or pasturing or water rights in the crater, the tribe had come to rely more and more upon tourism as a means for survival. And now even that had been taken from them. Since the government closed the crater two years ago due to the supposed outbreak, few tourists had come out to see the remnants of East Africa's once-most-powerful tribe.

The village was also smaller, less lively, with fewer children running around. The few that Donovan did see either clung weakly to their mothers' breasts or limped softly into view, usually peeking around the hips of their elders. Despite the efforts of industrialized nations over the last decade to bring life-saving drugs to the continent to combat AIDS, Ebola, and other diseases, far too little of the medicine had gotten through to the people who needed it most. Whatever corrupt government officials hadn't snatched up for themselves had been stolen by bandits. And despite their once-overwhelming power in the region, the Maasai had been no exception to the overall population drop in Africa.

Looking at the Maasai now, Donovan was reminded of the Native American reservations that he had visited with his father while they were living out west. The only thing that separated the Maasai now from those indigenous peoples was a few hundred years of history, a few hundred years of pillage, murder, slow death by disease and poverty. Except in the Maasai's case, they might not even last that long.

"Hey, Donovan," Benny muttered from the corner of his mouth. "You mind telling me why this dude's holding my hand?"

Donovan grinned despite himself. "He's leading you to dinner."

"I can see that," Benny said, nodding at the feast laid out before them. "But why does he have to lead me around by the hand like I'm his girlfriend or something?"

"The Maasai are a very affectionate people," Zell noted from his place in the procession. "Men often walk around holding hands. They're welcoming us into their family as honored guests."

Benny sighed. "I'm just glad the guys in my squadron can't see this. I'd never hear the end of it."

"But they're the ones missing out, Commander," Zell added. "You see, we've come on a special day. They're going to be initiating a new group of young men into the *morani*, the warrior class of the Maasai."

"You're kidding," Benny said as he took his seat at the banquet table. "So it's like a graduation or something?"

Soong laughed. "Not exactly."

Benny shook his head. "I dunno if I like the sound of that laugh. What am I missing? Do they haveta kill a lion or something?"

"In the old days we did," Badru noted as he sat next to Benny. "But conservation laws now restrict that. But there is one trial that the warriors must still endure."

"I hate to ask, but—"

"It's a circumcision ceremony."

"Oh no," Benny said, rubbing his eyes. "Somebody please tell me he's kidding. We're gonna see a bunch of kids get snipped?"

"Not kids," Donovan noted. "Most are about fourteen or fifteen; some are as old as eighteen. It all depends on when the elders of the tribe decide they need a new group of warriors."

"I think I'm gonna be sick," Benny groaned.

"I'd suggest you don't," Zell said, leaning across the table. "The morani can't so much as flinch during the procedure. If they do, they disgrace their families. If you do, you'll disgrace us."

Before them now were gathered the uncircumcised Maasai, known as the *laiyok*. Each of them wore long black robes and kept his hair long and oily as well. Soon, as Badru explained, their heads would be shaved to display their new status, and over the next few months they would be required to wear headdresses of birds' feathers.

"The boys who do not flinch at all during the ceremony are given ostrich plumes and eagle feathers," Badru noted. "And after the ceremony they'll go around teasing younger boys to go through the ceremony and not flinch."

"Talk about rough basic training," Benny said. "But how do they prove themselves as warriors?"

Badru sighed. "Again, the tests have now long since been banned. Once, they would kill a lion, armed with only a spear, and later they would be able to wear a headdress made from a lion's mane. Or they could prove themselves in battle. Now also outlawed."

"It seems like this teenage circumcision is a lot to go through nowadays," Benny noted, "with very few perks."

"At least for now," Badru remarked. "Perhaps someday we will be called upon to become true warriors again."

"What're they doing?"

Sherwood lifted his eyes from his binoculars and looked at Miller. "Nothing. Looks like they're getting ready to eat. We're not going to be able to get a shot at them now. Too much activity."

Miller grunted in agreement. "They want us to do this quietly. Knocking out a whole village might get the government's attention." Miller took the binoculars from Sherwood and peered through them at the village. "So we take them at the crater. Dispose of the bodies there."

"Our employer doesn't want them to reach the dig," Sherwood observed.

"We can get them as they enter the crater," Miller said. "There they'll just become food for the wildlife."

Chapter 20

September 12
Arusha, Tanzania
1:16 p.m.

"Colonel? They're on the move."

Mitch Casey snapped awake from his brief combat nap, stood up ramrod straight, and looked his lieutenant in the eye.

"Do we have confirmation?"

"We spotted a Jeep loaded down with equipment heading in the direction of the site."

Casey nodded, staring out at the midafternoon sun. "Then let's go get 'em."

"Yes, sir!" barked the lieutenant, then ducked out of the tent and began rounding up the men. Casey smiled. He had spent more than thirty-five years in service of his country, twenty-seven of those in special warfare, but he honestly felt this was the finest unit he'd ever led. On the books the team was known as Task Force Sierra—or the Sierra Club, as the boys in the teams liked to say—but to Casey and those around him, they were more commonly called the Wolverines, having adopted the ferocious mammal as their symbol. The name had come about as a result of the team's reputation for fighting tirelessly to the last soldier. In the team's seven-year history, they had traveled to some of the worst hot zones the planet had to offer and had taken down more than their share of heavy hitters. Before long, the word spread: if you wanted someone bagged, tagged, and brought home, you called in the Wolverines.

When Casey had gotten the call from General McKenna, he realized something serious was up. A team like his wasn't often contacted directly by the top brass, who always wanted to have as much plausible deniability as possible between them and whatever mission the Wolverines would be sent on. And what he learned from McKenna about this mission was almost beyond belief. A ship on the Moon. Time travel. Technology beyond belief. As crazy as it all sounded, since the pulse Casey found few things beyond imagining.

Yet the reasons behind this mission didn't matter now. All that he needed to know was that some folks had gone off the reservation. He and his men had to bring them back.

Which was exactly what he intended to do.

September 12
Ngorongoro Conservation Area, Tanzania
1:17 p.m.

The Jeep sped through the Serengeti Plain, kicking up dust in its wake. The vehicle had to be at least twenty years old and, from the way it was rattling over the terrain, seemed destined to fly apart at any moment.

"It figures we'd be ferried to what promises to be the most important dig of our careers in this rattletrap," moaned Zell. "It's something like poetic justice."

"I don't know what's worse," Donovan said, turning the vehicle onto a main road. "This car's clattering or your whining."

"Whining? Who's whining? I just think this journey would have been much more pleasant if we could have taken Jolene with us."

Jolene was a monster of a Humvee, which Zell had personally outfitted with the latest in hi-tech GPS, radar, and infrared technology, as well as numerous other gadgets—and creature comforts—that made remote digs a little easier. He had not yet had the chance to use the vehicle.

"Yes, Little Lord Fauntleroy's Twenty-First-Century Panzer Tank," Donovan quipped. "Just the thing for traveling incognito. We head out in that thing, and everybody from the Navy SEALs to the Cub Scouts will be on our tail."

Donovan took Zell's silence and the lighting of his cigar for acceptance.

"If I could interrupt for a moment," Soong said, leaning forward in her seat. "what's the game plan here?"

"Well, my dear, not for the first time do we find ourselves in uncharted waters," said Zell. "I've loaded this girl up with as much equipment from the institute as she could take. It's not a lot, but it should give us enough to analyze the crater site once we get there. After we find the ship, well, that's where the guessing games start."

With that, the group lapsed into silence, taking a moment to enjoy the sights around them. Donovan and Zell had been here before, but to Benny and Soong, the terrain was a wonderland of new discoveries. As far as their eyes could see, the shimmering plains of the Serengeti stretched out before them. In the distance, Soong could see scads of flamingos skimming down onto the waters of a lake, in whose reflection she could make out a silver line of sky. Soong's eyes flitted to the rearview mirror. At the same instant, Alan's eyes met hers in the mirror. He quickly looked away, concentrating a little harder on the road.

She in turn glanced out the window, letting herself get lost in the landscape.

September 12
Arusha, Tanzania
5:05 p.m.

"Something's not right here," muttered Mitch Casey. He and the team had been following their quarry discreetly for the better part of the day, lagging behind in their APC, which had been cleverly redressed as a tourist van. But now Casey was beginning to smell a rat.

"Sir?" asked the lieutenant, a young, dark-haired man named Kapoor.

"They're leading us in the wrong direction."

"I don't know, sir. They're with a guide. He knows the area."

Casey took another look at the map. "If he knows the area, then why are they driving away from the target area? Face it, Kapoor. We're being taken to the cleaners."

"Should we intercept?"

Casey scratched his chin as he thought on it. "Negative. They're already a little jumpy. We go in hot right now, and it could get bad really quick."

"What do you advise?"

"They're heading for that forest," Casey said. "The map calls it the Lerai Forest. My guess is they're going to make camp and figure out how best to ditch us for good." He turned to the driver. "Disengage, Corporal."

"Sir?" the driver asked.

"You heard me. Fall back. We're going to let them think they've lost us, then do a little snooping."

"And after that?" Kapoor asked.

"After that," said Casey, "we move in and put an end to this little safari."

September 13
Lerai Forest, Tanzania
6:16 a.m.

In Lerai Forest, a heavy mist clung to the trees. A lone figure stood at the campsite, stirring the dying embers from last night's fire. Suddenly the site was alive with red points of light as the Wolverines stormed out of their natural cover, the laser sights of their weapons pointed at the man's back.

"Freeze!" barked the team leader. "Get down on your knees, put your hands behind your head, and interlock your fingers . . . *now!*"

The man did as he was told, raising his hands with an obvious air of defeat. It was over. The team leader reached out, spinning him around by his shoulders. He stepped back, surprised at the smiling face in front of him.

"Vipi, rafiki?" Badru said. *What's up, friend?*

In response, the steady sound of clapping filled the morning air.

"Very clever," said Casey, walking toward Badru. "Very, very clever. So tell me, how long were you planning on keeping up this wild goose chase?"

"Until you ran out of gas or I ran out of interest, I suppose," Badru replied in a conversational tone.

Casey paused. "Let me tell you something. My mandate for this mission doesn't call for the use of terminal force." He moved in closer, face-to-face with Badru. "Unless I'm met with resistance. Interfering with a military operation. Jeopardizing national security. You're in dangerous territory, my friend."

Casey then became aware of subtle, almost imperceptible movements in the spaces between the trees. Moving soundlessly, a host of Maasai warriors emerged from the mist. Dressed in red robes, their faces painted in the traditional makeup of the warrior class, they looked like time travelers from an age long forgotten. They brandished spears, swords, and clubs confidently and with assurance. The lead warrior, newly inducted only two nights before, sidled catlike up to Casey and put his sword to the colonel's throat, his skeletal face locked in a determined grimace.

"No, my friend," said Badru. "I am afraid it is *you* who is in dangerous territory."

Casey paused a moment, reading the movements of his teammates. He had to admit, even after all the years of warfare and all the hot spots they'd been in, his men seemed frightened. He himself was not, having long since abolished fear from his genetic makeup. However, he knew enough to realize that should things take a turn for the worse, he could be looking at an international incident the likes of which could forever taint the office of his commander in chief.

In capitulation, he raised his hands. Almost in unison, the rest of the Wolverines performed similarly, lowering their weapons, if not their guard.

"That's better," said Badru. He looked at the warriors. "*Asanteni sana,*" he said with a wave of his hand, and they quietly stood down. Badru looked back at Casey. He clapped him on the shoulder warmly, then broke into a wide smile. "*Karibu, rafiki*. Do you like coffee?"

Casey paused in slight bewilderment. "Sure."

"Then sit with me, friend. And your men too. The fire's just getting started."

Badru took a seat on a rock and began poking at the fire with a stick. When Casey joined him after a moment, the suddenly stoic archeologist looked at the colonel and leaned in closely.

"And now," Badru said, "perhaps you can explain to me your interest in Alan Donovan."

September 13
Ngorongoro Conservation Area, Tanzania
6:47 a.m.

After a few more hours of driving through the mountain roads, Donovan and the others pulled off to an area alongside the crater wall. Their somewhat circuitous path to the crater cost them valuable time, but Donovan deemed the delay necessary. The main road into the conservation area was always guarded, even when it had been a tourist spot. Since its closing two years ago, the site was even more closely watched. Donovan opted to play it safe, after he was informed by Maasai scouts that he and his team were being followed.

"I think we're going to need to hike from here," he told the others flatly.

"What?" Zell roared. "And leave all this equipment behind?"

"Come on, Elias. You know we're being tracked."

Zell reluctantly agreed. He was frustrated, sneaking around like this, yet he was also reminded just how valuable the prize was.

The crater wall stretched up in front of them, more than sixteen hundred feet high and sloping at a steep angle.

"So we've got to climb this thing?" Benny asked, shouldering his pack as he peered up the crater wall.

"It's the only way," Donovan said. "Straight up."

"Great, great. So what happens when we reach the top?"

"Then, Benny, we head the only *other* way. Straight down."

Benny shook his head and began the hike up the crater wall. "This trip just gets better all the time."

The hike up was long, tortuous. But for all its arduousness, the climb provided many wonders as well. The forested woodlands of the crater wall revealed a primeval paradise that seemed untouched by the passing of centuries. As the travelers wound their way through rugged outcrops of rock and thick, riverine forest, they were treated to a number of thrilling spectacles. Poking up from the dense underbrush, Soong noticed the akimbo limbs of a wildebeest. She peered a little closer before the bloodied face of a lioness popped up. Her curiosity quickly vanished, and she froze a moment before Donovan's hand on her shoulder brought her back onto the trail.

"This isn't the place to sightsee," he said with a smile.

After a few more hours of hiking, they reached the rim of the crater. The view was spectacular. In the distance, they could see yellow fever trees, shining silver lakes, and verdant grasslands. Two thousand feet below them, they could just make out the crater floor, with herds of animals moving silently about.

Zell grunted. "Does it look like there's a virus loose down there?"

"We'll know soon enough," answered Donovan.

Later that night, Soong snapped awake with a jerk. For a moment, she thought she was still trapped on the Moon and fumbled for her lantern. After a second, she got her whereabouts and decided to step out and stretch her legs.

The night air was unseasonably cold, almost freezing. She wrapped her thick blanket more firmly around her shoulders and strolled over to the crater's edge. The Moon was bathing the crater in a soft-white glow and giving a blue tint to the land. The night was alive with the sounds of birds and various other wildlife. If she concentrated just a bit, Soong could almost imagine that this was what the world looked like at the dawn of history. A sobering and comforting moment.

She walked over to the fire, where Donovan was sitting and reading.

"Can't sleep?" she asked.

Donovan looked up from his book. "I guess I'm still on lunar time."

She laughed. "Mind if I join you?"

"Of course not." He gestured. "Pull up a rock. There's plenty."

Soong sat down, and the two took a moment in silence, enjoying the sounds of the night. After a moment, she spoke.

"What are you reading?"

Donovan looked down at the tattered paperback. "This? *The Once and Future King*."

"I hadn't pegged you for a fantasy fan."

He laughed. "I'm not. It's just, well, my father gave me this book when I was a kid. He used to read it to me a little at a time every night after dinner. Then, when things got bad, I had to finish it myself."

"I'm sorry."

"Don't be," he said. "The thing is, reading that book with him, hearing about Arthur and his knights, all of it—it took me to a different place. It was one of the only places I ever felt really safe. Except for archeology texts and history books, it's the only book I've read more than once. I still read it, over and over again. Especially when I've got something on my mind."

"So what's on your mind tonight?"

Donovan thought a minute, then looked at her. "This dig, whatever we're going to find. It's gotten past the point of the discovery for me. Whatever's down there, I already know we've made the find of a lifetime."

"Then why pursue it further?" she asked, moving slightly closer to him.

"My dad spent his whole life in pursuit of something. And like that, it was taken away from him. Everything he had sacrificed for was gone. In the end he was buried in a small cemetery outside of town. It seemed to Dad that his whole life, everything—it didn't have any meaning. And now it's down to me. I'm here because of him. So I guess in some weird way, I'm hoping that this find, this ship, will give his life the meaning he felt it never had."

"Maybe the meaning in his life came from having you," she said.

"Any son would like to think that," said Donovan. "But I know better."

He stirred the fire some more, lost in memory. "'Wherever you go, there you are,'" he whispered.

"What's that?"

"Something my dad used to say," said Donovan. "He just meant that there's a lot in life you can outrun, but you can't outrun yourself. So you'd better find a way to make peace with who you are; otherwise life's going to be a long damn journey." Donovan looked off in the distance. "Good advice, even if he didn't follow it himself."

Soong looked at him. "And have you?" she asked. "Made peace with yourself?"

Donovan was quiet; then a small grin appeared. "Ask me tomorrow."

The next morning, everyone was up early and ready to go. Benny was buzzing around the campsite, clearing up whatever he could, and then began hacking away the beginnings of a path. The group worked in relative quiet, knowing what a long day they had in store. Donovan and Soong made no mention of the previous night's conversation, but to everyone around them, they seemed much more at ease with each other. As the sun crept over the crater wall, Donovan clapped his hands together.

"Okay, everyone!" he called. "We've got to get moving. We've got a two-thousand-foot descent to make. Benny! Put down the machete and shoulder your pack!"

"Okay, Doc, okay," Benny said. "Lemme just—"

Benny never heard the shot. The bullet spun him like a top so violently that Donovan wasn't certain where his friend got hit. All he saw was Benny crumple to the ground and roll out of sight.

"Elias! Soong!" Donovan cried reflexively. "Get out of here!"

Soong and Zell didn't wait around to ask questions. The mission was too important. Gathering what they could, they left the clearing in a hurry. Donovan stayed a moment longer to check on Benny.

The assassin emerged from the woods. "Don't bother running," he said to Donovan.

In an instant, Donovan's eyes caught a log still smoldering in the embers of last night's fire. Almost by reflex, he kicked out his leg, catapulting ash and hot rocks into his attacker's eyes. Miller screamed in anguish and rage, clawing at his face. Seeing his chance, Donovan turned around and bolted before promptly catching his foot on a root and hitting the ground with an unceremonious thud. By the time he had caught his wind, Miller had regained his composure and was moving toward him again.

"You really, really shouldn't have done that," he said through clenched teeth. He unfurled a butterfly knife. "Now this is going to take some time."

The next sound Donovan heard took him a moment to process—a high-pitched chink mixed with a meaty thump of metal striking flesh and bone. His would-be killer's eyes went wide with surprise. Then he tilted his head down to gaze at the machete now planted firmly in his foot. Blood spurted gaily, running in rivulets onto the ground. Miller looked at the hand on the machete's grip, surprised to see that it was attached to the man he'd supposedly just killed, lying prostrate on the ground.

Miller jumped back, shouting an indistinguishable word that sounded to Donovan like "Gaug!" and brandished his butterfly knife. Benny struggled to his feet and snapped into a fighting stance.

"Run, Donovan!" Benny said.

Although he hated leaving his friend, he knew he was right. After hesitating a moment longer, he ran from the clearing and down the crater wall. Benny turned to Miller.

The hitman circled him, hobbling on his wounded foot. He lunged at Benny, but he telegraphed the move, and Benny sidestepped it easily. He countered with a left hook that crashed into Miller's right cheek. The assassin stumbled back, momentarily dazed, then quickly regained his senses and launched back into the fray. Even with only half a foot, he was fast. His leg snapped out in a roundhouse kick that collided with Benny's solar plexus, dropping him to his knees. Miller drew his gun.

Donovan caught up with Zell and Soong a few yards down the wall.

"I left him, Elias," Donovan said, seething with rage. "He saved my life and I left him."

"You did what you had to do," replied Zell. "If you had stayed, there's a chance you'd be dead too. And the whole mission would come apart at the seams. Benny knew that."

Donovan was silent a moment; then he turned around. "No. I'm going to get him."

Zell had begun to protest when the sound of a gunshot startled him into silence.

Chapter 21

"I only clipped you the first time," Miller said. "I won't make that mistake again."

He racked the slide on his HK and pointed the barrel at Benny's head. As he did, something stirred in the jungle off to his left. He jerked his head reflexively, only for a second. That was all the time Benny needed. With reflexes honed by years of training, his left hand darted to the sheath on his thigh and drew out his knife. In an instant, he twisted his body around and implanted the blade in Miller's right kneecap up to the hilt. Miller's shriek was high and impertinent, sounding more like an offended dinner guest than someone whose knee had just been maimed. He waved his arms wildly, discharging his gun into a nearby tree as he did. Benny stood up and eyed his opponent. He leveled one bone-crunching punch at Miller's jaw, and the would-be killer knew no more. He slumped to the dirt and lay there almost peacefully.

"Drop the knife, asshole."

Benny whipped around and saw a second man, dressed similarly to the one lying at his feet. Unlike his partner, this one had a cooler, almost passive disposition. His bald head and mirrored shades made Benny think of Mr. Clean turned rogue assassin. Benny noticed the USP in his hand and realized that things were about to go from bad to worse.

"Hey!" a voice came from behind Benny. The assassin looked up with surprise.

The hand axe whistled through the air with frightening intensity, striking the assassin in the chest with a thwack. The force of the blow drove him back at least three feet, and he came to rest underneath a fever tree, his eyes staring almost accusingly. Benny whirled around and was shocked to see Donovan coming up behind him.

"Jesus!" he said with a combination of surprise and relief. "Where'd you come from?"

"We heard the shot, and I had to do something," Donovan said. "I should never have left you in the first place."

"Can't say I disapprove of your choice. This one was fitting me for a zipper bag."

"Were you hit?"

Benny tore open the side of his shirt, now soaked in blood. "Creased me on the side, but it's just a flesh wound." He grinned at Donovan. "Just like the movies."

Donovan looked at Sherwood's body. "We'll dress your wound when we meet up with the others."

Benny looked around the clearing. "We got lucky with these two. But there's going to be more."

"We've wasted enough time as it is," Donovan said. "Better get going."

"Roger that, boss," Benny said, shouldering his bag and heading down the trail. He turned to Donovan. "Where'd you learn to throw an axe like that, anyway?"

Donovan smiled. "The benefits of a partial Canadian upbringing. Before we moved to Modesto my family lived for a time up in Kitimat.

I took first place in logger sports at the Skeena Valley Fall Fair two years running."

Three hours later the team had reached the bottom of the crater. They had said little to one another during their descent, primarily because they all had their own tasks to fulfill. As the only one with any combat experience, Benny agreed to take point and walked a dozen yards ahead of the others, his eyes on the lookout for an ambush, the gun taken from Miller ready at his side, his service sidearm in its holster as a backup. Soong and Zell followed next, occasionally calling out changes in their descent as they consulted their GPS devices. Donovan held up the rear, armed with a pistol dropped by one of their assailants.

The descent had been difficult. It was a hot late-summer day, and the crater was thick with the season's underbrush. Though hacking through the brush with their machetes was tiring, the group kept up a fairly steady pace and took little time to rest. Each of them felt they would be safer once they reached the ship. Sweat coated and burned Donovan's face, now lacerated with scratches. Mosquitoes swarmed around them, on their necks and arms, in their ears and eyes. In a way Donovan was glad to have such annoyances. They kept his mind off the killers they had confronted and the look in Soong's eyes when he and Benny told her what had happened to them.

Donovan had killed a man. He was so concerned with reaching the ship and keeping them alive he had hardly stopped to consider what he had done. He knew it was in self-defense and realized that the hired gun would've killed Benny in another second, but he could scarcely imagine that he had just ended a man's life. He wondered if Zell or Soong would make him talk about it—that is, if they got out of this crater alive. He didn't want to. He didn't see much of a point in such discussions. He suddenly felt a connection to his father, who must've killed untold numbers of people during his tour of duty as a pilot in Vietnam. He dimly wondered if his father had tried to blot out such thoughts every time he took a drink.

For the first time in his life, Donovan found himself not wanting to be like his father.

At the bottom of the crater, Zell called a halt and consulted his GPS tracker.

"This looks like the place," Zell said. He turned to Soong, showing her the coordinates. "You got the same thing?"

Soong looked at her own tracker. "It looks like we're up on the roof."

"Then let's look for the goddamn chimney," said Zell gruffly.

With that, each of them took a direction and slowly began to search for the entrance to the cavern. After several minutes of chopping through underbrush, Benny called out, "I think I've found it!"

The others rushed toward his voice. They found him on the edge of a clearing near a thicket of trees. Benny hardly noticed their approach; he was too busy tossing fallen tree branches aside, or at least what he had thought were fallen tree branches. Zell held one up and then another. Each of them had been cut down and placed there purposely. Donovan glanced down to see what the branches had been hiding—a rock pile some twenty-five by forty feet wide. Donovan tore at some of the grass beneath his feet. As he expected, hidden tire tracks were revealed.

"Well," said Benny, "looks like somebody didn't want visitors."

Zell sighed and pushed his hair under his cap. "What do you suggest now, Dr. Donovan?"

"We could blow it," said Donovan, "if we had any charges. I suggest we find another way in."

"That could take hours," protested Benny. "And with those spooks on our tail, I don't think this is the time to take the scenic route."

"If you've got a better idea, Benevisto, now's the time."

Soong reached into her backpack and pulled out what looked like a small car battery. She walked over to the cave entrance and sprayed the rock with some sort of resin. Soong then affixed the device to the boulder and stepped away, taking out what looked to be a cigarette lighter from the breast pocket of her shirt.

Soong popped the top and clicked the button on the detonator. There was a high-pitched whine that reached a crescendo with a pop. Instantly, the rocks covering the cave entrance were pulverized to gravel. The three men looked at one another with admiration.

"Dr. Soong, you are just full of surprises," said Zell.

The hole Soong had made in the rock was just wide enough for each of them to crawl through individually. Donovan agreed to go in first, to make sure that the cavern was safe enough for the others. He flicked on his flashlight and slipped through the opening. For about thirty feet or so, the opening was narrow enough that he had to walk sideways in order to pass through. He moved slowly, making sure to secure his footing on the incline before taking another step. After thirty feet the cavern suddenly opened up. Donovan flashed his light around the expanse and smiled.

"Son of a bitch."

A few minutes later Donovan poked his head out of the cave, grinning broadly. "You've gotta see this!"

The others gathered their packs and flashlights and followed Donovan inside. After clearing the first thirty feet, they found themselves inside a vast underground cave. Whoever had been down here before them had taken their time clearing and securing the dig site. A vaulted ceiling rose above their heads some forty or fifty feet, supported by massive I beams and trusses, which were riddled with catwalks, gantries, and ladders. The ceiling itself was rigged with the latest in halogen lighting. Off to one side near the entrance were several electric generators and an air purifier.

As they advanced farther into the cave, they came across two long rows of workstations. Some computers remained intact and looked as if they were waiting for their users to come back from a coffee break. Other stations were completely empty, with the exception of a few charred pieces of paper littering the ground. Adjacent to the workstations were a number of rooms, including a common meeting area, bathrooms with full showers, a kitchen, and several dormitory-style spaces with bunk beds, equipped to house roughly twenty people. Walking alongside the other bank of workstations, they found a machine shop, docking port, even a garage. An entire encampment placed underground and out of sight.

"This place is like a beehive," said Soong. "Some of these walkways stretch up to the ceiling."

"According to Badru," Donovan said, flashing his light around, "they were down here for two years."

"Looks like they made the most of their time," Benny mused.

"Let's just hope they left something for us," said Zell. He shined his light on a bank of computers. "If these are still working, we should probably check them for backup files."

"Got it," said Benny. "Let's just hope they haven't reformatted the hard drives."

"They're nothing if not thorough," Donovan said.

Benny grimaced. "Yeah, and I've got the bullet hole to prove it."

"But we need power first," Soong noted. "We can't do any meaningful search without lights."

"I'll head back to look at those generators," Zell replied. "Care to give me a hand, Commander?"

As Zell and Benny worked on the generator, Donovan and Soong ventured deeper into the chamber. Though their echoing voices had given some sense of just how vast this cavern was, the darkness surrounding them made it feel all the more immense. Donovan took Soong's hand as they advanced past the ends of the two rows of workstations. Soong glanced back. The hole she had blasted through the rock had become nothing more than a speck of light. Just as they lost whatever ambient light they were receiving from the outside world, Donovan stopped in his tracks. Soong watched as his flashlight's beam arched higher and higher about their heads. Thirty feet. Forty. Fifty. The cavern was even more immense in this location. Then Soong's eyes finally pieced together what Donovan's flashlight was revealing.

It was the *Eos*.

Soong felt her mouth go dry as Donovan squeezed her hand, a look of sheer delight in his eyes. "Alan, I can't believe it."

At that moment, piercing lights turned on all around them.

"Jesus Christ!" Donovan yelled as he covered his eyes. Blindly he reached for the radio clipped to his belt. "You could've given us a warning, Elias."

Zell's voice came back: "I wanted it to be a surprise. Find anything?"

Donovan and Soong smiled at each other as he clicked his radio again. "You gents might want to come down here."

Benny and Zell arrived a few minutes later and found Donovan and Soong standing before the unearthed *Eos*. The ship was almost obsidian in color and somewhat triangular in shape, dotted with bumps and ridges all along its hull. Although its nose was impacted into the ground, the stern rose up from the cave floor to the ceiling. Whole sections of the vessel were still buried in volcanic muck, but the vast majority of its front section had already been excavated. Ladders and gantries had been set up around the ship to allow access to its various sections. The *Eos* was as large as its sister ship on the Moon, a virtual skyscraper lying on its side.

Benny whistled. "Holy shit. When we were on the Moon, I never imagined these things to be so big."

"Looks like your theory holds water, Dr. Soong," said Zell. "This thing's big enough to pulverize a mountain."

"Or a volcano," Donovan observed.

"All right," said Zell. "Let's find the door. Benny, you've got the schematics from the *Astraeus*?"

"Right here, Doc," Benny said as he punched a few keys on his minicomputer. "Okay, on the other ship, the entry hatch was located on the port side . . . oh boy."

"What is it?" asked Soong.

"It's just that . . . the entry to the ship is near the stern," said Benny. He jerked his thumb toward the ceiling. "Up there."

Donovan scanned the ship with his light. Finally he found a massive scaffolding that rose up the length of its port side.

"There it is," he said. "Looks like we're walking."

After a lengthy climb, they arrived at the airlock. Benny and Donovan forced the door open, and the four explorers climbed in. The ship was in far less pristine condition than the *Astraeus*, having spent the last two million–plus years at the bottom of a volcano, but was still remarkably well preserved.

Donovan's light shone on a plaque at the airlock's entrance. "The *Eos*," he said, reading the ship's name. "Well, one thing about these people, they sure knew their classics."

"And were not without a sense of irony, it seems," answered Zell, looking around. "Now, which way to the bridge?"

"Where else?" Soong said, gesturing with her thumb. "Up."

As they walked up, the four of them noticed the evidence of the excavators' presence on board the *Eos*.

"They took just about everything that wasn't nailed down," Soong said. "That's going to make it harder for us to extract what we need."

"It also means that, whatever we know, they know more," Zell noted. "That could work against us if we try and go public with this stuff."

"Still," said Donovan, "if we can get anything, anything at all that proves what really happened on the Moon, I'll be satisfied."

"Let's just hope we don't become martyrs for the cause," Zell said.

Once they reached the bridge, the team began trying to work with what little had been left behind. Benny went about trying to power up the ship while Donovan, Zell, and Soong began searching for hard data.

"Got it," said Benny. "The damn thing's in sleep mode. Looks like they tried to kill the power at the source but couldn't bypass the main circuits."

"What do you mean?" asked Donovan.

"It's weird," said Benny. "It's almost as if the ship wouldn't *let* them turn it off." He turned around in his chair. "Like it was fighting to stay alive."

"How can that be?" Zell asked. "I thought we determined on the Moon that this technology wasn't intelligent."

"Nevertheless," Soong said, "how else can we explain it?"

Donovan scratched his head. "Very strange. On the Moon the ship's computers only seemed able to answer questions, not think independently."

"I dunno," answered Benny. "More likely it's some kinda default mechanism inherent to the programming. Ensures that, whatever trauma the ship endures, the data it's carrying will still be preserved."

"Makes sense, given what they were carrying," said Soong.

"So we're in business?" asked Donovan.

"Maybe," Benny replied. "They still managed to do a lot of damage. Whatever data I can get will be fragmentary at best."

As Benny worked, the archeologists decided to poke around the *Eos* a bit and see if they could get a better sense of what happened. Consoles were smashed, chairs uprooted. Papers, obviously left by earlier visitors, were scattered about the craft. To Donovan and Zell, seeing a site of such obvious historical value treated so abhorrently was dispiriting.

Given that the ship was on a more deliberate angle than the *Astraeus*, the three scientists felt themselves fighting against gravity at times. Once, Soong lost her footing walking up a passageway and slipped, skittering back down the slope until Donovan caught her arm. After a while, it seemed to them that up and down had sort of switched places. At times, the ship's angle was steep enough that they could practically walk up a wall with almost no danger of falling.

"I feel we've gone down the rabbit hole here," remarked Zell ruefully.

After an hour or so of nosing about, they came to what appeared to be the sick bay. It was in the same condition as the rest of the ship but promised to hold more tantalizing secrets. Soong walked over to one of the tables and began leafing through the charred pages that were scattered about its surface.

"Any interesting reading?" asked Donovan.

"Not much," Soong replied. "Just some notes from someone named Cuevas. Fragments, really."

"Keep 'em," Zell said. "We never know what they might tell us."

"Already done," answered Soong, zipping up her bag. She peered around the ship. "Judging from the condition of this room, as well as the rest of the *Eos*, I'd say our time travelers didn't last as long as those on the Moon."

"It's a miracle they survived at all," Zell said. "This thing must have hit the planet like a meteor."

"The question is," said Donovan, shining his flashlight about, "not how long they lasted, but what they did while they were here."

"We've got to move," Benny said, appearing behind them.

"Have you got the data?" asked Donovan.

"What I could. It's not much, but it should be enough."

"Why the hurry?" asked Zell.

"I was extracting the data, and I noticed that there was something embedded in the data stream. Subtle but still there."

"What was it?" Soong asked.

"A tracking signal. Obviously left by our friends. I guess they figured since they couldn't stop us from accessing the data, they could at least keep us from telling anyone about it."

"So we're going to have company," said Donovan. "Great. How long?"

"Your guess is as good as mine," Benny answered. "Twenty minutes. Ten seconds. Hell, they could be on their way up right now."

"Right," said Zell. "Gather whatever you can carry, and let's clear out. I suggest we split up, make for Dar."

Soong looked at him. "Shouldn't we head back to the village? Badru's still there, and the Maasai could—"

"My dear, based on what we've run into this morning, it's entirely possible that Badru's dead and his entire village wiped out. There's no telling how far these people will go to keep their secrets."

Donovan looked over at Zell. "You've still got that safe house?"

"But of course," his friend answered. "It's rather sparse, but I think it will suit our purposes well."

The team made their way out of the ship and back down the ladder. Before they left, Benny and Soong stopped to take one last look at the *Eos*.

"She's a thing of beauty, ain't she?" mused Benny.

"She is indeed," said Soong. "It's a shame that no one will ever see her."

"If we have anything to say about it," Benny said, "there's a chance she might never end up here at all."

"Change the present so this future doesn't exist." Soong laughed and shook her head. "Try as I might, I can hardly comprehend that idea."

"You and me both." Benny jerked his head toward the entrance. "C'mon, let's move."

As the two of them fled the cave, the last of their lights winked out, leaving the *Eos* as she had remained for millions of years: in total blackness, her stern pointing awkwardly up to the sky, poised forever for her final plunge into nothingness.

Chapter 22

September 15
Dar es Salaam, Tanzania
12:05 a.m.

The streets near the port of Dar es Salaam were quiet at this time of night, and a thick, warm sea breeze blew in across the bay from the Indian Ocean. Donovan made a left onto a side street and drove half-way up the block before parking in front of a dilapidated six-story warehouse. Soong stepped out of the Jeep and into the humid night air.

"Are you certain this is the right address?" she asked as she glanced up at the worn brick facade of the building.

"This is it," Donovan replied as he pulled his ancient leather knap-sack from the backseat. "Elias made sure I memorized the address."

"How does he know this place?"

Donovan smirked. "I think he owns it."

Soong met Donovan on the sidewalk. "It doesn't look like much."

He laughed. "I don't think supersecret safe houses are supposed to."

It was true: the building's facade *had* seen its fair share of bad-weather days. The crumbling bricks had left long streams of reddish dirt on the sidewalk from where the rain and wind had blasted the building for generations. The structure likely hadn't seen any real use since Tanzania's colonial days decades ago. Each of its street-facing windows was boarded shut with thick slats of wood. The iron gate on the loading dock and the office door were rusting off their hinges. Only a shiny new lock fitted into the old front door betrayed the fact that the building was still in use. Donovan pulled a freshly cut key from a pocket of his grimy khaki pants and fitted it into the lock. To their surprise the door opened noiselessly into a darkened interior.

Donovan took his flashlight from his knapsack and shone it around the room. The floor was bare except for a few empty packing crates and straw. Here and there a half dozen wharf rats sniffed around in a desperate search for morsels of food. Finding none, they scattered as Donovan and Soong made their way to the far end of the floor. The floorboards buckled under their feet, but Donovan was fairly certain they wouldn't give way.

A single bare bulb throwing off no more than forty watts revealed the elevator. Donovan slid back the creaking iron gate and pressed the button for the top floor. Not wanting to alarm Soong, he reached a hand into his backpack and gripped the pistol he had taken from one of the mercenaries. He took off the gun's safety and kept it at the ready inside the bag. If anyone had ambushed his friends, he wanted to make sure he would not prove as easy a target.

Upon reaching the top floor, the elevator door slid back, and Donovan pulled open the gate. He relaxed his grip on the gun when he saw Zell and Benny hunched before a large bank of computers, set up on folding tables and desks in the center of the floor. A faint smell of fresh paint and varnish caught in his nose. Off to one end, half-hidden behind mosquito netting, were four cots made up with clean white linens and warm cotton blankets. To the right of the elevator was a mahogany conference table and comfortable-looking leather chairs. To the left was a pair of couches, a sixty-inch flat-screen television mounted to a nearby wall, a wet bar, and complete kitchen. Somewhere a radio was playing "Moon River" and dulling out the sound of the industrial-strength air-conditioning Zell had installed.

Zell whipped off his reading glasses and glared at them. "Blast it, where have you been?"

Donovan put the safety back on the gun and tossed his knapsack on a nearby chair.

"I'll take that as your being worried about us, Elias."

Zell scoffed as he approached them. "Take that as me thinking you two went on a moonlight drive instead of showing up here when you were supposed to. We've been at it for two hours already."

Donovan glanced at his friend. Zell had changed his clothes, and his graying hair was darkened and still damp from a recent shower. Benny looked similarly refreshed. "Working for two hours, my ass. It looks like you two have been primping all this time."

"Well, I admit we did clean ourselves up a bit," Zell said, rubbing his recently trimmed beard, "but you two can feel free to use the facilities yourselves."

"As much as that appeals to me right now," Soong said with some exhaustion in her voice, "we didn't drive all around Lerai Forest for a shower."

Zell's eyes narrowed. "You weren't followed, were you?"

Benny swung around in his ergonomic desk chair. "Even if they were, they'd never know it. You oughta see the satellites we've got today. They can pick out a bug on your back."

Soong folded her arms across her chest. "So what are you saying, Commander? That there was no point in our being cautious?"

"I'm not saying that. All I'm saying is that if somebody really wants to track us, they can. And that there's not much point in our making any use outta those cots. Best guess is we've got a couple hours' lead time before we oughta be hightailing it outta here. So if you wanna take a shower, better hop to it."

"You're being paranoid," Soong said as she grabbed a Coke from the minifridge behind the wet bar. "Are you even certain those men were American agents?"

"You're kidding, right?" Donovan asked as he reached over the bar to grab a bottle of Jack Daniel's. "They weren't exactly your run-of-the-mill muggers."

Benny sat back in his chair, wincing at his still-aching side. "Definitely Special Forces of some kind. They had the skills."

"Which doesn't necessarily mean they're working for your government," Zell observed. "They could be mercenaries of some sort—perhaps even working for the men who were at the dig before us."

"In either case we can't say there won't be more of them." Donovan popped open a can of Coke and poured some of it into his scotch glass. "I agree with Benny. We should try to be out of here before anyone decides to come a-knocking."

"So you think they were American agents too? Aren't you taking your grudge with the American government a bit far?"

"Christ, Elias, this isn't about any grudge. Not anymore. But I think we have to go on the assumption that they were for now. After all, *somebody* didn't want us to get to the *Eos*. And it's somebody with a lot of frigging pull."

Zell nodded. "Fair enough."

"So you're on the run from your own government." Soong smiled. "Have you ever contemplated defecting to China?"

Zell pulled a cigar from the humidor on the bar and lit it with his gold Zippo. "I don't think it's gotten that bad, my dear."

Donovan wandered over to Benny's workstation. "So what've you got?"

"Well," Zell said, contemplating his cigar, "we've warmed up the computers and done tests on the data drives we generated on the *Eos*. They read just the same as the ones we generated on the *Astraeus*."

"But we never saw how those worked," Soong noted. "They were taken from us as soon as we landed back on Earth. All we ever saw of that information was what Benny and Yeoh copied onto a legitimate twenty-first-century flash drive."

"And don't forget," Benny added, "those drives we got off the *Astraeus* were fed straight into state-of-the-art government computers. No offense, Doc, but compared to that, we've got a pretty jerry-rigged setup here."

"None taken," Zell said as he approached Benny. "But we've got to hope that these generated drives are compatible with any twenty-first-century computer. After all, why would these people from the future allow us to be able to create such disks and not have them work universally?"

Soong put a gentle hand on Donovan's shoulder. "But remember, the *Eos*'s been exposed to both time and the elements, as well as a systematic dismantling."

"Well," Benny said, scratching his cheek, "the only way we're gonna know for sure is to try and open it. I'm game, even with reservations about the equipment."

"I agree," Zell said. "Not much point in almost getting killed several times and not trying to discover what you've been putting your life on the line for. When you're ready, Commander."

Benny swung his chair around and tapped out a few keystrokes. A list of files appeared on the screen in alphabetical order, featuring everything from "Air Supply" to "Zoological Surveys." Donovan leaned over Benny's shoulder to study the list. Though he was somewhat tempted by the "Zoological Surveys" file, he found another that was even more intriguing.

"Try the 'Ship's Logs.' We should start there."

"Okay," Benny said with a deep breath. "We should get another list of files, probably chronologically, on this screen."

As Benny clicked the icon, the lights dimmed suddenly. Computer monitors began flicking on and off throughout the room. The air-conditioning revved up, then slowed down before shutting off completely. The television and the radio turned off and on, bouncing through stations as they did. They squinted as a blinding flash popped out of nowhere in the center of the room. The group looked around them in astonishment as holograms similar to the ones they had witnessed on the *Astraeus* began to take shape around them.

"It shouldn't be doing this," Benny said as a choir of long-dead voices began to chatter all around them. "The system shouldn't have the power to do this."

Without realizing it, Donovan, Zell, and Soong found themselves crowding around Benny's chair in a circle, partially out of protective instincts, partially to watch every angle of the action. Unlike the holograms on the *Astraeus*, which were solid both to the eye and to the touch, these holograms were more ghostly and transparent in appearance. What was even stranger was the positioning of these holograms. Since they were not standing on the bridge of the *Eos*, these holograms had no consoles to hunch over or seats to sit in, so they sat or stood in midair in an eerie approximation of where they stood on the bridge of their long-dead ship. Donovan glanced at the far walls. Men and women were standing half-in and half-out of them and coming and going as if the exterior walls were merely leading to another place in their vessel. He wondered if there were holograms outside projected in midair over the street and below them on other floors in what would have been other areas of the *Eos*.

Where on Earth was all this power coming from?

"Benny," Donovan called over the noise. "Can't you clear up all this damn chatter?"

Benny stared at him. "You're kidding, right? I don't even know how the hell it's doing this."

Zell leaned over to Benny. "Can you at least isolate a specific date and play that? It looks like we're getting everything at once."

Benny whirled around in his seat and tried to isolate the individual ship's logs. After a few frustrated efforts he slammed his hand against the desk. "I can't. The frigging thing is corrupted somehow. It won't play any other way. It's as if every log is playing simultaneously."

Just as the din of the noise seemed to overwhelm them, the multiple overlapping images winked out of existence to be replaced by a single image, again of what they assumed to be the bridge.

"Report!"

The group turned to see a striking, tall, blond-haired woman with almond-shaped eyes sitting in midair. Like the captain of the *Astraeus*, she seemed to be in top physical condition and looked to be no more than twenty-five years old. She sat approximately in the center of the room—where the captain's chair had sat aboard the *Eos*.

A brown-haired man with bright-green eyes sitting in front of her spoke first. "We appear to have landed, Captain. Searching temporal database for time and spatial coordinates now."

"We didn't land; we crashed," the captain said, more to herself than anyone else. "I want a casualty update."

A blue-eyed black man to her left turned to face her. "We have reports of several injured crew members."

"Structural integrity?"

An Asian woman to her right responded. "Structural integrity is holding, but engineering is reporting that—" She pressed a hand to her almost-undetectable earpiece. "Captain, we've lost the temporal drive."

"What do you mean, lost?"

"Engineering is assessing the damage now. They're not sure if—"

"What is working around here?" the captain barked.

"Ship's computer is functioning, Captain," the woman to the right noted.

"Okay, then let's see what we can see," the captain muttered. "Main viewscreen on."

Donovan and the others watched as all holographic eyes turned in unison to stare at a point several feet above and behind their heads.

"Can you," the captain said with hesitation, "can you confirm if that is lava outside the main viewscreen?"

"AFFIRMATIVE. WHAT YOU ARE SEEING, CAPTAIN, IS INDEED MOLTEN LAVA."

"But where, ship? Where are we?"

"ACCESSING SPATIAL AND TEMPORAL COORDINATES NOW."

"Captain," the brown-haired man who had first spoken began with hesitation, "we're getting preliminary telemetry now. We're on Earth, in East Africa."

The captain's holographic image came out of her invisible chair. "When?"

"Captain . . . ," the brown-haired man said quietly as he glanced at his invisible instrument panel again. "This can't be right. Captain, ship's suggesting we're approximately two and a half million years in the past."

"How? How can we have been so off? Ship, I want you to run a diagnostic on the temporal drive. Make sure to—"

The scene winked out of existence, and the figures reappeared in different positions. A blond-haired man with dark-brown skin was standing next to the captain's chair and appeared to be holding something.

"—drive's out for now. We won't be sure how bad it is until the lava flows away from the stern so we can—"

"Captain!" the same young Asian woman called.

The captain turned to her. "Have you established contact with the Council?"

"No, Captain, but we *are* getting a response. It's the *Astraeus*. She's here, in this time. But—"

The single log playback disappeared suddenly and was again replaced by a squall of overlapping voices and a myriad of overlapping images. Faces and bodies blurred in and out of existence and ran into one another and over one another and through one another. Donovan squinted, trying to make sense of what he was witnessing. The bridge seemed chaotic, but he couldn't tell whether he was looking at something that had really happened or was merely seeing the result of too many ship's logs being played at once.

"Goddamn it!" Zell roared. "Benny, can't you clean up this goddamn mess?"

Benny cursed under his breath and vainly attempted to separate the fragmented bits of data into separate streams. As he worked, some images would disappear while others would freeze or speed up to a screech of sound and a blur of motion, almost as if Benny were playing several movies at once, pausing some and fast-forwarding through others.

Soong grabbed Donovan's arm and yelled over the noise into his ear as if she were at a rock concert. "It's no use! The files are corrupted—they've been exposed to the elements for too long! We have to shut it off before we lose all the data!"

For a moment it appeared to Donovan that she was right. The noise in the room had become almost deafening. Occasionally a fragment of conversation would come out clearly, catch their attention, and then disappear into all of the ambient sound.

"—*Astraeus* is trapped—engines destroyed on impact with the lunar—"

"—we shouldn't be here—"

"—we had to come—to assume—the *Astraeus* had failed in her mission—our time wasn't changed—"

"—wildly off course—we didn't account—positions of the Earth—that's likely why we crashed—"

"—can't be two million years in the past—all our tests—the temporal drive couldn't have miscalculated our arrival date by that much—"

"—ACCESSING TEMPORAL—"

"—damage to the hull is minimal—lava's receding—we should be able to—"

"—where's that—"

"—no, no, *no*—I—"

"—no, I want—"

"—isn't possible—"

"—negative, *Eos*. It's no good—we can't—engines are wrecked—"

"—Captain wants a status report on—"

"—is it possible to mount a rescue mission once we're—"

"—ten dead, sixteen injured—need to regenerate tissue on fourteen—"

"—I'm not going to sacrifice the lives lost—"

"—I agree—deaths can't be in vain—"

Then, just as suddenly, the multiple images and voices disappeared and were replaced by a single image of these descendants of humanity. The playback no longer appeared to be on the bridge, but in another part of the ship. Gone were the men and women hovering in midair at their invisible stations on the bridge. Instead, the captain was standing in the center of a room with her head down and her arms folded. Her face was anguished as she listened to three men in what appeared to be futuristic space suits. Each was holding a helmet under his arm. One of the men was speaking.

"Benny, did you do this?"

"It wasn't me, Donovan. It just cleared up."

"Quiet!" Zell demanded.

"—in a prehistoric jungle, Captain. The ship is right. From what we've seen, we're definitely in the distant past."

The tallest man spoke next. "We've found a variety of animals that existed about two million years ago. We've also come into contact with a tribe of our distant ancestors."

"Our distant ancestors?" the captain wondered.

"A type of australopithecine," the third man noted. "We'd have to get a closer look to be more specific."

"Are you certain?" the captain asked him.

"As certain as I can be from what I recollect from my evolution classes," the third man said with a firm nod of his head. "There's a tribe of at least twenty of them about twelve kilometers from our position. It appears that they were near the volcano when our ship crashed into it and are now fleeing the lava flow."

"Australopithecine," the captain muttered, her eyes brightening. "And a tribe of them right outside our door."

The first man stepped forward. "What are you thinking, Captain?"

She smiled dimly. "That we might not have to leave here empty-handed, gentlemen." She looked at the first to have spoken. "Munson, I want you and Dr. Maciak to meet me in my quarters in one hour. Bring all of your scans of the tribe with you. I'll be in engineering until then checking on the repairs."

The image disappeared again but this time was immediately replaced by another image. Donovan assumed it was in the captain's quarters, because she was there along with the crewmate she called Munson and another man with reddish hair and deep-set black eyes, whom he assumed to be Dr. Maciak. The latter man was speaking.

"—a risk, Captain, certainly. But it might work."

The captain leaned invisibly on what Donovan assumed to be a desk. "Then we have to take that risk."

Munson was leaning on what Donovan assumed to be a bulkhead, with his arms folded across his chest. "Even if what you say is correct, Doctor, we can't just test this theory on crew members—assuming that we'd get volunteers."

"We wouldn't risk the lives of the crew," the captain noted. "We'd have to first attempt it on the primitives, see if the process would work."

"So we'd have to capture some of them," Munson mused with his head down, "bring them back here, experiment on them, figure out if the procedure's safe for us, and then try it on ourselves?"

"You sound as if you don't approve, Munson," Dr. Maciak noted.

"I'm not sure if I do," Munson answered. "This would be . . . a crossbreeding experiment. A rather repugnant idea. And even if we could—"

"Do we have the right?" the captain said with a smile as she finished his sentence. "I'm not sure about this either, Munson. But we're out of options. The human race is going to die out if we don't try something. The engineers assure me that they can reverse the time warp and bring us back home. But I'm not willing to attempt another time jump to see if we can make it to the twenty-first century to warn the people of that time. It's a desperate choice, I know, but what other choice do we have?"

"Maybe the choice is to let the human race die out, Captain," Munson said softly. "We brought this on ourselves with all our genetic meddling. I don't see how more of—"

The captain stood up. "Munson, I appreciate your opinions. But we've lost too many people already—not just from the plague, but all of our crew members and those aboard the *Astraeus*. She'll never get back home. I'm not willing to sacrifice any more lives."

"Understood, Captain." Munson straightened up. "Just let me know when you want me to lead the recovery team."

"You leave in three hours. That will give Dr. Maciak and his team enough time to set up environmental blocks to prevent us from being exposed to the primitives' germs."

Munson turned to Maciak. "How many do you need?"

Maciak rubbed his chin. "As many as you can get. We'll need—"

The squall that hit Donovan and the others was murderous in its intensity. All of them winced in turn and covered their ears as the noise from so many overlapping recorded voices and sounds overwhelmed their senses. Benny tried to shrug off the increasingly chaotic din as he worked to separate the corrupted streams of information, but the noise was too much. As much as he tried, he couldn't pull his hand from his ear long enough to work the computer. Then he felt a hand on his shoulder and turned around. Donovan was jerking his head toward the center of the room.

Benny turned to see the image of what he first assumed to be an ape biting and clawing at the man the captain had called Maciak, followed by other images of more apelike creatures attacking other crew members. The images didn't last long, no more than ten or fifteen seconds. Only long after the images went dead and the noises disappeared did Benny realize he had been watching mankind's ancestors killing his descendants.

Chapter 23

Time had lost its meaning for them. Their self-imposed deadline for leaving had passed without a mention. After making another futile attempt to retrieve some of the missing ship's logs, the foursome had settled into the plush couches Zell had provided at the safe house to drink and piece together what they had seen. Donovan stifled a yawn and looked up with bleary eyes across the room, wondering if the sun had come up.

Zell sat with his arms across his broad chest, a chilled scotch glass in one hand resting against the inside of his elbow. For decades he had scoured the Earth searching for fragments of the past, for pieces of civilizations long gone. He had more experience than anyone else in this room, knew far better than all of them how nations rise and fall, how civilizations die. But even with that knowledge, even with knowing how fleeting empires had been throughout history, he had never expected to see the end of humanity itself. And he never would have assumed in his wildest dreams that the end of humanity would come at the moment of its birth.

Since viewing the *Eos*'s logs, all four had found it hard to understand what they were feeling. But the one feeling they had been trying to silence was a sense of defeat. Since the day the EMP signal had arrived from the Moon, they'd been facing death one way or another. They'd faced it, cheated it, and come out on top. Now, seeing those ship's logs, they wondered . . . They wondered if all of what they knew, all this building and striving for centuries, all the wars and the troubled moments of peace, and all the debates around all those tables about so many crazy issues mattered in the end.

For Donovan, the answer was clear: *Hell yes, it mattered.* He was unwilling to give up, even now in the face of all this. Between the files they had in their possession and the notes he had been frantically making for the last several hours, he knew he had enough to convince those fools in Washington of the dangers that lay ahead. And if he couldn't get to Washington, if they really were trying to kill him, he would go to London, to Paris, to the United Nations. He would get someone to listen. He would play the logs. He would *make* them understand. He had to. He had to keep fighting. They weren't dead yet.

All of them had made a considerable effort to get drunk in the last few hours, with little luck, even though they had made a fair dent in the bottle of Jack Daniel's Donovan had opened when he first came in. The bottle sat on the coffee table now, its contents barely reaching the bottom of the label at this point.

Sometime around four in the morning, the group had switched from liquor to coffee. On the bar sat a coffeemaker, its half pot occasionally hissing.

Soong picked herself up off the couch and wandered over to where Donovan was now sitting on the floor.

"You must be tired from writing."

He barely glanced at her. "I want to get it all down while it's still fresh in my mind."

"You should rest, Alan."

He smiled at her consideration and touched her arm. "I wish I could."

Soong frowned. "There has to be an easier way than taking down all these notes."

Zell cleared his throat, as if he was shaking himself awake. "Of course there is." He reached down and pulled a small digital recorder from his backpack. He looked at Donovan. "Try it my way for once, you Luddite."

Donovan chuckled. He tossed his pen across the coffee table, where it skittered momentarily before rolling under the couch. "Maybe just this once, Elias."

Zell placed the recorder down in the center of the coffee table and switched it on. Donovan sat back against the couch.

"Where do we begin?" Donovan asked.

"Who knows?" Benny asked with a smirk. "In the twenty-eighth century, or two and a half million years in the past?"

"The future," Soong stated. "That's where it started."

Zell relit his cigar. "From *your* perspective, Dr. Soong."

"But she's right," Donovan added. "What happened in the future influenced the past in this case."

"Okay," Benny said. "Let's go a step at a time. According to the intel we got from both ships, sometime in the twenty-eighth century a plague nearly wiped out all of humanity. They couldn't save themselves in the future on account of the fact that they had manipulated human DNA so much that they had somehow totally screwed with their immune systems. So they decide to take a little field trip back to the early twenty-first century to warn the people of our time not to muck with genetic engineering."

Donovan continued: "But both ships go wildly off course and crash into the Moon and Africa in approximately two-point-five million BC."

"However," Zell noted as he sat forward, "once the *Astraeus* had crashed into the Moon, it was unable to make another time jump. That crew set up camp under the lunar surface but likely died out within a generation. The *Eos* had fared better, but the captain of that ship was hesitant about attempting another time jump. Her engineers were certain that they could reverse the wormhole and get back to their time. So they tried to bring some hope back to their future. And they decided to do that by harvesting DNA from the immune systems of the closest relations they could find in the distant past."

Benny cleared his throat. "You mean those ape things we saw."

"Australopithecines," said Donovan.

"Do you think so?" asked Zell.

"The crew said as much," Donovan answered. "I'm inclined to believe them since they probably had uncovered more fossil records by their time. And there was no mention on the logs of toolmaking or any other kind of higher thinking that would put them in the *Homo* genus."

"You've lost me." Benny shook his head. "You guys really need to speak in something other than scientist."

Donovan stood up, pacing the floor in an effort to jog his mind. "Let me backtrack," he explained. "There are two classifications for ancient hominids—australopithecine and *Homo*. *Homo*, meaning man, are creatures which closely resemble human beings. They had higher intelligence that came from larger brain cavities—fifty percent bigger than earlier hominids in relation to their body size. Some of them could make tools with their opposable thumbs, communicate through symbols, interact socially. Australopithecines were basically still apes—upright-walking apes but apes nonetheless."

"But you don't know for certain," Benny interjected. "You seem confused by what you saw."

Donovan shrugged. "We've never *seen* a live one before, Benny, just fossils. There are only slight variations in the bone structures of some of these creatures, so slight that we'd have to dissect them to figure out where to place them on the evolutionary tree. Add to that the fact that many of these creatures lived at the same time, and it becomes pretty damn hard to guess the right one by looking at a few seconds of fragmentary images."

"In fact," Soong said, sobering up, "there were at least four different species of hominids living together in Africa when the first stone tools were forged. Any of them could've been candidates for the first toolmakers."

"But they *were* apes, these creatures," Zell noted. "Walking upright, yes, but five feet tall at best. But they had all the classic traits of australopithecines—short legs, a pronounced forward-leaning gait indicative of the fact that they sometimes used their knuckles to walk. They couldn't possibly have been any of the early hominids, especially not *Homo habilis*."

"The first toolmakers," said Donovan, "the first creatures to show signs of a higher intelligence."

"Hold on, hold on," said Soong, waving her arms, as if the gesture might clear her mind. "There's a missing link between the australopithecine genus and the *Homo* genus. Somehow these small semi-intelligent apes gained a knowledge they never had before and eventually evolved, ultimately becoming modern man. If we believe what we've seen on those logs from the *Eos*, the crew mingled their own DNA with that of these primates and enabled them to make that leap in knowledge." Soong gulped down some coffee. "Maybe it's conjecture, but it appears the crew of the *Eos* is the missing link. They gave rise to the human race."

Zell chuckled and blew smoke into the air. "Alpha and omega."

Benny glanced at him. "What do you mean?"

"Alpha and omega," Zell said with a smile. "The first and last letters of the Greek alphabet. The beginning and the end. Without realizing it, the crew of the *Eos* *made* the human race with their genetic manipulation . . . and brought about its destruction by the same means."

Benny massaged his temples with his palms. "My God, is that possible?"

"More like playing God," Zell exhaled. "The poor bastards were so desperate to save themselves that they probably didn't realize what they were doing. They probably figured on killing their primitive specimens once they realized the genetic mingling would take. Only they got themselves killed before they realized what they had done."

"And their weakened immune systems—" Soong began.

"Proved no match for the germs produced by this new species," Donovan concluded.

"And so," Benny continued, "*Homo habilis* went back out into the wild with this modified DNA, that ability for higher learning, the ability to make tools and all that crap, and—"

"Began the chain of reproduction that led to modern man," Donovan said quietly.

Benny shook his head. "But how can we be so sure that these couple dozen apes caused the evolution of the human race? How could that even be possible?"

"Evolutionary theory holds that humanity began in a central location," Donovan explained. "Most theories point to Africa as being that location. Only up until this point, nobody knew how it came about."

"Also," Soong noted, "the entire human gene pool has less diversity in it than a single troop of chimpanzees. Despite the fact that there are differences in appearance—what we term different *races*—there's very little difference between anyone on Earth at the genetic level. Differences, then, being only skin deep, we have to conclude that we all share a common point of origin."

"And this is the place," Benny mused. "The point of origin."

"The pieces fit," Soong said. "Let's take what we've seen on the logs and compare it to what we know. At some ambiguous point two and a half million years ago gracile australopithecines evolved into the first of the *Homo* species. Until now we had assumed that they developed larger brain cavities by scavenging for meat, eating the carcasses of animals, and smashing open their bones to suck out the marrow."

"Yes, of course. Bone marrow is essential for brain development," Zell said. "These australopithecines were too small and weak to combat large animals like predatory cats. Because they were desperate for proper nutrition, they cracked open the bones, ate the marrow, and placed themselves on another evolutionary path."

"At least that's how the theory went before now," Donovan addressed Benny. "With what we've seen on the logs, however, we know that they likely had a big push in that direction through the DNA they received from the crew of the *Eos*. This advanced DNA enabled them to develop those bigger brains, the ability to make tools—"

Soong's face brightened. "And the capacity for travel."

The men turned their attention to her. "Look at the fossil records. Two and a half million years ago all branches of hominids lived in Africa. Each of these lines eventually died off with the exception of one, our direct ancestors, and they eventually spread across Africa and Asia."

"My God," Zell exclaimed, "she's right. The crew of the *Eos* not only gave these creatures the capacity for higher thought, they gave them the desire to *explore*. Before that they were confined to their immediate surroundings by their mental and physical weaknesses."

"It's all making sense!" Soong said excitedly. "In 1960 Mary Leakey found the skeleton of a one-point-eight-million-year-old creature—*Homo habilis*—which she nicknamed the Handyman. And where did she find him?"

Zell and Donovan looked at each other. Donovan rubbed his chin and smiled at Soong. "In the Olduvai Gorge—not far from the Ngorongoro Crater, where the *Eos* crashed."

"Holy shit," Benny muttered. "Then Leakey's skeleton was the descendant of those apes that they screwed with?"

"Looks like." Donovan stood up and began pacing around the room. "The new species had the ability to adapt to new environments and situations—a fundamentally human trait."

"And before long *Homo erectus* was in China," Soong observed.

"And eight hundred thousand years ago, man's ancestors were in Spain, Italy, and Georgia," Zell said, wide-eyed. "And roughly four hundred thousand years ago, he was as far north as England."

"*Homo heidelbergensis,*" Donovan said, sitting up. "And they were more like us than any creatures who had come before. They used advanced wooden and stone tools and were able to kill their prey at a distance. They were able to communicate with one another through language; they had family groups. However, they still weren't quite like us—no evidence of symbolic communication or rituals."

"But that eventually changed." Soong turned to Donovan. "Eventually our ancestors communicated symbolically and displayed a talent for art, as evidenced by the numerous cave paintings that have been found over the years."

Benny sat back in his chair and looked at each of them. "So that's it. The only reason we're all sitting here is because those nuts from the future went back in time and screwed with our ancestors' DNA."

Donovan, Soong, and Zell looked at one another. A growing disquiet filled them. Evolutionary theory had seemingly been turned on its ear: humanity had in fact a prime mover. And that mover was man himself. For several minutes none of them could say anything, but each of them was thinking thoughts along the same lines. Could this possibly be true? Was humanity's story not a line but a circle? If they could hardly stand to accept this theory, after all their experiences, what would the world at large think?

Donovan, never a religious man, found his thoughts turning in that direction. "I guess this proves that there's no God."

Benny scoffed. "Or maybe just that he's got a sick sense of humor."

"I wouldn't say either of those things. None of this accounts for the origin of the universe or of life itself," Zell said, leaning his elbows on his knees. "Just because we know this now doesn't mean that the design of the human race is either an accident or a sick joke. Who are we to question the means of the Almighty?"

Donovan stared at him. “I never took you for religious, Elias.”

Zell grunted a laugh. “I’ve been praying all night.”

“I think we can debate the religious significance later,” Soong noted with some irritation. “We need to ask ourselves what we’re going to do with this information.”

“Are you kidding?” Benny asked. “We’ve gotta get on the horn to Washington and let them know.”

Zell shook his head at Benny. “And how do we know that it wasn’t Washington that was trying to prevent us from finding this information out in the first place?”

“We’ve gotta do something, Doc,” Benny roared. “For all we know they might not have a frigging clue as to what’s been going on here. We’ve gotta notify—”

“I say we take it to the United Nations,” Donovan said firmly. “This is information for the world, not just one country. Elias, could someone in the British government provide us with safe passage to New York?”

Zell rubbed his beard. “Possibly. I’d have to call in some big favors. And we’d have to make certain that His Majesty’s government isn’t working in concert with your own.”

“Okay,” Donovan replied. “Do what you’ve got to do. But we’ve got to remember one thing: whoever was trying to keep us from the *Eos* wanted to keep its secrets for themselves. Can you imagine how valuable their genetic techniques would be to a single government—or worse, some private company? The world deserves—”

The doors to the three main stairwells crashed open. A number of armed men dressed in black poured in. Benny jumped behind the couch nearest him and pulled his service sidearm from his shoulder holster. He got off two rounds, but they went wild, lodging themselves in the doorframe. *Damn,* Benny thought as automatic weapons fire flew around his head. Computer screens exploded and shed their glass and bits of hot metal all around him. Singed papers drifted around his head. The smell of gunpowder and fried electric circuits filled the air. He poked his head above the couch and fired off another round. This one found its mark in the thigh of the man nearest him, who went down with an agonized screech.

At the same time, Donovan had grabbed Soong and leapt behind the banks of computers. Zell ran toward the conference table and tossed it over on its side with a single massive shove. They were all in a group near one another. None of them was close to an exit, and even if anyone was, at least a dozen men were blocking their escape. They had circled the wagons, but there was no way they were going to hold off the hostiles without more firepower. Donovan looked around the immediate area for his backpack. He saw one of its straps poking out from underneath an overturned chair. He slid across the floor and pulled it out from underneath the chair. In a moment he had his gun and had flicked off the safety. *Two pistols against a dozen fully armed men,* he realized. After a pause in the weapons fire, he stood up. Part of a doorframe burst into splinters just above the head of his intended targets. More rapid automatic fire burst around them. Somewhere under the noise Donovan could hear Soong screaming. Suddenly another voice cascaded over the din.

"Cease fire! Cease fire, goddamn it! Who told you sons of bitches to fire?"

Donovan and the others kept their heads low, not knowing what to make of the command. Donovan had protected Soong from most of the flying glass. He glanced through a bullet hole in the desk and saw that Zell was in one piece, though half-buried in debris.

"Dr. Donovan? Dr. Alan Donovan?"

Donovan held Soong's head to his chest as he leaned against the back of a desk, his gun drawn. "Yeah?"

"We're not here to hurt you, Dr. Donovan. We've come to take you home."

"Sure," Donovan muttered, then yelled: "Dead or alive?"

"Dr. Donovan, trust me," Casey said from his position in the stairwell door nearest the elevator. "We don't want anyone to get hurt. My men were just reacting because you started firing."

"We started firing? You burst in here and now—"

"Donovan, would you shut the fuck up!" Benny yelled. "Who're you, asshole?"

"Colonel Mitch Casey, US Special Forces. From the mouthpiece on you I'm guessing you're our Lieutenant Commander Benevisto."

Benny laughed as he pulled two spare clips from his pockets. "Pardon me for not saluting, sir."

"Benevisto," Casey said from his corner, "you know better than anyone else here that if we wanted to take you out we could've done so already with ease."

"Tell that to your advance team," Benny smirked. "We took pretty good care of them."

"Advance team?" Casey wondered.

"Let's not play cute, Colonel," Zell called from his position. "We spent most of yesterday fighting off your men."

"There's a misunderstanding here," Casey said flatly. "We didn't send an advance team."

"Prove it, pal," Donovan replied. "There are two dead bodies in the Ngorongoro Crater that say otherwise."

Casey laid down his rifle and pulled his sidearm from its holster and held it away from him. "Donovan, I'm unarmed. I'm ordering my men to stand down. Don't fire. We don't want anyone else hurt."

"If this is a trick—"

"It's not." Casey stepped away from the doorframe and into the center of the room. "I'm approaching your position now."

Donovan peeked out from between the computers and watched a silver-haired burly man of about sixty years of age make his way through the shattered bits of furniture and glass and computers. His steps crunched the debris as he approached, giving both him and Benny an obvious target if they wanted to take him. Slowly Donovan stood up, his gun gripped in a sweaty but steady hand.

"I'm not going to just stand here and let you kill us," Donovan rasped.

"I'm not here to kill you, Donovan." Casey held his gun out to Donovan. "Take it if you don't believe me."

Out of the corner of his eye he saw Benny nod. Donovan took the gun from Casey. Its barrel was cool. It hadn't been fired.

"Who sent you?" Donovan asked.

Casey smiled, his hands still raised. "Friends."

Donovan kept his gun trained on Casey's head. "What friends?"

"Jim McKenna, for one."

Donovan laughed. "I wouldn't necessarily call him a friend. Name another."

"The President of the United States."

Donovan squinted at him. "The President?"

Casey nodded. "On her authority I am to give you safe conduct to Washington. She asked me to inform you that she will use all the power of her office to help you and our nation through this crisis."

Donovan smirked. "I'm supposed to trust a politician with what we've got? They're the ones that got us into this mess!"

"Then trust in the guns you have. I promise you my men won't relieve you of them. Consider me your prisoner if it makes you feel more secure."

Donovan glanced around him. The computers were smashed. Zell's digital recorder had been crushed by a broken chair. His notes were in charred fragments. All their proof, gone.

"You won't believe us," Donovan muttered, his voice cracking. "You've destroyed everything. You don't know—"

"About the ships you found?" Casey asked with a slight smile. "About the ship here in Tanzania and the one on the Moon? I've been briefed on the generalities, Dr. Donovan. I know."

"You can't," Donovan said with disbelief, finding it harder and harder to keep his guns trained steadily on Casey.

"I do, son," Casey said, dropping his hands slowly. "Please trust me."

Maybe it was exhaustion, maybe he was tired of fighting, or maybe, he thought, he actually did trust this guy. Whatever his reasons, Donovan slowly let his arms drop to his sides.

Chapter 24

September 28
Pennsylvania Avenue
Washington, DC
3:43 a.m.

A late-model hybrid town car sped through the early-morning quiet down rain-slicked streets. The only sound penetrating the armored vehicle was the rain beating a soft tattoo on the tinted bulletproof windows. In the backseat sat Benny, Soong, Zell, and Donovan, all puzzled as to why they had been called out of their hotel rooms at this ungodly hour. Of course, the blank-faced federal agents who were escorting them proved to be of no help whatsoever. Since arriving back from Tanzania, they had been subject to so many debriefings and depositions that they had almost become used to being at the beck and call of the powers that be. So here they were, bumping along the streets of DC on another rendezvous with God knows what.

"I wonder who's ringing us up now—NSA, CIA, FBI?" Zell grumbled as he peered through his window. "I don't know about the rest of you, but I'm growing rather weary of all this cloak-and-dagger shit."

"You are?" said Soong. "Since making your acquaintance, I've been in a bar fight, nearly incinerated by an exploding rocket, shot at, and stranded on the Moon! And while I know all of this is just an average day for the cowboys at the Zell Institute, it's a bit much for me."

"Come now, dear Dr. Soong," said Zell, "it hasn't been as bad as all that. After all, through all the hardship, at least you were treated to the pleasure of my company."

Soong shot him a chiding glance, then looked out the window. "Well, I see who's summoned us," she said. "Take a look."

The three men peered out the window and saw the familiar pillars of the White House on the horizon.

"Hoo boy," said Benny. "Things just got interesting."

Once they had arrived, the foursome was given over to two Secret Service agents, who led them into the library in the White House, where they were told to wait. Donovan paced the plush carpet as the others glanced around the room, looking at the paintings of long-dead presidents, craning their necks to read the spines of books. No one said anything, all of them secretly worried that whatever they said was either being recorded or monitored or both. Ten minutes later the doors opened and in strolled John Dieckman, Aaron Stein, and an elderly gentleman who no one but Zell recognized.

"Who's that?" Benny whispered to Donovan. Before he could get his answer, Zell stood up and walked over to the older man.

"Alastair, you old git!" Zell bellowed as he shook the man's hand vigorously. "Who'd you cheat to get this job?"

"Very likely the same people you cheated when you were given an OBE, old boy!" the man fired back. The two men shared a laugh, and then Zell turned to his three companions. "This is Alastair Brindle, an old friend and recently named British ambassador to the United States. His son studied at the institute for a few years." Zell turned to Brindle, grinning. "How is Nigel, by the way?"

"Doing well indeed," said Brindle. "Over on a dig in the South Pacific—Tonga, I believe."

"Is it just me," Benny asked in an aside to Soong, "or has *everyone* studied at the Zell Institute at one time or another?"

"I'm sorry to break this up," Stein said, "but there is a reason the President called you out here at four in the morning, and it's a rather pressing one."

Just then the President entered the room. Everyone stood as she swept by and took her seat, nodding in greeting to all present.

"Good morning," the President began. "First off, I should tell you that I am personally investigating all the evidence you've brought back from Tanzania. Ambassador Brindle is here to serve as liaison to the prime minister, who is heading up an independent investigation on her end. As Dr. Soong may already know, the Chinese ambassador was debriefed on the situation last night and has pledged his country's cooperation during this investigation. And as you might expect, owing to the extremely sensitive nature of the Tanzania dig, I would ask, though not demand, that you remain quiet about what you've seen and discovered until we can get all the facts on the table."

"That seems fair enough, Madam President," Zell said. "Most people wouldn't believe a fish story like that anyway."

The President smiled at Zell's remark and turned to Stein, who had pulled a pair of half-moon reading glasses from his breast pocket as he shuffled through an overstuffed manila folder. "What we've been able to divine, based on the fragmentary intel that you and the Sierra team were able to extract, is that the men who ambushed your site at the crater were outside contractors hired by Walker to suppress whatever you found there."

Benny folded his arms across his chest. "By suppress you mean they were planning to bump us off."

Stein cleared his throat. "Well . . . yes."

Donovan fidgeted in his chair. "Hired by Walker or TGI?"

"It would seem that Walker was acting primarily on his own," Stein explained, glancing over the rims of his glasses. "The site was owned and operated by TGI, but the more sensitive information, such as you described, hadn't yet reached their offices. We then did a back trace on Walker's financial holdings. It appears that, in addition to his stock in TGI, Walker held patents with a number of drug companies, as well as cord-blood registries and fetal-tissue research centers. Most of these companies operated below the radar and without FDA approval."

"So he hoped to steal this technology right out from under TGI's nose and sell it to the highest bidder?" asked Donovan.

"It appears so," Stein answered.

"Black-market genetic engineering," mused Soong. "What's next?"

"It should be noted," said the President, "that TGI is not without blame. They knew, at least in part, what Walker was up to. They gave him access to the site, high-level clearance at their labs. Hell, it even seems as if he was using some of their age-slowing technology on himself."

"Vainglorious bastard," cursed Zell.

"Needless to say, however minimal TGI's involvement may or may not have been, they're up to something shady, and I don't like it. I've authorized the Justice Department to open legal proceedings against them."

"What's your involvement in all this, Alastair?" Zell asked.

"As you know, Elias," he began, "I sit on the board of the British Museum and have a pretty good ear to the ground when it comes to news of an archeological type."

"Of course," said Benny, "all the better to tip off your old Oxford buddy."

"Well said," noted Brindle. "As odd as this is to imagine now in light of recent events, the British government had planned to ask the Zell Institute to investigate the Tanzania site when it was first reported by the Maasai two years ago. However, as Elias was then on a dig in New Zealand and out of contact, another team went out to the site to investigate. You can imagine my surprise when three days later they all turned up dead. That's when all the nonsense about that so-called plague started, and we haven't been able to get close since. The point is, if Cal Walker or anyone at TGI had a hand in this, they also have the blood of British citizens on their hands."

"Let me see if I understand this," Donovan interjected. "A British archeology team went to investigate what had been found in the crater and turned up dead. But then somehow this dig site wound up in the hands of Walker and TGI. Does anyone know how this happened?"

Stein cleared his throat. "That's what we hope to discover, Dr. Donovan. But the situation is more complicated than that. It appears that the dig site had been discovered about two years ago by one of the Maasai. It was at that point that the British team went to investigate and was found dead. TGI, through some contacts in the British and American governments, somehow gained access to the site—likely after they learned that a ship of some kind was found there. They planned on using the technology they found there to improve their own genetic-engineering techniques but made little headway until six months ago, when the pulse from the *Astraeus* activated the ship's systems."

Soong shook her head. "So what you're saying is that the two ships were connected?"

"In a way we can't even begin to understand. The pulse somehow turned on the *Eos*'s dormant systems, thereby allowing TGI access to its memory core. We suspect that Walker, once he knew of the existence of the Moon ship and in order to further his own ends, made sure he got involved in the Phoenix program to prevent us from ever learning about that second ship. Whatever technology he had procured, he wanted to make sure he had it all to himself."

"But I thought you had asked him to come on board, Deke," Donovan interjected.

"I did," Dieckman replied. "But I think I just beat him to the punch. We now feel that he was planning on getting involved, either personally or through his government contacts, one way or the other."

"This is nefarious," Soong muttered in disbelief.

"It gets worse, Dr. Soong," Dieckman added. "We also suspect that Walker had contacts in China who helped sabotage the Chinese moon program before our two countries joined forces."

"You can see where this is going," said the President. "People are dead, evidence has been destroyed, and now the governments of four nations—the US, the UK, China, and Tanzania—want answers. If this isn't handled with kid gloves, the Taiwan blockade will seem like a walk in the park. That's why we're asking for your cooperation. I assure you, this is not an attempt to cover anything up. I want the truth about these ships known as much as you do. But if we're careful and go about this cautiously, then we can prevent the future that you witnessed. In the end, what I'm asking for is your trust." She extended her hand to Donovan. "Do I have it?"

"Even if you didn't, Madam President," Donovan said, "I expect we wouldn't have a choice."

The President smiled slightly and nodded. "You have me there, Dr. Donovan. That's why this administration would greatly appreciate your understanding in this highly sensitive matter."

There was a brief moment of silence; then Donovan shook the President's hand, as did Benny, Soong, and Zell. They then turned to leave. At the door Donovan turned back to the President, who was still seated.

"There's just one thing that bothers me, Madam President."

The President lifted her head. "And that is?"

Donovan looked at Zell and the others, and turned back to the President after having received their unspoken support. "I think it's become clear to us that Walker had help in sabotaging the Moon mission—access to government property, top-secret intel, the works—from someone high up in the government."

The President nodded. "Yes, we're fairly certain of that. In order to inflict the damage to your spacecraft, Walker and TGI must have had help from someone with access to your ship's systems."

"And do you know who that person is?" Benny asked. "People died up there, Madam President. We can't just let that go."

The President shuffled fixed her gaze on Donovan. "I'm sorry to say that the operatives remain unknown."

Donovan shook his head. "They usually are, ma'am. But they don't always stay that way."

After Donovan and the others had left, the President, Brindle, Dieckman, and Stein began to discuss the issues that had arisen since the incidents on the Moon and in Tanzania.

"As you know," said the President, "the Chinese president is in agreement with us. The true nature of the *Eos*, and all traces of the world it came from, must remain buried. To reveal it would create a worldwide panic."

"I should say that it is the opinion of His Majesty's government that we shouldn't rush to hide the ship," protested Brindle. "We could learn so much from it."

"Though I'm loath to say it, the ambassador's right," argued Dieckman. "The scientific applications are too great. We should study it."

"Interesting you should say that, Deke," noted the President. "With the growing threat of chemical and biological terrorism, the genetic information recovered from the *Eos* has the power to save millions of lives. Not to mention what its technical specifications could do to solve energy problems, help the space program—the list goes on and on. I've struck a deal that will allow each of the four nations involved to benefit from the science and technology the *Eos* has to offer."

"What about Russia?" asked Stein.

"This is an . . . exclusive deal," said the President. "To bring them on board could create a rift with the Chinese."

"What about Zell and Donovan?" said Brindle. "Despite the trouble they've caused, they served both our countries well. I think some form of compensation should be in order."

"We're prepared to make a generous contribution to further Dr. Zell's research," said the President.

"Not that he needs it," muttered Deke.

"And the *Eos*?" asked Brindle. "When can we get a team out there to start excavating?"

"We'll have them in place within a week."

"Excellent," Brindle said, rising from his chair. "Well, then. Everything's in place, isn't it?"

"Of course," said Stein, "I should at least mention the fact that, by even allowing any trace of the *Eos* to survive, we could be setting in motion the downfall of the human race."

"That's one future, Aaron, and not mine," said the President. "We're taking the knowledge of events to come and using them to our advantage."

With a gesture, Dieckman led Ambassador Brindle out into the hallway. Stein stayed for a moment, gathering up his papers. The President watched him as he collected his things, knowing full well what he had on his mind.

"You might as well say it, Aaron."

Stein looked up from his papers quizzically. "Madam President?"

"You're still here because you want to talk about Jim McKenna again. You've made it clear enough that you don't approve of my solution."

Stein pulled off his glasses and tucked them back into his breast pocket. "No, ma'am, I don't. Putting aside the fact that he's directly responsible for the deaths of that British archeology team and the astronauts on the Moon, he betrayed this country. He betrayed *you*, ma'am, even if he ultimately confessed his involvement to you. Having him just *disappear* doesn't give justice to those people's families. And to top it all off, Donovan, Zell, and the others *know* someone on the inside was working for Walker. They just don't know it was the head of Space Command."

"And what would you have me do, Aaron?" the President asked. "Put him on trial for treason? Have him executed? Have the whole mess come out in the open after all the time and effort we've spent trying to keep matters hushed up?"

Stein flushed. "May I speak freely, ma'am?"

"Always."

He approached the President's chair. "This is about your friendship with McKenna, ma'am. This is about the politics of having one of your closest friends and advisers be revealed as a traitor to this nation. You feel like you owe him something, and you feel like you owe it to your political career to cover up a scandal."

The President stared at Stein for a long while with a pained look on her face. Stein wasn't sure what to make of such a look. He could be an inch away from being fired for speaking so boldly. Or he could be a moment away from being one of the precious few who'd seen this president with her guard down.

"Aaron," the President said, "the only reason we're having this conversation is because Jim McKenna confessed to me and helped us retrieve not only Donovan and the others but the ship itself. His actions helped a lot of people. His actions helped me. Maybe that means I do owe him something. But then so do we all. He's punished far above any verdict a jury could pronounce on him. He'll never see anyone he ever loved again, including the son he sacrificed everything for."

"I understand, Madam President."

"Thank you. Now please let's never speak of this again."

Two hours after the meeting at the White House, Soong emerged from a steaming bath in her hotel room and sat on the edge of the bed, wrapped in an oversized hotel towel. She could hardly believe the road that she had traveled in the last few months. It was as if the life before her training had belonged to another woman—a more innocent woman, perhaps, not someone who had walked the halls of power and flown to the Moon, definitely not the woman who had come to face the paradoxes of time itself. And yet, as she sat there brushing her hair, the time paradox seemed in a way no more complicated than the journey of life itself. Once, she had been a child living in a small fishing village, but since that time she had made the decisions that had brought her to this moment. She felt both small and a part of something greater, a mere piece of stitching in the fabric of the quilt of life and yet something intrinsic to the whole. The idea was remarkably comforting.

The hotel phone rang. She gripped her towel around her and picked up the receiver and was surprised to hear a very familiar voice at the other end.

"Bruce! Bruce, how are you?"

"Very good, I must say. Married life agrees with me."

She smiled at the idea. She had almost completely forgotten that Bruce Yeoh was now a married man. "Congratulations. I'm glad to hear that you're happy."

Bruce's tone grew serious. "I'm sure you know why I'm calling."

"I imagine you heard a very similar conversation to the one I heard this morning."

"As Benny would say, 'You got that right, chief.' I know we shouldn't really talk about it over an open line, but I wanted to call to see if you were okay."

"I am," Soong said quietly. "I'm a little surprised that I am. It's strange, but I was just thinking about that when you called."

"Maybe, then, we were meant to have this conversation," Bruce said with a laugh.

"So now you believe in fate, Bruce? That's somewhat hard to believe coming from a physicist."

"I guess it is. I really haven't quite come to grips with everything, but I am starting to wonder about a lot of things. Like the idea that time itself might not be a fixed thing. And the mere idea is making me reevaluate a lot of my beliefs."

"As our experiences should."

"It's more than just the idea that the decisions made in the last twenty-four hours could be leading to the creation of an alternate timeline. Perhaps it's simply the idea that we have more power over our lives than I have ever thought possible. That life can't be broken down simply into an evolutionist's idea or a priest's idea of the universe. That it could be an incredible combination of the two—design and evolution playing off one another in an eternal battle."

Soong was silent for a moment. "So where does that leave us, Bruce?"

He laughed again. "I don't know. Probably exactly where we were before we learned of all these things, searching for the meaning of existence."

"But don't we know the meaning of human existence, Bruce? It was all a tragic accident."

"That's an interpretation of an event. And the time paradox isn't the meaning of existence—it's simply how humanity began, not life itself."

Soong reflected on that for a time in silence. "Five minutes before you called, I was comforting myself with the idea that life was what we make of it. Now I'm not so sure."

"Why? Because I've challenged a—forgive me—pat conclusion? Here's a cliché, Yang Zi: Life is a journey. We have to make the most of it."

Soong smiled. "How are you going to make the most of it, Bruce?"

He laughed. "Do more research into what we've learned. Love my wife. Love the children we'll have. Learn to play the drums. And you?"

"Me?" Soong replied, curling the wire around her arm. "I'm going to take a risk."

October 7
Watergate Hotel
Room 304
Washington, DC
10:17 p.m.

It had been more than a week since the meeting with the President, and none of them had heard back about anything. Instead, day after day had passed of giving sworn testimony and telling and retelling their side of the story. As time wore on, they were all beginning to believe that they might never hear any news and spend the rest of their lives raising their right hands and speaking into recorders.

Thankfully, Donovan and Zell had been released from their duties that morning. Both of them were eager to get out of the Watergate Hotel and back to work. Donovan was poring over maps and schematics from Tanzania while Zell bustled about the suite straightening up when the knock came.

"Who could that be at this hour?" Donovan asked.

"Probably the concierge to talk about the liquor bill," said Zell as he opened the door.

"Good evening, Dr. Zell," said John Dieckman as he strode into the room. "I know it's late, but I didn't think this could wait until morning."

"Well, come in then," Zell said, gesturing with his hand. "There's scotch behind the bar. Help yourself."

Dieckman came in and poured himself two fingers. Donovan walked over to him.

"Good to see you, Deke," he said, shaking his hand. "But I've got the feeling you're not here for the scotch."

"No," he admitted. "The Justice Department's asked for a court order for TGI. They're required to relinquish all their files and provide full disclosure of their activities during the past sixteen months."

"You're not saying that like it's a good thing," Donovan said.

"Their lawyers have tangled up the process in red tape," said Dieckman. "It'll be years before they turn up anything of note."

"What about Cal Walker?" Zell asked.

"I had a feeling you were going to ask about him."

Zell rubbed his beard. "That doesn't sound good either. Where is he?"

"Gone," Dieckman replied. "His office in New York's been vacated, and all his numbers disconnected. He's vanished like smoke."

"That's it, then," said Zell, tossing ice into his glass with a clink. "The story ends."

"Not necessarily," Dieckman said. "Colonel Wilson's been released from the hospital. He'll probably walk with a limp for the rest of his life, but he's itching to get back into the action. The President has asked him to head up a task force with the sole mandate of trying to track down Walker and his cohorts. It might be like trying to track down

Nazi war criminals, but you know Wilson. The definition of tenacity has his picture next to it."

"Well, that's some good news, at least," Donovan admitted. "Wilson will get them, if anybody can. Got any other good news?"

Dieckman grinned. "I'm sure you know about my . . . promotion by now."

"Yes," Donovan said, shaking his hand. "I forgot. Congratulations. So they've gone and made you NASA's chief."

"We're heading up the Mars mission as we speak. We should make a landing there in four years or so. And while my mandate expressly forbids any touchdown on the Moon"—he paused for a sly smile—"they never said anything about satellite flybys."

"Spy satellites?" Donovan asked.

"We've got Skystalkers on the way already," said Dieckman. "It could be a while before we find anything interesting. But I promise you'll be the first to know when I do."

Dieckman drained his glass, then set it on the bar. He headed toward the door and put his hand on the knob. As he opened the door, he turned back to face them.

"For what it's worth," he said, "you've always got a friend at the agency."

"And you at the institute," said Zell, raising his glass. "If the face on Mars turns out to be a Mayan artifact, I trust you'll know who to call?"

Dieckman smiled and nodded, tossing them a salute as he cleared the doorframe.

The next morning Zell was enjoying the hotel's lavish buffet breakfast in the dining room when someone slapped a newspaper down on his table. Zell looked up to see Anthony Benevisto grinning at him.

"See anything you like?" he asked, gesturing at the headline.

Zell looked down to see the words staring back at him: "TGI Funding Bill Denied." His eyes widened at the headline, but it was the next line that really got his attention.

"Senator George Dieckman casts deciding vote," Zell read. "Well, well, well—I guess it does help to have friends in high places."

"It sure does," said Benny, taking a seat and helping himself to some coffee. "How else could a naval officer go AWOL, trade fire with Special Forces, and still end up with an honorable discharge?"

Zell cocked an eyebrow. "Discharge?" he asked. "So you're a free man. What are your plans?"

Benny paused. "Well, I'm going to Kansas. I owe it to Moose."

"Sure you don't want to change your mind? We could use a man like you in the institute."

Benny laughed. "I'm sure, Doc. I think I've had enough relic hunting to see me through the next few lifetimes." He paused, stirring his coffee thoughtfully. "Besides," he said, "I've got a promise to keep."

"Fair enough," said Zell as he raised his mimosa. "But don't be too certain about that relic hunting being out of your life. This racket has a funny way of drawing you back in."

"I can imagine," Benny said with a nod. "So what about you, Doc? What's next?"

"Me? Well, it's back to the institute for old Elias. I've got a lot of work to do."

"What kind of work?"

Zell topped off his drink and settled into his chair. "It seems that, given the rather . . . unusual circumstances surrounding our voyage *dans la lune*, the Zell Institute has begun to draw a slightly different clientele. To put it bluntly, every crackpot who's seen a UFO, were-yeti, or the Virgin Mary on a Triscuit has got an assignment for me. Most of them are barking mad, but a few are . . . worth following up."

"Paranormal archeology," Benny mused, smiling. "Sounds like it's right up your alley. I suppose Donovan's going along for the ride?"

"Alan?" said Zell. "No, Alan's heading back to Africa. He and Badru are going to squeeze every contact they've got in the region for more info on the *Eos*, TGI, the works." Zell looked back at the paper, studying the headline a moment. "He's just not ready to let it all go."

"I can understand, I guess," Benny said. "After all . . . we were close to something, weren't we?"

Zell gave a bemused chuckle. "In this game, Benny, you're always close to something." He sipped his mimosa quietly and looked out at the passersby. "Sometimes close enough to get burned."

"Another one, buddy?"

Donovan looked up from his drink at the bartender, then back at his rye and water.

"Nah," he grunted, slurring it a bit. "I think I've caught my limit."

"Sure, Mac," said the bartender, turning away. Before he did, he looked at Donovan, his eyes squinting with faint recognition. "Say, don't I know you from TV or something?"

Donovan threw back the rest of his drink, grimacing at the taste. "Yep," he said. "Reality TV."

Donovan tossed a fifty down on the bar and headed out into the night air. The cold breeze off the Potomac was like a splash of water to the face. *Summer's come to an end.* Not that it really mattered. He had a flight out tomorrow morning back to Tanzania. Whatever secrets the *Eos* had left behind, neither TGI nor the US government could bury them completely. If the ship's passengers had, through their deaths, set in motion the events leading to man's evolution, then Ngorongoro was only ground zero. The evidence would spread out from there.

He strolled along the banks of the river, lost in thought. When his cell phone rang, Donovan jumped about three feet. "Hello?"

"Ni hao," came Soong's voice from the other end.

"Howdy, yourself," Donovan replied. "I guess you heard the news about TGI, huh?"

"Yes," Soong said. "So it looks as if the future's changing already. Everything we did wasn't in vain."

"Maybe."

"You sound . . . unconvinced."

"There's a lot of money to be made in genetics. TGI's just one company. Who's to say stopping them alone prevents that future?" Donovan was quiet for a moment. "Still, I'm glad you called, Yang Zi. I didn't think I'd get a chance to say good-bye."

"Well, I must be honest, Alan. I want to shake your hand and apologize."

"For what?"

"For being wrong about you. For ever doubting that you are an honorable man."

"You don't owe me an apology, Yang Zi," Donovan laughed. "But I would like to see you again, to part as friends, though I suppose that's out of the question."

"Really?" said Soong from behind him.

Donovan whirled around to see her sitting on a park bench. Donovan shook his head, laughing.

"'Wherever you go,'" Soong said.

"'There you are,'" Donovan finished.

He walked over to where she was sitting and looked at her. She stood and extended her hand. He ignored it and hugged her for a long moment, and she hugged him back before letting him go. They walked for a time without speaking. After strolling for a bit, they stopped at a bridge overlooking the Potomac. Donovan tilted his head up, gazing at the Moon above them.

"They're still up there," he said with a sigh. "They came all this way just to . . . We owed them more." He shook his head again. "I'm finding it hard not to be angry, not to believe that we're just sitting on our hands as the politicians promise to make things right. We owed those people way more than we're doing now."

"There's still time to make up that debt," Soong replied.

"What do you mean?"

Soong picked up a stone and tossed it into the water, watching the ripples move out into the current. "By ensuring that the future they came from never happens."

"How?" Donovan asked. "There's no way we can be certain anything we do now will ensure that."

"I don't know about that. TGI is just one step." She took another stone and tossed it near the first, altering the movement of the ripples ever so slightly. "Things are already changing. We are already living in a different time." Soong turned to Donovan with a smile. "The future will take care of itself, Alan. But only if we make use of the lessons of the past, each one of us, in our own way."

They walked on a little longer. Donovan stopped and took one last look at the Moon.

"What are you thinking about?" Soong asked.

Donovan was quiet. "The future," he said. "The past. I want you to be right, that it all starts right here. With all of us. I so want you to be right."

Soong smiled at him and offered her arm. "Come, my friend," she said, "let's find out together."

They walked on, arm in arm. Over their heads, the Moon hung silent and stoic before passing behind a cloud and disappearing from sight.

ACKNOWLEDGMENTS

CHRISTOPHER MARI wishes to thank the following people for helping to make this novel possible: Jennifer Lyons, dauntless agent; Jason Kirk, risk-taking editor; Clarence Haynes, gentle master of the red pen.

Also and most especially: Ana Maria Estela, long-suffering beloved wife; Juliana, Olivia, and Luke Mari, trifecta of awesome kids; Kevin Mari, great brother and better friend; Chris, Andrew, and Jess Dieckman, Mike Mongillo, Meg Mullin, Dann Russo, always-got-your-back buddies; José, Rose Marie, and Joseph Estela, favorite in-laws.

And finally: Frances Benevisto and Regina Mari, late grandmother and mother but ever-present inspirations. Never give up.

JEREMY K. BROWN would like to thank Alli for being my audience of one and my tireless cheerleader. My boys, William and James, for teaching me every day how to be a better man. Jennifer Lyons for taking a chance on me, Jason Kirk at 47North for seeing in this book things even Chris and I didn't see, and Clarence Haynes, a true archeologist who helped us unearth the hidden story buried beneath our words. And thank you always to my whole family: my mom, Marilyn Brown; mother-in-law, Maureen Vincent; and to Allison, Phil, Peter, Maury, Kerby, Catharine, Sefita, Andy, Jack, and all my awesome nieces and nephews. Each and every one of you inspires me every day. And to my father and father-in-law, Kendall Brown and Peter Vincent. I hope they have hammocks in heaven and that you find a sunny spot to enjoy this story. Love you and miss you both.

ABOUT THE AUTHORS

Photo © 2016 Ana Maria Estela

CHRISTOPHER MARI was born and raised in Brooklyn, New York, and educated at Fordham University. He has edited books on a wide variety of topics, including three on space exploration. His writing has appeared in such magazines as *America*, *Current Biography*, *Issues and Controversies*, and *U.S. Catholic*. His next novel, *The Beachhead*, will be published by 47North in 2017. He lives with his family in Queens, New York.

Photo © 2016 Alli Brown

JEREMY K. BROWN has authored several biographies for young readers, including books on Stevie Wonder and Ursula K. Le Guin. He has also contributed articles to numerous magazines and newspapers, including special issues for *TV Guide* and the Discovery Channel, and recently edited a collector's issue on Pink Floyd for *Newsweek*. Jeremy published his first novel, *Calling Off Christmas*, in 2011 and is currently at work on another novel. He lives in New York with his wife and sons.